THE
BROKEN
SWORD

Tor Books by Molly Cochran and Warren Murphy

The Broken Sword
The Forever King
World Without End

THE
BROKEN
SWORD

MOLLY COCHRAN
AND
WARREN MURPHY

FIC
COCHRAN
1997

A TOM DOHERTY ASSOCIATES BOOK   NEW YORK

THE BROKEN SWORD

Copyright © 1997 by M. C. Murphy

This book is printed on acid-free paper.

Interior art by Ellisa Mitchell.

A Tor Book
Published by Tom Doherty Associates, Inc.
175 Fifth Avenue
New York, N.Y. 10010

Tor Books on the World Wide Web:
http://www.tor.com

Tor® is a registered trademark of Tom Doherty Associates, Inc.

Library of Congress Cataloging-in-Publication Data

Cochran, Molly.
    The broken sword: a novel of the return of King Arthur / Molly
Cochran and Warren Murphy.
        p.   cm.
    "A Tom Doherty Associates book."
    ISBN 0-312-86283-0
    1. Arthur, King—Fiction. 2. Arthurian romances—Adaptations.
3. Britons—Kings and rulers—Fiction. I. Murphy, Warren.
II. Title.
PS3553.O26B76   1997
813'.54—dc21   96-47188
                                                                    CIP

First Edition: April 1997

Printed in the United States of America

0 9 8 7 6 5 4 3 2 1

For Cynthia Fertal

ACKNOWLEDGMENTS

The authors would like to thank the following for their assistance and support:

Brian Murphy, Fred Koehler, Karen Hartman, Pat Hilliard, Megan Coles, Deirdre Abbots, Eleanore Muller, Eiko Nishimoto, Albert Neumeyer, Shirlee Kovacs, Penelope Lawbaugh, Ralph Rudolph, Jo Ann Jones, Barbara Conrad, and Joann Meier; the Moroccan Embassy in New York; and most especially, Sherry Schwartz.

THE
BROKEN
SWORD

PART ONE

THE
CUP

CHAPTER ONE

Marrakesh, Morocco

Beatrice listened to the distant strains of exotic music as she walked toward a food stall packed with Moroccan delicacies.

"Kibbee," the stallkeeper droned, somewhat less than enthusiastically.

"Kibbee!" Beatrice squealed. "I've heard of it, Grams. Oh, may I try some, please?"

Her grandmother looked askance at the array of aromatic dishes. "We don't know when this food was made, dear," the old woman whispered.

"Made fresh just now, beautiful ladies!" Meryat Haddish, the stallkeeper, waved a fan over the goods, momentarily dispersing the flies that had come to roost.

Ordinarily he wouldn't have bothered with them. They were English, for one thing. English women were always stupid about food. The old one looked as if she ate nothing but white potatoes, and the other was a girl who probably made faces at everything that wasn't pizza.

And they were rich. The price of the girl's dress alone could support Meryat's family for a month. What had her father done to pay for that dress? He hadn't stood over an oven all night with grease in his hair and sweat on his face, that was certain. He hadn't walked to the souks at dawn thinking about how his oldest son had cut the leather of his only pair of shoes to make room for his toes.

He sighed. There was no point in complaining about the strange ways in which Allah worked. Besides, the two English ladies might be the only customers he'd get all morning. The damnable Americans were parading their frail old ex-President through the bazaar, and the Secret Service was practically driving away the crowds at gunpoint. Meryat hadn't seen anyone except photographers and cameramen for the past half hour, and they never ate anything. Meryat could almost see his beautiful kibbee turning rancid in the sun.

"So, ladies," he said, forcing a smile at the approaching pair. "You try kibbee, okay?" He held up an aromatic stick, to which the wrinkled old bat responded as if it were a turd.

"I'm sure your . . . merchandise . . . is quite nice," Grams said, pulling gently on Beatrice's arm. "Oh, my, there's a stall filled with lovely pots and things. Shall we go over there?"

Meryat shook the meat stick gingerly. "No, no. No buy pots there," he whispered conspiratorially. "Is thief. Pots made in Taiwan. Only for tourists."

The old woman was staring longingly at the pot stall.

"You English ladies?" Maryat asked, waving the kibbee to distract her. "My brother, he go to London now ten years. Drive taxi." From beneath his counter he produced a British Union Jack and stuck it in a crack on the side of his stall.

"God save the Queen. Is beautiful lady." He broke off a piece of meat and held it out to her between grimy fingers. "Free sample. You like?"

"Gracious, no," Grams said.

"I would, please." Beatrice held out her hand.

She stood two feet away from the stall. Evidently the girl didn't want to venture too close to the natives, Meryat thought. The corners of his mouth turned down belligerently. If the English princess expected him to leave the counter and walk to where she stood in order to offer her a free piece of his delicious food, she would have a long wait. He crossed his arms. The girl stood in silence for a moment, adjusting her movie-star sunglasses, then finally took a step forward.

"Ah, the beautiful young lady, she knows the food is excellent." Meryat dropped the kibbee onto her palm.

"Oh," she said, startled. "I was rather expecting a pastry."

Meryat was incensed. "But you can *see*—"

"Don't eat it," her grandmother commanded.

"Is good," Meryat said, eating the rest of the piece himself. "Typical Moroccan dish, but better in Marrakesh than Casablanca or even Tangier. Meryat, myself, makes it best of all."

"Lamb," Beatrice said, sniffing the object. "And saffron, parsley, garlic, and—"

"It sounds perfectly dreadful," Grams said sourly. "Here's a handkerchief."

The girl popped the meat into her mouth just as her grandmother lunged to intercept it, knocking off the girl's sunglasses. Both of them immediately went to the ground, the girl's hands making broad sweeps over the dirt.

Involuntarily Meryat sucked in his breath. He hadn't guessed. The girl was so beautiful, with hair like spun gold and perfect white teeth and her rich-girl confidence.

She was blind.

"Now your hands are filthy," the grandmother chided, but the girl seemed to pay no attention to her. She found and replaced her dark glasses and smiled up at the stallkeeper. "Thank you. That was delicious," she said.

Meryat laughed to cover his embarrassment. "Did I not tell you my kibbee is the best? Now you buy some, please, beautiful lady. Only two dirham."

With a snort of exasperation, Grams reached into her pocketbook and gave him two coins. In exchange, Meryat handed her a greasy paper with three pieces of kibbee placed lovingly upon it.

The old woman grabbed Beatrice's hand and spread her flowered handkerchief over it before handing over the food. "I suppose it will be pointless to make plans for dinner now," she said. "I expect you'll be complaining of stomachache by this evening."

"Never a stomachache, beautiful lady—"

"Oh, do stop calling me that!" Grams snapped. "Excuse us, but we really must . . . Good heavens, that's President Marshall," she exclaimed.

Meryat peered past his awning. "Kibbee!" he roared. Quickly he replaced the Union Jack with an American flag.

"My brother, he drive taxi in New York ten years!"

Grams gave him a hard stare. Meryat shrugged.

"God bless America!" he shouted as the elderly English lady propelled the young blind girl toward the pot stall.

Former President William C. Marshall picked his way slowly through the bazaar, smiling genially for the photographers, trying without much success to hide the limp from his bad knee.

He was sixty-seven years old. It had been more than two decades since he had held any official position with the American government, but it seemed he was busier now than he had ever been. Despite a less than stellar reputation with the American press, he had been called upon more than fifteen times since leaving office to settle some disagreement or other in foreign countries ranging from obscure new African countries to international hotspots.

His own government had not sent him on these missions. They were too dangerous, the National Security Council said after the first foreign emissary had journeyed to Marshall's home in Pennsylvania. The United States would take no responsibility for his death while attempting to negotiate a peace in some unpronounceable country in which civil war had been raging for years, said the CIA. Aside from the usual Secret Service protection granted any former President, Marshall was to be on his own.

"He'll make a laughingstock of me," said the current President.

Yet Bill Marshall had succeeded alone where the entire political apparatus of the international community had failed. And he had done it fifteen times.

About fourteen times too many, he thought as he pretended to admire a ceramic incense burner. Who used incense, anyway, he wondered. If someone smoked a cigar or passed wind, you opened a window. You didn't stink up the place even worse with something that smelled like charred flowers.

Marshall set down the pottery after the cameras were finished with him and took out his handkerchief to wipe his face. It was hot as blazes out here, and his bum knee was killing him. This job, he decided, had even more of a downside than the Presidency. He still had to put up with the ill-mannered photographers and reporters, but his stints away from home were now measured in months, not days.

He missed his house on Apple Tree Road, where he had lived since he was a boy. He missed his wife, who had accompanied him everywhere when he was in office. It was too dangerous for her now. Without the extraordinary precautions taken for a visiting head of state, he was a sitting duck for any of a thousand terrorist organizations who wanted to get its name on the evening news.

That was especially true of this mission. The United Nations had long since abandoned hope of negotiating any sort of treaty between Israel and the Palestinians. In Marshall's own heart, too, he believed this effort would fail. He had been approached, not by a representative of either government, but by a contingent of rabbis and Islamic holy men. This would be a mission of peace, they had argued at the house on Apple Tree Road, brought about by men with differing faiths but the same God.

And so it had been for God that William Marshall had undertaken the task of meeting with both reluctant parties in the neutral setting of Marrakesh, because God could work miracles, and it would take no less than a miracle to pull this off.

But God and Man were two different species. No one was holding his breath on this one.

"Good heavens, that's President Marshall!" a refined-sounding old English woman shouted from the next stall.

Marshall sighed as the four Secret Service agents assigned to him closed ranks. They assumed everyone was an assassin, even white-haired old ladies who squealed at him in recognition.

She was towing an adolescent girl who didn't seem to be able to walk as quickly as the old woman might have liked. The girl tripped over some camera equipment and fell sprawling on the ground. Then the cameraman started shouting, the old woman shouted back, and the Secret Service agents were all over everyone like a coat of paint.

"For crying out loud," Marshall muttered. "She isn't—"

Something ripped into his chest. A split-second later, as he was falling backward into the pottery stall, he heard the report from the gun.

It all seemed to happen so slowly: The Secret Service men, forgetting the scuffle between the tourists and the cameraman, leapt up into a crouch as if they had been jerked upright on strings, their weapons drawn, their heads all swivelling in the same direction. On the ground, the teenage girl screamed first, followed by other, more distant shrieks. Marshall felt the flimsy stall counter collapse under his weight. One by one, the wares for sale crashed onto the ground. The incense burner which he had been holding flew out of his hands and glided past the stallkeeper, whose horrified expression seemed to be permanently frozen onto his face. Two of the agents broke into a run, their legs pistoning in unison as a leisurely stream of clay pots struck Marshall's pulpy, blood-soaked chest. Another flipped open a portable phone and barked into it. The fourth turned, with the slow grace of a dancer in a dream, and loped toward the ex-President.

He was thirsty. As he closed his eyes, Marshall saw an image of his house back in Pennsylvania. There was an old well up in the woods, now dry and boarded over, where his grandfather used to keep a bucket and a battered tin ladle. Occasionally the bucket would bring up a tiny spring frog or a dead junebug, but nothing tasted better than the water from that well.

Something warm was on his body. His hand closed around it. It was metal, like the tin ladle at the well. He squeezed it tightly, feeling the pulse in his fingers as his heartbeat ebbed. He tried to lick his dry lips, but found he lacked the energy. Blood was pooling on the inside of his cheek.

The two remaining Secret Service men were approaching him, and the souks had broken into a wild pandemonium, but Marshall no longer saw or heard anything.

The ladle in his hand was warming. Warming . . . getting hot . . .

An errant thought passed through his mind that it wasn't really a ladle at all, but some sort of battered metal cup. He wasn't back on Apple Tree Road. He was in Marrakesh, and he'd been shot in the chest by some invisible assailant, and he had lost a lot of blood. The wound was bad. Bad and getting . . .

. . . better . . .

Better?

Much better, Marshall thought with astonishment. He opened his eyes. An ambulance was blaring into the souks. Propping himself up on his elbows, he sat up. Immediately two Secret Service pushed him down again and then lifted him carefully, expertly, onto a gurney. One of them took the metal cup from his hand and tossed it away.

"The cup," Marshall said weakly, but no one paid attention to him.

As soon as he was in the ambulance, a paramedic cut open his shirt. The ambulance was already roaring out of the marketplace when the blood-soaked strips of broadcloth were peeled away and Marshall's chest swabbed.

The paramedic looked up, bewildered. "Where is the wound?" he asked one of the Secret Service men.

"For chrissake," the agent snapped. "Right—" A deep line creased his forehead. With his fingers, the agent probed around the iodine-tinted hair on Marshall's chest.

All he could find was a single puckered dent, like an old healed scar.

CHAPTER TWO

Inside the souks, a cameraman kicked the battered metal cup out of his way as he shot some footage of the blood-spattered stall where Marshall had fallen. The cup rolled along the ground, coming finally to rest beside the blind girl.

"Grams," Beatrice sobbed, casting about with her hands. She hadn't risen since she fell over the camera operator's equipment. Her white stockings were torn at the knee, and her sunglasses lay crushed a few feet away. "Grams, please be all right."

"I'm here, darling." The old woman's voice quavered above the wail of the ambulance siren She crawled over the rubble of fallen pots toward the girl and wrapped her arms around her. "Thank God you weren't hurt." Her tears fell on the dirty skirt of Beatrice's dress. "Oh, my, you've torn your stocking," she said, touching her handkerchief to the girl's scraped knee.

"What happened, Grams? Was someone shot?"

"I'm afraid so, dear. It was the American Pres . . . good heavens." She rubbed Beatrice's knee with her finger. Her glove had blood on it, yet the wound was gone. "Your knee . . ."

"Grams, something's happening to me," Beatrice whispered. Trembling, she sat upright. In her lap was a green-tinged metal cup. Slowly Beatrice's fingers closed over it. "It's coming from this," she said slowly. "It's warm."

"That? Why, it's nothing but an old . . ." She rubbed her fingers together. The blood on her gloves was still damp. ". . . thing. . . ."

"I can see," the girl said.

Startled, the old woman looked up. Her granddaughter's eyes, clouded and crossed from birth, were staring directly at her, blue as the sea. "You . . . Beatrice, you must be—"

"I can see you, Grams."

She stood before the mirror in the hotel room, touching again and again the smooth surface of the glass. The walk back from the bazaar had been nearly overwhelming for her: The riot of color and shapes and motion teeming around her was like suddenly finding herself on another planet. The sensations offered up to her had been so strong that she had felt neither joy nor fear, only immense surprise which compounded with every passing second.

But nothing had prepared her for the sight of her own face.

All her life, she had thought of her "self" as something internal— her thoughts, perhaps, or something beyond them. A being that only perceived, not an object in itself. And yet here she was, a girl who was nearly an adult, with creamy skin and red cheeks and frightened eyes the color of the sky she had seen this afternoon. And hair, gold-colored hair that hung down her back and tangled in front of her eyes.

"We should call a doctor," Grams said uncertainly, still reeling from the shock of Beatrice's revelation that her sight had been restored.

"No, not yet. I want to get used to things first. Everything's so . . . so strange."

It would have been different if she had been sighted at one time. She would have remembered what it was to see. But Beatrice had been blind from birth. She had never had a concept of the color red, never seen printing, never appreciated that old people looked very different from young people. She had not had time to prepare for the onslaught of visual sensations that had bombarded her from the moment she had picked up the rough metal cup, and the experience was at once magnificent and terrifying.

She turned the cup over in her hands. It was the simplest of containers, a plain bowl small enough to fit in the palm of her hand. Its exterior was bumpy, like a rock whose sharp projections had been worn away by time, but the interior was perfectly scooped, without a single chip or flaw. Its color was a deep blackish green and was translucent when held to the light, as if it were actually made of glass.

"Beatrice, are you sure . . ."

"Yes, Grams. I'm not making it up."

"Oh, I didn't mean—"

"No, of course not." She smiled at the old woman's guilty expression, and understood it. Her condition had been diagnosed as retinopathy prematura—massive hemorrhage in the retinal capillaries at birth—and was incurable. There had never been any hope that Beatrice would see. The doctors had made that very clear to the family from the beginning, and they had accepted Beatrice's blindness as she herself had.

But this was a miracle. As soon as the cup had warmed in her hands, it had become a part of her, as much a part of her as her arms or her organs. It was Beatrice's private miracle, and she would not let it go. Not ever.

Someone knocked, and the sound sent a jolt of terror through her. She had experienced the feeling only once before, on the night her parents were killed on a rain-slicked road twenty miles from home. Beatrice had been in bed, but the terror had been enough to send her screaming into the hallway.

She had been eight years old. Later, the psychiatrists who would become such a large and unwanted part of her life would say that she had imagined the premonition after the fact of her parents' death. They would explain away all of her special knowledge with the word "imagination."

But the danger inherent in the knock at the hotel room door was not imaginary, any more than Beatrice's certainty of her parents' doom had been. "Don't answer it, Gram!" she shouted, but by the time she'd found her voice, her grandmother was already turning the knob.

"No!" Beatrice leapt to her feet.

The door slammed inward, hitting the old woman's head. A gray-bearded man in Arab robes caught her as she fell with one hand and turned her frail, small body away from him. Then, pulling a long knife from the sleeve of his robe, he slashed once, powerfully, against her throat.

For a moment Grams hung suspended in the man's arms, her blood bubbling out of her, shooting across the room. A spray, ripe with the odor of her grandmother's warm blood, hit Beatrice's face.

For a moment the girl stood frozen, too shocked to utter a sound. Then she saw Gram's body slide out of the man's hands toward the floor.

Oh God, no, no, she thought as she backed away from the Arab.

He approached her slowly, his face as expressionless and efficient as the manner in which he had killed Grams. He lifted his robes as he stepped over the pool of blood that had shot out of the old woman's neck. With an almost elegant gesture, he flicked the blood from the long blade away from him so that it would not stain his garments. His eyes narrowed slightly.

He was trying to figure out how to kill her, Beatrice realized. She retreated further. Her back struck the open window; she could feel her buttocks trembling against the sill. Then the man's forehead cleared, and he took one step to the right. He had calculated the exact angle of his attack.

His arm drew back slowly, a small, economical movement in which Beatrice felt the man's complete concentration focus to a pinpoint. With a gasp, she scrambled onto the sill. Then, as he reached for her, she fell with a shriek toward the pavement four stories below.

She struck the stones of the courtyard with a thud and the sickening crack of broken bones. A smattering of people—a European nurse sitting on a bench beside a stroller, an old man reading, a young couple holding hands—leapt up at the intrusion. The young woman screamed. Beatrice sighed once, joltingly aware of the pain streaking through her body. When she opened her eyes, she saw the flap of a white robe from inside her hotel room. The man was coming after her.

Got to get up, she thought, dazed. The people in the courtyard were moving toward her, their movements slowed as if she were experiencing a dream. And while they were moving, their expressions stunned, their hands trembling, Beatrice felt her bones knitting, the warmth of the cup spreading through her injuries, healing the broken blood vessels, pulling her cells back together.

The cup. She was still holding it, clutching it so hard that her fingers were white. It throbbed hotly in her hands, singing to her as it did its work. The cup was what the man wanted. He had killed Grams just to get to Beatrice, to *this*.

Get up, she screamed at herself. *Get up now.*

Groaning, she pulled herself to her feet. The onlookers in the court-yard halted in their slow-motion pilgrimage toward her. The young woman fell to her knees, either in prayer or simple astonishment; the old man blinked owlishly. Around Beatrice were scattered droplets of her own blood, from wounds now entirely healed. She stared at them for a moment, struggling to believe her eyes, then lit out from the garden into the streets of the city.

Beatrice tore through the cluttered street, stumbling as she crashed into a stall where gaily colored scarves danced lazily in the hot desert air.

The stall owner shrieked at her in Arabic. Across the serpentine market street, two veiled women turned to one another, giggling. Be-side them, squatting before a blanket strewn with trinkets and glass beads, an old crone in a filthy burnoose directed a gesture toward Beatrice, hands brushing together as protection against whatever spirit had driven the European girl with the long golden hair crazy.

This might be a dream, she thought hopefully. It certainly seemed like a dream, from the shooting in the bazaar onward. Maybe she hadn't seen her grandmother murdered in front of her. Maybe she hadn't fallen four stories to a stone pavement and broken nearly every bone in her body. Maybe there was no cold-eyed Arab who moved with the grace of a dancer chasing her.

Let this be a dream, she prayed. *Oh God, yes.* She would wake up in the small squishy bed next to Grams', and daylight would be streaming through the window, and . . .

And I'd still be blind.

She pumped her legs faster, gulping for air. No, she had never dreamed like this. She had had running dreams before, but the land-scape had been entirely different. It had been the amorphous night-mare world of the blind, in which menace exuded from hidden sounds and smells and shapes that bumped her as she passed. This was differ-ent. Color screamed at her from every inch of the universe. Shapes were not something you felt when you drew near to them, but real objects that assaulted and intruded into you from a far distance. The buildings she saw were not the perfect monolithic structures she had imagined, but crumbling towers of stone and wood. And people in this new world were all strangers.

Behind her a shot rang out. Someone screamed.

Beatrice cast a glance backward and saw a woman fall. The people on the street looked wildly around to see where the shot had come from. Voices rose in a frenzied crescendo as the mob of terrified pedestrians trapped in the tight bottleneck of the ancient street sought to get clear. They ducked into doorways and flattened themselves against the sides of the narrow buildings, trying to make themselves invisible to the invisible gunman.

That was for me, Beatrice thought as she watched the woman's still body sprawled on the garbage-strewn street. The man in the white robes knew exactly where she was, and would kill whomever he needed to get to her. Her only hope was to manage somehow to melt into the panicked crowd.

"Thanatos," a woman shrilled as she crossed in front of Beatrice.

A man responded in English. "He's here?"

The woman nodded tearfully. "That is what they say. At the bazaar today, an American diplomat was shot. Assassination."

Just then Beatrice caught sight of her reflection in a small mirror hanging outside a rickety stall. The sight was terrifying. Blood painted one entire side of her face. Her yellow hair was matted with it. For a moment she stood still, frozen at the image of herself.

It was no wonder the man could spot her. Quickly she grabbed a loose garment from inside the unattended stall. The soft fabric stuck to her blood-sticky fingers.

Her grandmother's blood.

Beatrice choked back a sob. She had died in Beatrice's place, just as another woman had now died.

Leave the cup, she told herself. *Leave it and hide. He won't search for you in this crowd once he has the cup. You'll be safe.*

Her fingers trembled.

And blind.

"No," she whispered, her face set. The cup belonged to her, and so did her sight. If the Arab wanted either, he was going to have to kill her first.

As she ran back toward the crowd, an old beggar carrying a large sack over his shoulder crashed directly into her. Then everything happened almost too quickly for Beatrice to follow. A second shot rang out, this time very close. She felt a thud as the bullet tore into the rag bag the beggar had slung over his shoulder.

"Who . . . what . . ." she began, but the beggar fell with his full weight on top of her, then picked Beatrice up and ran with her toward the cluster of buildings just beyond the panic-stricken crowd. She struggled to get loose, but the old man's strength was astonishing.

There are two of them, she thought. "Help me!" she shouted, but the crowd of onlookers was too terrified to respond to her plea. She still held the cup in her hand. She brought it up and crashed it down on the old man's head with all her strength. The beggar staggered, and Beatrice struggled to wriggle free, but at that moment another bullet cracked behind them.

This time it smashed into the old man's back. Beatrice saw the coarse fabric of his robe fly apart in a gaping, smoking hole where the bullet entered. She screamed. She was still screaming when the old man fell at the mouth of a narrow alleyway.

Stumbling to her feet, Beatrice looked down at the old man, then in the other direction, toward the far end of the alley. Out there was freedom; the alley was certain capture and death at the hands of the white-robed man.

Hesitantly, she touched the old man's head. A vein throbbed in his temple. He wasn't dead yet, though with the bullet wound in his back, he would surely die soon.

Unless she helped him with the cup.

Three dead for me, she thought. *How many others will I allow to die so that I can keep the cup?* She looked again at the sunlight at the end of the alley.

Three is too many.

With a sigh, she knelt beside the beggar and gently turned him over. At least the cup would do some good before it was taken from her, she thought.

To her surprise, she could not find the wound. Then the old man sat up with surprising agility and smiled. He had wonderful teeth, Beatrice noticed.

"Thank you," he said in perfect King's English.

CHAPTER THREE

Hal pushed the last of the small change to the center of the table. "Three hundred eighteen dirham. How much is that in dollars?"

"Fifty-eight," the boy said automatically. "And thirty-two cents, at yesterday's exchange rate."

Arthur Blessing stood at the window in the cheap room the two had rented in the Medina, the Old City of Marrakesh. In the street, a crowd of people was shouting, running in all directions. "Something's going on. I heard gunshots."

"This place is getting to be as bad as the States," Hal said. He stretched on the rickety chair he was sitting on. It creaked portentously. "Speaking of which, maybe it's time we headed back." He said it as casually as he could, but he saw the boy tense. "We're not going to find her, Arthur," he added gently. "Not here, anyway. We've looked everywhere."

Arthur turned toward him. "But your old boss at the FBI said she'd come to Marrakesh. . . ."

"That was more than six months ago," Hal said. "And his information was old then."

"So maybe you could ask him again."

Hal shook his head. "I've tried. Koehler's retired." He forced himself to meet Arthur's eyes. "I didn't tell you because I thought you'd be upset."

"When?" the boy asked dully.

"A couple months ago." He fiddled with the coins on the table. "I couldn't get anyone else at the Bureau to talk to me." He smiled ruefully. Cashiered federal agents were as easily forgotten as dust under a bed. "I guess part-time auto mechanics don't carry a lot of clout in Washington."

In silhouette against the bright light from the window, the boy's shoulders slumped. "Do you think Emily's dead?" he asked.

Arthur was thirteen and small for his age, a redheaded urchin far from manhood, despite his lightning-quick mind. Sometimes it was hard for Hal to remember that the boy wasn't still the ten-year-old child who had followed him so trustingly through most of Europe and North Africa.

"No, she's not dead. She got herself lost, that's all. You told her how to do it."

"But three years . . ."

"Listen, Arthur, your aunt's all right. No one's come after us, have they?"

The boy shook his head.

"Then they haven't come after her, either."

Hal wished he could feel as certain as he sounded. Three years ago, when all their lives had become tangled in a nightmare too strange even for the police to sort out, the two of them had left Arthur's legal guardian, Emily Blessing, behind in a small village in England with instructions on how to erase her identity if that became necessary. Hal, meanwhile, took the boy into hiding.

After six months, when the danger to them had passed, they began to look for Emily. They'd been looking ever since.

"I just thought that by now she'd . . ." His voice trailed away.

. . . *she'd go back to her life,* Hal thought.

That was how it was supposed to be. Emily had had a good career with a solid future. Her only drawback had been Arthur. She had never wanted to raise a child in the first place; her sister had left the boy to her when she killed herself. It would not have been fair to take her from everything she knew to go to ground with a boy she had never wanted to raise and a man she had never wanted to love.

"Take it easy," Hal said. He got up and tried to put his arm around Arthur, but the boy shrugged him off. As a teenager, he considered himself too old for such overt affection.

And Hal? Was he too old, too? Emily Blessing had kindled a spark in Hal that he had believed to be long dead. The spark had flamed into one night of love before it had scared them both away.

It's too late, Emily had said as they lay in one another's arms. Too late for both of them.

And so he had let her go. Taken his unwanted love and her unwanted child and set out on a new life for them all.

Only it hadn't worked out that way. Emily had not returned to the think tank in Chicago where she had worked. As far as they could tell—with the help of Hal's former boss in the FBI—she hadn't even returned to the United States. Hal and Arthur had spent three years following a series of cold trails leading from London to Paris to Morocco. The last trail had ended here.

"With this money, plus what we've got socked away in the bank, we have enough to fly home."

"Home," Arthur said disdainfully. "Where's that, Hal? Chicago, where those people first started trying to kill me?"

"Nobody's trying to kill you now—"

"Do you plan to drop me off in some orphanage in Chicago? Is that what you're going to do if we can't find Emily?"

"Arthur . . ." Hal frowned, stunned by the boy's sudden vehemence.

"I suppose you've had enough of dragging a kid around with you," he spat. "A crazy kid."

"Hey." He tried to approach Arthur again, but the boy's angry scowl held him off. "Look, if you're crazy, then that makes two of us. I had the cup, too, remember?"

That was what had started it all, the cup. An unassuming little metal bowl that had changed their lives forever.

The boy stared out the window, then raised his hands to cover his face.

"It's gone now," Hal said softly. "The cup's gone. No one's going to try to hurt you anymore. And I'm not going anywhere without you."

This time it was Arthur's arms that flung around Hal. "I'm sorry for being such a baby," the boy said, sobbing into Hal's neck. "It's just that I don't want to be alone."

"You won't be," Hal said. "I'll never leave you. Never, as long as you need me. That's a promise."

There was a thump at the door. Hal scooped all the money off the table into his pockets.

"*Lahaza shweia,*" he growled in Arabic. "Hold your hor—" Before he could finish, the door burst open and a filthy old man tumbled inside.

Hal was on him in an instant, the crook of his arm around the beggar's throat. "I think you got the wrong room, buddy," he said.

"Gaaa," said the old man.

Arthur walked closer. "Hal, let him go."

"Oh, I'll do that, all right." He propelled the beggar into the hallway.

"No, stop. Hal! It's . . ."

The hood of the old man's robe fell backward, revealing a pair of bright blue eyes beneath a shock of white hair. "Taliesin," he said, dropping the old man at the threshold.

"Good heavens," the old man said, rubbing his neck, "what a coarse creature you turned out to be."

Hal crossed his arms. "After three years, you might have waited for me to answer the door."

"I was in a hurry." A broad smile lit up the old man's face. "Arthur! You've grown, boy."

"Where've you been?" Hal went on accusingly. "You said you'd catch up to us."

"So I have," Taliesin said. "Here I am. By the way, I've brought someone with me."

Hal peered out the door. The hallway was empty. "Someone invisible?"

"Of course she's visible. Beatrice?" He crooked his finger. "Come along, dear."

Hesitantly, the girl emerged from a doorway down the dimly lit corridor.

"Now, now, no one here's going to hurt you."

As she walked toward them, Hal and Arthur exchanged a glance. The girl was wrapped in some sort of cotton shawl with the pricetag hanging prominently near her right ear. Her face, or what they could see of it, was streaked with dirt and what looked like dried blood. She entered the room without speaking, her eyes downcast.

Hal glared at Taliesin. "How old is she?" he asked.

"Why, I'm sure I don't know," the old man said. "We've only just met. How old are you, child?"

"Twelve," Beatrice answered in a whisper. The shawl fell off her head, showing a cascade of long blonde hair. Arthur swallowed. Her eyes swept over him and he blushed, suddenly realizing that he'd been staring.

Her lower lip trembling, she straightened her spine and held her head high. "Well, now that you've got me here, I suppose you'll get what you wanted," she said.

Arthur's eyebrows rose. Taliesin smiled.

"And what would that be?" Hal asked, scowling.

From the folds of her robe she pulled out the cup and set it on the table, where it gleamed like the moon of a distant planet.

Hal's head reeled. He reached for the wooden chair and sat down. It broke under his weight. Taliesin burst into hearty laughter.

"It's come back," Arthur said softly.

Hal lumbered to his feet. "Get that thing out of here."

"That wouldn't be wise," Taliesin said. "It would only come back again, possibly at the cost of Beatrice's life. Or yours. Fate has a way of working itself out, you know. By the way, which way is the shower? I'm disgusting."

Hal folded his arms and glowered at the cup. "Down the hall. You'll have to pay the drunk at the desk five dirham to turn on the water."

Taliesin made a face. "What sort of holes have you been living in?" he groused as he swung open the door.

"For two more dirham, he'll give you a towel."

When he was gone, Arthur poured some water from a pitcher into a basin and produced a scrap of cloth, which he handed to Beatrice. "Would you like to wash your face?" he asked diffidently.

Beatrice tore her gaze from the cup. She looked stricken.

"I mean, you don't have to wash if you don't want to," Arthur waffled. "It's just that—"

'I'm not blind," she said with astonishment.

Arthur looked at Hal.

"That is . . ."

"You used to be blind," Hal said understandingly. "Until you found the cup."

"Yes." She touched her eyes. "I don't understand it. I thought I had to hold it for it to work. . . ." She looked searchingly from one face to the other. "Those people who died . . . my grandmother . . . Just because I wouldn't leave the cup behind. . . ." She began to tremble violently. "Because I wanted so much to *see*. . . ."

"Shh." Hal tore a blanket off the bed and wrapped it around her. "Whatever's happened, you'll get it sorted out. But for now, everything's okay. You're safe here, okay?"

"You're . . . you're not going to kill me?"

"No."

"But the cup—"

"Believe me, that's the last thing we want."

Arthur brought her a cup of tea. "Maybe this'll make you feel better," he said.

Beatrice looked at him for a long moment, then smiled. "Thank you," she said.

With those words and the beauty of her blue eyes, every molecule of saliva in Arthur's mouth dried up.

By the time Taliesin returned from his shower, Beatrice had recounted the events leading to her appearance in their hotel room—the attempted assassination at the souks, the white-robed man who had murdered her grandmother, the miraculous healing of bones she knew she had broken during her fall to the courtyard of her hotel, and her encounter with the beggar who had brought her to safety.

"Mr. Taliesin only told me that there was a place where I could hide, so of course when I saw you—"

"Ah! That feels better!" the old man boomed as he swirled into the room.

Beatrice gasped. The man who stood before them was someone she would not have recognized in a hundred years as the barefooted beggar on the street. From his snowy white hair to his Savile Row bermudas, Taliesin was the picture of colonial elegance. From the filthy bag he had brought with him, he took a pith helmet and placed it jauntily on his head. "How's that?"

"You planning to go on safari?" Hal asked.

"This is perfectly appropriate attire for the climate," Taliesin sniffed. "Whereas you, I see, continue to dress from the racks of the Salvation Army."

Suddenly Beatrice stood up. Her tea splashed onto the floor. "He's coming," she whispered.

Taliesin shivered. His eyes locked onto Beatrice's, which were staring blankly through him.

"Who's coming?" Arthur ventured.

"Never mind," the old man said, grabbing the cup. "Is there a way to the roof?"

"Sure. Up the stairs—"

"Go." He put his hands on Arthur's shoulders and propelled him toward the door. Hal followed. "You too, child," the old man told Beatrice. He took her by the hand. The moment he touched her, a thousand images sprang into his mind: a grove of tall oaks . . . the incessant drone of chanting . . . a circle of stones, impossibly high, suddenly ablaze with light from the first ray of morning . . .

He stared at her, his legs weak. "We have to hurry," he managed finally. He closed the door behind them and ran on silent feet with the girl up to the roof.

Within moments the white-robed man was inside the room. He tossed the meager contents of the drawers onto the floor, slashed open the pillows, checked the floorboards.

The cup was not there.

The concierge—or rather the diseased old sot that passed for a concierge in this flea trap—had said that one of them, the old man, was taking a shower, but there had been no one in the shower room.

Quickly the man raced to the top of the stairs and climbed up the fire ladder leading to the roof. It was empty. On the street below, he saw a battered Jeep drive off toward the north. In it were four foreigners—an old man, a young one, and a teenage boy and girl. Behind them ran an irate Moroccan, shouting and shaking his fist.

The man in the white robe blew out a puff of air in disgust. Finding them had been rather too much to hope for. Besides, he thought resignedly, it was probably for the best. Police were swarming over the area now. It was just as well they didn't find four fresh bodies in addition to that of the American ex-President.

Back in the abandoned hotel room, he removed the billowing white garment he was wearing and dressed in a nondescript brown shirt and trousers he had taped to his body beneath the burnoose. He peeled away the gray moustache and a small latex tip off the end of his nose.

The police were searching the area for a middle-aged Arab in white robes. Several people had seen him shoot the beggar with the girl. He took a quick glance in the mirror above the bureau to be sure all trace of the spirit gum was gone.

It was. No one would recognize him now.

No one ever did.

He had not expected to find them, really, not after what the concierge had told him. He had asked for the room where the beggar had gone with the girl. The concierge had told him it belonged to an American who was traveling with a boy. The boy had red hair.

He had known instantly who it was.

He did not need to follow them. *Let them think they've gotten away,* he thought with amusement. When the time was right, they would give the cup to him. And it would not be in a crowded city swarming with police over the assassination of some aged politician.

He picked up a piece of paper, set fire to it, then used the scrap to light a cigarette. Slowly, he walked around the room lighting the pillows and the thin cloth curtains. When the blaze became smoky enough, he went into the hall to wait.

All in all, it had been a good day's work. Marshall was dead and, in a happy coincidence, the cup had finally been located.

All the pieces were in place. The game was finally ready to begin.

At the first scream of "Fire!" he tossed his cigarette to the floor, crushed it with his shoe, and ambled outside.

CHAPTER FOUR

Hal pulled the Jeep to a stop some ninety miles northeast of Marra-kesh, at a gas station consisting of a mud-brick hut in front of which were stacked two pyramids of gasoline cans under a canvas awning. For the past several hours he had been driving back roads flanking the towering Atlas Mountains, but the mountains now loomed directly in front of them.

It had all seemed like a colossal waste of time to Hal, not to mention the fact that he faced time in a Moroccan prison for stealing the car if they were caught. And all because a teenage girl thought someone was after her.

He had been willing to believe her for the first few miles, but the Jeep had been the only vehicle on the road for the past hour.

"If someone's chasing us, he's a damn slow driver," he had com-plained, but Taliesin insisted that he go on. For some reason the old man was absolutely convinced that the girl was right. She had directed them onto this road, and Taliesin would hear of no objections, even after she'd admitted that she'd only been in the country for three days.

Still, the old man's instincts were good—actually, a lot better than good—and if he said run, Hal wasn't about to question him.

"Well?" he asked. "Where to now? Back to the hotel?" he asked hopefully.

"That way," Beatrice said, pointing straight at the snow-covered peaks.

"Those are mountains," Hal said, somewhat unnecessarily.

"Do what she says," Taliesin said.

"But . . ." He sighed. There was no point in protesting, he knew. He filled the Jeep's tank with eighteen laboriously poured cans of gas, then bought ten more to carry with them.

"We don't have any food or water, you know," he grumbled. "We'll probably be buried under an avalanche. Anything could happen to us in that wilderness, and we're not prepared for any of them."

"Yes we are," Arthur said quietly. "We have the cup."

That night they stopped near the village of Ait Haddus. They had tried for a hotel there, but since there was none in the tiny farm community, they had to resign themselves to a night spent in the open air. Fortunately there was a store in Ait Haddus, where Hal further depleted his meager resources to buy a couple of blankets to keep between their bodies and the rocky ground, as well as some dates, almonds, olives, three bottles of seltzer water, and, since there were no trees, an armload of dried donkey dung for a fire.

The dung briquettes, though aromatic, burned fairly well. As they ate their exotic meal around it, they watched the sun settle in a red haze over the mountain peaks. Beneath them spread the monochromatic village, a succession of squares and rectangles made of the same red earth on which they sat.

"It's magnificent, isn't it," Taliesin said contentedly, unwrapping a yellowed newspaper that contained the dates.

Hal grunted, thinking about his rock-pitted buttocks.

"One might never know western civilization ever existed. . . . Good grief." He parted the dates on the newspaper. "It's in English. The *International Herald Tribune*."

Arthur craned his neck to see. "Only the want ads. Oh, man." He grabbed the paper, scattering the dates onto the ground. "Hal, look at this."

"Look at *this*!" Taliesin shouted, gesturing toward the spilled fruit as Arthur scrambled past him.

"Work in Lichtenstein," Hal read from the black-bordered box ad on the center of the page.

"Not that. Here." He pointed to a small ad in the personals column next to it.

ARTHUR B, it began.
Meet me at seven at the Victoria Hotel in Tangier. I will stay as long as I can.
Your aunt Emily.

"She's alive, Hal."

Hal frowned. "I can't believe we happened to get this particular newspaper—"

"And she's looking for me."

"Right." He felt the texture of the paper. It seemed all right.

"What's the matter? Aren't you glad?"

Hal raised his eyes to the boy. Arthur's face was transformed with happiness. "Sure, kid. It's just that . . ."

That coincidences like this just don't happen.

Still, how could something like this have been arranged? They hadn't even known themselves which direction they were heading. He looked at Taliesin and arched an eyebrow. The old man shrugged. "Okay, I'm glad," he said, ruffling the boy's hair. "Damn glad." The two of them laughed, and Hal allowed himself at last to feel some measure of relief.

"Wait a minute. When did this run?" He checked the date. "It's from September of last year," he said. "That's three months before we ever got to Morocco."

"So? She might still be in Tangier."

Hal sighed. "I wouldn't count on it. Still, it may be a place to start."

"Tangier," Beatrice said, staring into the fire. "Yes, that's where it will begin."

"Where what will begin?" Arthur asked.

The girl blinked. "Did you say something?" she asked apologetically. "I must have been daydreaming."

"You said something would happen in Tangier."

"Did I?" She blushed deeply. "I'm sorry. I can't imagine . . ."

Taliesin was eyeing her sharply. "We'll go to Tangier," he said.

"Now wait a minute." Hal held up his hands. "We'll go, okay? But in a day or two, after we've had a chance to pack, check out of our hotel, go to the bank . . ."

"We'll go now," Taliesin said.

"Why? This newspaper's nine months old. A day or two isn't going to make any difference." He looked at Beatrice. "Or is it because of her?"

"Yes," the old man said impatiently.

Hal put his hands on his hips. "Are you saying that just because a twelve-year-old girl who doesn't even remember saying anything—"

"Yes. We'll go now."

"We can't," Hal explained, gritting his teeth.

"Why not?"

"Money, for one thing!" Hal exploded. "How are we supposed to live in Tangier? After buying food and gas for this car—which, incidentally, we can't keep in Tangier because it's *stolen*—I've got exactly . . ." He dug all his remaining Moroccan currency out of his pockets and fumbled through it.

Arthur glanced over his shoulder. "Three bucks. Twenty-seven cents."

"Three bucks!" Hal slapped the bills into Taliesin's hands. "*You* support the four of us in Tangier with three bucks!"

"Oh, don't be melodramatic, Hal," Taliesin said. He handed the dirham notes back to him, then extracted a wad of bills from his crisp khaki shirt. "Use this."

Hal leafed through the bills. "There's a thousand dollars here," he said, gawking at it incredulously. "American."

"Yes, I believe you prefer those."

Hal squinted. "How'd you get this much money?"

"What does it matter?" the old man said, yawning. "It's only paper."

"Only—"

"Shall we rest awhile before continuing on?"

Hal's arms flapped against his sides. "To Tangier," he said, defeated. "Quite."

Long after Hal and Arthur had fallen asleep, Beatrice sat silently gazing into the dung fire. Taliesin sat nearby, leaning against a rock. He had been watching her for hours, trying to understand why he felt such a sense of—*obedience* was the only word, really—around her. Hal was right; she didn't know what she was saying half the time. It was as if Beatrice were two people, one of them a frightened child, and the other . . .

It was the other who commanded him, though how and why he did not begin to know. "What do you see in there, child?" Taliesin asked. "You haven't taken your eyes off that fire since it was lit."

"It's just . . . so beautiful," she said, looking embarrassed. "I always thought fire was just *heat*—you know, invisible." She smiled. "I'm afraid I sound like a simpleton."

"Not at all," the old man said. "I've spent many an evening staring at fires myself. It gets cold in Wales."

"Wales! Is that where you're from?"

He nodded. "And you?"

"Dorset. Near the Somerset border."

Taliesin sucked in his breath. "Near Wilson-on-Hamble?"

"Yes. Do you know it?"

He nodded. "Have you heard about the doings on St. John's Eve?"

She laughed. "Of course. We all have. The ruins of Camelot are in our back yard. In midsummer, on St. John's Eve, the ghosts of the knights of the Round Table ride out in search of King Arthur. At least that's how the stories go."

"Do you believe them? The stories?"

She doodled on the soft ground with her finger. "I don't know. My parents didn't. They made fun of the villagers and their superstitions."

"Your parents!" Taliesin slapped the side of his head. "Good heavens, child, you haven't told them about—"

"There's no need." Her finger stopped moving in the dirt. "They died four years ago in a motorcar accident."

"Oh, my," he said softly. "I'm sorry."

"My grandmother raised me since then. And now that she's gone . . ." Tears sprang to her eyes and threatened to spill over.

"Beatrice . . ."

"No, I'm all right." She wiped her face. "It's just that I can't help but feel that I've somehow . . . traded her. For my sight."

"You mustn't believe that."

"But I do! Even when that man was . . . killing her . . ." She wept silently, her tears falling in dark circles on the ground. ". . . even then, all I could think about was being able to see."

"I understand," he said.

"No, you don't!" she shouted angrily. "You can't know what it's like to be blind! You've probably never even known a blind person."

"Oh, but I have. My teacher was blind."

"It's not the same." Beatrice sniffed. "Your teacher?"

Taliesin nodded.

"What did he teach?"

"She. My instructor—my master—was a woman." The old man cocked his head and smiled. "I suppose you'd say she taught life." He picked up a stone. It was gypsum, clear as water. He held it up to the slim bright crescent of light in the night sky.

"Selene," she said. "For the moon. It will bring clarity of vision."

"Why, quite right." He smiled delightedly. "You used the archaic term. Are you a student of the spiritual properties of stones? I understand there are quite a few of those these days."

She frowned. "No," she said, touching the stone with the tip of her finger as if it were an insect. "I've never seen a rock like this before."

There was a silence. Finally the old man said, "Ah, no matter. Someone must have mentioned it to you."

"Yes," she answered numbly.

Clarity of vision, she thought, looking into the fire. How had those words come into her head?

How had she come to know any of the strange things she had known all her life?

A psychologist had once asked her to describe her dreams. They were typical blind person's dreams, amorphous, filled with touch and sound. The only unusual thing was that several of them were recurring.

"There's a grove of oak trees," Beatrice explained. "It's around a circular clearing, with smoke rising up from the center of it. . . ."

"Yes? And are you in this dream?" the therapist prompted.

Beatrice nodded. "I'm dressed in a long woolen robe. It's raining, and I can smell the damp. The fire has been banked to embers, but there's something in it. . . ." She heard the swift intake of her own breath. "It's the heart of a stag, sacrificed for the festival of Midsummer. . . ."

The psychologist took notes in a leather-covered book. She looked up briefly. "What happened then, Beatrice?" she asked in a soprano singsong.

"Then . . . the magicians came."

The therapist's pencil stopped in mid air. "I beg your pardon?"

"The magicians. The sorcerers. They came to Mona. They killed my priests while I was in prayer. They burned everything."

The psychologist scribbled furiously. "Mona? Is that a place?"

"It was our place. Our last refuge." Tears ran down her face.

The therapist gave her a tissue. "Tell me, Beatrice," she asked, "do you sometimes feel that someone has taken your sight from you? The doctor who delivered you, perhaps, or your mother, or God himself?"

Beatrice only wept.

"Perhaps you'd like to think about that for next time," the therapist said, glancing at her watch.

"Mona," Beatrice whispered.

Taliesin started. "What did you say?"

She looked up, surprised to see him. She had been so absorbed in her own past that she had forgotten she wasn't alone. "I . . . I don't remember."

The old man's lips tightened.

"Yes?" Beatrice asked gently. "What is it?"

"You said . . . That is, I thought you said . . ." He blinked. "Listen, child, you'd best get some rest while you can. Tomorrow we'll take you to the British Embassy in Tangier and see about getting you back home."

She examined her hands. "I don't have a home," she said.

"But . . . Surely your grandmother made some provision . . ."

She shrugged. "I'm to inherit the estate when I come of age. Until then, I'll probably be sent to a boarding school under the aegis of some law firm." She turned away from him and lay facing the fire. "But that's not your problem."

"Well . . ." The old man cleared his throat. "We'll think of something."

He sat silently in the thick stillness of night.

"I really should be with you," Beatrice said sleepily, the flames dancing before her closed eyes.

"In Tangier."

"Yes."

"Why, Beatrice?" he asked. "Why Tangier?"

It took her a long time to answer. "Because the cycle is ending," she said at last.

"The cycle?" His voice was barely audible.

"The cycle that began on Mona."

Taliesin felt his heart thudding. He had heard her correctly, then. She had spoken the name of a place which had not existed for a thousand years.

Mona.

It had been so long since he had thought of it. So long . . .

This was the cup's doing, he knew that instinctively. The cup had come back, and whatever plans Hal and Arthur had made would mean nothing. The cup would do its work.

For surely, he thought, studying the slumbering girl, that work had already begun.

CHAPTER FIVE

Paris, France

The newspapers called him Thanatos, Greek for death.

How they had come to the conclusion that he was Greek was un-certain. A dropped exclamation in his native language, perhaps, during his younger days before he had learned how to be silent.

He was silent now, so silent that, in his other life, the life open to public scrutiny, he sometimes had to remind himself to walk so that others could hear him.

He opened the morning's edition of *Le Figaro*. There on the front page was the story of how the American ex-President had been the target of a would-be assassin.

Would-be, he thought, disgusted. This failure would ruin his repu-tation. He read on. By a seeming miracle, the story went on, William Marshall had escaped the incident uninjured.

He tossed the paper aside angrily. The bullet had entered Marshall's body cleanly, near the heart. He had seen it strike, had watched the blood boil up out of the diplomat's mouth. And then he had watched the cup heal him without a mark.

Thanatos slumped into a chair and threw his head back. His career as an assassin was over.

He sighed. It was of no consequence, really, to anything except his pride. Murder had always been more of a hobby than a career for him, anyway. He had certainly never needed the money. The fact that he was perhaps the highest paid professional assassin in the world was strictly a matter of prestige.

And excitement, he supposed. At least in the beginning.

His real name was Aubrey Katsuleris, and it was a famous one. Mounted on one wall of his bedroom was a blowup of a cover of *International Artist* magazine, bearing a self-portrait of Aubrey's face and the caption *Katsuleris: The Warlock Women Love*.

The original portrait was hanging in the Museum of Modern Art in New York. The Pompidou had offered a good price for it, but Aubrey felt the French had execrable taste in their museums. They hung as much as they could in any space available, without regard to the style of the artist. He could not abide the thought of one of his angular, dark paintings resting for the next fifty years beside some vapid neo-classicist.

He had taken the blowup and created another painting around it which itself was one of his most brilliant works. With color and the spiky acute angles which were his trademark, the painting conveyed Aubrey's very essence. For the people who saw it—and several collectors had already made six-figure offers for it—the painting was both disturbing and irresistible, like its creator.

"He is a twenty-first century Dracula," the magazine article had stated. Aubrey had smiled at that. It had described his Paris apartment as "Vampire Chic" and his sprawling villa in Tangier as "the Valhalla of the gods of darkness."

That last, perhaps, was truer than they knew.

The article had been tongue-in-cheek, written for a sophisticated audience, so Aubrey had smiled charmingly at the questions about his notorious private life. No, he was not a demon genius, he answered. He had had parents like everyone else, although fortunately they had been wealthy enough to raise Aubrey in an atmosphere of privilege in which he could pursue his talent.

The only son of an elderly Greek shipping magnate and an English countess with a passion for art—and artists—Aubrey had been reared in several magnificent homes around the world, all filled with priceless treasures. The house on the Ile St. Louis in Paris was decorated entirely in the Art Nouveau style, from the authentic Tiffany chandelier to the stained glass windows designed by Lalique and painstakingly reconstructed piece by piece. The home in Athens was a treasure trove of classical sculpture, as was the villa in the Apennine foothills outside Rome. The stately eighteenth-century stone mansion on St. James Square was filled with Joshua Reynolds' dogs and Gainsborough's pretty children. There was a house of Impressionists in Geneva, a Bauhaus structure in Berlin stocked with the best of the postwar modernists, a replica of a Chinese palace in Kowloon housing a fortune in Ming and Tang dynasty porcelain.

And in each of those marvelous houses had been a man to keep Aubrey's mother company. With her unfailing sense of order, Madame Katsuleris chose only those suitors whose work fit the style of the house in which she received them.

So it was that when she met the artist Saladin, whose work was unlike anything she had ever encountered, she had been obliged to build another home.

She chose Tangier, the most international of cities, as its location. The structure was a sprawling series of cubes designed by Saladin himself, and filled with his own work. From the beginning, Aubrey had been fascinated by the artist who resided in this unusual house. He was nothing like his mother's other lovers, who all seemed to be whining, spoiled children who deferred absolutely to Madame's authority. They fawned on Aubrey with a false and nervous concern, and Aubrey did his best to make them as uncomfortable as possible, treating them much as he did the constantly changing tutors who travelled with him and his mother. These men were little more than servants—the tutors for him, the lovers for his mother—and did not merit any more respect or attention than the groundskeepers or the kitchen help.

But Saladin was different. Everything about him was different. For one thing, the man was nearly seven feet tall. His long arms and delicate fingers were like the wings of some exotic bird. His skin—the little Aubrey saw of it, since Saladin preferred to dress in ornate Oriental robes of his own design—was as smooth as a baby's. He wore a moustache and an extraordinarily long goatee, which gave him the air of a Chinese mandarin.

But the most telling feature about him was his eyes. They were a killer's eyes, cold, intelligent, merciless. From the moment he met Saladin, Aubrey loved his eyes.

His work, too, was leagues apart from anything Aubrey or his mother had seen before. The paintings were done in an astonishing variety of styles, from Byzantine to abstract, in every conceivable medium. Yet even Aubrey, at the age of ten, knew that these were not imitations of old masters. Each bore Saladin's unmistakable stamp, which gave them all an air of foreboding and darkness and, for the boy, pure seduction. The first time Aubrey saw Saladin's abstracts—displayed, naturally, in a room by themselves—he experienced an erection of such power that he had been forced to leave the room in pain.

Saladin's work was death personified. Death as a beautiful, terrifying and inexorable force, death as lover. Saladin loved death. That was what showed in his eyes.

His last works, which he completed at the villa in Tangier, were painted plaster sculptures. Terrible, powerful sculptures, realistic in every detail down to the flash of shock in their eyes, of people caught in the moment of death. The poses were often hideous, but the workmanship and the painting were so glorious that they seemed more vibrant than living beings.

When Madame Katsuleris showed these pieces to a dozen international collectors in a private exhibition, their response was immediate and visceral. Aubrey, at the age of fourteen, could see in their eyes the same mixture of sexual desire and shame that he himself had felt. In the end, each one of the collectors had, very discreetly, purchased one of the works at an astronomical price.

It was shortly after this exhibit that Saladin left the villa. His departure was sudden. He took nothing except the money brought in by the sale of his sculptures. He left no note. Aubrey's mother was beside herself with what could only be called grief, eventually selling all her other properties and artwork and returning to her husband in Athens.

Although Aubrey's father was nearing eighty at the time, he outlived his young wife by two full years. Madame Katsuleris died without a further word from her vanished lover.

When Saladin finally did reappear, only Aubrey was left. He was twenty-one then, and completing a degree in art history at the Sorbonne while experimenting with painting. He had had no desire to continue his father's shipping business; when the old man finally died, Aubrey had been left with an inheritance of over three billion dollars.

One evening he walked into his Paris apartment to find all his paintings lined up against the walls, with a candle in front of each. Saladin sat in a slingback chair in the center of the room, his long limbs folded near his body like a great spider. He was smoking, and in the candlelight the effect was enhanced by the smoke curling white around him like a finely spun web.

"They're imitative," Saladin said, not moving from his position. "Fortunately, though, you've imitated me, so they're rather good."

After an initial moment of shock, Aubrey let out his breath with a grin. "Where in the world have you been?" he asked.

"Oh, nowhere in particular. I bought a house in the south of England. Hideous weather." He handed Aubrey the still-burning butt of his cigarette to put out for him. "How long has it been, really? You look older."

"Seven years," Aubrey answered, tossing the butt in the fireplace. "You left when I was fourteen."

"Seven years," Saladin mused. "You were still a child then."

Aubrey moved closer to him in the candlelight. "On the other hand, *you* look exactly the same," he said, nonplussed.

That was the amazing thing about Saladin. From the time Aubrey had met him at the age of ten, the man seemed never to have aged a day. "Just how old are you?"

The tall man laughed. "I lost count long ago," he said.

Aubrey had let it go at that. He brought out a bottle of good wine and poured a glass for each of them. "My mother died four years ago," he said quietly.

"Did she?" Saladin's voice exhibited only the most casual interest.

"Before she died, she sold all her houses except the villa in Tangier. Your paintings are still there, if you want them."

Saladin waved him away. "They were never of any importance."

"Would you like the house?"

Saladin thought for a moment. "Very well, that might be useful. I may have to evade the authorities for a time."

"The police? Whatever for?"

Saladin sipped his wine. "Do you remember my sculptures? The dead?"

"Of course. What was so wonderful about them was that they were so vibrantly *alive*—"

"Yes, yes. Well, one of them was broken in transit, and the police found the body inside."

Aubrey blinked. For several seconds he could say nothing. Finally he whispered, "The *body?*"

Saladin sighed. "It was The Washerwoman. I was never happy with the midsection. Too much fat."

"Oh, my God. That's why they were so realistic."

"It most certainly was not!" Saladin snapped. "Try covering a body with plaster, and see how realistic it looks. The body was a sort of joke, a little surprise. Rather like the inside of a Tootsie Pop."

Aubrey leaned against a table, resting his forehead in his hand. "How did you get them . . . her? The prototype of the washerwoman."

"I killed her, of course. Cleaved her chest with an axe. The impact of the piece was dramatic, but the axe threw the weight of the thing all out of balance. I'd never do that again, never."

Aubrey coughed. "Excuse me," he said, and staggered to the bathroom. When he returned, his hands were trembling and his breath smelled of mouthwash. Saladin laughed.

"You're suffering over the death of the washerwoman, I suppose," he said gleefully. "Were you very close? Or, like John Donne, does every man's death diminish you?"

"If you'll pardon my impertinence, Saladin, I don't find the act of murder quite as amusing as you do." Aubrey tried to affect a look of icy dignity.

Saladin laughed louder. "Do stop, Aubrey. The righteous pretense of the bourgeoisie doesn't suit you."

"There is such a thing as right and wrong!"

"Is there?" Saladin asked innocently.

"Yes. And the taking of human life is wrong."

"Except in war."

"Well, of course."

"Or when the victim is a convicted wrongdoer."

"I hadn't—"

"Or an unborn child. Or the holder of power. You know, here in Paris, the 1789 slaughter of thousands of nobles and their families is still celebrated with great fervor. The murder of the powerful is only considered assassination if the attempt does not end in the transfer of that power. If it does, it's called revolution."

"What are you saying?"

"And the murder of commoners is condoned as well, when it's done in the name of one's god. Witness the Crusades. The Spanish Inquisition. In virtually every ancient culture, innocents were viciously murdered as sacrifices to whichever deity was in fashion."

"Saladin—"

"In feudal Japan, it was entirely permissible for a samurai to test the blade of a new sword by beheading a member of the lowest class. In America, the physician who attended the broken ankle of John Wilkes Booth was nearly executed, even though he'd had no idea that his patient had shot President Lincoln. Don't prattle to me about right and wrong. You don't know the first thing about it."

"And you do, I suppose. Tell me, Saladin, how would you feel about your own death?"

Saladin blinked thoughtfully. "It's the most exciting thing I can imagine," he said at last.

Aubrey sighed and turned toward the window. Outside, the glittering band of the Champs Elysee brightened the dark night. "Why have you come here?" he asked. "Apparently it wasn't to see my mother. I suppose I should be grateful you didn't turn her into one of your statues. You could have called it The Countess."

Saladin smiled ruefully. "Your mother was a lovely creature," he said. "She would have made a marvelous sculpture."

Aubrey threw up his hands.

"Come with me to Morocco," Saladin said. "Until Interpol loses interest in me."

"Do you think I'm as mad as you are?" Aubrey snorted.

"You could be. I've always thought you held great promise. Come, Aubrey. Bring your paints. I'll teach you to be an artist."

"And a murderer?" Aubrey asked archly.

Saladin made an elegant gesture with his hands. "If you develop a taste for it."

CHAPTER SIX

At the villa in Tangier, Saladin taught Aubrey a great deal about painting. The young man learned to mix his own paints and use other media to better bring out the things he wanted to express. He discovered that a single line or a space between colors could speak volumes. Although his work still resembled Saladin's, it had begun to shimmer with promise.

In time, Aubrey forgot his distaste for his friend's past; or perhaps he had convinced himself that Saladin had lied about his murder of the washerwoman and others. The two of them lived an odd sort of monastic life revolving around the lofty ideals of art.

Then Saladin began bringing guests into the villa. They were all Arabs, what seemed to Aubrey to be a whole tribe of them, all with Saladin's strange killer's eyes. Though they were respectful of Aubrey, they kept distinctly apart from him. Even at meals—which had changed since their arrival from the delicate European cuisine he favored to platters of *mechoui* or *pastilla* served, to the chef's dismay, on a sheet on the floor—there was no conversation until Aubrey left the room. Then the chamber would explode in a din of loud talk. Aubrey, who was fluent in Arabic as well as a number of other languages, did not deign to eavesdrop on these conversations from which he was excluded. Instead, he returned to his paintings, telling himself that he was not jealous of Saladin, who no longer had the time to tutor him or share with Aubrey his vast knowledge of art and history.

Three weeks after the Arabs arrived, he made plans to return to Paris.

"Make it London," Saladin said in response to his decision. "It would be more convenient for me."

Aubrey closed his eyes with exasperation. "Difficult to believe as this may be, Saladin, my main concern is not with your convenience. If you must know, your . . . friends . . ."

Saladin laughed. "They are not my friends, darling boy, and I know they aren't yours. Let's call them relatives." He turned his hands palms up. "A necessary evil, eh? Besides, they may be of some use to you in the future."

"To me? What on earth would I want with them?"

Saladin shrugged. "What does one do with a virtual army of men who will obey one's every command?" He placed his hand on Aubrey's shoulder. "I have designated you as my heir. After I'm gone, their fealty will be to you and you alone."

Despite the fact that he could think of no circumstance whatever in which he would require the services of Saladin's noisy relatives, Aubrey felt oddly touched. "Why have you chosen me?" he asked.

Saladin laughed. "If I'd chosen one of them, the poor devil would have his throat cut within the week!"

Aubrey swallowed. "In that case, I may have to decline the honor."

"Oh, they wouldn't kill you." Saladin smiled. "Unless you let them." He cracked his knuckles. "You need to learn about power."

"Power? I hope you're not suggesting I become a politician."

"Real power, Aubrey. The power to manipulate not only men, but the universe itself. To master the laws of nature and defy them. To live, perhaps, forever."

Aubrey's eyebrows knitted together in an amused grimace. "Are you saying that's what it will take to control your relations?"

"I am not joking!" Saladin roared, his whole being transformed in an instant into something terrifying. Aubrey reeled backward involuntarily. "I am talking about magic," the older man said between clenched teeth.

"Magic . . . I see." Inwardly, Aubrey made a note to leave the house for the airport as soon as humanly possible. He would buy whatever clothing he needed in Paris. "If you'll excuse me for a moment—"

Like the talons of a great bird of prey, Saladin's hands snaked out with lightning-fast speed to grab Aubrey's shirt collar. The young man emitted a brief, horrified cry.

Saladin laughed uproariously. "What did you think I would do? Stalk you through the boutiques of Paris?"

"I . . . what . . . I . . ." Aubrey cleared his throat and straightened his shirt. "Stalk me where?"

"You were thinking of clothes shopping, weren't you? Of fleeing this place because I am obviously mad, and probably dangerous?"

The young man's mouth fell open. "You knew what I was *thinking?*"

Saladin sniffed. "That was nothing."

"It wasn't *nothing*. You may have guessed that I wanted to leave, but there was no way you could have known about the clothes. . . . What else can you do?"

The tall man smiled, seductively as a woman. "My boy, you have no idea," he said. "Sit down."

Aubrey eyed him suspiciously for a moment, then complied with a sigh. Saladin was no doubt going to try to talk him into keeping his dreadful relatives while he pranced off to London. "You know, I'd rather not—"

Saladin waved him down gently. "Tell me, Aubrey, what do you wish for most?"

"I beg your pardon?" Aubrey asked wearily.

"It was a simple enough question. What do you want out of life?"

It took a moment for him to answer. "I don't know, really. To paint, I suppose."

"You suppose?"

Aubrey made a noncommittal gesture.

"Come now. Surely even a spoiled princeling like you has dreams. Isn't there anything—anything in the entire spectrum of human achievement—that you truly desire?"

Aubrey felt the carpet with the toe of his shoe.

"To be a famous artist?" Saladin prodded. "A celebrity? A genius, perhaps?"

Aubrey looked up and smiled shyly, scratching the end of his nose. "That sounds awfully pompous."

Saladin shrugged. "It doesn't matter how it sounds. I only asked what you wanted."

"Just what are you getting at?"

"Is that your wish?" Saladin pressed. "To be a genius artist of great renown?"

"All right, damn it, yes!"

"Ah."

"I do hope there's some point to this line of—"

"Would you sell your soul for it?"

Aubrey laughed. "What?"

Saladin gazed into his eyes. "I asked if you would sell your soul to get your wish," he repeated slowly.

"Sell my soul? You mean to the devil?"

"Devils. There are more than one. But you would sell it to me."

Aubrey laughed again. "How bizarre."

"Is it?"

"What would you want with my soul, anyway? Provided I had one, that is."

"Oh, you have one. I would make an offering of it."

"To this vast array of demons you speak of."

"Yes." He grinned. "It would increase my own power. And it would initiate you."

"Initiate. As an artist and a devil."

"Umm. Do you agree?"

Aubrey rolled his eyes. "Why not," he said, rising. "You hereby have my soul. Now, about your relatives . . ."

"You won't ever have to worry about them again," Saladin said cryptically. "Go clean yourself up." Saladin placed a long bony hand on the young man's back. "I'm going to bring you into my life."

Aubrey hadn't thought much about where they were going—to dinner, perhaps, or to one of Tangier's famous if clandestine pleasure houses, though it was difficult to imagine Saladin taking pleasure in any mundane way. He refused to operate a telephone or drive a car. He never flushed a toilet, leaving the servants in the villa to follow, grumbling, after him. He expected them to bathe him as well, and dress him each morning. Aubrey could only imagine what a woman would think of his troublesome mentor.

And so he was dismayed when they entered not an elegant nightspot surrounded by bouganvillea and open to the stars, but a seamy dive in the old section of the city, where a one-eyed man opened the door to them and led them to a dirty table in a smoke-filled room.

The waiter brought them whiskeys. Aubrey's glass had some crusty substance dried onto its rim. He pushed it away in distaste. "I hadn't thought this would be the sort of place you liked to frequent," he said grimly.

Saladin only smiled. The two whiskeys sat silently unattended as Saladin looked slowly over the room. After a few minutes, the one-eyed man nodded from a faraway corner. Saladin rose.

"We've been announced," he said.

"To whom?" Aubrey was thinking that there was no one in the room he would even remotely like to meet.

"You'll see."

He led the way through the crowd of thieves and smugglers to a narrow door beneath a stairwell. As they passed through it into the darkness, Aubrey hadn't a clue what to expect—a Middle Eastern speakeasy, perhaps, or an opium den complete with wizened Chinese men smoking hookahs. But he was not prepared for what he saw.

The room was a cavern, with thousands of candles burning from tiny clefts of rock, dotting the dark chamber with eerie, wavering flames. In the center stood twelve men dressed in long black robes with hoods pulled over their faces. They were still as statues, and utterly silent.

Aubrey fell back while Saladin strode forward in measured steps. As he approached the men, one of them produced a black robe similar to the others and held it out for Saladin, who raised his arms and allowed himself to be dressed. The final touch was a large silver pentagram suspended on a chain. As this was placed over Saladin's head, the monks—which was how Aubrey had come to think of them—took up a chant.

The music was droning, like the buzzing of bees, its cadences rising and falling in rhythm almost like the Gregorian chants or those of the Russian Orthodox Church, yet this music held none of the serenity of any sacred liturgy Aubrey had ever heard. These sounds were disturbing in the same way Saladin's paintings were disturbing—dissonant, angular, frightening, irresistibly compelling. They sang in a language Aubrey had never heard, a mellifluous tongue with neither the harsh gutturals of Arabic nor the explosive tongued sounds of the Romance languages. Just listening to the unknown words chanted in their musical singsong brought to mind visions of ancient and secret rituals. As the chant grew in intensity and volume, Saladin took his place, not with the group, but standing in front of it. The others parted to form a vee with him at its apex.

He positioned himself directly in front of Aubrey and offered his hand. Smiling nervously, thinking that this must be some extravagant joke, Aubrey took it.

Saladin led him toward a low dais made of black onyx on which rested a large silver chalice. Two of the monks knelt before the chalice and lifted it toward the initiate.

"Drink it," Saladin said.

After a moment's hesitation, Aubrey accepted the vessel and drained its contents. It was wine, of a high quality, but with an aftertaste of bitterness.

"You've put something in it," he said. To his astonishment, his words were already sounding garbled, thick as bubbles made of honey, while the chant continued in the background. "What are you . . ."

He swooned. Several of the monks caught him before he fell. As his eyes struggled to open, they undressed him, then stood him naked upon the dais.

The chant felt like a tangible presence, enveloping him, holding him upright. In his narrowed vision Aubrey saw the music weave like silk scarves among the candles and the covered, faceless heads of the monks. The music and its words, the perfect, indecipherable yet oddly familiar words rose steadily, again and again, dancing like dark creatures. And then, more prominent than anything else in the cavern, were Saladin's eyes.

You are soulless, they said to him.

Despite his drugged state, Aubrey felt a small frisson of fear roll up his spine.

Don't resist the darkness. Embrace it, swallow it whole. It will comfort you.

Sweat trickled down the side of Aubrey's face.

Now you must become death. Saladin's eyes grew to fill up Aubrey's entire vista. They were hypnotic, luminous. They spoke to a part of his mind that had never before been used, opening it like a maidenhead. *To harness the powers of the dark gods, you must make them submit to your will. You must become Thanatos, bringer of chaos, who breathes fear and fire and snuffs out life with a touch of his hands. Thanatos, supreme god of death.*

"Thanatos," Aubrey repeated slowly. "I am . . . Thanatos."

Yes.

"Yes," Aubrey groaned.

I am death.

"I am death," he breathed.

I am the power.

"The power . . ." He felt the surrounding darkness enter him with an almost sexual penetration, and with it came the realization that he had been longing for this darkness all his life.

It was why he had loved Saladin's art from the time he first saw those terrifying canvasses. Saladin had known the great hidden truth, that somewhere within the horror of death was the power of the universe. Ordinary people avoided the power, feared it, and thus were at its mercy. Only by grasping death with one's whole spirit could a man overcome his fear. And once that fear was overcome, the power of death entered into his own body like the spirits of the dark gods themselves.

"I am death," he said, this time of his own accord. He became aware of his nakedness, and revelled in it. The sinews of his body stood out like ropes in the flickering light. His organ swelled, erect.

"Thanatos," Saladin said aloud.

Rising out of the monks' chant came the word again: "Thanatos."

In the newly opened corner of his mind, Aubrey realized with absolute certainty what he wanted above all other things. Not to be an artist or a celebrity, although those things would come to him. What he truly wanted was *this*. To be here, wallowing in the thick power of the dark, to live in the forbidden zone of existence.

"Thanatos," he repeated.

One of the monks approached the initiate holding a spitting black cat. Another presented him with a curved dagger. Aubrey picked up the cold blade slowly, clutching it so hard that it drew his own blood. Then, with one quick stroke, he disemboweled the creature, screaming as he struck so that his voice and the agonized wail of the dying animal melded into one sound, feeling its blood caress him with the touch of a lover.

And the chant droned on. "Thanatos," Saladin whispered.

"Thanatos," sang the monks.

Aubrey's eyes rolled back in his head. "Thanatos!" he shouted, and he felt the power surge through him like molten metal.

"Yes," Saladin answered softly. "You understand." With the cat's blood he traced a pentacle on Aubrey's forehead, and the young man fell to his knees in ecstasy.

When the ritual was ended, the monks parted again. A slab of rock covering a hole in the far wall was removed, and Aubrey walked out into an alley in the back of the building. He was alone in the night, and reborn. He found a woman among the lowest ranks of beggars, and had her for twenty dirham in the darkened doorway of a tumble-down building.

She was young, perhaps fifteen, although her teeth were already sparse. Her hair had been uncombed for days, and her arms were crusted with dirt. When Aubrey finished with her, she pulled herself up off the ground, clutching the coins in one hand, and loped down the alleyway, looking back once at the handsome young man who obviously had enough money for the high-priced bordellos.

She should not have looked back. For in that single glance Aubrey saw the girl's true heart, her longing for a better life, her hope. The hope sparked a fire in him that caused him to gasp aloud. In the instant of that glance, Aubrey was transported back to the stone chamber thick with the smell of the dead cat's blood. He heard the animal's wails as it struggled to hold onto the precious life which was leaving it with each beat of its heart. The girl's eyes held hope, and Thanatos had the power to take every last shred of it away.

With a spurt of energy he had not known he possessed, Aubrey sprang away from the stone wall and with two strides caught the girl by the arm. She turned toward him, smiling nervously at him through her mottled teeth while she hid the coins she'd earned behind her back. Aubrey grasped her by her hair. Then, hearing the chant of the black magicians drumming in his ears, he coiled the long black strands of hair into his fist and, as the girl began to scream, yanked her toward him with a violent tug that snapped the girl's neck.

At the moment of her death, Aubrey felt a satisfaction he had never imagined. He was Thanatos. He was death incarnate.

At dawn he walked back to the villa and began to paint.

CHAPTER SEVEN

The effect of the power on his work was immediate and startling. For the first time, his paintings were no longer a talented imitation of Saladin's, but branched into a direction that was his alone. Aubrey's lines were harder than Saladin's, his colors more vivid; and in the trapped, enclosed spaces between the tortured lines was the essence of the fear he had embraced with such love and awe on the night of his initiation into the dark world.

He painted all day and into the night without food or rest. In the evening, Saladin came into his studio wearing his customary robe and holding a glass of wine. "You smell like a woman," he said, sniffing with distaste. He flicked a finger at the oils Aubrey had finished. "These are better."

Aubrey put down his brush. His hands were shaking. "Saladin, I . . ." He swallowed. "Last night I killed someone."

Saladin looked up from the painting for a moment, then down again, smiling. "Have you developed a taste for murder, after all?" he asked.

Aubrey sat on the floor against a wall. "Is that all you can say?"

Saladin raised his eyebrows. "Should I say something else? You were the one who did the killing."

"Yes, you're right," Aubrey said numbly.

"Do you feel remorseful? Is that the problem?"

"Well, naturally . . ." He slumped forward, resting his chin on his arms. "Actually I don't. That's just it. I don't feel anything at all. I barely remember anything, except perhaps . . ." He swallowed. ". . . how enjoyable it was."

Saladin grinned. "Indeed. An uncommon pleasure." He lowered himself into a chair and sipped his wine.

"Even when I broke her neck, all I could think of was the chanting from last night, that strange music."

"Lovely, wasn't it? Egyptian, Nineteenth Dynasty."

"What did you *do* to me?" Aubrey wailed miserably.

"I? My dear boy—"

"I feel as if, between one day and the next, my life has changed completely. As if I've suddenly become this monstrous, amoral creature."

"And so you have," Saladin said, picking up a magazine and leafing through it. "You've given up your soul."

Aubrey sat in stunned silence. "You were serious."

"Of course I was. And so were you. Otherwise, you wouldn't be painting now."

"Then my wish . . ."

"You'll become a great artist, Aubrey," he said reassuringly. "And a famous one."

Aubrey stared ahead sullenly. "I might have done that anyway."

"It's rather late to have second thoughts about that, isn't it?" He laid the magazine on his lap. "Put some yellow in the upper right quadrant," he said, gesturing impatiently toward the abstract oil on the easel. "The balance is off."

Aubrey tapped his fingers to his lips, thinking. "Exactly what does it mean to lose one's soul?"

"Not much," Saladin answered. "Until you die."

"What happens then?"

"Nothing."

"Nothing?"

"According to the magicians with whom I studied, one forfeits any

life after this one, and therefore the opportunity to perfect oneself."
He shrugged.

"That doesn't seem like a very high price to pay," Aubrey said,
feeling better.

"My sentiments exactly. No choirs of angels with harps, no fellows
with pitchforks, no coming back as a snake or a tree or a one-armed
beggar. Just one jolly, self-indulgent life, and then . . ." He held out
his empty hands. "Nothing."

Aubrey stood up and walked to his easel. "A little more yellow, you
said?"

"Cadmium. Mix some burnt sienna into it."

Aubrey added a splash to the painting. "Saladin," he asked brightly,
"what did you wish for?"

The tall man stretched in his chair. "Haven't you guessed?"

Aubrey turned around, the brush poised in mid-air. Saladin's face
was as unlined as the day he had first met him, his hair as black, his
knowledge as profound. "You said the chant last night came from
Nineteenth Dynasty Egypt."

Saladin nodded. "The reign of Ramses the Second."

"Now, how would you know that?" Aubrey demanded. "No written
music from Pharaohnic Egypt exists. No one's ever heard it."

"Perhaps someone."

Aubrey closed his eyes with dawning understanding. "Good God,
you were there," he whispered. "Your wish was to live forever."

Saladin rose and walked across the room.

"But that's brilliant! What do you care about losing your soul? You'll
never know what it's like to die."

"I might."

"How? What can harm you?"

"Only magic stronger than my own. If there is such a thing."

"I doubt that."

"Hmm." He leaned against the doorway. "It might be nice if there
were."

"Nice? To die?"

The tall man shrugged. "A life that goes on too long ceases to seem
precious. It becomes a burden, like an overdue pregnancy."

Aubrey snorted. "Give it to me, then. I'll take it."

"Yes," Saladin said slowly, his ancient eyes shining with malevolent
humor. "I imagine you would."

* * *

Two months later Saladin was arrested in England for the murder of the washerwoman in the sculpture and eighteen others whose bodies had been similarly preserved. Aubrey never saw him again.

The paintings which had begun to take shape on the night of Aubrey's initiation into the coven in Tangier sold almost immediately. The name Katsuleris circulated quickly, first through esoteric European art circles, then on a broader scale. Within six months, a prominent gallery in Milan offered Aubrey a month-long exhibit for which people waited hours in line. *Time* magazine ran an article about the phenomenal resurgence of interest in the field of abstract art.

Through it all, Aubrey continued to participate in the rites of the coven. The rituals filled the places in his psyche that his work did not. They suffused him with energy and purpose; they focused his mind. They led him to a series of teachers around the world, all of them soulless as he was, all masters of the dark ways.

He excelled as a student. When he returned to the coven in Tangier, he took over as its leader, wearing the inverted silver pentagram that Saladin had once worn.

He became comfortable with the two lives he led, painting by day, then celebrating in the thick of night the magic rituals that brought him into deep communion with the powers of the demon gods.

And afterward, after each rite, he killed.

The killings were the great exultation of his new life. At first he murdered only women, and only for the pleasure it brought him. But women, he soon learned, were too easy to kill, and too easy to get away with killing. Aubrey longed to explore new frontiers in murder, to develop his skill to the level of an art form and to be recognized for his artistry.

And so, through contacts made in the coven, he added a third component to his life: He became an assassin known as Thanatos, and not even the people who sought his services ever connected him with the dapper young artist named Aubrey Katsuleris.

It came as a shock, then, when a young Arab appeared in the doorway of an apartment in New York City where Aubrey was staying.

"What do you want?" he hissed, maneuvering the man so that he would fall silently into the apartment when Aubrey killed him.

The Arab immediately prostrated himself on the floor, offering up a battered leather case.

Aubrey ignored it. "Who sent you?"

"My uncle, Hamid Lagouat, who follows the instructions of our patriarch, the High Lord Saladin."

For a moment, Aubrey could only stare at the man. Then, flinging himself onto a sofa, he burst out laughing. This was no terrorist seeking Thanatos. It was only one of Saladin's pesky relatives.

"I should have known. Well, get up, get up. What does Saladin have in mind now? Where the devil is he, anyway?"

The Arab raised his face from the carpet. "He is dead, Sire."

Aubrey blinked. "Dead? Did you say he was dead?"

"He was killed by an American FBI agent."

"But . . ." Aubrey felt dizzy. Saladin wasn't supposed to die, not ever. It was his wish, a wish granted in exchange for eternity. "How was it done?"

"He was beheaded, Sire."

"*Beheaded?* By the FBI?"

"My uncle saw it with his own eyes." He approached Aubrey once again with the leather case. "As Saladin's heir, the document in here is for you, Sire."

Slowly Aubrey took it. "That's right, he made me his heir, didn't he?" he mused.

"Yes, Sire. As such, my entire family—and there are many of us— stands ready to assist you in any way."

"Yes, yes." From the case Aubrey extracted a small notebook. It was a diary of some sort, its pages handwritten with a quill pen and interspersed with Saladin's breathtakingly realistic drawings. Among them were portraits of a man, a woman, and a preadolescent boy, as well as many pages—over twenty, rendered in colored pencil—of an oddly shaped container of some kind.

Aubrey flipped through the entire book first, then went back to the beginning. On the first pages was a letter to him.

My dear Aubrey,

I am writing to you because it is possible that I may at last have the good fortune to die. After you accept the gift implicit in my story— and you will, no doubt, accept it—you may also, one day millennia hence, come to long for death as I do.

My story is about a cup. A quite ordinary artifact, from its appearance, a small bowl of greenish metal; yet countless men have died for it. Wars have been fought, legends grown, kingdoms fallen over its existence.

At one time it was known as the Holy Grail, and in this connection was it stolen from me by a sorcerer named Merlin, who understood well the ways of magic. It was not for himself that Merlin took the cup, but for a king who, perhaps alone of all the multitudes who have ever lived upon this earth, did not desire to possess it and its wonderful gift. He feared that eternal life would corrupt him, as it had me. He never did embrace the darkness, which you and I have come to love so well. Rather than succumb to the temptation of the cup, he threw it away, and died young for his pains.

I wonder now if that king were not wiser than the rest of us.

His name was Arthur of Britain. You no doubt have heard the legend about the once and future king—the great ruler who would one day return to finish out his reign. For sixteen hundred years, the legend has been told and retold until it has become little more than a fairy story. Even among those who accept the possibility of reincarnation, no one believes that an individual can be reborn as himself, to continue a life begun in the distant past.

And yet that is what has happened. Arthur has come back.

He is a boy again these days, far from royal, and far from the land where he once ruled. What the gods have planned for him I do not know, but they have seen to it that the cup which I have possessed for five thousand years is now in his keeping.

The gods. The ancient gods, Aubrey. Are you familiar with them? Or are there no records of them left at all? The ancient gods, long vanquished and forgotten . . . I smell their presence in the air. Their magic.

If I die, it will be their doing.

And the cup will be yours—if you can find it and keep it. So you must find it, Aubrey. Find it and kill the boy. Discover, if you can, the instrument of my death and destroy it, for whatever the object is, the most terrible gods of all have placed their power in it.

And now, dear chap, farewell. If you are reading this, then I have already gone to the void, the nothing I was taught to expect. That is my only fear about dying—that there might be something other than a void waiting for me.

I do not wish to meet the ancient gods.

Aubrey closed the book. He tried to speak, but found that his lips and tongue were dry. He nodded curtly to the young man in dismissal.

"There is one more article I have been instructed to leave with you, Sire," the messenger said, producing an envelope. After handing it to Aubrey, he bowed. "Should you desire the assistance of my family, I will be nearby."

"Nearby where?"

"Wherever you are, Lord." The messenger performed a graceful salaam, then left.

The envelope contained a map. A map of a rural area in England, near the ruins of a fifth-century castle where Hamid Lagouat, who had ridden with Saladin on his last day of life, had seen a sword in a stone.

Aubrey left immediately for England, but he did not find the boy whom Saladin had described so well in his diary, nor the American FBI agent who apparently had cut himself loose from all ties to his past in order to protect him.

He did spot the woman in the drawings, however. She had remained for some time near the place where Arthur Blessing and Hal Woczniak had disappeared, although it quickly became clear from her actions that she knew nothing of their whereabouts.

He also saw the messenger who had visited him in New York to bring news of Saladin's death.

They may prove to be useful one day, Saladin had said of his relatives. He had been right. When the woman left the country in her own search for her nephew, Aubrey called upon Saladin's—now Aubrey's own—private army to track Emily Blessing in her wanderings.

She placed personal ads to Arthur in the newspapers of every place she visited. These the Arabs collected and sent to Aubrey. He instructed them to deliver copies of those newspapers to every village and community within a fifty-mile radius of those cities. It was a long shot, he knew, but worth the small effort. The woman was the key. Sooner or later, the boy would come to her. Aubrey would keep her in abeyance until then.

Meanwhile, there was the sword.

Find the cup. . . . Kill the boy. . . . Destroy the instrument of my death.

Of the three directives with which Saladin had charged his heir, only the third had been possible so far, and that had taken three years.

The weapon had not even been visible at first. Without the map, Aubrey would never have thought to look for it in the woods surrounding a field of ancient ruins. He would never have noticed one boulder among many, hidden in an overgrown thicket.

But he had Lagouat's map, and though he was skeptical about its authenticity, he followed it to the boulder and then dutifully broke up the five-foot-tall stone with a sledgehammer until its interior was exposed to reveal the hilt of a sword.

It was magnificent, made of pure gold inlaid with precious stones that had not chipped or lost their lustre when the rock had been smashed around it. But no matter how hard Aubrey struck it with the sledgehammer, the blade would not come free. It was as if the steel were bonded to the stone itself. Sweating, intensely disliking the hard work and the effect it was having on his sensitive hands, Aubrey finally tossed the sledgehammer away and grasped the hilt, hoping to break it from the blade.

Its touch was like an explosion. With a cry of pain, Aubrey flew backward, his feet off the ground, and crashed into a tree trunk.

When his head cleared, he got on all fours to examine the ground. Someone—Lagouat himself, perhaps—had obviously planted a device, a land mine of some kind . . .

But the ground was unbroken.

Then, with his magician's senses, he heard the hum of the buried blade, saw the tendrils of energy curling like smoke up the golden hilt.

The ancient gods, long vanquished and forgotten . . . Was this their work? Had the terrible gods whom Saladin so feared forged this sword against him and his kind?

He was certain of two things: that this was the weapon which had killed Saladin, and that nothing short of the strongest magic he could summon would destroy its power.

For the task, Aubrey collected twelve of the most deadly magicians he knew. They were difficult to find, even more difficult to persuade to help him. But three years and several million dollars later, they arrived.

In a rite that began at midnight, the thirteen sorcerers circled the sword, chanting, calling on their demon deities, building their power until Aubrey felt the dark forces inside him spill out of his eyes and ears and mouth like oily liquid. He became Thanatos the death god, ruler of the soulless places. His senses quickened until they were those of a beast; his very hands seemed to transmute into claws. With them he grasped the golden hilt and poured his evil into it.

The sword crumbled under his touch.

Later, after the magicians had gone, Aubrey went back to collect the dun-colored fragments. Why, it wasn't even real gold, he thought. The gems had been shattered; their dust lay sparkling in the dirt. The rock which had once encased the long blade so tightly now fell away beneath his fingers like rotten plaster.

He felt slightly cheated. After spending a fortune to bring the magicians to this place, the sword had given up its power almost at once. Aubrey wanted to kick himself for assuming he needed the help of those greedy old men. The thing had probably given off its last spurt of magic on the day he'd discovered it.

It had all been so damnably, disappointingly easy.

As he swept the last particles of the sword into a pouch, he imagined Saladin at the end of his life, fearful, cowering at the thought of retribution by some ancient and forgotten gods.

"They were nothing," he said aloud, hefting the pouch. "Here's the proof of it."

Shortly after the ritual with the twelve magicians, Aubrey was called to Marrakesh for a fairly routine assassination. He would not normally have accepted the assignment—he was rapidly becoming bored with his gun-for-hire hobby and, besides, he was acquainted with the family of the man he would have to kill—but he agreed, finally, because he thought it might distract him for a time from his frustrated quest for the cup.

He was beginning to wonder if Saladin hadn't made the whole story up just to send him on a lifelong wild goose chase when he saw William Marshall sit up after experiencing the impact of a bullet in his chest. A green metal cup which exactly matched Saladin's detailed drawings had rolled off Marshall's body as he was carried into the ambulance.

Aubrey very nearly shouted with delight then and there, before remembering that he was viewing these events through the telescopic sight of a semiautomatic rifle. He would have to wait, he decided. Not long, just until the police and those Secret Service fools left . . .

And then, just as he was about to discard the rifle, he saw a young blind girl pick up the cup.

Aubrey groaned. The look on the girl's face was unmistakable. She knew what she had.

Doggedly, seething with impatience, he got rid of the weapon, exchanged one disguise for another, then followed the girl and the old woman with her to their hotel where, to his eternal shame, he had failed both to secure the cup and to kill the girl. The very memory made him writhe with embarrassment.

Nevertheless, some good had come of the encounter. He knew where the cup was. He had found Arthur Blessing and his protector. And by a stroke of luck, the Arabs had just informed him that morning that the whole carload of runaways had spent the night in Ait Haddus, where a nine-month-old newspaper containing a personals ad for "Arthur B" had been used to wrap a pound of dates.

Things were looking better, after all.

Aubrey uncoiled himself from his chair and dialled two numbers. The first was to the nearest of the Arab relatives, to whom he dictated a letter. The second was to a woman in London, a woman whose friendship Aubrey had been cultivating for the past month in anticipation of this day.

Her name was Emily Blessing.

He would wear silk tonight, he decided, doodling idly while he waited for the clicks and pauses in the telephone connection to end.

"Hello?" Emily answered, sounding, as she always did, like a scared mouse.

"Emily," he purred. "This is Aubrey Katsuleris."

He heard her soft intake of air. Then a deferential "Yes?"

What a bloodless woman, Aubrey thought. American, intellectual, and thoroughly dull. "I've found your nephew," he said.

"Oh, my God," she whispered. "Is he with you?"

"No, he's in Tangier. We'll meet him tonight."

"Tangier!"

"I'll pick you up."

"I . . . I don't know how to thank you, Mr. Katsuleris."

"Aubrey, please. I told you I'd find him, didn't I?"

"Yes, but I never imagined—"

"I'll come for you at five o'clock. We'll have dinner at the Victoria Hotel." He hung up.

He would take her to Tangier, and make love to her beneath the Arabian moon. Then, after she got the cup to him, he would kill her.

CHAPTER EIGHT

Arthur!

Emily sat down and clasped her trembling hands together. Was it possible? Had the search finally come to an end?

She tried not to hope. Yes, Aubrey Katsuleris was a rich and influential man with contacts all around the world, but how could he have found Arthur within a month when she herself, in three years of constant effort, had not?

It's got to be the wrong boy, she told herself. All she had given Mr. Katsuleris was one photograph taken when Arthur was ten years old. He would be thirteen now. He had probably changed a great deal. . . .

If he's still alive.

Emily shut her eyes, trying not to hope too much.

Arthur had left a note for her presupposing his and Hal's death. The note said that if the man named Saladin who had been pursuing them for Arthur's cup managed to kill them, then Emily's own life would still be in danger. The secret of the cup was too great to trust to even one other human being. Saladin would make sure that everyone who knew about it did not survive. And Saladin had had a great number of men at his disposal.

Arthur, meticulously brilliant as always, gave detailed instructions on how she could lose herself in any large city. "After a year," he finished, "you'll be free to go back to work and try to have some kind of normal life. I know now that will never be possible for me. I'm sorry that I've put you through so much grief. Love, Arthur."

They had drugged her before they left, so that when she first read the note, she could not fully grasp its content. But she did not sleep. Through that night she sat awake at the window of the inn where she and Arthur and Hal had stayed, staring at the bed where Hal had made love to her once, only once. . . .

At dawn the next day she had read the note again, and howled with grief.

"Arthur," she sobbed, hating herself for her belated concern. Where had she been during all the years he'd needed her? Where had her love for the boy been then?

He had known that she resented his presence. When Emily's sister jumped off a bridge five days after giving birth to Arthur, the burden of raising the child had gone to Emily. She had been on the fast track at a national think tank at the time, assisting a scientist who later earned a Nobel Prize for the work Emily had done. With her new responsibilities as an unwilling mother, her career had virtually ground to a halt. She was no longer able to work the long hours that were necessary for advancement in the competitive field of pure science.

Her anger at having had her career interrupted by the burden of raising her dead sister's child had been all too clear from the beginning. Arthur had spent most of his life with strangers, waiting for her to return from work, and the other half watching her boil with self-pity for the time she was forced to spend with him. If it had not been for the cup, their lives might still be forming that same dull, aching pattern.

But the cup had changed everything. It had made her realize that Arthur was more important to her than the lost Nobel. And it had brought her the love of a man. It had, for the briefest moment, connected Emily Blessing with the human race.

And then the cup had taken it all away.

The police found the smoldering remains of a burned mansion inside of which were several bodies. None of them had been children; neither was one the remains of a seven-foot-tall man named Saladin. Some distance away, perhaps coincidentally, an abandoned field bore the hoofprints of hundreds of horses, although no one in the area had seen them. Scotland Yard sent a man to investigate, but after three months he had turned up nothing except the weird account of a village boy who claimed to have witnessed a great battle on the site, with knights on horseback and Saracens wielding scimitars.

"The villagers here are superstitious," the investigator told her. "They believe this was the site of the original Camelot, you know."

"Oh?" Emily said without interest.

The detective smiled. "Part of the legend is that on St. John's Eve, the ghosts of King Arthur's knights of the Round Table go out riding, looking for their missing king. Arthur was supposed to come back, you know. Rather like the Second Coming."

"So they think ghosts made the hoofprints."

"I'm afraid not much goes on in Wilson-on-Hamble," he said apologetically.

The Yard called their investigator back shortly afterward. Their conclusion was that Saladin had died, probably in transit with the bodies of Arthur Blessing and Hal Woczniak.

"I'm sorry," the Scotland Yard man told her on the day he left the village. "We might be wrong. We'll keep the case open."

Emily nodded dully.

That afternoon, she went back to the meadow. It was September. The summer had been dry, and the muddy earth, churned by the hooves of those never-found horses, had dried as a testament to the mystery which had occurred there.

She cried. For the past, for the future which would be just like it, and for the tiny window of hope in which Hal and Arthur and Emily would be together again, a window which now was closed forever.

"Excuse me, m'um," a youthful voice said behind her. Emily gasped at the stark interruption of her thoughts, and the boy quickly removed his hat and bobbed at her.

"What do you want?" she asked, embarrassed by her tears.

He was around twelve or thirteen years old, she had guessed, a little older than Arthur at the time. His pants were worn and too short for his lanky legs by a good three inches. The sight of the boy's exposed pink ankles broke Emily's heart. She would never see Arthur during the coltish, awkward years of adolescence. Back in Chicago, his room would be filled with reminders of how much Emily had missed.

"I'm Tom Rodgers, m'um, and you'd be the lady from America," he said nervously. "There's been talk that the police have done aught to find your boy."

"The inspector from Scotland Yard just left," she said. "The investigation is over."

"Aye. I'm sorry to hear it, too. That's why when I seen you I decided to come talk."

"About what?" she asked. Then she remembered what the inspector had said. A local boy had claimed to see the ghost-horses in this meadow. "Look, Tom Rodgers, or whoever you are," she snapped. "You probably thought it was fun to joke with the police, but it's damn cruel to try it with me."

Tom backed away from her as if her words had been physical blows, removing his cap and clutching it over his stomach. "I know as how you might not take me serious," he said meekly. "There's most in the village think I'm daft. But I seen what I seen. And so I won't trouble you except to say that your boy's all right." He tipped his hat and walked away.

"Wait!" Emily called, running after him. "Please wait." She grabbed his arm. "What do you mean he's all right? Did you see him?"

"Aye, I did. Him and the American bloke, and the old man, too."

"What old man?"

"I don't know what his name was, but he's some kind of wizard, I'll tell you that," the boy said. "And there was a castle, and knights in armor, and a bunch of wogs that looked like Ali Baba's forty thieves—"

Emily shook her head. She did not want to hear the boy's fantasies. "Tell me about the boy," she said. "Where did he go?"

"Dunno." He shrugged. "Him and the American took off down the road after it was all over. The castle disappeared, and so did the knights and the others. Only the old man was left." The boy chuckled. "And he was laughing like a loon."

"Did they—the boy and the American—did they have anything with them?" Emily asked. "Like a cup, or a bowl?"

"No." The boy frowned, thinking. "No, they got rid of that. Birds come for it."

Emily stood in silence for a long moment, a thousand thoughts racing through her mind. If they were alive, why hadn't Hal and Arthur come back for her? Where had they gone? Who was the old man?

And where was the cup?

She shook her head. This was ridiculous, she told herself. Young Tom here was obviously demented. Knights. Ali Baba. "Thank you," she said, and watched him as he walked away across the field. It was as easy to be crazy in a small town as in a big city, she decided. With a sigh, she went back to the hotel.

There was nothing for her to do besides go home. Back to Chicago and her job at the Katzenbaum Institute.

How little that meant to her now.

Him and the American took off down the road after it was all over.

What if Tom Rodgers wasn't crazy? she thought, her heart racing. What if he really had seen them leave?

Then he was just looking for attention, she told herself. Or playing with the emotions of a tourist.

And who was the old man?

She had only met one old man since their arrival in England, a professor named Taliesin who had vanished at the same time Arthur had been kidnapped. The police had never found him, either.

And then, with utter certainty, she knew. Arthur and Hal—and perhaps Taliesin, too—had left her at the inn because they were still in danger. The danger was to themselves; Emily herself knew next to nothing about Saladin or the cup. They had abandoned her in order to spare her life.

The village boy was telling the truth.

Emily finished packing her bag and left the inn. But instead of heading back to Chicago, she took a train to London and began her own search for her nephew.

That search had continued for the past three years. When her savings ran out, she took a job as a chemist in a small London paint company specializing in artists' oils to support herself while she scoured the streets and took out ads in every newspaper in Great Britain and the Continent searching for them. She never bothered to change her name or find a new identity. No one was interested enough in her to kill her.

And if they did, Emily didn't really care.

Then, just one month ago, she had met Aubrey Katsuleris. He had come to the paint company to commission a new color. He wanted a red the exact color of human blood.

When he was escorted into the small laboratory where Emily worked, he had begun to explain, then stopped in frustration. "The problem with blood," he said exasperated, "is that it changes color with each moment of exposure to air. I can make those changes; it will be the point of my painting. But I need the original color to begin with."

Patiently Emily had shown him the palette of reds, trying to arrive at a base color, when Katsuleris suddenly grasped an X-Acto knife and cut open the vein of his left wrist. Blood poured onto the white countertop in a gush.

While the president of the company scurried away screaming for bandages, Emily could only stare at the artist in shock, watching with fascination as his blood poured out of him.

"That is the color I want," he said.

She considered for a moment, then picked up a beaker and mixed into it a compound made from different tubes and vials in the lab. Then she poured it on top of the spilled blood.

When the president and his secretary arrived back with a bottle of iodine and some gauze bandage, Emily had gone back to her desk.

"What did she do?" the artist asked as he offered up his arm to the clucking secretary.

"Who?" the president asked. "You mean Emily? I'm sure I've no idea. Emily, call someone to have this mess cleaned up."

"Don't touch it!" Aubrey shouted. "Don't you see? The color is exactly the same as it was when it came out of my vein. See this blood, here." He pointed with his chin toward another spattering of blood. "And here. It's already darkened. But this . . ." He touched his finger to it and drew a line of red across the countertop. The president and his secretary exchanged disgusted glances.

"Er . . . Quite right," the president said. "And you say Miss Blessing had something to do with this?"

"I applied a fixative to it," the mousy woman answered. She had an American accent. "He wanted the exact color . . ."

"He doesn't want to paint with blood!" the president hissed.

"Oh, but I do," Aubrey said. He dipped his finger in the color again. "I do very much."

The president's face broke into an ingratiating grin. "Then we shall by all means provide you with all the color—"

"I can prepare the fixative," Emily said. "But I will not mix the blood."

"Fine," Katuleris said, smiling dreamily at her. "I'll take a pint."

Her eyebrows raised. "That would be enough for twenty or thirty gallons."

He shrugged.

"Where will you get the blood?" she asked.

"I'm sure that's none of your business, Miss Blessing," the president said, ushering the artist out of the lab.

That had been the beginning of her relationship with the artist. She had tried to forget the incident, but found Aubrey Katsuleris' face returning to her again and again.

For one thing, he was famous. Even Emily, who had never taken any interest in the arts or in popular culture, had heard of him. He had been called the Picasso of the jet age. Many critics said that Katsuleris was overrated and that the prices of his paintings were out of proportion to their intrinsic value, but others touted his work as a pure reflection of the post-Vietnam generation. Even the British Museum had purchased some of his canvasses.

For another—and Emily was ashamed to admit this to herself—she found him charming. Of that there was no doubt. Aubrey Katsuleris was as well known for his good looks and success with women as he was for his talent.

He had come into the paint company several times after that first encounter, each time bringing with him some small but lovely gift for her: a box of chocolates from Geneva, a single rose which he claimed to have plucked with his own hands from the gardens of the Duchess of Kent. Nothing expensive or personal enough to warrant returning; just enough to keep her awake nights with thoughts of him.

Through it all, she continually asked herself what on earth he could possibly see in her. She was no beauty. Oh, she had felt like one once, when she had been with Hal. She had even given in to one night of abandon in a creaky bed at a roadside inn.

Hal had thought she was beautiful.

Hal . . .

She slammed her fist on the arm of the dusty secondhand sofa. Hal was gone. He was gone, and so was Arthur, and for three years Emily had been so lonely, so terribly lonely. . . .

And so, when she'd run into Aubrey Katsuleris a couple of weeks later in Regent's Park on her way home from work, she had told him about Arthur. She hadn't mentioned the cup, only that her nephew had been kidnapped by a man named Saladin, and that she had been searching for him for years.

"Scotland Yard thinks he's dead," she confessed.

"But you don't believe he is." Aubrey was quiet, compassionate, intensely interested.

"No."

Aubrey swooped her up in his arms and spun her in a circle. "Darling Emily, you're wonderfully stubborn. And I love this mystery about your nephew. I think I shall help you find him."

"It's not a game," she said, unimpressed by his enthusiasm.

"Forgive me. That was callow. Nevertheless, I'd like to try. Begin some inquiries, that sort of thing. Would you object?"

"I wish it were that easy," she said.

He smiled. "It might be."

Apparently it had been that easy. Two weeks afterward, Aubrey rang her apartment bell at exactly five o'clock. A plane was waiting at the airport to take them to Tangier.

CHAPTER NINE

Beatrice could barely contain herself as she sauntered with her companions through the *Grand Socco* in Tangier. It was a feast for newborn eyes, from the magnificent carpets laid out on the ground to sacks of almonds and chickpeas piled into hills twice the height of a man. The air was thick with scent—saffron, cumin, pepper, ginger, verbena, cloves, orange flower . . . she could identify each with her nose, but it thrilled her to actually see them, to examine each box filled with buds and roots and dried petals. Weaving among the stalls were peasant women wearing the red and white striped *foutas* peculiar to Tangier, their heads covered by broad hats sporting huge blue pom-poms. The large baskets they carried were filled with dates, olives, pots of henna, wool, flasks of rose and jasmine extract, mint, kohl, amber, or musk.

"Oh, look!" she squealed, pointing to a boy dressed in a bright red costume jangling with bells. Across his back was a pole with buckets at either end. "What's he doing?"

"He's a water carrier," Taliesin said as the boy ran past them. "The musicians are calling him over."

Not far away, a group of dignified-looking men squatted on the ground playing a variety of strange instruments while a belly dancer gyrated around them. Around the corner, a public scribe was writing a letter on a portable lap-desk for an unlettered customer while a storyteller entertained a group of wide-eyed children.

Hal looked at his watch. "It's almost seven. I think we ought to be heading for the hotel," he said.

They had left the Jeep on the outskirts of the city, then walked through the crowded market district in case the police spotted the vehicle. Hal was grateful for the walk. It gave him a chance to think.

He was not happy with his thoughts. They all revolved around the cup, and the danger it had brought them in the past.

He had told himself over and over that finding Emily's message in the old newspaper had been nothing more than a coincidence. If they hadn't had the cup, he might have accepted it as such.

But they did have the cup, and someone had already tried to kill Beatrice for it.

The Victoria Hotel was built on a cliff overlooking the Strait of Gibraltar. Behind its white domes the sun was setting, turning the sea to gold. Docked near the picturesque oceanside walkway bordered by palm and banana trees were cargo ships flying flags from all over the world. In the far distance, the shimmering hills of Andalusia rose out of the water.

Hal wanted to see Emily, ached for her. That, too, fueled his sense of unease. The fact that he *wanted* the ad to have been a coincidence— hell, he wanted her to be in the Victoria Hotel waiting for them, wanted it more than he had ever wanted anything in his life—made him suspicious of his own actions. Had he placed Arthur in danger by coming to Tangier because he himself had needed to make certain that Emily wasn't there?

"You okay, Hal?" Arthur asked.

Hal stopped in his tracks. "No," he said. "No, I'm not." He gathered Arthur and Beatrice to him. "Listen, guys, I don't like this."

"Why not?" Arthur asked.

"I don't know why, okay? Call it paranoia. All I know is that if this is some kind of setup and the four of us walk in that place together, it won't be good."

"Hal—"

"He's right, Arthur," Taliesin said. "The two of you should wait—"

"The *three* of you are going to wait. Over there by the docks." He pointed toward the ships. "I'll go in alone. If everything's all right, I'll come back for you."

Arthur scowled. "What if it's not all right?"

"It will be." Hal ruffled the boy's hair. "Who knows, Emily might still be there. I'll bring her out to see you, and then we'll all go have dinner, okay?"

Arthur only stared at him.

"Come along," Taliesin said gently.

Hal watched them walk over the embankment toward the docks as the sky melted from red to indigo. Just before they descended out of sight, Arthur turned to look at him again.

Hal ventured alone into the hotel.

"Are you sure they're coming?" Emily asked for the fourth time, peering through one of the tall windows in the Victoria's dining room.

"Don't worry about a thing," Aubrey answered automatically, although his sensitive hands had begun to perspire.

It was possible that they hadn't seen the ad in the newspaper. Still, they were definitely coming to Tangier. It was the only place where the road that passed through Ait Haddus led. Saladin's relatives were stationed all over the city. If the four travelers didn't come to the hotel tonight, the Arabs would find them by morning. Either way, none of them would leave Tangier alive.

"You're lovely," Aubrey said, thinking that Emily's dress must have been designed by a tentmaker. "Americans have such a unique style."

She smiled nervously, adjusting her neckline. It was the only garment she owned which might be termed dressy, although now she thought it might be more suitable for a funeral than a dinner date.

She was frumpy, she decided, no matter what Aubrey said. Actually, she had always been frumpy, except for the weeks she'd been with Hal.

Hal had made her feel beautiful. She would not have worn this dress with Hal. She would have dressed in pink silk with flowers. She would have painted her toenails and showed them. She would have run naked through a rainstorm.

Hal. She saw her arms trembling. Tonight she would see Hal again.

It's all right, she told herself. *You're a grown woman. He left you, but that isn't the issue here. You're going to get Arthur back. Hal doesn't figure*

into it one way or the other. You'll be polite, and then take your nephew
and be on your way. Thank you very much, Hal, and good-bye.

Yes.

She was trembling harder than ever.

"Are you cold?" Aubrey asked.

Emily shook her head. She glanced at her watch again. Seven oh
four. Hal was late. "How do you know they'll be here?" she asked.

"Because they'll want to see you," he said, forcing a smile.

"I need to go to the ladies' room."

"Emily—"

"I'm sorry," she said, pushing her chair back with a squeak. It was
just too much for her. In the washroom she applied her lipstick twice,
straightened her slip, fixed her pantyhose, washed her hands.

Don't worry about a thing, Aubrey had said. He had made all the
contacts, through a friend who knew a friend, who knew someone else.
She had read once that anyone in the world was only six links removed
from anyone else. The problem was finding the six correct links.

But Aubrey had found them, and at the end of that chain of contacts
were Arthur and Hal and another chance for Emily's life.

Please come, she begged as she walked back, feeling her knees knocking together. *Please, please come.*

She was passing by a beefy waiter carrying an enormous try on his
shoulder when she spotted Hal. He was walking beside a railing, looking up at the tables on the mezzanine. He was alone.

"Hal!" she called, but she found her voice had left her. She signalled
frantically, her elbow bumping into the waiter. The waiter stumbled
over her, nearly dropping the tray.

"Oh, I'm so sorry," she said. The waiter gave her a withering look.

Hal had not noticed the scene, but Aubrey had. From the table he
nodded almost imperceptibly to a busboy polishing silver in a corner
of the restaurant. The busboy, whose eyes, Aubrey noticed, looked just
like Saladin's, set down the handful of utensils he was holding and
pulled a gun from beneath his apron.

A woman sitting near the bus table screamed. Instinctively Hal
dived to the floor, catching sight of the busboy as he fired two shots
at the spot where Hal had been standing. The bullets hit the waiter
instead, in the back of the neck. As the gunman fled through the
kitchen, he threw two small containers resembling balloons at the long

draperies. They caught fire immediately, and the room burst into pan-demonium.

The waiter fell, the heavy tray clattering to the floor as a fountain of blood gushed out of him, spurting onto the diners as they ran screaming toward the exit. They smashed into Emily, who craned backward, trying to see past the crush of people around her.

"Arthur!" she screamed. "Are you here? Hal?"

Someone knocked against her, hard. She lost her footing and slipped. The next moment she was on the floor, screaming helplessly as strangers ran over her, heedless, no longer concerned that she was a human being, sensing her body only as an impediment to their escape from the suffocating heat and smoke.

She felt a bone snap in her leg with agonizing clarity, and another in her hand as she tried to pull herself upright. She screamed until her throat was raw, but even she could not hear the sound she made amid the din of exploding windows and crackling flames.

Then by some chance she was lifted up off the floor. Emily never saw who her rescuer was; the hands had remained on her only long enough to set her back in the middle of the panicked stampede. The press of bodies carried her along as if she were a piece of flotsam on a wave, her ribcage all but crushed, her broken bones shrieking with pain as two hundred people tried to squeeze through one set of doors. Barely able to breathe, she was finally propelled into the lobby, where the hotel guests were also evacuating, and finally out the main exit.

Some of the guests were dressed in nightclothes; others carried hast-ily stuffed suitcases or towels filled with valuables. One elderly woman was wandering around in circles, her hands clutching strands of pearls and gold jewelry.

The police and fire engine sirens were coming closer. A cluster of English people standing near the marble column where Emily had propped herself chattered excitedly about a witness having seen the gunman take off in a German-made car toward the interior.

"Why do you suppose he shot the waiter?" a woman asked in hushed tones.

Hal, please be all right, Emily thought, thumping her head against the pillar.

Within minutes an ambulance arrived, and she was carried gingerly inside.

She never saw Aubrey Katsuleris again. And though she tried for several years afterward to establish the six links that would bring her back to Hal Woczniak and Arthur Blessing, she was not able to accomplish that, either.

As soon as the draperies caught fire, Hal knew what was going to happen. There were only two exits from the dining room, and the killer had gone out through one of them. Nearly everyone in the room would rush for the grand, although not particularly wide, double doors leading to the lobby.

Besides, he had no illusions about whom the shots were meant for. He hadn't recognized the gunman, but he doubted that the man was anything more than a hired shooter. When he'd missed his target, he had opted to run rather than try again—the mark of a professional who had blundered. If the so-called busboy had known about the cup, he would have taken Hal in the melee that followed.

And that, he was sure, was what whoever planned this setup was about to do.

While the diners were still rising from their seats, Hal swept a pink tablecloth out from under its burden of dishes and threw it over his head. Then he leaped toward one of the huge windows feet first and fell in a spray of broken glass into the garden below.

He shook the glass out of his hair. The fall had been a good one. Out of a dozen cuts and scrapes, not one was serious. He looked up at the broken window. No one was in it looking for him. Probably covering one of the exits, he thought, or both. Taking a final look around, he sprinted toward the docks.

Taliesin and the children were waiting on the dark side of a moonlit cargo ship.

"Where's Emily?" Arthur asked.

"It was a fake," Hal said. "Look, I think—"

"Someone's coming," Beatrice whispered.

Hal whirled around, but he was too late. Something kicked him in the small of the back, sending him tumbling down the pier. In another second, Aubrey stood behind Arthur, a gun with a web silencer to the boy's head.

"You know what I want," he said casually. "Let's not try any heroics."

"He's . . . he's just a little boy," Taliesin whispered. Aubrey turned slightly and fired at the old man's shoulder. The fabric from his tweed jacket burst into a tuft of charred threads. With a groan, Taliesin slapped his hand over the wound. Blood flowed out from between his fingers.

Arthur tried to wrench himself away, but Aubrey grabbed the boy's hair and jerked his head back, the smoking silencer jammed into his cheek. "Will there be any more discussion?" he asked crisply.

"Give me the cup," Hal ordered.

Beatrice held it out. "He's going to kill us anyway," she said, breaking into sobs. "All of us. It won't matter. . . ."

Hal snatched it out of her hands, then extended his arm over the edge of the pier. "Okay, here it is," he said. "If you shoot any of them, I'll drop it. If you shoot me, I'll drop it. Either way, you aren't going to get this cup without a team of scuba divers and the permission of the Moroccan government."

"You'd better give it to me, Hal," Aubrey said patiently.

Hal spoke without taking his eyes off the other man. "Get out of here, Taliesin. Take the girl with you." When no one moved, he snapped, "Now! Get out of here!"

The old man put his good arm around Beatrice, who had covered her face with her hands.

"Now the kid," Hal said. "Let him go. When he's out of the way, you can have the cup. And you can have me."

"No, Hal—" Arthur cried.

"Shut up. Is it a deal?"

Aubrey half smiled. "A deal," he said. He released Arthur.

He would kill the boy, of course, just as soon as he had the cup. Hal knew that from the man's easy manner. An amateur would not have released Arthur so easily. He would have argued, threatened, maybe even have taken a couple of wild shots.

But this was no amateur. He had shot the old man without blinking an eye. And he had aimed for Taliesin's shoulder. Enough to cause alarm without real panic. And now he was calmly watching Arthur trot down the long pier, where he would eventually find him and kill him, along with the others.

Yes, Hal thought, he was very good.

And so while Arthur was still an easy target with nowhere to hide, just a moment or two before Hal would have been expected to turn over the cup, he dropped it to the pier with a clatter, then threw up one leg in a high three-sixty roundhouse kick that knocked the gun out of the man's hands.

The move took Aubrey completely by surprise. He had been expecting a retired FBI agent with the reflexes of a walrus, but the American's timing had been a work of art. Before he could recover from the first blow, Hal grabbed him by the throat and pummelled Aubrey's head into the splintered boards.

And the cup rolled on, down the pier, slowing as it crested each warped plank, veering first right, then left, glinting dully in the moonlight, until it came to rest at Beatrice's feet.

She picked it up, unbelieving, then held it up to show Arthur.

"Hal!" the boy called. "We've got it! Come with us!"

Hal looked up. It was only for an instant, but an instant was all it took for Aubrey to grab the gun lying on the pier. He smashed its stock across Hal's cheek.

As Hal reeled backward, Aubrey caught sight of the boy and took careful aim. Hal lunged at him on all fours, like a wild bull, dragging him down. A shot fired into the air as the two men rolled over one another toward the edge. Then, as Arthur watched, rooted to the place where he stood, Aubrey kicked upward with both feet, sending Hal hurtling over the edge.

Staggering to his feet, Aubrey aimed at the water and fired. Once, twice. Then he turned and crouched, directing the fat web of the barrel directly at Arthur.

Something slammed the boy to the wooden slats just before the muffled report from the gun sounded, then dragged him up a gangplank.

"Hurry," Taliesin whispered, pointing his chin toward the open hold of a ship. The interior was stacked with crates. He shooed Arthur and Beatrice up the ramp and over the crates into the darkness of the hold, where they sat in numb silence.

In the distance, some sailors were walking and shouting goodnaturedly to one another in what sounded like English. Arthur stared into the blackness of his hiding place, hearing them but unable to concentrate on their words. Unable to think of anything but the sight of Hal windmilling into the water, and the two shots that had followed.

They were both gone now, Emily, who had raised him from infancy, and Hal, who had been the only father he'd ever known.

Hal . . .

Hal was dead.

In time, the sailors walking down the dock approached the ship and finished loading the crates. Their ribald jokes and loud voices turned the atmosphere around the pier from silent terror to a workaday warmth, but Arthur felt none of it.

For him the world had ended, and when Beatrice reached out in the darkness to clasp her hand over his, he felt only the hot tears of his loss running down his face.

On the dock Aubrey waited, his jaw clenching both from the pain in his face and from his impatience. He had expected the drunken sailors to pass the ship where the old man and the children with the cup had entered. He stood in the shadows, feeling the blood harden in the fine lines around his eyes, as the men took their time loading the hold.

He did not mind the pain; Aubrey knew he deserved every bit of the beating the American had given him. He should never have depended on Saladin's relatives to kill for him. The gunman who had come so highly recommended by the Lagouat clan had failed miserably, and would never be seen again.

It had been essential that the American be killed first. With his protector dead, the boy would have led Aubrey straight to the cup. Then three shots in the darkness, and the cup would have been his, with no witnesses, no problems.

He would never use the relatives again.

"Hey, you!" one of the sailors called, pointing unmistakably at Aubrey. "What do you want, huh? You got a problem or what?"

Cautiously, Aubrey took two steps forward—not enough to show his face, but enough to allay any fears the sailor might have. "Where is this ship headed?" he asked pleasantly.

"Port of New York."

"Ah." From where he stood, he could see the ship's name, the S.S. *Comanche*, on its prow. "The container port in Newark?"

"Yeah," the sailor answered. "And we're shipping out now, so get your ass out of here."

"Certainly," he said genially. He walked back along the dock to the place where the American had fallen. It had been difficult to see, particularly with blood running in Aubrey's eyes, but he had sensed that one of the bullets had struck.

The tide was going out. With the active surface current in the Strait of Gibraltar, the corpse had probably already begun its journey down the twelve-mile-wide channel separating Tangier from Spain. By daylight, it would be swallowed by the vastness of the North Atlantic.

So all there was to do was to reach the United States and wait for Arthur Blessing and his magic cup when the S.S. *Comanche* docked. Despite Aubrey's colossal frustration, the thought of taking the cup in America was rather thrilling. In a country where violent crime was so commonplace, it would be easy to kill two children and an old man.

He would find someone—no Arabs, please, not after tonight—to get rid of the girl and the old man. But the boy's death had meant a great deal to Saladin. Aubrey would kill Arthur Blessing himself. He would take his time, find some inventive method of doing away with the little bugger.

For old times' sake.

As the ship pulled out, its foghorn booming, Aubrey saluted it with a little wave of farewell.

PART TWO

THE
SWORD

CHAPTER TEN

Dawn was breaking, and Hal was cold. It had been nearly seven hours since he had emerged, frantic and gasping, from the grip of the undertow that had carried him away from shore.

The first few moments had been a welter of confusion and despair. Images of the past hour—the waiter's blood spurting out in the dining room, the panicked stampede to the exit after the fire started, the dark man's smile as he held the gun to Arthur's head at the pier—came to him in a jumble, mixed with the sensation of the water and the sound of Katsuleris' two bullets thudding into the pylon near him as the current carried him under.

His only thought at the time was to breathe as the riptide smashed him against underwater boulders and tangled him in kelp. Afterwards, he wondered why he had bothered; and yet he had fought against the current, fought with all his body and will for one gulp of air before the tide grasped him again, pulling him out farther, farther into the cold black water of the channel.

The second time he came up, he was nearly unconscious. The black water had melted into the starless sky seamlessly. Hal was not aware of when the current had let him go, or of when he had started to breathe again. All he knew was that he was floating alone in the channel with a piece of rotted board under his head. Both his shoes and one sock were missing. So was his watch. Dim lights were scattered like pinpricks in the black shroud that surrounded him. There was a larger light somewhere to the left of his big toe: The lighthouse in Tangier, he presumed.

Miles away.

He might have slept then; he didn't remember. Then, as the sky was changing color from black to cobalt and a thin, sparkling line of light appeared on the waves in the east, he heard something. It was only momentary. When he strained to hear it, the sound was gone, drowned out by the susuration of the waves. Still, Hal was certain he had heard something.

Then he saw it, off to the west, barely visible against the still-inky sky: a boat. It was a trawler of some kind, steaming toward him. As it neared, the noise Hal had heard grew steadily louder, then stopped abruptly as the trawler's engine was cut. The men on board were shouting to one another in a language Hal didn't recognize as they lifted a net heavy with fish onto the deck.

He tried to signal to it, but found that his arms were too stiff with cold to lift. He struggled in the water, managing only to knock away the board on which his head and chest were resting. With the effort, his legs stiffened with cramps, and he felt himself going under again, flailing, gasping for breath.

"Hey!" he shouted. "Over here!" He heard his voice ring across the water with a curious loudness before being silenced in the swell of a wave. Water washed over his head. He sputtered and coughed, then went under again.

It would be an easy death, he thought.

And Arthur? Was he dead, too? During his last moments on the dock, Hal had been the only thing between Arthur and the killer.

But they had the cup. Yes! Arthur still had the cup, and Taliesin was with him. The old man would look after Arthur until Hal found them. Suddenly he wanted very much to live.

"Help!" he yelled, disappointed that he sounded so feeble. His voice had seemed loud only a moment ago.

Or was it an hour . . .

His last conscious memory was the sound of the trawler's engine starting up again.

*   *   *

The castle was filled with ghosts.

In the Great Hall, Hal sat among them at the Round Table, uncomfortable in the big chair. They watched him, these long dead men dressed in chain mail and leather, their eyes attentive. The chair had stood empty for sixteen hundred years, while one of their number had gone into the world, born and reborn, again and again, looking for their lost king.

Then, as they watched, a swirl of moondust encircled the Siege Perilous and the visitor who sat upon it. Hal gasped as light frozen from a time which had passed into legend a millennium before burst into life and gathered around him.

"Galahad," one of the knights whispered. He was Launcelot, first among the Companions and father to the young knight who had been chosen for this special, earthly quest. Launcelot had recognized him even though his son now bore a different face and a new body.

"Galahad!" the others affirmed, their voices deafening in the cobwebby silence. They raised their swords to him.

"But I'm not . . ." Hal protested. "You don't know . . ."

But they drowned him out, calling the name again and again because they remembered, as he himself did not, that the name was his own, and that he had indeed, after sixteen centuries of searching, found the king.

Water gushed out of his mouth. Hal came to, coughing, his eyes streaming. He gulped a mouthful of air, convinced with half his mind that it would kill him, but unable to resist.

It tasted of fish. It gurgled in his lungs and he coughed again, so hard that it drew his shoulders up off the hard surface where he lay, then thumped him back down again.

Someone had covered him with a blanket. Hal could not yet feel its warmth, but his arms registered the prickliness of the wool. A stranger's face moved in front of him, very close. Its skin was lined and brown from a lifetime in the sun, with two deep creases between the palest of blue eyes. Softly the man said something in the strange language Hal had heard on the sea, then turned his head to repeat it to a group of men who had gathered behind him. Slowly they came into focus, each of them frowning down at Hal.

"O Borracho?" the man asked. Hal shook his head. The man said something else, waited in vain for a response, then sighed.

"Americane," one of the men behind him said, holding up Hal's wallet. The man with the blue eyes stood up stiffly and examined it, glancing at the wad of hundred-dollar bills inside, riffling through the documents attesting to Hal's existence: a New York driver's license, an out-of-date voter registration card, the business card from his last place of employment—a garage in Tangier specializing in European cars—and a torn piece of old newspaper. "Arold," the blue-eyed man read, trying to sound out the name on the driver's license. "Arold Wocks . . . Wuzzi . . ." Shaking his head, he handed the wallet somberly to Hal.

"Woczniak," Hal said. "Thank you." His throat still burned from salt water. Blinking hard to keep his thoughts in focus, he fished half the bills from his wallet and offered them to the man. "Hey, thanks for helping me out," he said, struggling to rise. "I'd like to . . ."

The man with the blue eyes shook his finger at the money, then gently pushed Hal backward so that he was leaning against the cabin wall. He adjusted the blanket around him and made a gesture for Hal to rest. Then he turned away and shouted at the others.

Hal watched for a few minutes while some of the men gathered up thousands of sardines from the deck of the boat and tossed them into a hole in the floor and others untangled the big nets, readying them to cast once again into the sea. The blanket and the sun overhead were beginning to warm him. The gentle motion of the boat was lulling and comfortable.

He did not know when he fell asleep, but when he awoke, the sun was nearing its zenith and the boat heading toward land. It was not Tangier. The houses of the small village along the shore were not Moroccan, and the people he saw at the dock were white. He had gone to the other shore, then. To Spain? But the language was not Spanish. The musical tongue spoken by the men on the fishing boat sounded, to Hal's untrained ear, like an admixture of French and German.

After unloading the trawler's catch into a van filled with ice and lined with plastic shower curtains, the man with the blue eyes helped him to his feet and led him off the boat.

On the dock, a man cooking eels on a smoky grill waved to them. The sailor with Hal waved back, then gestured expansively at the collection of crumbling stone and plaster houses on the cobblestone street above them. "Santa Amelia," he said lovingly, leading Hal up some rickety wooden steps. "Portugal."

"Portugal?" Hal repeated. "I can't be in Portugal."

He looked up and down the road. Behind the sardine van, which was heading into the inland hills, walked a mule led by two children. Two boxy women wearing cotton dresses and ankle socks smoked cigarettes beneath a weatherbeaten poster with the symbol of the Communist hammer and sickle on it. "American Embassy?" he asked.

The fisherman held up a finger and nodded, the universal symbol for "wait." Then he took him by the arm and led him up the street. "Olazabal," he said, thumping his chest.

"Olazabal? That's your name?"

The fisherman nodded. "Juan Marco Olazabal." His lips curved into something almost resembling a smile on his taut, sculpted-stone features, then thrust his chin at Hal. "Arold," he added.

"Hal. Call me Hal."

"Hall. Okay."

Olazabal's house was on the village's main street. Made of stone, it was immaculately whitewashed, with a garden in back. The fisherman threw open the front door with a bang and a shout. His wife, stirring a pot of some fragrant stew over a woodburning stove, smiled shyly, wiped her hands on the stained apron she was wearing, and came to take his hat. She bowed politely to Hal, then immediately placed two wooden bowls filled with clams and sausages in red broth on the table, along with a basket of crusty bread and a bottle of pale wine, which she poured into coffee cups. Olazabal wiped his hands on a rag and sat down, gesturing toward Hal's bowl.

"*Ameijoas,*" he boomed, smiling.

Hal tasted it and thought he would die of happiness. As he ate, he realized that it had been his first meal in more than two days.

"*Bom?*" Olazabal asked.

Hal nodded. "*Bom,*" he repeated. "Very good."

With a roar of good humor, the Portuguese slapped him on the back so hard that the piece of bread in Hal's mouth flew across the table. Then he laughed some more.

By the time dinner was over, Hal could barely sit upright. "I have to get to the Embassy," he said breathlessly. "I floated over to Portugal without a passport, and I've got to get back."

"*Passaporte. Si,*" Olazabal repeated, holding his finger up again.

"Ah." His stone features broke into a gap-toothed smile as the wooden door creaked open and a young woman walked in.

"Antonia!" he shouted.

"Papa," she answered breathlessly, removing a scarf from her head. "Mama." She nodded at Hal, but no one introduced him. Both Olazabal and his wife shouted a torrent of remarks, gesticulating freely toward their unexpected guest. As they spoke, she looked over at Hal, her expression alternately friendly and appalled.

"My father says he found you in the ocean," she said, sitting down at the table across from him.

"You speak English."

"Yes. I work in Faro, a short distance. Many English come there. Also Americans. How did you come to be in the ocean so many miles away?"

"I fell in. Off a dock in . . . Tangier. . . ."

"Tangier! But you should not have lived!"

"You're not the only one who feels that way," Hal said.

"No, my English is not perfect. I meant it is very far to Tangier. A long distance to stay in the ocean." She smiled. "Do you have family in Tangier?"

Family. Arthur was as close as Hal had ever come to having a family. Arthur and, he had once hoped, Emily. Were either of them still alive?

He couldn't think about that, he told himself. It would do no good. He would have to assume they were, that Emily had gotten out of the hotel, and that Taliesin had taken Arthur and Beatrice out of the city to a place of safety.

The question was, where?

Antonia was still smiling sweetly, waiting for Hal to answer her question. "Uh . . . no," he said. "I was just passing through."

"Then perhaps you were meant to come here. To help someone."

Her gaze could have bored holes through him. She was looking at him so intently that he was tempted to check over his shoulder, but suppressed the urge. "Yeah, maybe so," he said, trying to be agreeable.

Olazabal said something lengthy and mellifluous, accompanied by a variety of gestures. When he was through, Antonia nodded. "My father insists that you spend the night here, but I will take you to my place of work in the morning, if your health is good."

It seemed like an odd invitation. "Well . . ."

"I work in the passport office. You have lost your papers, yes?"

"Oh. Yes. Well, just my passport. I've still got my driver's license and things like that."

"Then it will not be a problem." She patted his hand. "You wish to go back to Tangier, yes?"

"Yes," Hal said. "Thanks."

Tangier was as good a place as any to start looking for Arthur.

But first he would find the bastard who had thrown him off the dock. Whoever he was, he knew about the cup, and would go after Arthur until he got it.

The cup, the damned cup! Hal almost hoped Taliesin would just leave it for the man to find. But he wouldn't do that. The old man knew even better than Hal what would happen if the cup fell into the hands of someone like the man on the dock. It was a vessel of dreams and wonder, too precious and too dangerous to be set loose in the world.

He sighed. He wished he'd never set eyes on the thing.

During the evening, the small house was filled with neighbors coming to get a look at the strange visitor who had been fished out of the sea like a sardine, but shortly their fascination for him diminished. The men played a poker-like card game called *mus*, and the women gossiped in whispers, standing or seated on stools around an old woman draped in black like a nun. She was apparently the local wise woman who, according to Antonia, dispensed advice on every subject from giving birth to winning at cards. Occasionally one of the men would excuse himself from the *mus* table to consult with her as well.

"Dona Theresa is a *bruxa*," Antonia said. "A witch. They wish for her to tell them how to win at the cards."

"What happens if they lose?" Hal asked.

Antonia shrugged. "Perhaps she will give them better advice next time."

At the end of the evening everyone bowed graciously and clasped Hal's hand. Some embraced him; others made a point of rubbing his back or chest or hair.

"I feel like the family dog," Hal said after the guests left.

"They were waiting all evening to do that," Antonia told him. "To touch a man who has been saved by a miracle is great good luck."

Olazabal offered Antonia's bedroom to Hal for the night, but Hal insisted on sleeping on the divan in the parlor. It was made of wood, but Mrs. Olazabal covered it with thick wool blankets so that it was reasonably comfortable, although too narrow to accommodate Hal's body. He squirmed, shifting from one side to the other, trying to keep his limbs from going numb, for most of the night. At last he got up and moved the mass of blankets onto the floor beside the fire and sat there, poking the embers with a stick.

"I see you also cannot sleep." Antonia pulled a tattered robe closer over her nightgown and sat down beside him.

Hal looked into the fire, remembering his dream on the ship, in which he had sat in a place of honor with the ghost-knights of the Round Table. It had not really been a dream, he knew, but a memory of another life.

The first time he experienced the dream, three years before, he had been awake. Even so, he had dismissed it. The idea of his having lived before had been too outlandish for Hal to believe. But little by little, he had been shown the truth.

He had once been privileged to serve a great king who, rather than compromise his soul, had refused the cup of immortality. Yet there had been a prophecy that Arthur of Britain would come again, and so his knights waited at their Round Table, their spirits thin as air, while one of their number, whose name had been Galahad, returned to the world of men to wait for his king's return.

"Galahad!" the knights called, their voices an echo of the far distant past, inaudible to any ears but Galahad's own, while moondust swirled around him in the Siege Perilous of the ancient hall at Camelot.

Hal looked up with a start. Antonia was staring at him. "Am I disturbing your private thoughts?"

"No, nothing like that. I was just . . ." He shrugged.

"Excuse me if I seem to pry," she said tentatively. "But you said you have no family in Tangier."

"That's right," Hal said.

"Then your business is there?"

Hal shook his head.

"Your home?" she asked.

He held up his palms. "Hotel room."

"I am sorry," Antonia said quietly. She looked around the shabby room. "A home is important. Family, children, parents . . ." A tear coursed down her cheek.

"Hey, it's okay," Hal said. "I've gotten used to it."

"Yes, yes." She brushed the tear away. "I apologize. I have not been good company for you," she said huskily, and rose. "We go early to the passport office. Then you can go back to Tangier."

"Right," he mumbled. Back to Tangier. To kill a man.

For the cup.

Again.

Two hours later they were in Antonia's ancient lime-green Fiat.

Her tears had sprung up again as they ate breakfast. Antonia hugged her parents fiercely at the door, then began to sob loudly as she started up the car. A fresh torrent of noisy sobs burst out of the woman as they crested a hill overlooking the seacoast village they had left. Hal thought the Portuguese had to be the most emotional people he'd ever met.

"Is there something bothering you, Antonia?" he asked politely.

She blew her nose. "My home, my home," she wailed.

He looked behind them. "Just how far is it to the passport office?"

"Twelve kilometers." She honked noisily into her handkerchief.

"Twelve . . ." He stifled a laugh. "Not to be nosy, but do you go through this every day?" Antonia answered with a fresh wail. Hal decided not to press her on the subject.

She seemed to calm down somewhat over the next couple of miles, until the Fiat's engine sputtered and died in the middle of a flock of geese.

"My car!" she moaned. "Not my car!" Her voice had an hysterical edge to it.

Hal leaped out. Anyone who reacted to leaving for work in the morning the way Antonia did might well go off the deep end over a stalled engine. "Relax," he said. "I'll have a look at it. I'm a mechanic."

He opened the hood. Steam shot up in a cloud. When it cleared, Antonia was standing beside him.

"It's no big deal," Hal said. "Leaky radiator, that's all. It'll start up again in a couple of minutes. We can get a patch for it at the next town."

"You say you are a car mechanic?" she asked.

"At your service."

"*Deo gracias,*" she murmured, closing her eyes rapturously and making the sign of the cross.

"Uh . . . yeah."

Antonia's eyes were brimming again. Hal bent over the engine with feigned interest before she decided to kiss his feet and declare a miracle.

"It is a miracle," she said.

Hal wiped his forehead. "Antonia, it's a cracked radiator, not the Shroud of Turin, okay?"

"Dona Theresa—the *bruxa*—said that someone would come to help me. That is you, Senhor Hal."

"And if it weren't me, it'd be the next guy who drove by. Anybody could do this, believe me."

"No, the miracle is not with my car," she said. "Dona Theresa was speaking about my plan. You have come to help me with my plan."

"Your plan to get to work?"

"No. I have already quit my job. Today I will travel to England."

He looked up from the engine. "What?"

"And I will remain there." Her eyes began to well with tears.

Hal replaced the radiator cap quickly. "Maybe you'd better tell me while we're on the road. Mind if I drive?"

She blew her nose and shook her head. Gratefully Hal led her to the passenger seat and hopped behind the wheel. The Fiat started up immediately. After a few minutes he spotted a sign that said *Faro 8 k.* He gunned the engine. He figured that the faster he drove, the less time he would have to spend listening to Antonia cry. "Okay, go ahead," he said, pushing the car to its limit. "Did you tell your parents you're moving out?"

She shook her head. "That is what makes it all so sad. But there is no other way. You see, I am married. But secretly. Papa does not know."

"Does he know the guy? I mean, your husband?"

"He hates Franco." Antonia hiccupped loudly. "He used to love him. Franco was like his own son. He grew up on the fishing boats with my father. It was my father himself who announced our engagement. But Franco could not remain a fisherman. He is a thinker, Franco." She tapped her forehead with meaning. "A scholar. One day he will be a great man."

"What did he do?" Hal asked. "To make your father hate him?"

"He went to accounting school."

"Ah," Hal said.

"In the Algarve. The English sector. For a man from my village, this is like treason. We have hated the English for centuries. But it was an Englishman, not a Portuguese, who offered Franco a chance to do bookkeeping for his business. When Franco did well, the Englishman lent him the money to go to school," she said hotly. "Yet still my father will not forgive Franco for leaving the village. He says his daughter would never be given to an Englishman's slave in marriage." She wept into her hands.

"But you married him anyway."

Antonia nodded. "Two months ago. I told my parents I had to go to Lisbon for the passport office. But I met Franco instead. To become his wife."

"Why didn't you go to England then?"

"Franco was still a student. I have some savings, but he would not allow me to support us. But now he has a good job in a big company in London."

"An accounting firm?"

"No, a sporting goods store. He is the manager," she said proudly. "It is one of the Englishman's businesses."

"Sounds like this guy's taking pretty good care of Franco."

"He is a good man. Were it not for him, Franco and I might have grown old thinking the way my father does."

"Your father's a good man, too, Antonia," Hal said. "He saved my life."

That had been a mistake. Antonia burst into tears and wailed annoyingly for the next five miles. By the time they reached the passport office at Faro, the Fiat had broken down twice more. Hal couldn't wait to get out.

"Well, thanks for the lift," he said breezily. As a second thought, he took some bills out of his wallet and held them out to her. "Here, I'd like you to have—"

"You are coming with me, no? After your passport is replaced?"

Hal cleared his throat. "Well, actually, I hadn't planned—"

"But Dona Theresa said you would come." She looked suddenly frail, like a wounded child.

She *is* a child, Hal thought. A little girl running away from home. "Antonia," he said gently, "maybe you'd better reconsider this trip. I don't think you really want to leave your parents."

"But I must," she cried. "I am . . ." She looked at the ground. "I am with child."

Oh, great, he thought. A pregnant little girl running away from home in a jalopy that wasn't going to make it through town without breaking down. "I can't," he said at last. "I've got to get back to Tangier."

"Why?" she demanded.

"To . . . Never mind." He waved the bills at her again. "Take the money. Please." He looked over the car dubiously. "And stay on the main roads."

She pushed his hand away. "Perhaps it was another whom Dona Theresa meant." Her lip quivered.

"Yeah," Hal said. "That's got to be it."

He went into the passport office feeling like a heel.

An hour later he emerged with a new passport and the disheartening news that the only rental car in town had crashed into a tree the previous night. The Faro passport office had, however provided him with a map. The nearest ferry to Tangier was a hundred and six miles away.

Hal thrust his hands in his pockets. He was crossing the street when a green Fiat swerved wildly to avoid hitting him.

"What the hell were you looking at?" Hal shouted from the gutter where he had flung himself. Then he recognized the car and its sobbing driver.

"Deo, forgive me!" Antonia wailed. "I was not watching . . ." Her tears suddenly stopped. "Senhor Hal, it is you."

"Unfortunately, yes."

"I will take you to the rental car office, okay?" she offered helpfully.

"There is no rental car."

"Oh?" Her face broke into a broad smile. She looked a lot prettier when she wasn't crying, Hal thought.

"I can take you to the next town," she offered. "Of course, if you would rather go to England . . ."

Hal rolled his eyes.

"Please, Senhor." She clasped his hands prayerfully, her tears already dripping off her chin. "You have no family in Tangier, no work, no home. I beg of you. My unborn baby begs of you—"

"Enough! Enough!" He threw up his hands. "All right, I'll go."

Antonia shrieked, weeping rapturously. "Oh, Senhor Hal—"

"On two conditions," he said. "One, we stop at a garage. We need to get the radiator fixed."

She nodded, wiping her nose delicately.

"Two, you have to promise me not to cry until we reach your husband. For any reason. Understand?"

The hanky stopped in mid-blot. "Okay," she squeaked.

With a grunt, Hal got in the Fiat. "I mean it," he said. "If you let loose with so much as a sniffle, I'm out of here."

Five days and twenty-six breakdowns later, they arrived in London. Antonia's husband wept for joy when he saw them, which came as no big surprise to Hal.

"How can I thank you?" Franco effused tearfully. "You would like a jogging suit, perhaps? No charge."

"That's okay," Hal said. "I'm not doing a lot of jogging these days."

"But I must repay you," Franco wailed, stricken.

"I'll take a cup of coffee," Hal said.

Franco sprang into action like a man possessed, fiddling with an old percolator while Antonia filled him in on the perils of their motor trip, extolling Hal's genius with a wrench while sobbing intermittently about her lost family in Portugal. Hal decided to absent himself from the commotion by browsing through a copy of the *Observer* on the kitchen table.

"You must stay with us for as long as you like," Franco was saying. "If you need work, perhaps I can help—"

"It's June twenty-third," Hal said, noticing the date on the newspaper.

"What did you say?"

Hal didn't answer. On page three was a small article about a village called Wilson-on-Hamble on the border between Dorset and Somerset counties.

It read: GHOST RIDERS TONIGHT? VILLAGERS EXPECTANT.

Residents of Wilson-on-Hamble are gearing up for an age-old phenomenon: the midnight ride of King Arthur's knights. The village is one of several area communities which claim to be the location of Camelot. On this night each year, according to long-term residents of the hamlet, the ghosts of the ancient knights leave the ruins atop what is now Cadbury Tor to gallop their steeds through the countryside in search of their king who, legend has it, is destined to reappear one day.

Many villagers claim to have heard the ghostly horses. In 1958, a team sent by the London Museum made a tape recording of the village's Front Street between 7 and 9 P.M., when the residents traditionally remain inside their homes to clear the way for the fast-moving ghost riders. Although the recording did pick up noises which "somewhat resembled" a muffled pounding of horses' hooves, the results were inconclusive, according to museum officials, since the sounds may have come from a nearby riding stable.

Nevertheless, the denizens of Wilson-on-Hamble will keep watch once again this evening, perpetuating one of the oddest of Arthurian traditions.

"The twenty-third, yes," Franco said, checking a calendar on the wall. "St. John's Eve, it says. In Portugal, it would be the festival of—"

"Can I get to Dorset on the train?"

"Dorset! But you must stay with us!" Antonia exclaimed. "At least for supper. After such a long trip—"

"Maybe I'll come by this way again. I'll stay then. Promise." He left hurriedly, before Antonia started blubbering.

CHAPTER ELEVEN

St. John's Eve. The last time Hal visited Cadbury Tor on this day in
midsummer, he saw a vision that had changed his life. On a deserted
field, amid a pile of ancient rubble, Hal had seen a castle rise. A castle
filled with ghosts who had called to him as if he were one of their
own.

There were no ghosts this time. He sat on a rock in the field, watching while the afternoon sun grew from a bright disk to a fat, lazy ball
on the horizon. The wind blew around him in a low whistle. The sun
set. Hal had never felt so lonely.

Suddenly he heard a groan nearby, and jumped to his feet.

"Aahhggh," came the voice, followed by the unmistakable sound
of retching. Hal squinted into the glare of the setting sun to see a
figure rising from among the windswept bushes at the base of a line of
fir trees.

Hal smelled him from fifty feet away. "You all right?" he called,
hoping the answer would be yes. The idea of touching anyone who
could produce such a stench filled him with dread.

"Blimy, what an ale head I've got." The creature was an old man
dressed in dun-colored rags. His face—what Hal could see of it against

the fierce dying light—was crusted with dirt and all manner of bodily effluvium which Hal preferred not to think about.

"How long you been there?"

The man scratched his beard, coughed, spat several times, and scratched his thigh while considering. "What day is it now?" he asked finally.

"Tuesday," Hal said.

"Ah." The old man picked something from his head and chewed on it. "Can't say as I recollect, then. Say, friend, got a tenner on you, by chance? For a bit of supper."

"A ten? Where do you eat, the Ritz?"

"I'll make it worth your while, so I will." He gave Hal a broad wink.

"Right. Here, take this." He handed the man a pound note.

The old man spat through a space left by a missing tooth. The stream shot over Hal's shoulder. "That all you can spare?"

"Sheesh." Hal gave him another.

"That'll do."

"Glad to hear it." Hal headed off toward the rental car.

"Wait!" the geezer called, loping after him. "I said I'd make it worth your while, didn't I?"

"What are you, a pervert?"

The old man laughed wheezily. "Got something for you." From the pocket of his Huck Finn trousers he took a hunk of brownish metal. "Found it yesterday." He frowned. "Or sometime. It brought me luck."

"I can tell," Hal said, edging downwind of the man.

"Found a quart bottle half full of Gilbey's in this very field not an hour later, so I did."

"Keep the rock, Pop. Your good fortune may strike again."

"Cross my palm with another quid, and I'll say it did."

Hal sighed. He took out another note and handed it over. "Okay, get out of here."

Chortling, the old man danced off.

"Hey, your rock," Hal shouted, but the beggar had vanished into the mist.

Mist?

In the encroaching twilight, the big fir trees surrounding the meadow were swathed in moving vapor. Tendrils of fog snaked around their low branches and crawled across the grass toward a pile of ancient cut stone in the center of the meadow, where they met and fairly exploded into a circle of frothing mist that extended outward with amazing rapidity in all directions.

"What the hell is this?" Hal whispered as the mist rolled out toward him like a surf, engulfing his legs up to the knees and then moving beyond him, back toward the trees, toward the road.

The rental car which he'd parked on the side of the lane was no longer visible. In another moment the trees, too, were obscured by the rising mist. Hal felt himself shrinking inside it, caught in the vortex of this strange force, feeling its power swirling around him.

He looked down at his hands. In them was the misshapen piece of metal the old man had given him. It was glowing bright red. Then, as he watched, its color transmuted into a vibrant orange, then changed again to yellow, green, blue, violet. He felt as if the top of his head were exploding into space as the nugget changed once more, this time to brilliant white, brighter than the light of a thousand suns.

The light blinded him. For a moment he could see nothing except a sea of dazzling white. Then it dimmed, and through the mist he saw, rising out of the thin air, a castle made of stone.

Red and gold pennants fluttered from its crenolated ramparts, flanking a great broad banner depicting a golden dragon on a scarlet background. Above a wide moat which encircled the building, a drawbridge held by chains with links the size of a man's forearm lowered with a thud onto the bank, and two massive oak and iron doors creaked open. From within Hal could hear voices shouting and the whinnying of horses. Then, traveling in a unit like one lone beast with footfalls of thunder, rode twelve men in armor.

Hal stood awestruck and terrified as their horses crossed the moat and pounded toward him. With a swift motion, one of the knights raised his visor. His eyes, blue as the sea, glowered with a cold fire.

Hal recognized him. He was Launcelot, First Knight and Galahad's own father. This man, in a long-ago vision, had charged Hal with the safekeeping of his king.

And Hal had failed.

Launcelot bent over, his arm outthrust, and lifted Hal off the ground. Panicking, Hal clutched the knight's metal-sheathed back as Launcelot spurred his stallion. The horse leapt forward into a gallop.

Beside them, a knight bearing the red and gold Pendragon banner gave a shout. The other horsemen tore off behind Launcelot and his frightened passenger, the animals' hooves digging up the dry grass beneath them, speeding over the meadow as if charging into battle, racing through the wall of mist that separated Camelot from the rest of the world.

"Hey!" Hal found his voice at last. "What do you think you're . . ."

On the other side of the mist, he saw the village of Wilson-on-Hamble in the distance, shimmering like a mirage.

". . . doing . . . ?" Hal finished absently. Because the village *was* a mirage, he realized. As they drew nearer, he saw that the houses and shops and automobiles parked along the sides of the streets were transparent. He could see through them to the trees and rivers beyond, as if the town and its inhabitants were no more substantial than holograms. In the middle of the main street stood a figure listing precariously, as if he were deciding whether to walk forward or fall in a heap. Hal recognized him as the old man from the meadow.

The beggar, who was as unreal and ghostlike as the rest of the village, solved his dilemma by having a drink. As the horsemen galloped on a direct course with him, the old man threw back his head and tilted the bottle skyward.

"Get out of the way!" Hal shouted. The old man paid no attention. Hal pounded on Launcelot's back. "Slow down!" he screamed into the knight's ear.

Launcelot twitched in his saddle.

"You're going to run him down, for chrissake!" He leaned over, trying to grab the reins away from the knight, but succeeded only in throwing himself of balance and nearly falling off. By the time he righted himself, the riders were almost on top of the drunkard. Hal watched with horror as Launcelot's stallion bore down on the old man. . . .

And rode through him.

The knights never slowed for a moment. With a gasp, Hal craned his neck to look behind him. The old man was still guzzling from his bottle, oblivious to the fact that he had just been run through by a dozen horses.

"What is this," Hal breathed, and felt himself trembling.

The knights stormed through the make-believe streets, listening to the tinny, distant shouts of make-believe people. At the far end of the village, beyond the last dim street lamp, a young mother stood on the corner of the sidewalk, holding the hand of a small girl no more than four years old. As the knights rode by, the child held out her arm and pointed at them solemnly. The mother looked around, an expression of bewilderment on her face.

Within minutes, the village had receded into the distance. The knights rode on, over plains and hills, through farms and valleys and industrial parks.

By nightfall they had veered into the forest, cantering expertly through the foliage.

"I get it," Hal said. "The village back there wasn't a mirage. Those people who looked like ghosts—they were real. They're real, and you're the ghosts, isn't that right?"

No one answered him.

"Of course it is. It's St. John's Eve. You're looking for Arthur, right? The way you do every year." He had been bouncing behind Launcelot for hours. His thighs felt as if they'd been brushburned. "I suppose you're taking me with you because I'm the one who lost him."

They rode on in silence.

Slowly now, the horses exhausted, they headed toward a meandering stream, where Launcelot finally allowed his stallion to drink. The knight himself hung his head with fatigue and disappointment. The others milled around or dismounted, leading their steeds to water.

"Can I get off now?" Hal asked.

Launcelot half turned in his saddle and cuffed him with his forearm. Hal tumbled off the horse onto the mud of the bank.

"Look, I know you're pissed that I'm here without Arthur!" Hal shouted. "Well, you don't have to find him, I do! You can go on your little once-a-year ride, and then disappear back into dreamland, but I can't!"

Some of the knights, removing their helmets, turned to stare at him.

"I can't . . ." His voice cracked with emotion. "And I don't even know where to start looking."

He staggered to his feet and lumbered away from the men. This had to be some kind of dream. Maybe he had fallen asleep here in the meadow sometime in the warm afternoon, before he'd ever met the beggar. Or maybe he was still lying half dead on the Portuguese sardine boat. Or maybe, with some luck, he was sleeping in a cheap hotel room in Tangier with Arthur in the next bunk.

Let that be it, he thought thickly. *Make it so Arthur's still here.*

Someone clasped his arm at the elbow. Hal turned around and saw

Launcelot, bare headed, his long sandy-colored hair plastered down with sweat. Dirt accentuated the lines around the piercing blue eyes. Those eyes no longer challenged Hal with anger. They showed only weariness and despair.

Wordlessly he led Hal back near the stream, where some of the others had started a fire. It felt warm, the motion of the flames almost hypnotically restful. Hal lay back on his elbows, enjoying the feeling of the springy grass against his skin. A young knight no more than twenty years old, with hair the color of summer corn, reached across with a smile to offer Hal a piece of dried meat. He ate it gratefully.

"Why are you camping out here?" Hal asked suddenly.

The other knights all looked up from their rations. Some of them glanced at one another.

"Well?" he persisted. "Don't you have to be in the castle by morning or something? What about that wall of fog? Don't tell me it was just the weather."

The young blond man's eyes traveled from Hal's face to Launcelot's.

"Come on, guys." He tried to laugh. "What's the big secret?"

Launcelot rose and gestured with his arm toward a clearing among an outcropping of boulders in the woods behind him. A clearing scattered with the dead twigs of what had once been a dense thicket. Piles of rock and rubble lay over the twigs.

Hal squinted. The place looked oddly familiar. He walked over to the area and picked up one of the stone pieces. "It's got marks on it," he said, dropping it and collecting several more. "They all do. It's as if someone smashed up one of these boulders on purpose. . . . Oh, no." All of the pieces but one fell to the ground.

From a place deep, deep inside him, a well of panic and despair began to rise. In his hand was a slab of rock bearing the imprint of a jeweled sword hilt.

"Excalibur," he whispered.

That night, when Hal could finally sleep, he dreamed about Taliesin.

The old man, dressed in a flowing blue robe embroidered with silver half-moons, sat on a wide stone bench against a background of a city skyline at night.

"And I thought the pith helmet was bad," Hal said.

Taliesin sniffed. "As if you knew anything about clothes. This garment is far more comfortable than those trouser things you're so fond of. Besides, it is a mark of my status."

"Your status as what, a trick-or-treater?"

"As the Merlin," he said with icy dignity. "How easy it is to forget one's betters."

"Oh, I didn't forget who you were. While I was freezing to death in the ocean, I cheered myself up by recalling that I knew a real live wizard who wasn't lifting a finger to help me. It was heartwarming."

"Testy, testy," the old man said. "You found a boat, didn't you?"

"After two days!"

"Well, then, I don't know what you're complaining about."

Hal emitted a squeak of exasperation.

"Be that as it may—"

"Hold on. I'm not done complaining yet. The sword in the stone is gone."

"Yes, yes," Taliesin said calmly. "It's why I came to fetch you in Marrakesh, before we got sidetracked. Ah, well. No matter. You're here now."

"Okay," Hal said slowly, trying to follow the old man's drift. "I'm here, and the sword isn't. Are you saying you want me to go look for it?"

"Oh, that wouldn't be of much use. The sword hasn't been *taken*, you see. It's been *destroyed*. Broken into fragments and swept away. You had to be here for the Companions."

"Whose companions?" Hal asked, confused.

"Good grief, Hal, but you're thick as a plank. The Companions of the Round Table, naturally."

"Them?" Hal asked, appalled. "I spent two days as fish food for a bunch of *ghosts?"*

The old man folded his arms across his chest. "Now, that's a fine way to talk about men who've fed you and welcomed you to their fire."

"But they're not real! That is . . ." He grimaced. "You're right. I've been with them all night." His face blanked. "Does that mean *I'm* not real, either?"

Taliesin glared at him. "Please try not to be such a dolt, Hal. In the first place, they've always been real, at least for the past sixteen hundred years. They've just been existing on a plane other than yours. Except, of course for the summer solstice."

"Which is now?"

"This year it is," the old man answered. "Once a year, through the power of Excalibur, the Companions have been able to pierce the veil between the two planes in order to search for the sword's rightful owner."

"Arthur."

"Who is still a child, having returned to the world of men rather recently. You were to look after him until Arthur reaches an age when he is able to lead his knights again."

"Yeah, I've really been a swell guardian," Hal said wretchedly.

"Well, that couldn't be helped. You didn't know someone would toss you into the sea."

Hal stared at the old man accusingly. "And I didn't either," Taliesin added emphatically. "Even a wizard can't foretell the future, you know. Too many variables. Choice. Free will." He slapped the bench he was sitting on. "Confound it, the point is, with the sword missing, the doorway into your plane—what you arrogantly refer to as reality—was closed. Rather a letdown, I'd say, for soldiers who'd waited sixteen centuries to ride with their king again."

"But they're here," Hal said. "They're still ghosts, and they made their usual ride last night."

The old man laughed. "Because of you, Hal. You were carrying a piece of Excalibur when you walked into the meadow. It was in your pocket."

"My . . ." He remembered the lump of metal the beggar had given him. "That was just a little nugget."

"Unfortunately, yes. There was only enough magic in it to open the door once."

"Are you saying they can't get back?"

"Quite. I'm afraid that when the knights of the Round Table rode out from Camelot this time, it was for good."

Hal stared at him for a long time. "You mean . . ."

"I mean they're real, Hal, even from your narrow perspective."

"What's going to happen to them? They can't just go on living in the woods."

The Merlin scratched his nose. "Why, I've no idea. I suppose they'll stay with you."

"With me? What am I going to do with them?"

"Why, you'll find Arthur, of course. It's what all of you want."

"I can find him myself. Just tell me where he is."

"You know where he is. He's with me. You don't think I'd leave him on his own, do you? By the way, I wish you'd hurry. I think the fellow from the dock in Tangier knows where we're going."

"Well, I don't!" Hal shouted. "For God's sake, you crazy old coot! Where can I find you?"

"Quiet down before you wake everyone," the old man said. "I'm right here, you see? Hal, use your eyes. Right here . . ."

"*Galahad.*"

The old man vanished.

"No! Taliesin, come back! You have to tell me . . ."

"Galahad." The voice was deep and resonant, tinged with a sight accent. Hal's eyes flew open so suddenly that he caught himself in the middle of a snore.

Launcelot was standing over him. "Up with you. It's full dawn."

Hal blinked, surveying the site. Around the charred remains of a fire, a dozen men in strange attire yawned as they washed their faces in the stream or gnawed on pieces of hard bread. Nearby, their horses whinnied and stamped in the woods.

"You're . . . you're all still here," he said wonderingly. "Where's the castle?"

"Gone," Launcelot said, looking into the distance. "The whole world, it seems, has disappeared."

You got the boys out, and now they can't get back in.

Hal reached into the pocket of his trousers for the nugget the beggar had given him.

It was gone.

"Oh, Jesus," he said.

The big knight clasped his shoulder and held it, as if to impart his strength to Hal. "Ah, well," he said softly. "Perhaps it's time we rode together again."

CHAPTER TWELVE

It was as if the new day had lifted a veil of mist from around the men in camp. Hal realized that the night before, he had been the only one to speak. But today the camp was bustling with sound as the strange horsemen prepared for the day, talking, shouting, joking, occasionally swatting each other in irritation.

"Have a biscuit?" offered the blond boy who had given him a piece of dried meat the night before.

Hal blinked at him. Without his armor, the young man was dressed in the oddest garb he had ever seen: His legs were covered by ragged breeches that ended somewhere around his ankles, while over it he wore a shapeless tunic of coarsely woven yellow cloth. On his feet were shoes that resembled leather bags, tied with cords. He thrust the crust of bread at Hal again.

It was hard and dry as a rock, and one corner was covered with blue mold. "Pity we haven't got some ale to go with it," the boy said with a grin. "Drank the last of it last night."

"No need to fret over that, Fairhands," called a stocky bantam of a man in a thick Irish brogue. "I spotted a pub in the village yonder."

He swaggered over and clasped Hal's shoulder, which was at the level of his own black-curled head. "What say we ride over for a decent breakfast, eh, Galahad?"

"Galahad," Hal repeated. "That's the name you know me by."

The man burst into hearty laughter. "If you'd rather we called you something else, I'm sure we could come up with something, couldn't we, Agravaine?"

A young, lean man with a wicked-looking hook in place of his right hand cast them both a disdainful glance and went about saddling his horse.

"Agravaine . . ." Before, when he had first seen the spectral vision of the knights, Hal had thought of them only as spirits. But they were real now, truly real, men of flesh and blood and speech, with histories and personalities and names. "I know Launcelot," he said. "But you . . ." He looked at the young blond man. "He called you Fairhands. . . ."

The handsome youth smiled. "Gareth Beaumains," he said. "I'm called 'Fairhands' because I bear the king's standard in battle. And because MacDaire won't speak a French name," he added with a wink.

"MacDaire? Is that who you are?" Hal asked the Irishman.

"Is that who I am?" the stocky man shouted feistily. "Who else would I be, you brainless pup? You act as if you'd never heard the name Curoi MacDaire!"

"Well . . ."

"Don't be hard on him, Irish," Fairhands said. "He's been gone from us a long time."

"Hmmph. Long enough to have forgotten his sworn brothers, looks like."

Hal closed his eyes. This wasn't happening. These were not King Arthur's knights talking to him in broad daylight as if he were a compatriot of theirs.

"Ah, well, I expect you can make it up to me by buying a spot of breakfast. You'll do that much for an old friend, won't you, Galahad?"

Hal rubbed his eyes. MacDaire and the young knight exchanged a meaningful look.

"I'll warrant it has been a long time, son," the Irishman said, tousling Hal's hair. "We'll have a horn of ale and catch you up. Go fetch the others," he said to Fairhands, then turned back to Hal. "Mind you, you're still paying."

*   *   *

The pub, known as the Motte and Bailey, delighted the knights. They held their factory-made beer steins up to the light as if they were jewels, marvelled at the brightly colored signs advertising liquor, and watched with fascination as the plastic clock with "Guinness" on its face slowly marked the passage of time.

"Like a church, it is," young Fairhands said with wonder as he surveyed the colored cellophane pasted to the window facing the street.

"Nectar." MacDaire quaffed a glass of ale, his eyes closed in rapture.

Even Launcelot, who had been so stern the night before, loosened up after three beers and a plate of bangers. Within an hour, the bar was heaped with dirty dishes and more glasses than the barman could keep up with. Three men at a table and two regulars at the bar gave up their own conversations to stare openly at Hal and the weirdly dressed, long-haired fellows who sat or stood around him, grabbing sausages by twos and threes with their bare hands and belching contentedly while they downed gallons of beer and ale.

The Irishman named MacDaire introduced Hal around. In addition to Fairhands, there were four other youths among the Companions: Bedwyr, a strapping twenty-two-year-old with a bush of blond hair and a mischievous grin, who proudly announced himself as Master of Horse; Tristan, who resembled a young Tyrone Power and was apparently famous for his exploits with women; a spindly young fellow called Geraint Lightfoot; and Agravaine, the saturnine youth with the hook.

Among the older men, there was a soldier with a bald head the shape of a dum-dum bullet and a prodigious capacity for drink. Graced with the unpronounceable name of Gwenwynwyn ap Naw, he granted Hal the right to call him Dry Lips. "So long as the name's not used in jest," he warned, pulling out the heavy spear he kept strapped to his broad back. "I was the King's champion at the battle of Culhwch, and I'll not be spoken of in jest." He fixed Hal with a steely gaze above his glass.

"Wouldn't think of it," Hal said. "Sir."

MacDaire coughed delicately. "Since you've not quite come to yourself yet, I'd suggest you use the same restraint with Lugh there."

"Lugh?"

"Lugh Loinnbheimionach," MacDaire said, nodding toward a huge, wild-haired dirtball who occupied a corner table alone except for several empty platters of sausage. "Lugh's a good-hearted sort, really, but he likes a fight. Wouldn't you say, boys?"

"That he does," Fairhands agreed.

"Aye, he's a beast." Dry Lips quaffed another beer. "Never seen a man to live after a beating with that mace of his."

Hal looked over at the dirtball again. Propped against the chair where he sat was a wooden handle attached to a ten-inch-wide iron ball bristling with spikes. "He fights with that?" he asked.

The three knights nodded thoughtfully. "Doesn't need to, though," said a big bluff man whom Hal had not yet met. "His hands'll do the job just as well." He put his meaty arm around Hal. "Remember me, Galahad?"

"I don't think so," Hal said. "Even though you all seem somehow . . . familiar. . . ."

"You'll be familiar with Kay soon enough," MacDaire said with a chuckle. "On a winter day at dawn, you'll be cursing the day he was born."

"Kay," Hal whispered. He remembered the name from a Walt Disney movie from his childhood.

"The drillmaster. It's me keeps you boys from turning into wild bandits," he said with a grin. "Got to keep up the practice, you know. That's what we'll be doing as soon as we get back to the . . ." He cocked his head at Launcelot. "Well, I suppose we won't be getting back to the castle, will we, seeing as how there is no castle." He burst into loud guffaws and pounded his fist on the bar for another drink.

"Weren't you Arthur's stepbrother?" Hal asked. "That is, the king was raised in your household, wasn't he?"

"That he was," Kay pronounced somberly. "Brought to my da by the wizard, he was. Said we was to foster the babe as if he was a proper nobleman's son. Hah!" He slammed the stein on the bar. "Turned out 'twas the son of Uther Pendragon himself, but the old devil wouldn't tell us that."

"You mean Merlin," Hal said.

"See, he's getting back his memory already," MacDaire said. "Have another ale, son."

"Aye, the Merlin." Kay wiped a foamy moustache off his lip with his forearm. "When me da told him to be off with the child, the sorcerer took the very moon out of the sky. Said he wouldn't give it back until Da accepted the fostering."

Hal smiled. No doubt Taliesin had timed his visit to coincide with a lunar eclipse. "He's a sly one, all right."

"Oh, those druids are not to be crossed," Kay went on, shaking his head. "They'll turn you into frogs soon as look at you. Me, I'm a Christian, myself." He set down his glass momentarily to make the sign of the cross. "Still, the wizard never struck me down for it. Decent sort, at the bottom of it all."

Hal ventured a question. "Do you know where he is now?"

MacDaire laughed. "Know where the Merlin is! Why, you might as well try to find the wind." He threw down the dregs of his ale. "Had a dream about the old dear last night, so I did."

"You did?" Hal asked. "Where was he?"

Kay scratched his beard. "Odd. I dreamed about him, too, come to think of it. He was in a strange place, like a city, but in the sky."

"The sky, that was it!" MacDaire exclaimed. "I swear, there was windows lit clear up to the moon and beyond."

Hal frowned. "That's right," he said. "It was a city of some kind. But there wasn't any noise."

"And it was in the sky," MacDaire added.

"All cities are like that now," Hal said, disappointed. "The buildings are called skyscrapers."

"Skyscrapers," Fairhands said, savoring the word. "I wish I could remember my dreams. Maybe I saw it, too."

"Wait a minute. All of us couldn't have had the same dream," Hal said. "What'd he say to the rest of you?"

"Nothing," said a sad-faced man in a green tunic who had stood drinking in stoic silence since they had entered. "He was talking to you, Galahad. Telling you to take us along to find the king, he was." He finished his glass. "From a city in the sky."

"It *was* the same dream," Hal said. "But that's impossible. . . ." The knight in green gave him a doleful look.

"Mayhap," Kay said stolidly. "But if Gawain says it's so, then it's so. He wouldn't take the trouble to speak a fancy."

Finished with the conversation, Gawain held out his glass to the barman. But as it was being refilled, he set it on the bar and cocked his head toward the door.

"What is it?" Kay asked.

"The horses," Gawain said. "They're skittish."

The two of them were drawing their swords when the door opened and two portly, pink-faced men in their sixties walked in, fairly steaming with irritation. "What are all those scrofulous horses doing in your car park?" one of them demanded of the barkeep. "We had to park nearly two blocks away." The other scowled sympathetically. Side by side, wearing the same expression on their faces, Hal saw that they were twins.

"The horses are ours," young Bedwyr said, springing up from his place at the bar.

"Well, get them out," one of the twins insisted. "They're a nuisance, and quite illegal, I'm sure. . . . I say, that's a smashing looking broadsword." He took a step toward Gawain and his unsheathed weapon. Instantly the two newcomers had clearly forgotten all about the horses in the parking lot.

"Tenth century?" the second twin hazarded.

"Oh, earlier that that, I'd venture. Look at the scrollwork on the hilt." He reached out to touch it, but Kay stepped forward to bar the way with his own sword. "Oh, my," the man went on, switching his attention to Kay's sword. "Look at this one. Now this is definitely early medieval. Fifth century, I'd wager."

"Saxon, perhaps," his brother agreed eagerly.

"Saxon?" Kay roared. "Are you calling me a Saxon then, you wrinkle-nutted arse licker?"

Hal choked on his beer. From his corner table, Lugh Loinnbheimionach looked up, grinning.

"Hey, guys . . ." Hal began, but he was pushed out of the way.

"I'll not be having talk of Saxons in my presence," Dry Lips said as he rose majestically from the bar stool, spear in hand.

Bedwyr leaped up on a nearby table. "And I'll not have the king's horses insulted!" He drew his own sword.

The pink-faced men smiled indulgently. "Quite good replicas," the first twin said, addressing Gawain. "Are you here for some sort of festival? We have so many of them, my brother and I can hardly keep track."

"That's it," Hal said, seizing the opportunity. "They're actors. Just trying to get into their roles. You know how it is." He chuckled feebly.

"Lugh!" MacDaire called as the dirty giant hurled himself toward the twins. He managed to land on both of them at once, knocking them to the floor like two large bowling pins.

"What in . . ." one of them protested as they tried to right themselves. "This is most . . ."

"For the love of God Almightly, keep your bloody head down!"

MacDaire shouted. A split second later, Lugh's mace whistled through the air and embedded itself into the doorjamb with a thunk.

Both twins screamed at once. The other patrons ducked under the tables.

MacDaire looked at the mace, then at the grinning man who had thrown it. "This isn't the time or the place for that, Lugh," he said patiently. Lugh's face fell.

Kay burst into hearty laughter, and the others joined in, slapping Lugh on the back. His spirits revived. "How think you, boys?" Kay boomed, aiming his spear at the two terrified men on the floor. "Ought we finish them off now?"

The knights responded by banging the hilts of their swords on the tabletops until the walls shook. All but Gawain, who rolled his eyes, put away his weapon, and went back to his beer. And the barman, who lay prostrate behind the bar. And Hal, who struggled vainly to push his way toward the hapless twins. "Get them out of here!" he shouted to the Irishman.

At that moment Lugh, showing all three of his brown teeth in a display of gleeful anticipation, emerged from the crowd like a bull from its pen to remove his mace from the doorframe with one mighty, timber-splitting pull.

"Methinks you chaps might do well to be on your way now," MacDaire whispered to the twins with a wink.

The two men scrambled to their feet and threw themselves outside with the speed of Olympic sprinters. Lugh lumbered after them, swinging the mace as he walked. The twins screamed again. Finally Hal, who had at last broken through the knights, leaped skyward and grabbed the handle of the mace. The movement caught Lugh off balance, and the weapon dropped heavily to the ground. The twins took the opportunity to dash, shrieking, down the street.

"What do you think you're doing?" Hal shouted, throwing his arms up in the air. "You could have killed them with that thing! This isn't the fifth century anymore, you know. Nowadays . . ."

Lugh interrupted his tirade with a weirdly yodeling battle cry that originated in the pit of his massive abdomen and reverberated through his cavernous open mouth. Hal had never heard a sound like that before. It made the spittle dry in his throat.

"Okay, okay," he said, backing up. "We'll talk. We can work this out. No big deal. I see where you're coming from, and . . ."

Lugh repeated his statement, this time accompanied by a galloping lunge, his hairy arms on a level with Hal's neck.

Without thinking, Hal grabbed the giant by the wrist and elbow and flipped Lugh over his head. The knight landed on the gravel of the parking lot in a cloud of dust.

They were beginning to draw a crowd, including the ancient drunk from the meadow. "He'll kill you for sure now," the beggar chortled, sitting on a bench in front of the pub and taking a long pull from a pint bottle of gin. The other knights, now assembled outside the doorway, agreed enthusiastically.

Hal tried to swallow, without success. As Lugh propped himself up on his elbows, Hal danced backward, his hands loose and ready. The big man shook his mop of wild black hair, checked the stability of one of his teeth, then threw back his head and laughed.

"It's happy I am to see you again, Galahad," he said sweetly. He extended his arm to Hal. Hesitantly Hal took it and pulled the big man to his feet. As the rest of the knights gathered around them in goodwill, Lugh embraced Hal in a powerful bear hug that squeezed every last particle of air out of Hal's lungs.

"You guys had better clear out of here before the cops come," Hal said.

"Cops?" Lugh asked.

"The police." Lugh's face was blank. "The authorities. The law." He looked at the others, who stared at him incomprehendingly. "Look, those two guys you terrorized are going to complain to whoever's in charge in this town."

"But we're the king's men," Dry Lips said.

"It doesn't matter. If those guys say you bothered them, someone will come and take you all to jail."

Dry Lips knitted his eyebrows threateningly. "They can try."

"Perfect," Kay said, laughing. "We'll be needing a morning drill anyway."

"Come on, guys," Hal said in exasperation. "Just go, okay? I'll join you after I pay the bill."

One by one the knights mounted their steeds and ambled off toward the meadow. As Hal was walking back into the pub, the old drunk on the bench snorted and spat. "Didn't give us much of a show," he said.

"Go haunt a house."

* * *

The bill for the food and drink, combined with the barman's estimate of the damage done to the door, totalled nearly four hundred pounds. After laying out the money for food, gas, and hotel rooms en route to Tangier, his and Antonia's expenses on the motor trip to England, and the rental car from London to Dorset County, the thousand dollars which Taliesin had miraculously produced in Ait Haddus had dwindled to nearly nothing.

He counted out all the money he had left. Eight pounds. Barely enough for a train ticket for one back to London.

Well, why shouldn't he go, he argued with himself. He didn't owe the Companions anything. He wasn't the one who'd wrecked the damn sword. For all he cared, they could go play in the cemetery with the other ghosts.

Now, that's a fine way to talk about men who've fed you and welcomed you to their fire.

Men. Hal felt ashamed remembering Taliesin's words. The knights weren't ghosts anymore. They were men, strong men who could break doors with iron-studded weapons, but who would not be able to survive a single day in the twentieth century on their own.

No, he would not leave the Companions. Inadvertently or not, Hal had opened the door to bring them into this world, and they were his responsibility now. He would just have to face the fact that he was stuck in the village of Wilson-on-Hamble with eleven half-civilized men and no money. Never mind the train ticket; eight pounds wasn't enough to provide Lugh with an afternoon snack.

With a sigh, he slapped the notes onto the bar. "For your trouble," he said.

"Thank you, guv." The barman picked it up with a smile. "This village hasn't seen so much excitement in a long while. The Swithingtons'll be telling the tale to their dying day."

"Swithington? Is that the name of the two guys we almost killed?"

The barman nodded. "Twins. They own an antiques shop on Front Street. Very posh. Come down from London a few years ago."

"Do you think they'll call the police?"

The barman smiled and began washing out some glasses. "I'll put it this way, Cap'n. If I was you, I'd cancel whatever festival your actors are signed up for and move on. Get my drift? Just a suggestion."

Hal considered his future as a fugitive, skulking indefinitely through the English countryside with a bunch of men whose idea of fun was to kill strangers in bars. It was a grim thought.

With them to take care of, he would probably never find Arthur.

"Thanks," he said to the barman.

"Righto."

Outside, the old drunk was still sitting on the bench in front of the pub's window. Inside the window was a poster for Gilbey's gin showing a bottle suspended over a city skyline at night, its flowing contents a river of liquid silver on which jungle beasts wearing festive hats stampeded toward the high-rise buildings below. *Gilbey's,* it read, *For the Discriminating Party Animal.* The addition of the filthy old man guzzling Gilbey's product in front of the poster gave the ad a new dimension.

"I could use another tenner," the beggar said. He stuck his tongue inside the neck of the empty gin bottle and tilted it hopefully. The position of the bottle matched the one in the poster exactly.

"You and me both," Hal said, then froze in his tracks.

"What is it?" the old man said, feeling the top of his head. "It's not a spider, is it? Don't like spiders."

Hal pushed him aside abstractedly to get a better look at the poster. "Manhattan," he whispered. "The city in the sky."

"I quit drinking once, and spiders came a-crawling all over me," the beggar said. "Took it as a sign that the Lord didn't mean for me to live dry."

"And this is the bench he was sitting on. A stone bench."

"Figured if God wanted me to keep on drinking, who was I to say Him nay?"

Hal looked at him suddenly, frowning. "What?"

"I said God wants me to keep drinking," the old man said with conviction. "So I'd like a tenner to go about the Lord's business."

With a grunt of irritation, Hal reached into his pocket for the small change left over from the bar bill and handed it over to the old man. "Go for it, champ," he said, and jogged back toward the meadow.

Arthur was in New York. Hal knew that, knew it as well as if Taliesin had telephoned him from Grand Central Terminal.

He also knew that he had to get eleven men who hadn't existed before yesterday across an ocean.

CHAPTER THIRTEEN

When Hal arrived back at the meadow, Launcelot was currying his horse with a handful of dry grass.

"I know where Arthur is," he told the knight.

Launcelot's eyes immediately locked into his own. "The city in the sky?"

"New York."

The knight furrowed his brow. "York?"

"*New* York. It's not in England. Somehow we've got to get over there, but I don't know how," Hal said disspiritiedly.

Launcelot caught Gawain's eye and beckoned him over. Gawain strolled over carrying the leather and chain mail helmet he was oiling. He cocked his head at Hal in question.

The two of them must not speak fifty words a year, Hal thought. "I've figured out where Taliesin—er, the Merlin—was telling me to find Arthur, only I don't know how we're going to get there."

"York," Launcelot elaborated. "A new one."

"How far from the old one?" Gawain asked, squinting.

"About two thousand miles, across the Atlantic Ocean. A big sea."

"Two thousand!" Launcelot and Gawain exchanged glances. Then

Gawain whistled for the others to come over. With his chin, he gestured again for Hal to explain their predicament to the others.

"We'd be needing a boat, then," Kay said. He surveyed the trees around them. "It'd take time, but I suppose we could build one."

"The Atlantic's too wide and rough for any boat we could make," Hal said. "We'll have to buy tickets . . . pay passage to get over. But we don't have any money."

"Money?"

"Currency. Coin, I guess you'd call it. We need coin, plenty of it. And we don't have any."

"Speak for yourself, son," Dry Lips said. He unfastened a pouch at his waist and poured out a pile of bright gold coins. Hal picked one up. It bore on its face a likeness of a man's head adorned with leaves. The inscription was in Latin.

"This is a Roman coin," Hal said in wonder.

"Aye, but it's still gold," Dry Lips said. "The filthy scoundrels left something behind, at least. Well, come along, the rest of you." He gestured impatiently to the others. "I'll not be the sole benefactor of this expedition."

While Hal picked up one coin and then another, the others dumped their money onto the pile. Some of the older knights carried substantial sums, although none as great as Dry Lips', while the younger members could only offer a few.

"This says Caligula," Hal said, picking up a shiny piece on which the stamping still looked fresh.

"The names don't matter," MacDaire explained. "It's the weight, Galahad. The weight's what counts. I'd say there's a goodly sum there."

"Enough for a boat, I'll wager," Kay said.

Hal sifted through the coins. "This has got to be worth . . ." He looked up blankly, his heart skipping. "The twins."

"Who?"

"Those guys you almost killed. They're antique dealers."

"Don't be worrying about them, lad," Dry Lips said confidently. "Those two couldn't wring a chicken's neck between them."

"No, I mean . . . Never mind." Hal scooped up the coins. "Is there something I can carry these in? They weigh a ton."

Bedwyr, the Master of Horse, picked up a pair of leather saddlebags and emptied their contents. "How's this?" he asked.

"Great. That is . . ." Hal looked over at the grazing horses, remembering the bone-jolting ride of the night before.

Bedwyr placed a blanket and a small curl of leather over the back of a chestnut stallion.

"Is that a saddle?" Hal asked.

The young man blinked. "It is," he said politely.

Hal tried to mount, but succeeded only in pulling off the saddle. He attempted the maneuver again, with the same result. The third time, he sat on the ground, fuming. "Aren't there supposed to be ropes or something holding the thing on?" he asked.

Bedwyr struggled to keep a smile from spreading across his face. "Have you not ridden for a while, then, Galahad?"

"A few lifetimes," Hal said grumpily.

In the end, it took four men and thirty minutes to mount Hal and his booty. In addition to the coins, the knights had also reluctantly parted with their armor, although they never quite believed that they would not be permitted to cross the ocean in it.

"I'll ride with you, if you like," Bedwyr offered delicately. "With this much coin, you may be waylaid by bandits."

"Or gravity," Hal muttered.

The Swithingtons' shop was a crowded melange of fragile and lovely items arranged artistically among vases filled with fresh flowers.

"God's blood, it's a treasure house," Bedwyr said, looking through the window. "I'll wager some of that belongs to the King in taxes." He reached for his sword. Hal grabbed his hand and forced the weapon back into its scabbard.

"I think you'd better wait out here," he said flatly. "To guard the horses." He took the saddlebags. "And please . . . don't kill anyone," he pleaded. "Just stand there, okay?"

"Aye, that's what I'll do," Bedwyr said affably.

"Good."

"Unless I encounter evil or misdeeds. It's the vow, you understand."

"The vow?"

"The Companions' vow. We took it when we joined the Round Table."

"Oh, that vow," Hal said. He went into the shop, whispering a prayer that no one would indulge in evil or misdeeds within a two-block radius of Bedwyr for the next few minutes.

One of the twins was dusting a Russian samovar when Hal walked in, accompanied by a tinkling of tiny silver bells. The shopkeeper looked up with a smile, which transformed immediately into a mask of terror.

"Cedric!" he shrieked.

The other twin rushed in. "Good heavens, Sidney, what's—"

"They're back! This is one of them!" Sidney pointed an accusing finger at Hal, then at the window, where a young blond man in a Dutch-boy haircut stood holding the reins of two horses. "And there's another!"

"Ring the police," Sidney commanded as he rummaged through a drawer in a cherrywood rolltop desk. "Tell them . . . Damn it to hell, where is that gun?"

"Look, fellas . . ." Hal began.

"Here it is." Unsteadily, Sidney brandished an Arostegui dueling pistol. "Now don't try anything foolish, young man."

"I'm not going to hurt you," Hal said, backing up. "I only came to show some . . ."

"Stop!" Cedric threw down the phone as Hal crashed into a table filled with gladiola and silver Victoriana. A Delft ginger jar which had held the flowers shattered on impact. The other pieces remained intact until Hal landed on them. The saddlebags flew out of his hands and spilled their contents among the debris.

"My crumber," Cedric moaned, moving toward the wreckage with outstretched arms.

"Move aside!" his brother snapped, darting about the room to get a clear shot of Hal.

Cedric picked up what looked like a tiny silver dust pan, now flattened. "I don't suppose it matters to people like you that this was used in the royal household," he shrilled, poking it under Hal's nose. The handle popped off. Cedric closed his eyes in despair.

"Get out of the way, I said!" the other twin complained. "The way you're writhing about, I'm as likely to shoot you as him."

"For God's sake, Sidney!" Cedric said indignantly. "That thing hasn't been fired in a hundred years. Think of the porcelain." He rummaged around the mess on the floor for the crumber handle. "Just call the . . . what's this?" He picked up a coin.

"It's part of what I came to show you," Hal said.

"A First Century Nero!" Cedric's voice was hoarse with passion.

"A what?" Sidney laid the gun atop a walnut lap desk and fell to his hands and knees. "Good God," he said. "A hundred-sesterce gold piece."

"Who's on it?" his brother asked, grabbing for the coin like a child. Sidney snatched it away. "Can't tell," he said, holding it to the light.

"Claudius!" Cedric exclaimed as he picked up another. Then his eyes slid slowly toward Hal. "Did you say this was *part* of what you were offering?" he asked softly.

Hal nodded. "That's what I said. Would you like to see the rest?"

The twins looked at one another, then nodded in unison. Hal waved to Bedwyr standing outside, and the young knight brought in the parcels from the horses.

"This one nearly filleted me," Cedric said, recognizing Bedwyr as he tossed the armor in a heap on the floor. "Oh, my stars! A Boudiccan helmet!"

"Do you want them or not?" Hal asked.

"Yes," both men chanted in unison.

An hour later, Hal and Bedwyr were riding back to the meadow with a cashier's check in place of the gold coins.

"The two of them seemed in better spirits at the end than when they first saw you," Bedwyr said.

"Dropped all the charges against us." He patted the cashier's check in his pocket. "And they got the money out of their own savings. This all worked out great."

"Mayhap," the young knight said, looking uncomfortable. "Though 'tis hard to believe a piece of paper can be worth all that gold. There was enough coin in these bags to buy an indulgence from the Pope himself."

"But a check's just like real money. Trust me on this."

"Oh, I've no say in the matter. But when Launcelot hears of this trade . . . Well, begging your pardon, but I hope you're better at selling gold than you are at riding."

Hal laughed. "I hope so—riding!" He pulled up short, and his stallion reared up. Hal was slipping precariously of the saddle when Bedwyr finally calmed the animal down. "We've got to get rid of the horses," he said.

Bedwyr chuckled. "You'll get the hang of it soon enough. It's practice with the hands you need, that's all. Now, when—"

"No, I'm serious. We can't keep the horses."

Bedwyr shook his head. "Well, then how do you propose we travel once we get to York, on foot?"

"*New* York, I keep telling you! And I don't know how we'll get around. But it can't be on horseback. There's a law or something."

"A law against horses! Do you take me for a fool? I suppose there be a law against swords in this godforsaken swamp of yours as well."

"As a matter of fact . . ."

Bedwyr rode off without him.

"A scrap of paper!" Kay boomed when Hal got back to camp. "Aye, young Bedwyr's told us, so there's no point in denying it."

"And about the horses, too," the young man named Agravaine said, sharpening his hook.

Kay slapped him across the back of his head. "I'll handle this." He gave Agravaine an evil glance, and the young man walked away.

"No, I will." Launcelot walked forward and beckoned Hal toward a cluster of trees out of earshot of the others. When they were alone, the knight's sad eyes searched Hal's. "We want to be of help to you," he said softly. "But you'll have to explain yourself to me. You can start with the coin."

Hal sighed. "Okay. I traded the coins for modern currency. This," he said, showing Launcelot the check. "I can take this to a bank— sort of a counting house, I suppose you'd call it. And the bank will give me ten thousand pounds for it."

"Ten thousand pounds of gold?" The knight looked incredulous. "Even the king's own treasure house does not contain that much."

"It's not the same kind of pounds," Hal said. "But it's still a lot of money, and it's waiting for us." He saw that his explanation wasn't reaching Launcelot. "Because that money has already been placed in the bank by the guys who gave me this piece of paper."

"Were these noble and honorable men?"

"They seemed all right," Hal said. "Actually, they were the twins who came into the pub this morning."

Launcelot stepped back a pace. "The ones who attempted to raise an army against us?"

"No . . . Well, they were going to call the police, but they changed their minds after seeing the coins."

"No doubt they did!" The knight wiped his hand across his face.

"Galahad, I fear your purity of heart has blinded you to the ways of men."

"No, you don't understand," Hal explained. "It was business, that's all. People don't have to like each other to do business. It's just like buying a pig."

"I would not buy a pig from a man who wished to have me imprisoned."

"The point is, if he stole your money you could have *him* imprisoned. There are laws that take care of people doing business."

"And the keeper of the counting house? Is he also ignoble and dishonorable?"

"I'm telling you, it doesn't matter. The money's all kept track of through compu—machines that count. Anytime we want to take it out, we can. Please trust me on this, Launcelot. I know what I'm doing."

The knight took a deep breath. "I'll have to take you at your word, since what's done is done. But the horses—"

"We've got to sell them," Hal said. "We can't take them where we're going."

"Then how shall we move about?"

"In taxis, I guess. Cars. Machines with wheels that can move faster than any horse."

The knight blinked. "You ride on a machine. A machine counts your coin. A strange and frightening land, indeed."

Hal felt his uncertainty. "That it is," he said quietly. "Frightening." He looked away. "Hell, I shouldn't even be taking you. It's a different world now, filled with problems you guys have never dreamed of. But I don't know what else to do. I've got to get to Arthur. . . ."

"Have your machines not yet driven the wicked from the earth?" Launcelot asked.

"No," Hal said, smiling. "Not by a long shot."

"Then we shall come with you." The knight touched Hal's shoulder. "This time you will not be made to face this strange new world alone."

Launcelot ordered that the horses be sold, and sent Curoi MacDaire to locate a farm where they might be of use. Meanwhile, Hal took a pouting Bedwyr back into town to see about renting a truck to transport them all to London.

"Does the machine resemble a horse, at least?" he asked despairingly.

"Not really. It's got . . . well, there's one." He pointed to a car coming toward them down the road.

"I've seen them!" Bedwyr shouted. "Bloody little moving houses. A man wouldn't so much as feel the wind on his face in one of those." He scowled. "And the smell! A great smoky farting thing . . ."

"We're here," Hal said when they approached the E-Z Trail Discount Truck & RV rental agency. Bedwyr was looking with disdain at the small wagons that dotted the front of the establishment, as well as the automobiles of its employees. It was, Hal realized, the hurt pride of a young man who had lost a hard-won position of honor. Bedwyr had been Master of Horse for the Round Table. Now he was nothing more than a common foot soldier.

"I don't suppose you'd like to look at one up close," he said.

Bedwyr turned his back.

After arranging for the rental, Hal drove the truck around front and swung the passenger door open. "Get in."

Bedwyr blinked at the truck. " 'Tis of greater girth than the others," he said, unable to conceal the admiration in his voice as he stepped up into the cabin.

"It's a big mother, all right." Hal let out the clutch and they rolled into traffic.

"Zounds! We are moving more swiftly than the very wind!" Bedwyr clutched the dashboard.

Hal laughed. "Just wait," he said, downshifting as he veered onto the open road. "Turn that crank. It'll open the window."

Bedwyr leaned into the rushing wind, whooping in exultation. "This machine is faster than even Launcelot's stallion!" he screamed, flinging his arms over his head.

"It's faster than six hundred horses pulling at the same time."

The young man pulled his head back into the cab, his hair wild, a red glow in his cheeks. "Six hundred horses! And as gentle a ride as a baby's cradle."

Hal turned on the air conditioning. "You're going to love this," he said.

Bedwyr was awestruck by the suddenly cool breeze. "It changes the weather, too."

Hal turned on the radio. They were blasted with a chorus of Steppenwolf singing "Born to be Wild." Bedwyr gasped, shrinking back into his seat and staring at the glowing numbers on the dial.

"Sorry," Hal said. He turned down the volume and switched on a station playing sedate chamber music.

"No." Bedwyr pushed Hal's fingers aside and adjusted the dial back to "Born to be Wild." "It is warrior music," he said reverently, closing his eyes and shaking his head to the beat.

Hal smiled as he turned onto a country lane with a vista clear of traffic. "Want to drive?"

Bedwyr looked at him in amazement. "I?" he asked quietly. "You would permit me this?"

"You're Master of Horse, aren't you?"

"I . . ." His lip trembled. "Aye, Galahad. That I am."

Hal stopped the vehicle. "Just do what I tell you. And call me Hal."

They screeched to a halt a half hour later to the strains of Aerosmith exhorting the battalion to "Dream On."

"What wonder is this?" Fairhands asked as Bedwyr leaped out the driver's side with a swing of his blond hair.

"This is our new transport," he said, opening the hood with a flourish. "It has the power of six hundred horses."

Fairhands touched the engine, then withdrew his hand with a yelp. " 'Tis fiercely hot," he said.

"The inner place of it is for the Master of Horse alone," Bedwyr said loftily. "And for Sir Galahad, of course," he demurred. "Hal," he added with a smile.

CHAPTER FOURTEEN

By nightfall the entire clanging, cursing company reached London. They tumbled out the back of the E-Z Trail, stiff from squatting in the cargo area throughout the jostling ride.

"Power of a hundred horses. Pah!" Dry Lips spat, hobbling over to Hal. " 'Twas like riding in a barrel."

"I'm sorry, guys . . ."

"Find us an alehouse, and be quick about it!"

Hal groaned as one of the men pointed enthusiastically to a sign bearing the picture of a coat of arms.

"Hey, come back, all of you!" he shouted as the knights stampeded past him and darted into the street to the accompaniment of blaring horns and cursing drivers.

"It's no use stopping them," Curoi MacDaire said with a grin. He looked around. "So this is Londinium. It looks a sight more habitable than it did."

"You've been here before?" Hal asked.

"Aye. Many a time, and I've got the scars from cutthroats to prove it."

"That bad, huh?"

"All the cities left by the Romans turned into cesspools, so they did. Nothing but thieves and murderers in them." MacDaire cocked his head. "Good for a spot of fun, though, if you knew where to look."

Hal laughed. "Go on into the pub," he said. "Have the Companions wait for me there. Oh. Here's some money." He handed the Irishman a fistful of notes. "If the bill comes to more than that, I'll pay the balance when I get back."

"Saying your good-byes to a ladyfriend?" MacDaire gave Hal a lewd wink.

"No such luck, I'm afraid. I've got to find a way to get passports for all you guys."

"Passports?"

"Documents that allow people to travel to other countries."

"Letters of safe conduct." MacDaire nodded sagely. "But you haven't got the king to sign them. That's the problem."

"What? Oh. Yeah. Something like that." *Plus the fact that none of these jokers actually exists*, Hal thought glumly. The British passport office was going to love that.

The hood of the truck popped open. In front of it, Bedwyr stood with the owner's manual in his hands, comparing the engine with a diagram at the front of the book. "What is the purpose of sparkplugs?" he demanded.

Hal closed the hood. "Take him with you," he told MacDaire.

"Passports?" Antonia repeated. "For eleven men?"

"Eleven men with no proof of citizenship in any country," her husband Franco said, chuckling.

"I thought there might be a problem with that." Hal turned back to Antonia. "So I wanted to know what you did at the passport office when people came in without proper documentation. People who don't legally exist."

"Ah, yes," Antonia said. "There are many from my village who can boast neither a driver's license nor a birth certificate. They have lived in the old way."

"That's exactly the case. How would people like that get passports?"

Antonia shook her head. "They would not," she said softly. "Unfortunately, all governments are quite insistent on correct documentation. In my office, we have even had to turn away grandmothers who wished to visit distant relatives because they could not produce any papers. It is quite sad."

"Are these eleven men ancient ones also, my friend?" Franco asked.

Hal cleared his throat. "Well, they're older than they look. That is . . . They're in good shape. For how old they are," Hal fumbled. "They're athletes."

"A team of some sort?" Franco asked.

"A team? Oh, right," Hal said, brightening.

"What is their sport?"

Hal's face went blank. "Er . . ." His eyes fastened on a photograph on the wall showing the hills of central Portugal. "Skiing. They're a ski team. I'm training them for the Olympics."

"How wonderful, Hal!" Antonia's face broke into a warm smile. "I had thought you to be a lonely man with no connections."

"Well, this . . . came up suddenly."

"Skiing," Franco mused. "An odd sport for the English. Their country has no mountains."

Hal coughed. "That's why I have to get them to the United States. To practice."

"Ah." Antonia frowned. "And not one of them has ever worked, or voted, or been in military service?"

"Nope," Hal said, rising. "They just ski." It was clear that this was not working. "Well, thanks for your time. I've got to get going."

"I am sorry we could not be of more help to you," Antonia said.

"Please," Franco said, pressing his business card into Hal's palm. "Come to my store. Select a jogging suit. I will not rest until we can repay our debt to you."

"Sure. Thanks," Hal said.

At the pub, the knights had taken over the bar, shouting noisily and throwing back pints of Guinness as fast as the barman could serve them.

"That's him," Dry Lips shouted, wiping a foam moustache off his mouth. The barman moved toward Hal, crooking his finger at him sternly.

"Beg your pardon, sir, but these men say you'll be paying for their drink. I should tell you there's been quite a bit of it."

Hal looked around. "Where's MacDaire?" he demanded.

Bedwyr wiped the foam off his mouth. "He told me to come in on my own. Said he had business to attend to."

"What the hell kind of business would he have in London?"

Bedwyr shrugged.

"Another tankard this way, if you please!" Dry Lips shouted, thumping his glass on the bar.

The barman narrowed his eyes. "I gave one of the guys the money to pay the tab," Hal said. The barman set his jaw. "Oh, forget it." Hal doled out a hundred pounds. "Will that cover it?"

"For the moment," the barman said. "What'll you have?"

"A gun. To shoot myself."

"Beg your pardon?"

"Nothing. I don't want anything." He turned around and leaned backward against the bar. He had no idea where to begin looking for MacDaire. Like the rest of the knights, the Irishman was as innocent of the world as a newborn baby, and a lot more likely to get into trouble.

"I'll be back," he told the barman, laying out another hundred pounds as a deposit on the next hour's refreshments. He had almost reached the door when MacDaire walked in.

"Hail, brother!" he called out heartily, slapping Hal on the back. "I'll wager you'll be glad to see me."

"Where in hell have you been?"

"Why, I was off being of service to you, methinks." He smiled slyly. "Were you able to get our letters of safe conduct?"

"That's nothing you have to be concerned with."

"Well, did you?"

"No," Hal said miserably.

"Then my time wasn't wasted." He reached into his tunic and extracted a brown envelope. "Fine paper they make here," he said, rubbing his fingers along the flap. Then he opened it. Inside were a pile of British passports. "Fine work, wouldn't you say?"

"What?" Hal blinked once, then closed the flap quickly. "How did you get these?" he whispered.

MacDaire chortled. "We're in Londinium, lad! The place may have changed summat, but there's still no shortage of rotters who'll supply a man with whatever he wants for a price."

Hal flipped through the pages of one of the passports. They were blank. "These are illegal," he hissed. "We could be put in jail for just having these, let alone using them."

"Then again, we might get away with it." MacDaire winked.

"Oh, brother." Hal pictured all twelve of them with numbers across their chests.

"We've got to find the King," MacDaire reminded him softly. "That's what this is all about, isn't it?" The Irishman put his arm around Hal. "Galahad, me boy, you're a good fellow. I know you were picked by no less than the ancient gods themselves to find the Grail because of your pure heart. But when your path takes you smack in the middle of a tree, you can take the time to cut it down, or you can just go around it. Which do you think will take you where you've got to go faster?"

Hal looked at him, thinking.

"Aye," MacDaire said softly. "And methinks the old gods wouldn't mind, either. After all, it was them put the tree in your way in the first place, to see if you can think on your feet."

He patted Hal's back. "By the way, the swine what sold these to me wants more gelt. Says he'll fill in the missing parts as soon as we bring him pictures and five thousand pounds. 'Five thousand,' says I, 'why, ye must be a thief!' And he laughs. Wouldn't come down in price, though. So I figures we'll take Lugh along to persuade the gentleman to be more reasonable."

"No . . . no, we'll pay him." Hal peered again at the illegal passports. "I just hope your gods keep us ahead of the cops."

Three days later, outfitted by Antonia's husband, Franco, who received a whopping commission for selling most of the merchandise in his store, the unofficial Ski Team of Great Britain boarded a British Airways jet en route to New York.

CHAPTER FIFTEEN

Taliesin and his two wards spent nearly two weeks in the hold of the cargo ship where they had gone to seek refuge from the killer on the docks in Tangier.

The life of stowaways was not the hardship they had expected, since the old man quickly found a way onto the poopdeck, and Arthur and Beatrice both turned out to be excellent burglars. Within a few days they had all the blankets they needed, more food than they could eat and, since the discovery of a box of candles in the ship's galley, did not have to live in total darkness.

"I've got you now," Beatrice said, moving a chess piece made out of candle wax on a board drawn with charcoal on the floor.

"Are you sure you want to move your queen there?" Arthur asked.

"Oh, is that the queen? I thought it was the bishop's pawn." She picked up the piece and examined it in the candlelight. It melted in her fingers. "Oh, dear, I've killed her," she said, giggling.

Arthur smiled. "That's okay. She was a drip, anyway."

Beatrice laughed, and the flame from the candle between them cast its light on her face, making her skin look like velvet.

"Shall I make another?" she asked.

"Maybe we should play checkers." Arthur made a fist and squashed his rook into a flat disk.

"What a smashing idea!"

Arthur groaned.

"Shh." She pointed to Taliesin, who was snoring in a makeshift hammock some ten feet away. "The poor dear must be awfully tired. This is the first I've seen him sleep since we left . . ." Her eyes registered the memory of that terrible day. ". . . Marrakesh. . . ."

Suddenly all the fun that had bubbled out of her during their game seemed to dry up. "Well, then," she said, trying to ignore the pain she felt. "Would you rather be red or black?"

"I know how you feel," he said. "I do."

"Yes, I know you do," she whispered. "Hal was all you had, just like my Grams."

He looked away.

"The difference is, Hal's going to come back."

"No, he isn't," Arthur hissed. "You don't have to say things like that to make me feel better. I'm not a little kid." He rolled over in his bedding.

"Oh, Arthur, I wasn't patronizing you. Please believe me."

"Then why'd you say it?" Through his anger, a glimmer of hope appeared in his eyes. "Did Taliesin tell you?" If the old man said Hal was alive, then he was. Taliesin knew everything.

"No."

"Oh," Arthur said, disappointed.

"But I know it."

"Okay," he said, trying to smile.

"I know you don't believe me. I'm not putting it into words very well." She searched his face. "It's just that sometimes I get a feeling of . . . of watching something happen, although I can't see it with my eyes. It's as though a puzzle is coming together. Hal is a piece of the puzzle, and so is Mr. Taliesin. But you're the most important piece of all, Arthur. Everything that's coming is because of you."

Arthur swallowed. He knew what Beatrice was talking about, even if she herself did not. He knew who he was, what he was. He knew why Hal and the old man had come into his life.

What he didn't know was what he was supposed to do about it.

"What's coming?" he asked, desperately wanting to hear the answer.

"A beginning," she said. She touched her fingers to his cheek. "You're going to do something wonderful."

"Like what?"

She shrugged. "You'll have to decide that, I imagine." Beatrice got gracefully to her feet. "I want to give you something." She went over to her bedroll, then came back carrying an object in her two hands. It was the cup. "This was meant for you. I'm sure of that."

He held it. "You wouldn't be giving me this if you knew what it can do."

"Oh, I know. It will keep you alive forever."

Arthur shook his head, then offered it back to her. "I don't think I want that."

"Keep it anyway, Arthur. It's part of the puzzle."

The candle guttered. "Oh, man," he said. "Where'd we put the matches?"

"I'll get them for you if you want, but I'm going to bed."

"Oh. Never mind, then."

He heard Beatrice walking confidently through the darkness, using the senses she had depended on long before she gained her sight. Arthur curled up in his blanket, picturing her face in the firelight, then went to sleep.

When Taliesin awakened in the middle of the night, she was squatting near his hammock, her face on a level with his.

"Good heavens, child, you startled me!" he said, swinging his legs to the floor. He stood up and lit a candle which he had placed on one of the wooden crates in the hold. Beatrice didn't move. "Is something on your mind?"

"Mona," she whispered. "I've been thinking of Mona."

The old man felt a shiver. "How do you know about that?"

"Do you remember?" The girl stared straight ahead, her eyes open but focused far away, past Taliesin's face, to a place deep within his private memories. Those memories were from more than a thousand years ago, but they still burned in his mind, intense and immediate.

"Yes, I remember," he said quietly. "It was the most beautiful place I had ever seen. Perhaps the most beautiful place on earth."

"You were little more than a boy when you came, a joker and a balladeer."

Taliesin stiffened. "You could not know that!"

She smiled, an impish grin that make the old man's heart skip.

"Who are you?" he demanded.

The girl did not answer. *Her eyes,* the old man thought. If he had not known that Beatrice was sighted, he would have believed she was still blind.

He had been a bard.

That was the only way he could think of to make a living away from the court after King Ambrosius died. Out of love for his youngest and brightest child, the King had given young Taliesin the title of Prince and a place in the castle—a gift which had proven to be a curse rather than a blessing.

As a bastard, Taliesin was viewed as a threat by Ambrosius' eldest son, Uther, even though three other legitimate heirs stood between Taliesin and the rulership of Ambrosius' chiefdom. Perhaps it was the open affection the king had always shown this child of his old age, whose mother had brought him a happiness unlike any he had known with his queen while she was alive; or it might have been Taliesin's particular gifts—his gentleness, his prescient sensitivity, his stunning capacity for learning—that singled him out as a target for Uther's hatred. For whatever reason, Uther had always made it clear that his much younger half-brother would not be welcome in the court after Ambrosius was gone. As the old king's strength began to fail, Taliesin began to notice Uther watching him through narrowed eyes, as if he half expected his father to name the unwanted child, rather than Uther himself, as his successor.

Not that Taliesin ever harbored pretensions toward the throne. He was a scholar by nature, not at all inclined toward leading men into battle or engaging in the niggling demands of statecraft. His position in his father's court had allowed him the opportunity to explore the world of the mind through the voluminous scrolls left by the Romans and the rarer and subtler texts of the mystical Irish writers. Too, he studied the properties of herbs and spirit-healing from the wise women who lived in the countryside, the anatomy of the human body from the surgeons who accompanied soldiers into battle, and music from the traveling entertainers who stopped by King Ambrosius' stronghold during times of peace.

This was what he loved most. During the evenings when the bards came to bring news of neighboring chiefdoms or sing the ancient histories of Wales, Taliesin would sit motionless for hours, his eyes smarting from the smoke of the torch fires, as he committed each line to memory.

He taught himself to write in his native language, using the simple Roman alphabet to sound out the complex Welsh words in order to remember the hundreds of songs extolling the heroic exploits of brave Welsh warriors and wicked kings (they were all wicked, except for Ambrosius, he noted, assuming the bards changed the names of the villains and heroes with each castle they visited). And he taught himself to play instruments—a harp he constructed from a piece of pine and strings of squirrel gut, several flutes and drums, and a long, shallow basin in which strings resonated against hammered bells.

These were all he took with him when he left the castle after Uther tried to kill him.

The attempt on his life had not been unexpected; when Uther took time out from his new duties to go for a morning ride in the mountains with a fifteen-year-old boy whose company he had never sought before, Taliesin knew that he would end up either running for his life or losing it.

As it turned out, Uther's lack of interest in his imagined rival was what saved Taliesin. Believing the thin, unathletic boy to be frail and unaccustomed to the outdoors, he led his young bastard half-brother to the wilds of Gwynedd, in the western part of the kingdom, where the hills were rugged and the snow fell early, and the howling of wolves pierced the silence of the long nights. There, in the evening fog that confused the most experienced huntsmen, Uther sent Taliesin into a valley to investigate what he said might be a wild boar in a thicket. When the boy returned to the rise where he had left Uther, the crown prince was gone.

With a sigh of relief, Taliesin dismounted and led his horse to a nearby stream to drink. So this was all it was to be, he thought, making a sign of gratitude to Mithras, the god whose stream this was. Disdainful of actually murdering him, Uther had simply left Taliesin to die of exposure or wolves.

Neither was a real possibility. Taliesin knew the west intimately. He had traveled often to these parts to consult with the wise ones—the midwives and herb-healers who journeyed here for the rare flowers and grasses that made up their apothecaries, the hermits who chose to live in the west because of its loneliness and harsh beauty, and the druids who passed through one by one, always solitary, on their way from the island of Mona which was the beating heart of their community.

For the druids, the few inhabitants of the area came two or three times a week to set food beneath the worn stone shrines to Mithras at the sources of the mountain streams. The druids were always being called by some king or other to cast spells for victory in battle or for a queen's delivery of a strong boy-child. Sometimes those calls were heeded, sometimes not. No one except the Innocent, the druids' term for the first among their number, told these magicians where to practice their art, and not even the Innocent could order the results.

Consequently, the local herders and fishermen felt a strong combination of fear and divine protection from the wizards of Mona who passed through their bleak land on the way to castles or religious enclaves in more hospitable climates to the south and east. To ensure their goodwill, the precious and scarce food was set out even in the foulest weather to feed the magicians or their gods or, more often, the wolves who, according to the druids, were also a part of All That Is.

Armed with this knowledge, Taliesin spent the night in a cave near the Mithras shrine, well fed and protected from predators by a fire created with tinder and flint left conveniently nearby, and considered the urgency of his departure from his father's court.

During that night, he heard music from the druids' island of Mona. It was a chant of sorts, the ancient and wild music of the earth itself. He had heard people speak of it before, this office that took place at the quietest hour of the night, but he had not come close to imagining the music. Sometimes it was harsh, as forbidding as the countryside from which it originated; then, later, the sound grew serene as angels' wings, with lilting high voices of women encasing the low baritone cry of the druid men.

He heard it again the next morning, at dawn, when the fog settled thickly into the valleys like pools of milk. The Salutation to the Sun, sung in ancient syllables no longer recognizable as Welsh, drifting in patches like puffs of wind across the water and the cold mountain air.

Mona, he thought, staring out into the fog toward the source of the song. Every word spoken or sung there was magic. The island was the great repository of truth, of all the knowledge in the world worth keeping. It was not stored in books, as were the histories and poetry of the Irish; the barbarian Saxons had plundered Ireland's sacred places and used those precious parchment tomes to start their cooking fires. No, the wisdom of Mona was not trusted to written symbols which might be destroyed in a moment or misinterpreted through centuries. It was kept, intact and perfect, in the minds of all its druids. Each gray-hooded disciple, young or old, male or female, devoted his life to absorbing Mona's knowledge until he was himself that knowledge, a living embodiment of the power of All That Is.

Taliesin closed his eyes to better hear the music. The druids were not of the world. Their discipline took them out of the sphere of men to become part of a greater whole, their wizardry the magic of the universe. Mona was where he belonged, where he wished to be more than any place else on earth.

With an inrush of air, he ran to untie his horse. He would go there now, straightaway, and ask to be admitted as a student or a menial. Mentally he went over his qualifications: He could read and write; that would be an asset to the community. He was already self-trained in the use of herbs and medicines. His knowledge would be laughable compared with that of the disciples at Mona, but at least he was not completely ignorant. And he was stronger than he looked. Yes, he would . . .

Just before the crest of the hill where his horse waited, Taliesin stopped with a gasp. A wolf had walked unseen out of the fog and now stood directly in front of him, its long shape barring his way, its head turned to face him.

The animal was old, he could see that from its grizzled white muzzle, but it was not lame or ill. Oddly, it exhibited no sign of fear at seeing him. Its fangs were not bared, and its ears were not slanted back; nor had its body assumed the crouched position of attack. Then, with a sudden ray of sunlight that shot over the horizon, Taliesin noticed something else about the wolf.

It was blind.

A creamy blue film completely covered its eyes. The wolf seemed to be looking at Taliesin through two shafts of moonlight.

Maybe he doesn't know I'm here, he thought wildly. If I'm still, if I'm very quiet . . .

Go to your father, a voice said.

Involuntarily, Taliesin snapped his head around. There was no one besides himself and the wolf in the still valley. Yet the voice had been so clear!

The animal was still facing him calmly, those blank, unseeing eyes seeming to peer at him from the depths of the universe.

He is dying. Make your farewells. Go. Mona will wait.

A thin cry of fear and confusion escaped from the boy's throat. The wolf blinked its slitted eyes slowly. Then, with a graceful swoop of its long tail, it walked back into the fog.

Taliesin stumbled toward his horse and untied it with wildly shaking hands. Of course the wolf had not spoken, he told himself. No one had. The voice, as he remembered it, had been neither young nor old, male nor female. Not a real voice at all, but some trick of the imagination borne of the cold and the mystery of this deserted place. It would be foolish to go home now, to give Uther another chance to kill him.

As he mounted, he heard again the weird, compelling music from the island, and it broke his heart.

"Mona will wait," he whispered.

He turned his horse toward the east and, with the rising sun stinging his eyes, headed at a canter back toward Ambrosius' castle.

He remained at court only long enough to say good-bye to Ambrosius, who had raised his bastard son like a prince. Uther, who had scowled in suppressed rage when the boy rode into the castle gates, was finally appeased when Taliesin rode back out with nothing more than his instruments and a few books. He was, in fact, so pleased with his half-brother's voluntary banishment that years later, when Taliesin's name was known throughout Wales and his songs were remembered and sung in places as far away as Cornwall and Scotland, Uther invited the famous bard to sing at the castle where the two of them had once shared a father.

And Taliesin had accepted, as he had accepted the invitations of all the petty chiefs who called themselves kings, though they all knew that, since the Romans, there had been no real king to rule Britain.

The Romans had come some four hundred years before. They had built roads, established cities, introduced bathing, brought books, even officially recognized some of the local kings as honorary citizens of Rome. An ancestor of Ambrosius himself had been granted this honor generations before, which was why his chiefdom had been permitted to stand. The machine-like invaders from their warm land to the south had deemed this family "civilized"—meaning that the clans so honored were less likely to attack the Romans as they went about the business of Romanizing Britain.

Or tried to. They had been trying for centuries to instill the Pax Romana on the wild tribes of this northern land. Beginning with Vercingetorix of Gaul, the Romans had systematically eliminated every leader capable of uniting the disparate chiefdoms. They had burned the villages of the rebellious, starved the uncertain, murdered by the thousands the women and children who wandered as refugees, preferring to live off the meager fruits of the uncultivated earth rather than look to their conquerors for succor.

But their efforts had been for nothing. The wide Roman-built roads went unused by the proud Britons. Their magnificent baths were smeared with dung. And the populace, from farmers armed with wooden pitchforks to the educated honorary Romans and their genteel wives, had never, not in four hundred years, ceased to fight.

By the time Taliesin was born, the Romans had all but vanished from Britain, maintaining only a small number of garrisons in England to protect their towns populated almost exclusively by Romans and their mixed-blood descendants. In Wales, the soldiers were almost never seen.

"It is because of Mona," the Welsh whispered among themselves. "The druids keep them away with their magic."

Any Roman worth his salt wages would have laughed at such an idea. The druids were of no consequence, the useless relics of an ancient folk religion whose tenets were so lost in time that the people no longer knew what they were. Oh, the warrior chieftains occasionally prevailed on the gray-robed holy men to cast some sort of spell or other (which, more often than not, didn't work), and the farmers in the barbaric countryside still coupled with their women in the fields, believing that the act of procreation would bring about a good harvest, but there were no services in this dying religion, nothing to connect the druids with any sort of reality. No, despite the fierce patriotism of its inhabitants, the real reason the Romans had abandoned Wales was that there was nothing in that desolate land worth taking.

Still, the stature of the druids grew during the Empire's slow retreat from Britain. When Rome itself began to suffer from constant attack by nomadic barbarians and the far-flung legions were recalled home one by one to defend their besieged city, even the conquered Britons in places as Romanized as Londinium began to believe that this had been the work of the druids who manipulated the stars of destiny from their mysterious island.

"If only the holy men could give us a king to unify the chiefdoms," mused the people from one shore of Britain to the other.

This was not lost on the hundreds of rival chiefs. A unified land would ensure that no invaders would ever again occupy Britain. And the man who brought about that union would be the greatest king who ever lived. In consequence, the departure of the Romans signalled a new era of civil warfare which divided and weakened the nation more effectively than any assault by a conquering foreign army.

"Britain is ripe for invasion," Taliesin warned Uther during a private moment. "While we fight among ourselves, ruining our crops, wasting our weapons, and killing our best fighting men, any half-organized army could come in and take us with one hand."

"The Romans will not be back," Uther said, drunk enough from the evening's mead to pass a few moments of idle talk with the half-brother he had once so despised. "They know better than to fight us again."

"It wouldn't have to be the Romans. Before long, the whole world will know of our pitiful condition. Already the Saxons are making their way toward us. The chiefdoms along the eastern seacoast have already seen fighting."

"The Saxons!" Uther roared with laughter. "A Saxon couldn't win in combat against a Welsh farm girl!" He waved dismissively at Taliesin. "Go play your music, bard. Sing songs of my conquests, and leave your political opinions in your weakling's mouth, where they belong."

Taliesin did as he was instructed. He lifted his sweet, high voice in songs of brave deeds tailored to his audience, as he had for the past six years. In that time he had crisscrossed Britain, from its filthy cities to the sleepy farms in the plains; from the wild highlands of the Scots to the sea-swept rocks of the south. They had been wonderful years, filled with adventure, brimming over with worldly pleasures. He had dined with more kings than he could remember. He had ridden into battle, his harp bouncing against his horse's flank, his blood on fire. He had lain with women, spoken with scholars, formed friendships with men who would have torn one another apart on sight, yet opened their hearts to a visiting bard. For six years Taliesin had gobbled up life with both hands, and a full banquet was still before him.

And so it had been so very strange, that night in Uther's court, when he realized with a dreadful suddenness that his life as a bard was over.

It had occurred in a moment, at the mention of a single word. . . .

Tintagel.

It was Uther's new castle to the far south, acquired through a series of conquests and alliances. Taliesin had known about it; indeed, much of the stronghold in Wales where they were presently gathered was in the process of being packed up for the journey to Uther's new lands, which afforded him a better position to jockey for the title of High King. But it was Uther's own utterance of the word that struck such a weirdly resonating note in Taliesin that the song he was singing died in his throat, and the last chord he had plucked upon his harp rang out in solitude for a moment, then faded away.

Uther continued talking briefly, until the weight of the sudden silence caused him to turn his head in the direction of the bard, whose eyes were staring back blankly at him.

"Well?" he snapped irritably. "What is the problem?"

Taliesin himself did not know what the problem was. He was, in fact, unaware that he had even been eavesdropping on Uther's conversation. Usually while he sang, there was nothing in his mind except the song itself, its music transporting him back to whatever state he had been in when he composed it. But when Uther had spoken the name "Tintagel," the word had cut like a sword through every association in the bard's mind, taking his spirit out of the castle where he could see his physical body holding the harp on which the strings of the last chord plucked upon them still vibrated.

He found himself on a boulder-strewn shore, looking up at the stone fortress of Tintagel. There was no wind; the place was silent except for an eerie, rhythmic sound like muffled drums. As he watched in awestruck wonder, twelve arrows leaving trails of blinding white light fell out of the sky, sweeping across the horizon until they were out of sight. Then, before his eyes, the castle crumbled and vanished, leaving behind its single occupant, a young man wearing a circlet of gold upon his head. The rhythmic sound increased, and Taliesin realized that it was the man's beating heart that he heard, filling the very sky with its power.

Bewildered, Taliesin tried to get to shore, but he lost his footing on the boulders and fell, nearly tumbling into the ocean's waves. He cursed while he wrung out his sodden sleeves, then pulled himself up onto one knee before realizing that he was not alone on the treacherous rocks. The old blind wolf he had encountered years before sat quietly on its haunches on a flat stone in front of him. This time Taliesin knew better than to fear the animal's presence.

"Who is he?" he asked quietly, knowing the wolf would answer.

He is your destiny, the white eyes communicated. *And you must forge the tools to prepare for him.*

"How? With my music?"

No, your life in the world has ended for a time. You must follow me now.

"Where?" he asked, confused. "Where do you wish me to go?"

The wolf rose from the rock where it had been and walked away, over the water into the setting sun.

"I will do as you will, but I must know where to go!" Taliesin shouted after the retreating from of the wolf.

He heard nothing more until Uther asked him dryly: "Well? What is the problem?"

Taliesin looked around at the faces staring at him, then strummed a chord on his harp. He began another song, since he had no idea what he had been singing since he fell into his waking dream.

A dream, he thought. Yes, that must be it.

His arms were cold. He looked down. With each chord he played, droplets of water from his wet sleeves spattered onto the instrument.

Although he had been planning to remain at Uther's court for several more days, he left immediately after that night's performance. In his mind, the moonlight eyes of the old wolf pulled at him like a magnet, even though he did not know where he was being pulled; and so he followed the moon.

It led him to the crest of a hill, the first of the foothills leading south to the mountains. Taliesin smiled and shook his head. But of course the wolf would have led him here! It was in these fog-enshrouded foothills that the creature had first spoken to him of Mona.

Mona will wait, the wolf had said with its blind yet all-seeing eyes.

Then he heard it again, for the first time in six years, the ancient chant of the druids during the darkest hour of the night, drifting faintly toward him from the island of magic. It filled him to trembling. Its awesome perfection was no less wonderful to him now that he was a grown man and a musician rather than the raw boy who had first heard its strains, and its pull on him was no less compelling than it had been then. He only wondered how he could have forgotten it for so long.

Taliesin rode the rest of the night to the shore and sold his horse to the innkeeper who offered him the night's lodging. In the morning, before dawn, he hired passage on a small boat and, with the sound of the druids' Salutation to the Sun ringing loud in his ears, finally made his crossing to Mona.

CHAPTER SIXTEEN

The candle in the ship's hold had burned down an inch or two. Outside, the wind buffeted like pounding hands against the hull, but the ship was large, and held steady.

Beatrice's eyes, still transfixed, were beatific and calm.

"By all that's holy, I do know you," Taliesin whispered.

She smiled softly.

It was the second time he had recognized her. The first was sixteen centuries ago, in Mona.

By the time he reached the island, the druids had stopped singing. So silent was the island that, watching the retreating shapes of the boatman and his vessel rowing back across the channel to Wales, Taliesin wondered if he had come to the right place.

It was said that druids could make themselves invisible at will. It was also said that anyone who dared invade Mona would suffer the unbridled wrath of their fearful and powerful magic. Taliesin felt his skin crawl as he walked down the foot-worn paths searching for some sign of life. There were no buildings here, not even the great hall where the Innocent spoke to his disciples. Yet the wooded paths, indented to trenches, spoke of years—perhaps centuries—of use. Every single rock large enough to sit on had been worn smooth with use. No, they were here, he was certain of it. They just weren't showing themselves to him.

Surely he would not be considered an invader, he told himself. The wolf had led him here. In his vision it had walked westward into the setting sun. Westward, to Mona.

The wolf . . .

Would even a druid laugh at his tale of a blind wolf who spoke to him with its eyes? Had he just imagined it all in his poet's brain?

He leaned against a tree and closed his eyes in anguish. "I am a fool," he whispered.

And a voice said softly behind him, "That is a beginning."

He whirled around to face a man in a gray hood. His face radiated such serenity and goodwill that Taliesin's fears immediately evaporated. "Were . . ." He hesitated, but could not keep himself from asking. "Were you invisible?"

The druid smiled. "No. I was still."

Years later, Taliesin would also know the secret of the druid's stillness, a stillness that originated in the very essence of his body and soul, a stillness so perfect that he could stand in a crowded room without being noticed by anyone. But at the moment, he could only tremble in fear at the wizard's magic.

"Come," the druid said. "The Innocent has been waiting for you."

"Waiting? But I didn't say I was coming."

The druid's expression was amused. "Nevertheless, I was asked to watch for you," he said.

Accompanied by the druid, Taliesin now saw not dozens, but hundreds of gray-robed disciples walking calmly about the island, talking together or sitting silently in meditation upon the smooth rocks. It struck him that Mona was one of the most populous places he had ever seen, and wondered how he could possibly have missed such a dense collection of individuals.

But where did they live? Nowhere, among all the humanity that teemed on the island, was there a single building.

Perhaps they didn't need them, Taliesin thought as he followed the druid past lakes and streams as undisturbed as if no human had ever set foot near them. Mona was the pinnacle of the druids' achievement of mind: Here was where the chief druids from thousands of enclaves throughout Britain and Gaul gathered to renew their powers; here was the place where those raised from childhood to the life of the spirit came to undergo initiation and testing. Here lived the Innocent himself, who understood the innermost mysteries of the higher realms, surrounded by his chosen disciples. Perhaps at this level, shelter from the elements was no longer a necessity.

But again he eventually saw the truth, and was surprised by it. When the druid knelt to enter the sod-covered opening of a cave, Taliesin noticed that the area was covered by tall mounds. Mounds! He almost laughed aloud. They lived in turf-roofed mounds, probably of the same design as the dwellings of the very first humans in Britain.

Even the great cave where he entered was part of a hillside, all but obscured by living grass and new flowers. It smelled of the earth, clean and fresh as the outdoors. And so he understood from the beginning of his time in Mona that the druids, for all their learning, dwelled upon the land like the most humble of creatures.

The interior of the cave was as simple as the outside. Aside from a fire that vented through a hole in the sod above it, almost no effort had been made to make it resemble anything other than what it was. The walls dripped with damp; overhead, bats circled. Their backs to the entrance, ten druids flanked a large granite altar, in front of which stood a frail old woman, her bony arms outstretched in silent prayer.

The Innocent.

The druid with Taliesin pressed him forward. He could barely bring his feet to move. None of the fantastic stories he had heard about the great wizards had shocked him more than this. A woman!

The Innocent lowered her spindly arms and laughed. "While you are here, you will have to examine all your values," she said in a resonant voice completely at variance with her effete appearance. Then, slowly, she turned to face Taliesin so that he might feel the full effect of her eyes.

They were blind, as milky and opaque as the wolf's, and yet they seemed to stare right through him into his very soul.

Taliesin felt himself shaking uncontrollably.

"Do you know me?" she asked.

"I do," he answered hoarsely.

"Do you know why I have called you here?"

"The dream," he stammered. "I had a dream while playing music. . . ." But of course she would know that. "There was a man in it, a man you called my destiny."

"So he is. Though the man has not yet been born, he will one day become king of this land, a king who will bring order out of chaos and elevate the whole of mankind with his life. And you, my singing poet, must prepare to teach him how to do it."

"I?" he asked. "But I know nothing about . . ." He looked at his hands. "I know nothing at all."

The Innocent smiled. "Then you shall have to work very hard at learning," she said gently. "Are you ready to begin?"

Taliesin fell to his knees. "Yes, master," he said. "I am ready."

"I was twenty-one years old when I came to Mona," the old man said. "When I left, I was forty."

Beatrice took his hand. "Were they very difficult, those two decades?"

"Yes. I remember thinking bitterly that you'd shrunken me to a seed."

"A good analogy, Taliesin. You should have told me."

"As if I had to tell you anything," he said, giving Beatrice's hand a squeeze.

"Although an egg might be better."

"An egg?"

"You did hatch, you know. You became the Merlin, the great magician of the gods."

He smiled. "The Merlin. It is a title I have never deserved."

"Oh, I think you have. You gave up much for the magic—the love of women, the joy of raising sons and daughters, the companionship of friends. These were never yours. There was only the magic." She touched his hand with one delicate finger. "Was it enough, little bard?"

Taliesin looked into the girl's blank, impossibly old eyes. *Was it enough?*

He remembered the years of loneliness during which he'd envied the poorest peasant for the simple joys he himself could never have. Yet in that loneliness, the magic had brought him moments of transcendent happiness.

"Who can say whether it was enough or not?" the old man answered quietly. He sighed. "I think I might have preferred to remain an egg."

*   *   *

In order to become the Merlin, Taliesin had to first discard everything else that he had been. It was the first step in his journey toward the holy life, and the hardest task he had ever faced.

He was no longer the brilliant bard known from one end of Britain to the other. He was not permitted to play his instruments, lest his pride be bolstered by those who might take pleasure from hearing his music. To lose the arrogance of his intellect, he was denied the use of books or paper so that he would not be tempted to read or write. He was forbidden to use his knowledge of herbs to treat his sick brethren, even when all other attempts had failed. To forget that he had been a king's son, the other druids were ordered to shun him and behave as if he were invisible. He was allowed to attend the druids' services, but not to participate. Each dawn, when the community gathered to sing the Salutation to the Sun, Taliesin could only stand outside the circle of initiates, his eyes cast down in acknowledgment that he was an outsider.

Each week he was brought before the Innocent to confess his faults.

"My mind wandered during the moon reverence," he said at his first confession. It was the only thing he had done which could possibly be construed as a fault.

The Innocent fixed him with her blank, blind stare. "What were you thinking?"

"I . . . I was remembering the first time I heard it. I was lost in the foothills on the mainland—"

"You will no longer be permitted to attend the moon reverence," she said.

Shocked at the severity of her punishment for such an insignificant transgression, he willed himself to perfect concentration during all of the services left to him. When he came before her the second week, he said with all sincerity, "Master, I have done nothing wrong."

For his arrogance, the Innocent removed his right to attend the Salutation to the Sun.

The third week, he confessed to being lonely. His sleeping blanket was taken away. It was late fall, and he shivered so much that he could not sleep.

By the fourth week, he was angry.

"What are your faults?" the Innocent asked.

"Whatever they are, I will be punished with unnessary harshness for them, so do what you will," he said.

The cold eyes stared, unblinking.

Taliesin was made to remain in a sod mound in the earth which was too small for him to stand erect in. He could not build a fire. His blanket had not been returned to him. A meal of bread and water was left outside the mound-dwelling once a day, and once a day the container filled with his bodily wastes was removed and replaced by invisible hands. In his earthen prison, with only worms and insects for companionship, he could barely hear the faint strands of music from the Salutation to the Sun, and he never saw light.

It was the life of the living dead Taliesin lived, and more than once he wished that he was truly dead. His body itched with vermin. His mouth was filled with sores. For weeks—or months; he quickly lost all track of time—he waited patiently, penitent for his outburst, comforted by the certainty that this was a trial and that it would pass. At times he would weep without realizing it, his tears falling on his arms and legs like foreign objects.

When his food came he crammed it into his mouth with his fingers and drank his small ration of water, longing for more. He retched when he carried the clay pot filled with his excrement into the tunnel leading to the outside. In time he stopped taking it out at all.

One day he began to scream, and found that he could not stop himself from screaming. The rage inside his heart poured out of him like venom, wordless, pointless. This was not punishment. It was torture. He had not deserved such terrible injustice. It was not his fault that he had been born into the nobility. His talent and intellect were not faults; they were gifts, gifts that anyone with eyes in her head could see were useful and good!

He felt some measure of guilty pleasure at the thought of the words *eyes in her head*. The Innocent had no eyes, in more ways than one. She was nothing more than a wicked old woman wreaking revenge on men. It had probably been a man who blinded her.

What of the male druids who served her? he wondered. Had they, too, submitted to this humiliation? Were they so spineless that they believed torture was the way to enlightenment? Or were they the sort who enjoyed abuse?

He crawled to the entrance of the mound. Like a mole, he thought, or a beaten dog. His legs were like dead weights. Well, he would force them to stand when he got out. He would walk out of this nightmare

with the dignity of a man. The world outside was waiting for him. It
hadn't changed. . . .

Nor have I.

The thought occurred to him just as his hand reached the light of
the entranceway. He turned his arm back and forth slowly, watching
the play of sunlight on his filthy skin.

It was hard to think. His mind had become undisciplined in the
hole where he had allowed himself to degenerate into the creature he
had become.

"The dignity of a man," he repeated aloud. He had no dignity. She
had taken it away from him. *She,* the blind bat who had sent him to
this torture. She, who had made him crawl for so long that he had lost
the use of his legs.

Taliesin shook his head. His legs . . . It wasn't about his legs, really.
He did not need legs to possess dignity, any more than the Innocent
needed sight.

He had been told to live in the earth, but not in squalor. His books
had been removed, but no one had told him not to think. He had
been prohibited from playing music, but not from hearing it in his
soul.

And yet he had done none of those things. He had changed nothing
about himself to adapt to what was, but had merely waited and railed
and wished for what was to become something else.

The Innocent had done nothing to harm him, Taliesin realized: He
himself, alone, had possessed the power to make him something less
than a human being.

And he alone could make him something more.

He went back into the darkness, to the stinking chamber pot that
crawled with maggots, and brought it into the tunnel. When he came
back into the mound, he reached up to its roof with tentative fingers.
He had been told to remain inside, he realized, but he had never been
forbidden to change the mound itself.

"The darkness," he croaked, scratching furiously at the hard-packed
earth. "I never had to accept the darkness."

His heart racing, he picked up a rock and dug faster, laughing as
clods of soil fell onto his upturned face. When he finally broke through
to the surface, he gasped at the feel of the cold air on his hands, the
welcome stretch in his spine. Taliesin wiggled his fingers, feeling as if

they were the fragile stems of some new plant, pale shoots growing between blades of grass.

And I am their root, he thought.

Between his fingers shone a single star. He cupped his palms around it. "Thank you," he whispered. "Gods of my spirit, gods of the earth and the universe, thank you for giving me so much."

With some turf he scrubbed his body until it smelled of green grass. When his meal came, he used the water to wash his face and hands. He placed the bread outside, as an offering to the gods. Then he closed his eyes and listened to the music of his mind.

It was exquisite, the song of his first night on earth. And when the moon passed over his tiny window above his head, annointing him with silver light, his song blended with the distant druids' moon reverence to create a music more moving and lovely than he had ever dreamed could exist.

Later, at the most silent hour of the night, it began to snow. It fell lightly over Taliesin, making a circle around the place where he sat. He opened his mouth to taste the perfect crystals on his tongue, and rejoiced to feel their coldness. He filled his lungs with healing air, then sang the song his spirit had created, the wild, perfect melody that captured all the joy and wonder that he felt surging through him like liquid light.

As the music poured out of him, the snowflakes seemed to change into stars that fell from the sky in a glittering column, descending into his very essence. He gasped, feeling the pillar of starfire alight inside him, filling him, burning him pure. His hair stood on end; his fingernails melted. He felt himself shrinking, shrivelling, drying to white ash. Then, cell by cell, he felt himself growing again, becoming someone he had never known. Not Taliesin, although he would use the name for all his life on earth, but someone—something—utterly different, a creature made of snow and moonlight and filled with music.

He cried out once in happiness, then wept, conscious of every joyful tear.

"What were your faults?" the Innocent asked gently.

Sunlight streamed from the hole in the turf above Taliesin to bathe him in warmth. It spilled over onto the old woman, who crouched in front of him like a wolf on its haunches.

"My ingratitude, Master," Taliesin answered, "to receive the gift of growth without appreciating it. My arrogance, to think I did not need the things of the spirit. My foolishness, to believe I needed anything else."

The Innocent turned her face toward the opening in the roof.

"My torpor, in not trying to reach the gods, though they were waiting always to help me." He turned his open palms up into the shaft of sunlight. "It took so little effort to bring this light."

"And so much to live in the darkness," the Innocent said.

CHAPTER SEVENTEEN

The ship bearing Taliesin and his two wards docked at the Port of New York the next day.

They were awakened by the jostling of the ship and shouting from outside. The old man sat bolt upright. Arthur was a few feet away, rubbing his eyes.

"Where's Beatrice?"

The boy looked around. "She was—"

"I'm right here," Beatrice answered. And she was. Right on the pallet of blankets where she had gone to sleep the night before.

"That's funny. I didn't even see you," Arthur said.

Few would have, Taliesin thought. He alone had noticed the almost imperceptible shift the girl had made from perfect stillness to waking vibrancy.

"Arthur, listen to me," he whispered. "When the hold is opened, you must find a way to slip out unobserved. It won't be difficult—the crates the stevedores will be unloading are large, and they won't be expecting to see anyone."

"Then what? Once I'm out, someone's bound to see me."

"Just pretend you've wandered onto the docks by accident. Say you

were looking for someone. You're a child with an American accent—
they may accept your story. If not, try to make a run for it. We'll meet
you in front of whichever building is closest to this place."

"What about you?" Arthur asked, alarmed. "And Beatrice?"

"We'll be all right. Now get behind that box near the hatch. When
they move it out, stay behind it."

Arthur nodded, then made his way toward the cargo near the hatch.

"Now you," Taliesin said to Beatrice. "Help me move these blankets
and things into a corner where they won't be spotted for a while."

She obeyed, bundling up the candles and food they had removed
from the galley inside a sheet. "But Mr. Taliesin," she whispered.
"What shall we do when the stevedores come?"

"We, my dear," he said with a smile, "shall become invisible."

Beatrice looked at him dubiously. "Invisible?"

"Come, now, you just did it. The stillness, girl. The way we did in
Mona."

"What's Mona?"

"What's . . . But we talked all about it!" he sputtered. "Almost all
last night . . ."

"But you were asleep when I went to bed." Her expression revealed
nothing but bewilderment.

"Asleep . . . Oh, never mind. Go with Arthur. Where's the cup?"

"Arthur's got it." She headed for the hatch, but after a few feet she
turned around to face him. "Are you sure you'll be all right, Mr. Taliesin?"

"Of course I will! It's you I'm worried about. Just keep quiet. Let
Arthur talk." He shooed her away.

When the hatch opened, the two children scrambled out like crabs
behind the first big box onto the dock.

"Hey, what are you kids doing here?" an angry voice shouted.

There was a long pause. "Go on, Arthur, talk!" Merlin goaded in a
whisper from inside the hold.

"We're looking for our dad," Arthur said with just the right touch
of street toughness.

"Yeah? What's his name?"

"Art Blessing."

"Blessing? Don't know him. He union?"

"Naah. He don't work much. But we already checked the bars."

"Good," Taliesin murmured. "Very good, boy."

"We don't use nobody outside the union here. How'd you get in?"

"Fence. No big deal."

"Well, you could be arrested for being here. So blast off unless you want to be in big trouble."

The fence, Taliesin thought as he heard their running footsteps. He would look for a fence.

Just then two men walked into the hold of the ship, and Taliesin willed himself to stillness. He slowed his breathing until the very air around him quieted. He made his heart beat so slowly that a physician would have declared him dead. His senses, too, shut down one by one, to be replaced by a different means of perception: Instead of vision, Taliesin recognized the solid objects around him by the movement of their molecules and their displacement of space. He shrank the aura surrounding him, that emanating band of vitality that signals one's presence as surely as a shout, so that he became as outwardly lifeless as a rock. Then, with his new spirit's eyes, he moved past the men.

They were no more than energy forms to him now, their speech and laughter explosions of color which Taliesin felt throughout his body. Outside, the gentle water at the docks gave off the tremendous power of the ocean's hidden life. The concrete beneath his feet shone with the slow, eternal vibrations of its component minerals. Far in the distance, past the heavy, squat buildings guarding the dock like sentinels, a line of trees breathed the joyous essence of wood and green leaves. And beyond them, hundreds of miles past the streets and automobiles and the jagged yellow lines of electricity and the millions of human beings throbbing with life inside their sturdy cement walls, were ancient low mountains.

He could see everything

Arthur and Beatrice, their unique energies as familiar to Taliesin as his own, were climbing over a chain-link fence which gave off the spirit-scents of iron and aluminum. As he approached, the two forms leaped to the ground in a cloud of exhilaration.

Taliesin remembered his first day on Mona, when he had appeared as just such a form to the invisible druids who had watched him with their inner vision.

No more nor less than a blade of grass or a star, he thought as he melded himself with the fence and moved through it to the other side.

* * *

"You are no more nor less than a blade of grass or a star." The Innocent walked beside him through a field of flowers. "All being is eternal, and part of All That Is. Understand this, and in time you shall harness the power of the universe." She disappeared before his eyes.

When she reappeared a moment later, it was on a hilltop miles away.

"How can you transport yourself like that?" Taliesin asked when he caught up. "It is impossible, against the laws of nature."

The Innocent laughed. "Which laws are those? The same ones that insist the earth is flat? Or the laws announcing that the sun moves around the earth?"

Taliesin had been studying the night sky from the druids' standing stones, and knew that neither assumption was true, even though they were so accepted in the world that any word to the contrary was punishable by death. So the druids kept this knowledge to themselves, just as they kept their knowledge about fortelling the future and calling up magic. A gigantic observatory at Stonehenge had been standing for millennia so that men could see for themselves the truth about their planet's place among the stars, but even that had had no effect on mankind's perceptions of the "laws of nature."

"It is not the same," he said. "In the observatory, I can see with my own eyes that the earth revolves around the sun."

"But even the most ignorant herder has seen the sun rise and set. To him—and to the mass of men—that is indisputable proof that the earth is the center of the universe, and that our arcane observations are false."

"Are you saying that what you did was a trick? That there is no such thing as truth at all, but only perception?"

The Innocent smiled. "Oh, there is truth, to be sure. But it lies only in the things that cannot be perceived." She walked to a boulder that stood taller than she, then disappeared inside it and emerged out the far side.

"You walked through solid rock!" Taliesin whispered in amazement. "How is that done?"

She made a dismissive gesture.

"How did you walk through the rock?" Taliesin shouted. "You must tell me!"

"I can tell you, but my words will not help you. To make magic, you must not think, but *become*."

"Become what?"

The old woman put her hand over his heart. "Become a blade of grass," she said. "Or a star."

"Where'd you come from?" Arthur asked, startled at the sight of the old man at the fence beside him.

"The ship, naturally," Taliesin said. "And now we must find a place to stay, if we ever expect Hal to find us."

"Hal?" Arthur's fingers gripped the wire of the fence. "Hal's alive?"

"Heavens, yes. Didn't you know?"

Arthur fought down his irritation. "No," he said. "I didn't. And you didn't tell me."

"I did," Beatrice said softly.

"Well, no matter, eh?" the old man said heartily. "All's well that ends well."

"Where is he?"

"Who, Hal? He's on his way. Needn't worry about him. What we've got to find now is a room, preferably with a bath that isn't down the hall—Oh . . ." A soft pop sounded from somewhere nearby. The old man fell to the ground.

"Taliesin!" Beatrice shrieked, kneeling beside him. "Oh, God, Arthur . . ." She held up her hands. They were soaked with the old man's blood.

Arthur fumbled to get the cup out of the pocket of his jeans. With shaking hands he placed it over Taliesin's bloody chest.

Across the street, a man with blond hair got out of a battered blue van and ran toward them. "Someone's coming," Beatrice whispered.

"See if you can keep him away. I don't want to have to explain this."

Beatrice stood up, prepared to intercept the stranger. "He's all right," she shouted. "It was just . . ." Then she screamed.

Arthur looked up. The blond man lunged at Beatrice. Grabbing a handful of her hair, he dragged her behind him as he moved toward the fence.

"Bea!" Arthur left the cup with Taliesin and ran toward the attacker. Out of the corner of his eye he noticed that the street was empty. There were no police here, not a soul except himself to hear Beatrice's screams.

At that moment, the doors of the Port Authority building swung open and two young people holding flowers spilled out, chattering and laughing. Their merriment died away abruptly as they took in the sight of a man who was obviously trying to abduct a child.

The man saw them as well. He hesitated for the briefest moment— long enough for Arthur to take a flying leap at him, and for the pas- sersby to drop their flowers and stampede toward them in a rage.

"Let go of her, you geek!" shouted the woman, running toward them in a sprint. She wore her hair in braids, which streamed out from her head like serpents. In a single motion, she unshouldered a huge back- pack and smacked the blond man across the face with it.

As he reeled away from the blow, a skinny young man still bearing the marks of teenage acne gently untangled the blond man's fingers from Beatrice's hair. "This is your *soul*, man, don't you get it?" he asked earnestly. The blond man kicked him in the groin.

"Bad karma," the skinny man wheezed as the girl picked up a rock and threw it like a hardball into the assailant's forehead.

Blood flooded the blond man's face. He shoved Beatrice away from him and fled back to the blue van.

"Get the license number!" the woman with the braids shrilled.

"Got it," grunted her companion, wincing as he pulled himself to his feet.

Arthur jogged back to Taliesin, who was pulling himself up to a sitting position beside the fence. "Are you all right?" he asked.

"Yes," the old man said dazedly. "Yes, I think so, although I'm not quite sure what happened." He picked up the cup, which had rolled into his lap, and slipped it into the sleeve of his shirt.

"It was just a mugger, I guess," Arthur said. "But why would he mug us? We look like bums."

Taliesin rose to his feet. "A mugger? I think not."

"What do you mean? The guy in Tangier? That wasn't him. I re- member his face."

"So do I. I also remember the dock workers shouting that the ship we were stowed away on was headed for New York. This chap was expecting us, Arthur."

Beatrice ran into Taliesin's arms, sobbing. Behind her were the two people who had helped to turn her attacker away. "There, there, child," the old man said with a smile as he enfolded her in his arms. "No harm seems to have come to either of us."

"You've been hurt!" the braided woman gasped, seeing the blood on Taliesin's shirt. "We've got to call an ambulance. There's blood all over you."

"It's quite all right, miss," Taliesin said, doing his best to cover the red stains that covered his entire torso. "The wound was no more than a graze, I assure you."

"A *graze?* I'm sorry, but I was a medic in the Peace Corps. A graze doesn't bleed like that." She swooped at him like a vulture and yanked open his shirt. Frowning, she explored the old man's unbroken skin. "There's no wound," she said in amazement. Slowly, she looked up into Taliesin's face.

"Maybe he was hit someplace else," her friend said, limping past her to take a look at Taliesin. "Is your head okay?" he asked. "Kate's right, you know. We should get you to a hospital. Or do you want to talk to the cops first?"

"No, no hospital," Taliesin managed at last. "And no police. Please. We'll just be on our way."

The girl with the braids narrowed her eyes. "Where do you live?"

"Well, er . . ."

"You're street people, aren't you," she said flatly.

The old man looked to Arthur for an explanation. "Homeless," the boy said. "She thinks we're homeless."

"Hey, that's okay," the pockmarked young man said. "That's cool. We know where you're coming from."

"You do?"

"He means he understands," Arthur translated.

"We sure do," the woman in braids said. "The cops aren't going to do a thing for you. And by the time a hospital gets around to treating you, you'll either be healed or in a coma."

Taliesin brightened. "Ah. Well, that's settled, then. We'll be on our way. Thank you for your help."

"You're coming with us," the woman said with finality.

"I beg your pardon?"

"Zack Diamond," the young man said, extending his hand. "This is Kate Marshall. We've got a place for you to stay if you need one. It's in Manhattan, but there's plenty of room, and it won't cost you anything." He flashed them a friendly grin. "But you'll have to pitch in with the chores. We all do at the Center."

"The Center?" Taliesin asked.

The skinny man with acne assumed a serious expression. "The Center for Cosmic Consciousness," he said importantly. "CCC for short."

Arthur and Beatrice exchanged glances, trying hard not to laugh. "No, thanks," Arthur began. "We'd really better—"

"We'd be delighted," Taliesin said.

"The Center for Cosmic Consciousness," Arthur muttered as they followed their new acquaintances to the bus stop.

"CCC for short," Beatrice added, giggling.

"The ingratitude of youth," Taliesin pronounced loftily. "After what just happened, I should think you'd see that fate has sent us a lightning bolt of good fortune in those two helpful individuals."

"But they think we're homeless," Arthur said.

"They are quite correct."

"But we're not destitute or anything. I mean, it's not as if we have to stay in some *center*."

"Oh?"

Arthur squinted at the old man. "You know what I'm saying." He cast a sidelong glance toward Beatrice. It was important, he knew, that no one guess who Taliesin really was, or what he could do. "Like the money in Morocco," he said out of the side of his mouth. "Maybe you could . . ." He spun little circles with his hand. ". . . come up with some money."

"Just like that?" He laughed. "Good heavens, boy, what do you think I am, a wizard?"

Arthur inhaled noisily. "It's just that after living in the storage area of a cargo ship, I was kind of hoping for a hotel room."

"Mmmm," Beatrice mused. "A bath with bubbles in it. A feather pillow. Tea with scones . . ."

"To be followed quickly by another visit from our violent friend, or someone just like him," Taliesin finished. "Whom do you suppose will be sent next time—a room service waiter with a stiletto under his napkin, or a chambermaid wearing shoes that shoot poisonous darts? Because without doubt, my greedy darlings, the fellow is already becoming acquainted with the city's major hotels."

After a silence, Beatrice spoke. "He's right, Arthur. The man in Tangier knows we have the cup. He's not going to stop looking for us now."

"Well, who's to say he's not watching us right this minute?" Arthur argued.

"Oh, we're safe from him at the moment."

"How do you know?"

The old man put his hands on his hips. "Because there is a massive traffic jam three blocks away," he said, peeved. "Anyone going in that direction would be caught up in it."

Beatrice's head snapped toward him. "How would you know that, Mr. Taliesin?"

"Er . . ."

"Yeah," Arthur said with feigned innocence, enjoying the old man's discomfort. "How would you know that?"

"He saw it with his mind," Beatrice answered breathlessly. "That was it, wasn't it? You saw it . . ." She blinked slowly. ". . . when you walked through the fence . . ."

Arthur and Taliesin looked at one another.

"He didn't walk through any fence," Arthur insisted, trying to protect the old man's secret. "He came through the gate."

"But there wasn't—"

"Shhh," the old man said, touching her shoulder lightly. "I knew about the traffic jam because I could hear the noise from the automobiles."

But Beatrice continued to stare at him, because she knew, in a place inside her so deep and forgotten that the knowledge was no more than the breeze created by a blade of grass bending, that Taliesin's feat had been real magic, and that she had taught it to him.

CHAPTER EIGHTEEN

It took Taliesin years to master that first magic, born of stillness; and more to learn the others, for which he needed every resource of his mind and body.

Through those years he came to love the Innocent more than he had ever loved anyone. Like a mother, he supposed, although he had never known the woman who had died giving him birth, and he doubted that most mothers would order their sons, as she had ordered him, to render service to the gods by engaging in copulation.

"At Beltane, you will embody the reborn aspect of the god," she told him simply.

Taliesin had been shocked. Beltane was a festival of drunkenness and licentiousness, hardly the sort of celebration one would expect from the disciplined druids on Mona. His memories of the event were of unruly peasants dancing in the streets, dancing, fighting with one another, and tumbling whatever girls happened to seize their attention. Since all rules of social conduct were suspended for Beltane and rape a normal part of the festivities, the only women who remained outside after the innocent morning maypole dressing and afternoon feasting were unsatisfied wives looking for a diversion from their husbands. The maidens, along with the grumbling prostitutes who could not hope to earn a penny on this day of free love, shut themselves in their chambers before nightfall and remained there until the following morning, when the peasants went home with throbbing heads and the innkeepers set to repairing their establishments. It was no wonder the saintly Christians, who balked even at the excesses of the Roman holy days, positively railed against Beltane.

Taliesin himself had found it a rather pleasurable amusement once he was of an age to participate, but that was when he had been out in the world, not a seeker of enlightenment. Since his arrival on Mona, he had never held so much as a lustful thought toward the women who served the gods as he did . . . although he had, on occasion, found his mind wandering during the druids' processionals, when the shapeless gray shift he happened to walk behind would unexpectedly move with a fluidity and fullness that reminded him of his maleness.

"Beltane?" he whispered hoarsely. "You celebrate Beltane here?"

The Innocent laughed. "We invented Beltane, little bard. It is the ancient rite of spring, when the great earth mother becomes a maiden once more and renews her fertility by taking a husband. Of course, we no longer follow the old custom of sacrificing the husband at the end of one year. After the festivities, you will return to your life as a servant of the gods."

"But . . . what will be expected of me?"

"Nothing is expected. What happens is what the gods decree. Beltane is their time to speak."

They did speak that year, although Taliesin was not to know it for decades to come.

What the gods said to the island of Mona was good-bye.

But that first May, when the streams bubbled with clean water and the apple blossoms blew across the island in fragrant blizzards, Taliesin could not imagine a place more favored by the gods.

On the day of the Beltane celebration, he remained inside the cave of the Innocent, naked and in prayer, while the others carried out the long ritual: First, nine kinds of wood were gathered and dressed with wildflowers and straw ribbons for the great Beltane fire. These were arranged around the sacred circle, a ring of dark, lush grass growing in a clearing in the ancient forest of oaks which was at the physical and spiritual heart of Mona. In the center of the circle was a wreath woven of every flowering plant and herb on the island, and suspended over it, held aloft by two thin ropes of woven grass, was the severed trunk of a young fir, stripped of all its branches and bark and covered with a white cloth to symbolize the body of the Earth's lover, who had lain dead through the cold winter.

Each step of the ritual took hours, with incantations and offerings of salt, with chanting and song and the unceasing, six-word prayer for the earth which began with the Salutation to the Sun at dawn and was carried by one voice after another through every activity of the day:

Mother bring us life from death

In the cave of the Innocent, purified by fasting and water, Taliesin heard the prayer with every beat of his heart, heard it until it sang through his very blood. While the other druids took their meal of white asparagus and strawberry wine, a lone singer remained at the sacred circle to sing the endless prayer until sunset. *Mother bring us life from death.* . . . Taliesin's lips moved with the words. His body felt numb, anesthetized by the droning plea. His mind, once full of questions about what would befall him in the sacred circle, was now quiet.

He knew he would make love with a woman, if he was able; that much had been made clear to him. His questions revolved around how that would become a sacred act. Try as he might, he could not rid himself of the memories of Beltane as a tawdry display of people's basest inclinations. At one point he had even asked the Innocent to excuse him from the duty, but she had refused.

"You fear you will enjoy the act of love," the Innocent said, without a trace of mirth.

"The problem is, it wouldn't be love," he offered miserably. "I wouldn't even know the woman. It would be like . . . like tumbling with a whore. The pleasure would be for me as a man, nothing more." He hung his head. "I would insult the gods."

"I told you that the gods would decree what would happen. It was they who selected you, not I. And I doubt that they would choose to be insulted by their chosen."

"Do the gods speak through you?" Taliesin asked, trying to understand. It was the way all the petty kings thought—that their every wish was the decree of the highest deities. This was the kind of thinking that enabled them to wage war on lesser tribes for the sole purpose of increasing their treasuries and massacre their women and children for sport. He had thought the Innocent above that.

"Not through me," she explained softly. "They speak directly to me. It is my gift. It is why I am called the Innocent." She closed her opaque eyes. "And why I am blind."

"Because you can see the gods themselves, but not their creations," Taliesin whispered.

"That is so. And they have made it clear that it must be you who plants the seed of the future into the earth mother's body."

He hesitated for a moment before speaking. "Will you tell me why?"

The Innocent smiled sadly. "That is a burden I will not ask you to bear," she answered. "Go now, and let the gods unravel their plan in their own time."

And so he waited in the sanctified cave hour after hour, listening to the prayer for the earth.

Mother bring us life from death

In time, he sensed the Innocent's presence coming nearer. She never made a sound when she moved, but so great was the strength of her aura that even with his eyes closed Taliesin could feel it, like the heat from the sun.

She said nothing as she stood before him, offering a bowl filled with mushrooms. Taliesin recognized them. They were the tiny, disfigured earth-fruit that grew in rings in the forest—fairy rings, the country folk called them. On Mona, these mushrooms were sacred, and therefore never eaten by anyone except the Innocent during her times of solitude in the wilderness, when she lived alone and unsheltered in the elements and consumed no other food for the cycle of one moon. Now she was allowing him to feed on the gods' food.

He knelt and ate them, one at a time, until the bowl was empty. Then the Innocent handed him a vessel filled with water. It was carved from alabaster, and so ancient that the hands which fashioned them had belonged to a race of men no longer extant, the small, dark people known as the Tuatha de Danaan, whose priests first uttered the cease-less prayer to the earth mother in spring.

When Taliesin had drunk its contents, the Innocent left without a word, and four druids came to paint his naked body with blue woad and anoint his eyelids with oil made fragrant with the essences of marigold, thyme, hollyhock, and grass. As they worked, they joined the lone voice outside in the prayer for the earth, transforming it from a pure tenor line to a broader spectrum of sound resonating with bass and baritone undertones.

They led him outside. With each step he felt the effects of the mushrooms he had eaten take hold, sharpening his senses. The colors of the sunset pierced his eyes with an intensity that was almost painful after the long hours of darkness. His legs felt as if they were made of rubber and would bounce to the moon if he did not restrain them. With each breath he tasted the salt from the sea. And all around him, filling him utterly, was the prayer for the earth, now taken up by every voice, male and female, and loud as thunder.

During the last moments of daylight, when the setting sun seemed to melt into the far horizon, the druids stepped one by one inside the circle, each clasping a stone knife. They stood before the dressed fir, the effigy of the dead god, to give him their blood. With a single stroke each man and woman, undifferentiated beneath the gray robe of the holy seeker, slashed open a vein and spattered blood upon the white cloth of the sacrificial fir until it was bright red and steaming with spilled life.

The sun disappeared. Within minutes, the sky darkened. The first stars shone.

Then the wood surrounding the sacred circle was set ablaze.

It was time for the dead god to come to life.

As Taliesin took the final steps of his journey to the flaming circle, he saw for the first time the woman who would receive his seed. She was naked, as he was, painted and oiled so that her skin shone with the luminescence of the moon. Her dark hair, crowned with a circlet of apple blossoms, hung loose in wild waves down her back. Her eyes were glassy, distant, but her gaze met his, and in that moment Taliesin ceased to be a human man. He was the god of the sky, come to pour lightning into the earth. His desire welled up like a rage inside him; he had to be restrained from running to her.

As he struggled to break free, a drum began to beat. The rhythm was a palpable thing: Taliesin could see the air explode in bright bubbles with each blow of the mallet on the cloth-covered log. Around the great oaks, tendrils of life snaked like smoke. The trees were alive, and their being welled up into the chant and the beating of the drum.

In the middle of the circle, the blood-soaked trunk quivered as the grass ropes suspending it over the ground were pulled taut by the druids' stone knives. In another instant the ropes gave way and the tree descended through the wreath of flowers beneath it, penetrating like a phallus into the waiting earth.

Taliesin's own manhood stood rigid. Sweat ran down his body. His limbs trembled. Then, through the heat of the fire, he saw the goddess moving toward him.

With a cry of anguish, he tore himself away from his captors and walked through the flames to meet her.

He took her in the sacred circle as the god, drunk with the new life that surged through his body. They fell on the ground in a rush of wild hunger, oblivious to the presence of the others who closed the circle around them, aware only of the chant that beat through their veins with the drumbeat, the chant that was the prayer for the earth.

Mother bring us life from death
Mother bring us life from death

He rode the pliable earth goddess in a fury. Life in death . . . He was reborn, potent, whole, inexorable.

Life from death
Life from death

With a shout of triumph, he poured his seed into her, clinging fast to her flesh, to the soft earth. To life.

Mother bring us life from death . . .

The chant swirled around him like petals on the breeze. He rose above them, spiraling higher, above the body that lay spent on the ground beside the limp form of a woman, above the music and the drumbeats. There was no time here, no sound, no imprisoning flesh.

He was free.

Life from death.

It was the voice of the Innocent, but she spoke without sound, directly into his soul.

"Am I dead?" he asked.

We never die, little bard. Even though the trappings of our lives fall away to dust, yet we remain, as do the gods.

Taliesin felt himself being lifted higher until he was soaring through space, surrounded by the limitless stars. He flew toward one, the brightest, until its light enveloped and blinded him. There, on its surface, he trembled amid mountains of clear crystal born of pure, airless light. For this was the resting place of the gods, and their power shook him like thunderbolts.

Far in the distance, the blue world of the earth, his home, faded into darkness.

"What have you done?" he whispered.

It was the Innocent's voice which answered. "They are leaving us. The gods wish to die. And when they go, they will take their magic with them."

Taliesin looked for her, but he knew that he was alone in this wild, cold place. "But you said we never die!" he shouted.

"That is so," the Innocent said. Her voice faded away.

"Wait! I don't understand . . ." He looked around helplessly. There was nothing here, nothing . . .

Then he caught a glimpse of something inside one of the crystal mountains, something that glowed with a brilliance more exquisite than the star itself.

With a thudding heart, he saw it was a man. Dressed in black, with a thin gold circlet around his forehead, Taliesin recognized him as the man who had appeared in the vision he had experienced at his brother's castle, the vision that had caused the bard to leave behind all he knew to come to Mona to serve the gods. The figure in the mountain stood perfectly still, holding aloft a magnificent sword.

He was waiting to be born.

"But how will I find him?" Taliesin asked.

From inside the solid crystal, the man lowered his sword and pointed it toward the earth. A solitary beam of light traveled from the sword's gleaming metal tip into the blackness of space, to rest at last as a bright pinpoint on the darkened planet.

Hesitantly, Taliesin followed the beam of light, flying, floating free again in empty space, descending giddily, faster than a comet toward the tiny dot of light, until he saw the earth spread beneath him, its oceans blue as jewels, the land green and fragrant.

Mother, bring us life from death . . . The chant pounded in his ears. *Bring us life from death* . . . *life from death* . . .

The light ended in a tangled thicket in an old forest, on a slab of stone from which a great jeweled sword protruded, the same sword whose light had directed him here. There was no space between the perfect blade and the rock in which it had, quite impossibly, been buried; there was no human way to extricate it. And on the stone was engraved a message, covered with moss and lichen and eroded with time:

Whoso pulleth this sword from this stone
Shall be named rightwise King of England

So this was where it would begin. With a single point of light.

He awoke back in the sacred circle, and he was alone. Sweat dripped blue off his painted body. Surrounding him were the last glowing embers of what had been the great Beltane bonfire, now scattered red eyes winking at him in the night.

On wobbly legs he righted himself and walked slowly out of the clearing.

What did she mean about the gods' dying, he wondered.

When they go, they will take their magic with them.

A breeze rustled through the tops of the ancient trees. On their branches sat a full moon, fat and orange-colored. Beside him, a stream gurgled over stones grown smooth with centuries. He knelt beside it and drank. The water was cold, delicious.

This is their magic, he thought. It is all right here.

"Remember that, little bard."

He looked up, startled. It was the Innocent, standing across the stream from him. Taliesin had not heard her come, but then he never did.

"One day I will have to leave this place," he said.

She nodded.

And so his time in Mona would end, as it had begun, with a vision of a man he was yet to meet.

"Can the gods die?" he asked.

But the Innocent had already vanished.

PART THREE

THE
MAGICIAN

CHAPTER NINETEEN

The Center for Cosmic Consciousness turned out to be less eccentric than Taliesin had imagined. Located on a respectable block in Manhattan's west fifties, it was distinguishable from the other three-story apartment buildings lining the street only by a small brass plaque near the door.

"Most people we bring here expect something a little more woo-woo," Zack Diamond said.

"Woo-woo?"

"Meta. You know, metaphysical. Black walls with Day-Glo stars and incense in the corners. I guess it's the name."

"Corny, isn't it?" Kate mussed his hair affectionately. "See you later," she said, striding toward the stairs. "And welcome!" she called out behind her.

Zack laughed self-deprecatingly. "I guess she's right about the name, but I wanted to remind people that we're all in this together. That we're here for a reason, and that every one of us *belongs*. Do you know what I mean?"

"Cosmic consciousness," Arthur said. "C.C." Beatrice giggled. Taliesin glared at them both.

"Good people live here," Zack went on. "The retired minister who lived in the apartment where you'll be staying spent every day visiting hospitals, talking with people who didn't have anyone else."

He led them to a door just left of the foyer. "He died last week at ninety-eight. There were so many people at the funeral service that they couldn't all fit into the church."

"Good show," Taliesin said, touching the young man's arm. "Not a bit woo-woo."

"Glad you agree." He unlocked the door. "This is a nice room," he said. "It's just like mine, on the other side."

"Does it have a bath?" Beatrice asked longingly.

"Yep. They all do. No kitchen, though. I wanted to make as many units as possible. We all eat together, in the big room across from the front door. It's fun."

"I'm sure," Taliesin said graciously.

The apartment Zack showed them was sparse but clean, with a comfortable old chair in the corner and a threadbare sofa facing a fireplace.

"It works, too," Zack said, putting his foot on the grate. "Not that you're likely to build a fire in June—"

"Get away from there!" Beatrice shouted.

Zack leaped aside. "Is something wrong?"

"Wrong. Yes." Beatrice stood as if she were frozen, her gaze trained on the fireplace. "A dark place . . . underground . . ."

"Wow, you can really pick up on vibes," Zack said admiringly. "This building was built over the site of a witches' coven. That's what somebody told me at the municipal building, anyway."

"The city government here must be very thorough," Taliesin said.

"Oh, every building has a history. I had to go through a lot of red tape to renovate the place, so I spent a lot of time looking through records. I found out about the coven stuff then. But that went on hundreds of years ago. The original building was burned in the 1800s. In fact, another building was built over it before this one."

He leaned down so that his face was level with Beatrice's. "Besides, witches aren't so bad. They were just nature worshippers, kind of like the old druids. Ever hear of them?"

The girl's head snapped up imperiously. "These were not druids!" she spat. She closed her eyes. "And not witches, either."

Zack laughed uncomfortably. "Jeez, I wish I could give you another apartment, but—"

"No, no. This one is quite lovely," Taliesin said, offering his hand to the young man. "We will try to be good guests. And we shall do our best to earn our keep. When are we to report for duty?"

Zack grinned. "After dinner, in the kitchen behind the dining room. There'll be other volunteers." He turned back to Beatrice. "Are you sure you're okay about this?"

She blinked. "What? I'm sorry. I think I was daydreaming."

"About the . . . oh, it doesn't matter." He turned to Taliesin. "Hey, I think I can get hold of some clothes for you. A lady on the second floor collects stuff for the Salvation Army. You want to come up with me?"

Taliesin shot a quick glance at Beatrice. The girl seemed perfectly normal now. "Delighted," he said.

When they were alone, Arthur stood by the wall studying Beatrice, who was inspecting a pot of silk flowers on the windowsill. "It's much nicer than I expected—"

"Bea," Arthur said softly. "What were you saying about the fireplace?"

"The fireplace?" She looked at it. "It seems fine. Do you think it works?"

Arthur took a deep breath. "Zack said it did."

"Did he?" She clapped her hands together. "I get the first bath."

"This looks disgusting," Arthur said, swabbing out an enormous pot containing the burnt remains of pea soup.

"And it tasted even worse," Beatrice added.

Taliesin adjusted the waistband of a pair of jeans donated by the woman upstairs. "I certainly can't dispute that," he said quietly. "Ah, Zack."

The young man was carrying a tray of salt and pepper shakers. "How'd you like dinner?"

"Splendid," Taliesin lied. "We were just talking about it."

"I made the soup myself," Zack said proudly.

"In that case, I'm glad I missed it." Kate came in and helped Zack put the shakers away. "Sorry I'm late. I was studying."

"Want a sandwich?"

"Maybe later." She smiled at Taliesin. "How's your wound?" she asked.

"Wound? Oh, yes, that. It's fine. That is, it was only a scratch."

She stared at him. "I didn't even see a scratch."

Taliesin cleared his throat. "Yes, well, um . . . That is, there was rather a lot of blood, but the source of it was negligible. Almost impossible to find, in fact." He made a great clatter washing his pot.

Kate opened her mouth to argue, but the old man prevented her. "Tell me, Kate, are you a street person as well?"

She smiled and shook her head. "No, I can't say I am. I'm not rich, but that's a choice I made. I grew up with a lot of privileges."

Zack, who had ambled over, stuck his hands in his pockets and laughed. "I'd say that's an understatement," he said. "Kate's father was President of the United States."

Arthur screwed up his face. "Well, what are you doing here?" he asked. Beatrice nudged him, but it had never occurred to him that he was being rude. He simply wanted to know.

Kate grabbed one of the pots and a rag and joined them in their work at the sink. "You can't spend your life just being someone's kid," she said with a shrug. "I left home as soon as I was out of high school. I joined the Peace Corps and went to Africa. Then I bummed around Europe for a few years. So now I'm twenty-five years old and a starving student."

"She's working on her Master's at Columbia," Zack added.

"And my parents don't support me. I work for my room and board here, just like you."

"Does everyone stay here for free?" Arthur asked.

"Every last one of us," Zack said.

"How can you afford that?"

"Arthur, please," Taliesin said.

"That's all right. It's a natural question." Zack leaned against the sink. "I don't own the building. I only manage it for a friend."

"A rich friend," Kate said.

"The place is a tax-write-off for him or something." He smiled. "And it helps a lot of people. Good karma all around."

"Come on, give these a swipe with the dishcloth," Kate said, handing him a rag. "You, too," she said to Beatrice, who had ceased working to stare at Kate through narrowed eyes.

"Your father," Beatrice ventured timidly. "Would he be the man who was shot in Morocco?"

"He wasn't shot," Kate said, not looking up from her pots.

"But . . ." Beatrice pressed her lips together. "I'm glad he's well," she said finally.

"He's perfect." The dishrag hung suspended in Kate's hand.

Zack smiled sympathetically. "Kate has a hard time believing in miracles."

"It wasn't a miracle. It was a heart attack. The doctors all agree. Someone near him got shot, and blood spattered on my dad's clothes. The shock of it all brought on a mini heart attack."

"That's not what he says."

"Well, he's crazy, all right? My dad's sixty-seven years old, and he's losing it."

"Look, he's not the first person to have seen the Grail. . . ."

"He didn't see any Grail, Zack!" she shouted. "He believes he was healed by something that looks like a nut dish!"

Slowly, Beatrice looked at Taliesin. The old man shook his head in a barely perceptible gesture.

"Hey," Zack said gently, placing his hands on Kate's shoulders. "You're upset. Let me give you a love bomb."

"Oh, get off it, Zack," she snapped, brushing him off. She threw down the dishcloth. "Love bomb," she muttered as she left the room.

Zack shook his head sadly. "I keep telling her, you have to believe in magic for it to work."

"What's a love bomb?" Beatrice asked.

Taliesin held up one finger. "Later, child." His voice was somber. "Tell us first, Zack, about this Grail."

Zack grinned. "Oh, you haven't heard about that? The Holy Grail?"

"I believe I've heard of it. The magic cup that was the object of King Arthur's Quest."

"That's the one. Some people think it's back in circulation."

"Which people?" the old man asked tensely.

Zack spread his hands. "Lots of us. Kate's dad, for one. He was shot point blank in the chest. Four days later he was back in Pennsylvania without a scratch. He says a cup fell on top of him and miraculously closed his wound. The government won't believe him, of course, but that doesn't mean anything."

"Was President Marshall the first to tell you about this . . . article?"

"Oh, man, no," Zack said. "I've been hearing about the Grail for over three years. Nobody knows where it is, exactly, but it's back. And it'll come to light in time for the new millennium."

"What's one got to do with the other?" Arthur asked.

"Everything," Zack said, his eyes sparkling. "The whole planet's changing, all of us who call ourselves human beings. Think about it. We started out as a pretty nasty species, killing everything we didn't understand, even each other. But that's changing. Slowly we're evolving into something different, a different kind of homo sapiens that can look beyond anger and fear and territoriality, into the very heart of God." He looked at each of them in turn.

"That's the purpose of this center, and other places like it. To foster that new kind of human being. And we're everywhere. We're housewives and corporate executives and artists and doctors. . . . All over the place, people are beginning to experience things they'd never dreamed possible—seeing visions, getting messages from spirits, weird things. We're getting in touch with something bigger than ourselves, and a lot of us are being called crazy, and a lot of us *feel* crazy while these things are happening, but they keep on happening. And sooner or later, we're going to realize that we've become something completely different from the human beings we used to be. That's when the Grail will appear."

Taliesin stared at him, blinking, for a moment. "Ah," he said at last, unable to think of anything more eloquent in response to the young man's empassioned soliloquy. "Then the cup—the Grail—may or may not really exist."

"Oh, it exists, all right. It's just a question of when we'll be ready for it."

"I see," Taliesin said, remembering a time long ago, when a great king had turned the Grail away rather than see it misused by mankind.

"May I ask about the love bomb now?" Beatrice whispered, interrupting the old man's thoughts.

Zack laughed. "Sure. Now like I said, you have to believe it'll work for it to work, okay?"

"You're going to give one to me?" she squealed.

"It won't hurt. In fact, it'll feel good. It's *love*."

"All right." She held herself stiff and scrunched closed her eyes, giggling. "I'm ready."

"Here it comes," Zack warned. He nodded vigorously toward Beatrice and grunted. "Did you feel that?"

Beatrice peeked out of one eye. "Oh, you've done it already?"

"Guess she didn't feel it," Arthur commented drily. Taliesin thumped him on his head.

"Let's try again." Undaunted, Zack began hyperventilating noisily.

"It's like . . . gathering all your energy . . . up in a ball . . . and then . . . throwing it at someone," he explained between exertions.

"Just like baseball," Arthur said, ducking out of the way before Taliesin could bonk him again.

"Get ready!"

Beatrice could barely stop herself from jumping up and down.

"Here goes!" Zack screwed his face into a mask of concentration, then threw his arms out in front of him as if pushing a column of air toward Beatrice. When he was finished, he staggered back to the kitchen sink, panting. "There, did you feel that one?"

Beatrice smiled. "Well . . . I think perhaps a little."

"Oh, brother," Arthur mumbled.

"Now throw it back to me," Zack said.

Beatrice giggled.

"Just concentrate," Zack urged. "That's it, close your eyes. Now pull your energy together and—" With a shriek, he flew backward across the room and thudded against the far wall.

"Did you feel it, Zack? Did you . . ." She uncovered her eyes. "Oh, dear."

Zack slapped one hand against the wall and tried to pull himself up, but his legs were too wobbly to support him. "How did you do that?" he whispered.

"I . . . I don't know. I just . . ."

In an instant Zack was flying upward, skittering along the wall like a spider. His arms and legs were outstretched, his face a study in exultation. "It works!" he cried, jubilant. "It really works! Wait'll I tell the other tenants! We've got to do this on TV!"

Taliesin turned to Arthur. "Perhaps you'd better take Beatrice to our rooms," he said quietly. Then, with a twitch of his fingers unnoticeable to anyone, he felt the thickened column of air emanating from the middle of Beatrice's forehead and severed it. Zack slid to the floor.

"Marvellous!" the old man said, beaming, as he helped his host get to his feet. "Zack, you must tell me how you accomplished that!"

CHAPTER TWENTY

"What did you do back there?" Arthur asked when they were both back in the room.

"I honestly don't know," she said, mystified. "I felt this . . . sensation from Zack, a little thing, really, and I tried to throw it back at him . . ." She looked at Arthur. "Something's happening to me," she said softly. "I've always had a sense of things that other people didn't understand, but I thought that was because I was blind. When I got my sight, I thought I'd lose that other sense, whatever it was."

"But you haven't."

"No. It's gotten stronger. "Sometimes I have dreams. . . . Oh, Arthur." Her eyes welled with tears. "Terrible dreams . . ."

Arthur took her hand. "Nightmares can't hurt you," he said.

"They're different from nightmares. I'm not even afraid while they're going on, only after I wake up. In them, an old woman is talking to me."

"Your grandmother, maybe?"

"No, it's not Grams." Beatrice swallowed. "The old woman is me. She's *me*, Arthur, and she's telling me to get ready."

"For what?"

"For death," she whispered.

Taliesin walked in, fuming. "Please don't ever do that again, Beatrice," he said irritably. "Zack was about to have your love bomb performance broadcast on television!" He mopped his forehead with a handkerchief. "It was all I could do to convince him that he, and not you, was the originator of the incident."

He sat down heavily. "Now he believes he's tapped the power of the universe. In celebration of his triumph, he's invited you both to go out for ice cream." He waited for a response. "I say, are you two not feeling well?"

"What do you think, Bea?" Arthur asked. "I haven't had ice cream for a while. How about you?"

She smiled. "Not for years. Grams didn't like it."

"Then we'll go. And don't worry. I won't let anything happen to you."

"Is something going on that I should know about?" the old man asked. "Good heavens, where's the cup? You didn't have it with you at dinner."

"I put it in the flower pot by the window," Arthur said. "I figured it would be safe there, and I wouldn't have to explain to people why I had it hanging from my belt."

Taliesin walked to the window and picked up the plastic flowers. In the base of the pot was the cup. The old man was replacing the flowers when he stopped suddenly and turned around. "You oughtn't have left it here," he said.

"Why, is the cup gone?" Arthur jumped up and hurried to the window. "No, it's right where I left it, see?"

"That is not the point," Taliesin said angrily. "You were responsible for it, and you . . ." He sighed. "Oh, be off with you," he said, shooing them away. "I shall be glad to spend an evening without your adolescent voices dinning in my ears."

"Should we go to Zack's room?"

"Immediately, if you please. And Beatrice, you are not to discuss the event that occurred in the kitchen, understood?"

Beatrice nodded uncertainly. "Of course, Mr. Taliesin," she said. "But why? It seemed harmless enough."

The old man did not answer for a moment. "Because you have a gift," he said at last. "And there are those in the world who will hate you for it."

"The dark magicians," Beatrice breathed. "Yes, I've felt them. Here, in this place." Slowly she walked toward the fireplace and stood facing it. When she spoke again her voice was hoarse and cracked, the voice of an old woman. "One of our own shall kill the gods."

"Bea!" Arthur shouted, but she was already oblivious to his presence.

As soon as the Innocent saw the baby her heart was filled with fear, for she saw the mark of the gods upon its face.

It was a boy, the son of the young bard and the druid priestess who had been selected to represent the Earth goddess during the festival of Beltane. It was a handsome child, with chestnut-colored hair and long fingers. The women who attended his mother cooed with delight as the infant wailed for nourishment. As they laid him upon his mother's breast, the Innocent saw that the child's aura was black, as dark as the void of space between the stars. The void was in his eyes, too, ancient eyes filled with misery. This, she knew, was the embodiment of the gods themselves who knew it was their time to die, and would commit the act upon themselves through this child.

And what of us, she thought. *Must we die, too, your priests and priestesses to whom you have given the gifts of Sight and prophecy? Will all our knowledge be lost?*

But it had not been a question, not really, and she did not wait for an answer because she knew it already. The gods would die, and they would take her and all her kind with them, and the time of magic would pass from the world.

"Bea!" The boy grabbed her shoulders and shook her gently. "Bea, it's Arthur!"

She blinked, startled. "No, I won't talk about the love bombs. I don't know how it happened, anyway. . . ." She looked from Arthur to Taliesin. "I had another lapse, didn't I," she said quietly.

Taliesin nodded.

"They're happening more often. It's as if I'm losing hold of who I am. Sometimes I think I may disappear altogether." She tried to smile, but her fear was evident. "I wish I knew what to do."

"Go have some ice cream," the old man said gently.

As soon as they were gone, Taliesin took the cup out of the flower pot and held it up to the light.

It was perfect, he thought. The shape, the color, even the weight. Only its aura was missing. Only its magic.

He knew immediately that it was a fake. And he had sensed the presence of danger, just as Beatrice had.

From the fireplace.

He walked over to it and knelt, his hands extended over the cold grate. He shivered. There was something wrong here, something that the girl had noticed from the beginning.

He wished he had listened to her then. He had believed, like Zack, that her extraordinary sensitivities were perceiving the atmosphere of a disbanded witches' coven. But what he felt now went far beyond witches. On the far side of this wall was a force so unnatural that it terrified him.

Still on his knees, the old man backed away. He was sweating. *Hurry, Hal,* he pleaded.

At least the children were gone. He had a little time.

The question was, did he possess enough magic to fight whatever was behind the wall?

He breathed deeply, filling himself with energy, becoming still. First the stillness, he told himself. First . . .

Too late, old man, a voice said inside his mind as the brickwork of the fireplace burst apart and Taliesin felt the sting of a needle shooting into his heart.

CHAPTER TWENTY-ONE

Kate sat in a bathtub filled with lilac-scented bubbles. She had brought a book to read—her eyeglasses were perched on the end of her nose—but she couldn't concentrate on the words. All she could think about was the old man's chest. His clothes had been covered with blood, yet there hadn't been a mark on his skin.

Just like her father.

And just like her father, the old man had possessed a cup. She had seen it with her own eyes before the Englishman hid it.

A battered thing without a handle, made of a greenish metal. You know, what it looked like more than anything else was a nut dish.

A nut dish. It was no wonder that no one in the government believed William Marshall.

He'd started raving about the nut dish in the ambulance on the way to the hospital in Tangier, and had never stopped. During his four-day debriefing, he had insisted that he had been healed by a nut dish, even after a psychiatrist explained to the former President that he'd probably never been shot at all, that he had doubtless been sprayed by blood from a bystander and had collapsed from a minor heart attack brought on by shock.

He had been so adamant about the miraculous nut dish that the State Department had been left with no choice but to force Marshall to sign a statement promising never to reveal any aspect of the aborted peace mission to Morocco, so that his insanity would at least be kept from the press. Still, word got around in the foreign service, and "nut dish" jokes circulated around Washington's hipper dinner parties for some time, usually in reference to aging politicians who had lost their edge.

Nevertheless, there were some who did not discount Marshall's story.

Of the four Secret Service agents with him in Tangier, two had been reassigned to duties in remote outposts in Asia. The other two— those who had seen the bullets thud into the former President's chest—were granted early retirement, with honors and a lifelong pledge of secrecy.

The physician who read the results of Marshall's MRI after the nut dish incident also departed government service following a severe reprimand by the hospital's board of directors for losing Marshall's test results and lab work. The images from the MRI, CAT scan, and blood analysis purported to belong to William Marshall were clearly from a much younger man, the board contended. Not only had these tests shown no damage to Marshall's heart, but a healthier heart than the statesman had possessed before he went to Morocco.

No legal action, however, was taken against the doctor, who returned to a thriving private practice in Georgetown. Because of Marshall's deteriorating mental condition, the tests were not repeated.

A Moroccan paramedic, who was a Christian, told his priest that he had heard what he had thought to be the American President's last words: "The cup . . ." The priest had been moved to tears by Marshall's devotion to God.

"This man of peace believed that in the cup of communion was a miracle, a miracle that would save his life," Father Idris said during his homily that Sunday in Marrakesh. "And, in a way, it did."

A couple in the congregation exchanged glances. They had just returned from England, where they had watched a television program titled "Camelot: Legend or History?" on which a sixteen-year-old farm boy named Tom Rodgers had related a vision he'd had—"plain as the nose on me face"—of knights in armor riding out of a castle that grew out of the mist to attend a wizard and a young boy holding a magnificent sword.

"There was a great battle took place, with the knights and them knocking one another about, all over a cup. It was a special cup what heals wounds, and the wizard wanted the boy to have it. But the boy didn't want no part of it, so he didn't, and he made the wizard get rid of it. So in the end it was the wizard called over a great flock of birds, he did, and they carried off the cup for parts unknown."

A well known British psychic, who had also watched the program, dashed off a quick note to a colleague, an American astrologer who had made headlines several years before when it was discovered that the then-First Lady had consulted her about her travel plans.

The astrologer, whose numerous clients included the wives of several Washington dignitaries, related the psychic's message about the TV show to a woman who had attended the first dinner party at which the nut dish incident had been revealed. The woman's husband, who had also heard the remark, was a prominent cardiologist who had recently been told that the tests he had performed on William C. Marshall were inaccurate because they had shown no damage to the patient's heart.

He and his wife had not laughed at the nut dish incident.

Neither had the astrologer.

Nor the couple in the Catholic Church in Marrakesh.

Nor the Moroccan paramedic.

Nor the British psychic, whose transatlantic note had read: *I think the Holy Grail may have surfaced at last.*

Another person had seen the British television program. As Emily Blessing sat in her small London apartment, her leg and hand encased in plaster casts, she watched an English country boy tell the world about a boy he had seen three years ago in a meadow. A boy with a magic cup.

Had Arthur been in the hotel in Tangier? she asked herself for the millionth time. Had Arthur died then? Had Hal?

Six people. Only six people between herself and everything that made life worth living.

She switched off the television and sat motionless in the darkness.

"Six people . . ." she whispered.

* * *

"It's the Grail, sir. You touched the Holy Grail."

Kate had suffered a moment of intense embarrassment when Zack uttered these words. Her father had been President of the United States. He was a nominal Episcopalian, and a practicing pragmatist. He did not believe in ghosts, angels, or the Easter bunny, and certainly not in the Holy Grail.

"I'm telling you the truth," Zack went on earnestly. "There's a lot of talk about it these days. People have—"

"Zack," Kate interrupted with a warning glance. "I think Dad's pretty busy just now. . . ."

"You think that nut dish was the Holy Grail?" Marshall asked, tight-lipped. "As in Jesus Christ and King Arthur?"

Kate sighed. She should never have let Zack come with her. But he had been there when the evening news showed footage of Marshall stumbling backward into the stall, his shirt covered with blood. He had been there during the subsequent frantic telephone calls between Kate, her mother, and the State Department, which seemed not to want to give out any information other than the fact that Marshall was still alive. Zack had been there when Kate finally got word that her father was being flown into Walter Reed Hospital, and drove her there from New York in a rented car so that she would not have to face the trip alone.

Zack had always been there for her, ever since they both started at Columbia as freshmen, and that was why she let him come with her to her parents' house in Pennsylvania for her father's birthday cele-bration.

She had known that Zack would not make a terrific impression on her father. He was not the type of person William Marshall referred to as "good stock." That accolade was reserved for poli-sci majors from wealthy families with a long history of public service. Zack Diamond, a barber's son who had entered Columbia on scholarship at the age of twenty-four to become an English teacher, definitely would not qual-ify. His only saving grace, which Kate had made a point of telling her mother when she called to say she was coming, was that he had no romantic ties with Kate. She did not mention that Zack would have married her in a moment if she ever gave him any encouragement, which she did not.

Even so, she hadn't expected Zack to be quite so goofy. His prat-tlings about peace and love and the universal life force of the cosmos were fine over a joint and a bottle of wine, but she never thought he would bring up his New Age hippie wacko ideas here, in her parents' two-hundred-year-old house.

"Really, Zack," she said, "maybe we should—"

"Will you please be quiet!" her father demanded. "I want to know what the man thinks."

"You do?" The question had been involuntary. It just slipped out of her.

"Yes, I do," Marshall growled. "Every doctor, psychiatrist, military man, and politician I've talked to thinks I'm a lunatic. Maybe it's time I talked to a lunatic."

"Dad!"

Zack laughed. "Sounds like good reasoning to me."

"You believe me, do you?"

"That a cup mysteriously healed a gunshot wound? Yes, sir, I believe you."

"Why?"

"Because I believe in miracles," Zack said gently. "That's the main reason. The secondary reason is because there have been a lot of rumors lately about a magic cup."

"The Holy Grail."

"That's what they say. There's supposed to be a whole cult of people in the Middle East somewhere who claim to have seen it. And there's a kid in England who swears he saw a flock of birds carry it away." He shrugged. "Who knows? Maybe they dropped it on you."

"It would take a hell of a bird to fly from England to Morocco," Marshall said.

At that point Kate's mother had called them in for dinner and, to Kate's relief, the discussion about the nut dish had ended.

She hadn't known that in less than two weeks she would see a cup bring a dead man back to life.

She reached behind her in the bathtub and pulled out a dented metallic object with a greenish cast.

This cup.

She had taken it from the loaner apartment after its three occupants had gone to the dining room. Zack's key had fit the door perfectly.

It resembled a nut dish. It throbbed in her hands.

The Holy Grail, she thought, holding it up to the light.

* * *

Of course it wasn't the Grail. It wasn't possible.

Was it?

Kate lowered the cup into the water and sank further into the tub.

Zack would believe it, of course. Zack believed everything. He was the best friend Kate ever had, but he was a fool.

He had always believed in magic. "Good magic," he called it, as opposed to Black Magic.

As if Zack would know the difference.

"You can be in the middle of good magic and not even know it's happening," he told her after they'd gone to see *Pulp Fiction* at the big Loew's on Times Square. Kate had liked the movie. She found it funny, raunchy, and upbeat, despite its violence. Zack, however, had regarded the film as a milestone in his spiritual growth. He had been transported into a state of bliss.

"Don't you get it?" he shouted on the street, waving his arms wildly. "They were all *agents of God*, every one of them! Ordinary people—crummy people, even—who went in and out of each other's lives thinking they were following their own agendas. But what they were really doing was magic stuff, avenging, destroying, redeeming one another . . . It was like they were angels, even though they looked like street people. I think we're all like that, at least a little bit."

"Angels," Kate said.

"Agents of God. I like that. I really do."

An agent of God, Kate thought, wrapping a towel around her. *Maybe that's what I am.*

She heard the doorbell. "Go away!" she shouted out the bathroom.

"It's Zack. Feel like going for ice cream?"

"I'm in the tub."

"I can wait," Zack offered.

"No, thanks. I'm tired."

"Man, you should have stuck around. We were shooting love bombs—"

"I told you I was tired, Zack. Can you tell me about it tomorrow?"

"Sure, Kate. Hope I didn't disturb you. There was like this mental *juice*—"

"Tomorrow, okay?"

"Hey, no problem."

Why did he have to be such an *ass?*

"Oh, by the way, Aubrey called. He wants you to get back to him. Right away, he said." There was no answer. "Did you hear me, Kate?"

The towel had dropped to the floor. Kate stood naked, her fists clenched at her sides, trying to stem the flow of her tears.

"Kate?"

"Yeah. Okay, thanks," she called out finally.

"It wouldn't hurt if you played a little hard to get," he offered.

A little mirthless puff of air escaped from Kate's lips. Then she crumpled onto a heap, sobbing.

No, she was not an agent of God.

She belonged to Aubrey Katsuleris, and he was the devil.

CHAPTER TWENTY-TWO

Aubrey. Dark, mysterious, handsome, fascinating, evil . . .

Evil, yes. She was sure of that now. Now that there was no way out.

Kate had met him in a course called Medieval Rites and Rituals—Columbia's high-brow offering to students who had been weaned on self-help books and consciousness expansion. Zack had talked her into taking it with him.

A European of indeterminate origin, Aubrey had apparently decided to take the course as a lark while spending a few months in New York. He already knew a great deal about rites and rituals, and his presence in the class transformed it from a dry series of lectures and textbook reading into something resembling a ritual itself.

Aubrey always wore black, and before the first month was out, everyone in the class took to dressing in black. He liked classical music, and soon the weekly Baroque Society concerts, which had never before been well attended, were playing to SRO audiences made up of students from the Medieval Rites and Rituals class.

It was not as if Aubrey organized these outings, or even persuaded anyone to follow his example. On the contrary, he rarely spoke about anything aside from the subject matter of the class. But people flocked around him nevertheless. They were drawn toward him like dust to a powerful electric current. Everyone wanted to be with him, to be like him, to follow him. Within a few weeks, even the professor relinquished his position of leadership in the class in deference to the brilliant young man who seemed to understand the very depths of ancient magic.

Before long the class expanded, first to weekly and then nightly sessions at Aubrey's Fifth Avenue apartment. He was rich, and Kate had gone, like many of the others, just to sample the hundred-year-old brandy he served; but there was always a core of students who followed Aubrey's every word with slavish devotion.

Zack was one of these. He began to quote Aubrey during the course of ordinary conversation. He lost interest in his other classes, spending his days reading about magic and his evenings at Aubrey's apartment. When the Rites and Rituals course ended, Zack dropped out of school altogether and worked at menial jobs, living for the night hours when he and the other acolytes made their pilgrimage to sit at Aubrey's feet.

"But what do you do there?" Kate asked, exasperated.

Zack had smiled. "I'm learning to dream," he said.

Kate was incensed. "Oh, great," she said, "that's just great. Look at where you live, Zack. This place is a hole! You were a year away from getting your degree. You could have been a teacher. Instead, you're—just what is it you're doing now, anyway? Bussing tables?"

"It doesn't matter what I do," he said sagely. "It's what I know."

"For God's sake, listen to yourself!"

"Come with me, Kate. Hear him, and you'll understand."

"I've been there, and I've heard him. Philosophy and history. You've thrown away your future for some sophomoric discussion group!"

"It's different now. Come with me. I promise, your eyes will be opened."

And they were. What she discovered was that the group that followed Aubrey had subtly changed in its makeup from the homogeneous group of dressed-down but unmistakably middle-class college students to a strange mix of men. One was well into his fifties, his thinning hair grown long to comb over a bald spot. Another was a young man in a cheap suit who, when he spoke, exhibited an excess both of bad grammar and bad teeth. There was an elegant fop wearing jewelry, and a number of the sort of men Kate would have been afraid of on a darkened street. There was a dry, academic sort and an actor who claimed to be working in an off-Broadway play.

Kate's first impression was one of utter confusion. What in the world did any of these men have in common?

"What would you like most?" Aubrey said to the group at large.

"He always starts out this way," Zack whispered.

"Anyone? What do you want, Bill?"

The man in the cheap suit jerked a thumb at Kate. "Her," he said. The others laughed.

"Her hair," the elegant one said. "On the condition that her hairdresser dies a slow and painful death." He leaned toward her. "Is that actually a barrette?" Seeing that it was, he withdrew, clucking.

"Harold, what about you?" Aubrey asked the balding man.

"Same as always. This apartment. Or one just like it."

Kate looked around. It was a striking apartment, all right, in a frightening kind of way. All of the surfaces were reflective—black leather furniture, glass tables, a lacquer floor polished to a high gloss, metallic wallpaper. The only items in the room with any texture were the artwork, and most of that was white plaster accented by smears of black or red the exact color of blood. In one corner stood a sculpture of a gardener with a hoe in one hand and his own disembodied head in the other.

Suddenly, coming so swiftly that it shocked her, Kate realized what it was that bound these men together.

They were not nice.

Kate's first reaction to her epiphany was to be ashamed of herself. Throughout her childhood, she had heard her mother rail against people who weren't "nice." Her mother's damning criteria included dressing incorrectly, speaking loudly, espousing political views which were extreme in either direction, rejecting God or embracing Him too fervently, and a host of other innocuous offenses. Once she had finally escaped the suffocating and privileged nest of her parents' home, Kate had made a point of not judging by appearances or first impressions. Or second impressions, for that matter. Kate was determinedly open-minded, and fiercely respectful of others' individuality. Still, there was something in this group beyond bad tailoring and rough laughter that brought bile into her throat.

They were not nice. And Kate was afraid of them.

She saw Aubrey's eyes on her, and felt herself sweating. He smiled.

It was her imagination, of course, but she was certain—no, no, she told herself, she was *imagining*—that Aubrey Katsuleris knew exactly what she was thinking and feeling.

"Tell us, Miss Marshall," he asked politely, "what it is you'd like most in life."

She shrugged disdainfully.

"Please," Aubrey persisted. "There must be something you want so badly that you'd sell your soul for it. Isn't there?"

Yeah, she thought. *I'd like to see Bill get hit by a truck.* "World peace," she said quickly.

Aubrey laughed aloud. The others joined him. They laughed, she supposed, because her wish had been so predictably Pollyanna College Girl. But Aubrey had kept his eyes on her the whole time, and she understood, with a pang of shame, that his laughter had been for a different reason. Aubrey had laughed because he knew that her voiced wish was false.

"Let's get out of here," she muttered to Zack.

"We haven't even started," he protested.

"Then I'll go alone." She stood up, swinging an enormous carryall onto her shoulder. "I've got a test tomorrow," she said, not caring if she sounded convincing or not.

Zack sighed and stood up. "I'll see you home."

"Where do you live?" Aubrey asked.

Zack answered for her. "Near Columbia. It's not a good neighborhood."

Kate was already out the door. "You don't have to walk me back," she said testily when he caught up with her.

"I know. I'd just feel better if I did."

"Suit yourself." She headed for the subway on Sixth Avenue, with Zack trailing silently behind her.

When they got to the station, Zack put two tokens in the style, then walked to the platform with his head hanging and his hands in his pockets.

"I wish you would have given him a chance," he said quietly.

"Those goons? Give me a break."

"Not them, *him.* Aubrey. It's Aubrey I go to see. There's something . . . special about him." He gestured with his hands, creating little imaginary clouds. "Sometimes I almost feel as if he's reading my mind."

Kate inhaled sharply.

The train roared in, and they boarded. It was late enough that there wasn't much of a crowd in their car, so they were able to sit together. "About reading your mind," Kate said slowly. "You don't really think Aubrey can do that, do you?"

Zack smiled, the way he always did, like a little kid. He wasn't handsome, not by any standard, but Zack had the kind of perfectly ingenuous smile usually found only on very good-looking men who know what to do with their faces. "Well, yeah, in a way. It's funny, but he always seems to know what I'm going to say before I say it."

"Oh," she said, relieved. "But he doesn't actually hear your thoughts, or anything like that."

"Of course not. No one can do that. I mean, we're entitled to some privacy, aren't we?"

She hugged him. She wished then, as now, that she could love Zack. Zack was kind and sweet and generous. He would never hurt her, or anyone.

"You don't belong there, Zack. Those men . . ." She shuddered. "They all gave me the creeps."

Zack shrugged. "Jesus didn't just talk to holy people, either."

"Aubrey Katsuleris is not Jesus," Kate said flatly.

Zack stared out the far window of the subway car. "I don't know. It's time for something to happen. You can almost smell it in the air. All over the world, people are beginning to recognize their own inner power. . . ."

"Oh, please. Not that again."

"But it's true. Alternative medicine, astrology, yoga, even martial arts . . . they're all a part of this spiritual awakening. It's as if, after thousands of years, God has come back."

"In the person of Aubrey Katsuleris?" Kate folded her arms in disgust. "Or was it Bill, that cretin whose greatest wish was to dig his dirty fingers into me?"

"I'm sorry about that, Kate."

She deflated, feeling her anger soften. She could never stay mad around Zack. "It's okay. The world's full of people like him. It's just that I can't believe you hang out with him. Or the rest of them. You talk about a spiritual awakening, but did you listen to what they were saying? I want, I want, I want. It definitely was not a spiritual discussion, Zack."

"I know. But it could be. If you wanted the right things."

"Come again?"

"Aubrey tells you how to get what you want."

"Like a self-help program? Positive attitude and that kind of thing?"

"No. He teaches spells."

"What?"

"Magic, Kate. I'm talking about real magic."

"Oh, for God's sake."

"And it works. Harold—the older guy—he's made more than fifty thousand dollars in the stock market in the last two months. Sean, the actor, got a part in a play."

"Those things *happen*. Every day somebody makes money in the stock market."

"And Geoffrey, he's—"

"Let me guess. Geoffrey's the one who wanted my hair. What'd he get, a season ticket to the opera?"

Zack was quiet for a moment. "That was a joke about your hair. What he wanted was money. A million dollars, to be exact. He said that two weeks ago."

"Well? Did he get it?"

Zack nodded. "His uncle died and left it to him."

"Which proves squat."

"His uncle was only forty-five years old," he said quietly. "He died in a freak accident."

Kate felt a shiver of unreasonable fear race down her spine. "It still doesn't mean anything, Zack. Really."

He shrugged.

"Well, why don't you have what you want, then? Whatever that is."

He ran his hand through his hair and stood up. "This is your stop."

Outside, the night air was crisp. A sheen of frost glistened off the cracked sidewalk. Zack breathed deeply. "Sometimes the city actually smells clean," he said.

"What do you want, Zack?" she asked quietly. "I've never known."

He laughed softly. "You," he said. "You're the only thing I've ever wanted. But I'm not going to use a spell to get you." She put her arm around him and rested her head against his chest while they walked.

CHAPTER TWENTY-THREE

Kate picked the bath towel up off the floor and dried her eyes with it. There was no point in crying. Not anymore. She opened her closet and began to get dressed.

Oh, she wished she could have loved Zack.

But she didn't love Zack, couldn't love him.

She could only love men like Aubrey.

Kate had believed that she fell in love with Aubrey the first time she'd gone to bed with him; but the truth was, it happened before that.

It happened when she first saw him kill.

It had seemed like an accident.

The cab had come skidding around the corner just as Kate and Zack began to cross it. Zack threw his arms around her and pushed her back to the curb. She dropped her handbag.

"Zack! Hey, Zack!" The cab was screeching to a stop, and the man was already halfway out the door. "Wait a second!"

Zack narrowed his eyes to see down the dimly lit street. "It's Bill," he said.

"Oh, great." Kate moved to pick up her bag, but Zack threw her backward again. She landed flat on her rear with a shriek as the second vehicle came by in the opposite direction.

It was a noisy, primer-spotted Chevy half-ton with a missing headlight. It must have been doing fifty when it hit Bill. He flew up in the air like a tumbler toward the streetlamp, and for a moment the stark light captured perfectly the man's expression of utter surprise. The truck never stopped.

When it had roared away, the street became so quiet that the squeak of the cab door opening sounded loud. Bill, wearing a trenchcoat over his cheap suit, lay in a weird position on the asphalt, his eyes open and crossed, trickles of blood oozing out of his mouth and ears. The cabbie got out and looked around, his arms rising in a gesture of helplessness.

Kate's bag had been run over. Its contents—a broken lipstick, three notebooks, a cassette tape of B. B. King, and a thick wad of assorted papers—were spilled on the street. For a second or two, nothing moved; then a gust of wind sent the papers whirling. One of the loose pieces of paper blew against Bill's body and stuck there.

Zack was the first to venture near the corpse. He told the cabbie to call the police, talked with the officer, gathered up Kate's things and stuffed them back into her bag while the ambulance arrived, walked her to her apartment, made her a cup of tea, and kissed her on the cheek before leaving.

All Kate could do was remember something she had thought sometime during the evening:

I wish Bill would get hit by a truck.

"He was hit by a truck," she had said, first to the policeman and then to Zack over her tea. It was the only sentence she'd spoken since witnessing the accident.

But it hadn't been an accident. She knew that, even then.

And when Aubrey came to her later that night she opened her door to him, staring at him with wide, unfocused eyes, her spine trembling.

"You did it, didn't you?" she whispered hoarsely. "You weren't driving, but you did it all the same."

Aubrey had smiled, a little crook of his lips. "What else do you want, Kate?" he asked. Then he took her in his arms and though Kate was shaking so hard that her cotton pajamas were fluttering, she pressed her lips against his and felt the wild violence of his power.

"I hate you," she said, trying to pull away.

"No." He pinned her arms at her sides. "No, you don't hate me. You fear me. And yourself."

"Let me go!"

Aubrey laughed, raising his hands in surrender. She spat in his face. He slapped her. She hit him back, so hard that her palm stung. Then he moaned softly and nuzzled his face against her neck. She wrapped her legs around him and cried out with pleasure.

He took her on the floor with no more words, nothing but his skin soft over hard muscle, his dark hair falling over her eyes, his power, his power pumping into her like a heartbeat, pumping, shooting into her, skewering her like a bug.

No words at all.

When it was over, when she lay alone on the floor of her apartment, she cried.

She didn't see Aubrey again for two weeks. For those two weeks she never left her apartment. She missed two important tests, and didn't care. She ate nothing. She forgot how to use a comb. She never changed her clothes.

The phone rang often—it was Zack, she knew—but she didn't answer it. When Zack came by to see if she was all right, she only opened the door a crack, enough to tell him that she wanted to be left alone.

"You don't look good, Kate," he said through the narrow opening.

"Yeah, well, I caught a cold or something."

"I'll bring you some soup from the deli down the street."

"No, thanks. I just want to get some sleep."

"Please, Kate. I know you're bothered by the accident we saw. I am, too. We should talk about it. It would be good—"

"No, it wouldn't." She closed the door.

Nothing would ever be good again. Because it wasn't the accident that was troubling her. That was an incident out of the past, no more real to her than an episode from a TV series. In her mind she replayed the scene over and over, seeing Bill tumbling effortlessly through the air, his cheap suit shiny in the light of the street lamp. And dubbed over it was the sound of her own voice:

I wish Bill would get hit by a truck.

That was the part that made her want to scream every hour of the day. That she had wished, during a wanton moment, that a man would die, and he did.

It didn't matter that the idea obsessing her was impossible. Her reason told her that what had happened was simply a coincidence, and held no more meaning than the bald guy making money in the stock market or the actor getting a part in a show. Her reason was baffled by her reaction to an unfortunate but patently accidental occurrence.

But Kate's reason had not looked into Aubrey's eyes. Another part of her mind, darker, knowing, had connected with the frightening being that was Aubrey Katsuleris. Connected with him, body and soul.

What else do you want, Kate?

That was a tease. He knew perfectly well what she wanted, what she needed in order to keep living.

She needed him.

For two weeks she fought the need, but there was no point in it. During their lovemaking, Aubrey had planted a seed in her womb—not the seed of a child, but of some unnamed evil that she felt daily growing inside her like a dark flower unfolding, taking her over. It, the evil, blossoming thing, was what brought her back to Aubrey's apartment, her face flushed with shame, her body trembling with raw yearning.

Zack was delighted to see her. Cheerfully he introduced her to a new member of the group, a young, light-haired thug whose fingers twitched nervously throughout the evening. Three times Kate caught the man glancing over at her, but as soon as her eyes met his, he averted his gaze.

Zack left the group early. Afterward, Aubrey recited some foolish-sounding incantations which the men repeated. Kate sat silently, thinking only of the man with the twitching fingers.

"He's the one you sent to kill Bill, isn't he," Kate asked Aubrey later, after they had made love.

"Hold still." He was braiding her hair, entwining rosebuds into the thick, silky brown rope that hung down her back.

Sitting naked on a chair in front of a mirror, she spoke to his image behind her.

"Is that something they have to do to enter your inner circle? Murder for you?"

"Don't be boring." He caressed her breasts with one of the roses. "I just give them what they want." Kate shivered, feeling the evil flower within her growing, reaching out again to Aubrey's hot darkness, hating herself for wanting him so.

"Did Bill say he wanted to die?"

"Of course he didn't say it. In the beginning, they always say they want money."

She turned to face him. Some of the buds fell out of her hair. "Then he didn't want to die at all. It was just you."

"Why would I want Bill dead? I couldn't have cared less about him one way or the other." He sighed and turned away from her. "You're too talkative. I've lost interest."

Aubrey walked, naked, over to an easel with a half-finished oil painting on it. Thoughtfully he picked up a long brush and daubed spots of yellow on it. Not very much, and not in any discernable pattern; just enough to make the painting scream.

"The truth is, Bill was a heroin addict. He had AIDS. He was going to be sent to prison for shooting two people in a gas station last year. At thirty-one, his life was over. He was terrified of suffering a lingering death behind bars."

"So you had him murdered."

Aubrey took another brush and coated it with red paint. "It wasn't really for him. That is, I wouldn't have bothered to have him killed if you hadn't wanted it." He turned around, grinning. "Poor Bill. All the time, he thought he was going there to kill Zack."

Kate's mouth was suddenly dry. "Zack?"

"Without Zack, Bill assumed he would be able to rape you without interference," Aubrey said casually. "Bill believed he wanted that at the moment, if you'll recall." With four strokes, he created a crimson bird, at once perfect and evil. "Fortunately for you, his death wish was stronger."

As Kate watched the painting take shape, she thought, *This is unreal. It wouldn't have made the slightest difference to him if Bill had lived and Zack had been killed. Or me . . .*

Aubrey laughed softly. "Of course it would have made a difference. I sent the other, didn't I? Bill owed him a debt, incidentally, which he wasn't about to repay, under the circumstances. Everything worked out well."

"Stop it!" Kate shrieked, slapping her hands over her ears. "You can't know what I'm thinking! You can't!" She bolted out of bed and pulled on her jeans. "I'm calling the police."

"Oh? And what will you tell them? That a hit-and-run was engineered by a mindreading acquaintance of yours?" His laughter rang in the room.

She covered her face with her hands. Aubrey walked over to her slowly and stroked the little wisps of hair on her forehead. "Kate," he said as if he were speaking to a pouting child. "It's understandable that you would be confused now. This is a time of transition for you. It will pass. You'll grow to like who you are. What you are," he added in a whisper.

"What does that mean?"

He was silent.

"Answer me," she screamed. "What have you done to me?"

"Shhh. There's no need for histrionics." He pulled her back on the bed, kissing her, soothing her as if he were comforting a child. "You're lovely, Kate. Your nipples are lovely. I used to watch you on television, playing with the royal dog, or whatever that thing was, and I'd imagine what sort of nipples you'd have. . . ."

"What have you done?" she repeated between clenched teeth.

With his finger, he drew a reversed five-pointed star on her belly. "I've taken your soul," he said, regarding her steadily. "Do you understand what a soul is?"

She heard her breath come out in a quiver.

"It's the part of you that's eternal," he said softly. "The part that is reborn in life after life. Each life offers its own obstacles—troubles, tragedies, suffering, what have you. None of it is very pleasant. But slowly, as people learn their lessons, as it were, in a nearly endless series of paltry existences, their souls grow a little older, a little wiser, until at last they no longer have to look forward to another horrid seventy or eighty years of constant tribulation. They finally become free . . . but at the cost of countless agonizing existences."

He retraced the pentacle on her belly until it showed red against her skin. "I've saved you that effort, Kate. Without a soul, you will never have to be reborn again. This lifetime will be your last. And in it, all your desires—everything you wish for—will be yours for the taking."

Kate sat up slowly. "Is this supposed to be some kind of joke?"

He shook his head. "No, Kate. Why should I joke with you?"

"But you can't . . . just take my *soul*. Just like that."

"I didn't just take it. I gave you something in exchange for it. A wish, remember? I asked you if there was anything you wanted so badly that you would sell your soul for it. And you answered—"

She backed off the bed. "You're crazy."

"Am I?"

The mark on her belly burned. "What about Zack?" she demanded shrilly. "Are you going to talk him into believing you've taken his soul, too?"

Aubrey crossed his arms over his chest and assessed her, his eyes smiling. "That ridiculous creature really does mean something to you, doesn't he?" he declared with admiration. "Most women in your situation would only be concerned for themselves."

"Yeah, well, let's just say that Zack's more easily convinced than I am, and I don't want you messing with his head."

"Wish it, Kate," he said, taunting her.

"I wish you'd drop dead!"

He looked into her eyes. "You shouldn't have done that, my darling." His face went ashen. With a small sound, he sank to the floor.

"Aubrey?"

His breathing was labored.

"Oh, God, what's happening?" she squeaked. "Aubrey!"

Suddenly he sat up and grabbed her, laughing in big booming peals as he threw her on the bed. "*That* won't work," he said.

She shoved him backward. "I almost believed you."

Gently he pulled the braid of her hair forward to rest upon her breast. "Just be careful what you wish for, Kate," he said.

It was raining on the way home from Aubrey's apartment, and by the time Kate reached her own walk-up in Morningside Heights, she was chilled to the bone.

What I'd give for a tub of hot water to be waiting for me, she thought.

It was.

The first thing she saw when she opened the door was the carpet, steaming like a primeval swamp. Some books lying beside the couch were soaked through with moisture. Dark stains crept halfway up her beanbag chair. From the bathroom, she heard the sound of running water.

"Oh, shit," she muttered, her feet making squishing sounds on the saturated rug.

By the time she reached the bathroom, her feet were burning. The hot water had loosened the floor tiles. The wallpaper had peeled completely off, and floated in loose rolls on the two-inch-deep water. Slabs of plaster had fallen from the ceiling into the tub, where they lay surrounded by a colony of dead cockroaches. The tap, when she was able to grasp it with the aid of a towel, spun around uselessly while the water continued to pour out of the faucet.

Finally Kate called the superintendent, who called a plumber, who turned off all the water to Kate's bathroom for the next five days.

"All I wanted was a bath," she complained as she carried her eighteenth bucket to the kitchen sink.

By midnight she had finished the monumental job of mopping the floor and getting the living room carpet down to the sidewalk. Exhausted and sweating, she tumbled into bed, tearing off her soggy clothes on the descent. As she was drifting off to sleep, she saw the star Aubrey had scratched into the skin of her abdomen. It had raised in a red welt radiating out from her navel.

"What a jerk," she mumbled, uncertain whether she was referring to Aubrey or herself. She had lost two weeks of her life mooning over a one-night stand that had happened to take place on the same evening she had witnessed a terrible accident. In her freaked-out condition, she had put the two events together to create some kind of wicked fantasy, and Aubrey Katsuleris was ready and willing to play his part in it to the hilt.

"Looks like a goddamn tattoo," she said, touching the hot red mark. She thought briefly—very briefly—about getting up to swab it with peroxide, but discarded the idea. If it got infected, it would be no more than she deserved for letting anyone doodle on her body.

"I wish he'd just go away," she said. Three seconds later, she was asleep.

"Kate!"

Zack's pounding on her door woke her up.

She checked the alarm clock. Nine thirty. She'd already missed two of her classes. "Oh, God," she moaned. She padded to the door, yawning.

"I've brought coffee," Zack said, exactly as if he had brought the crown jewels of England. "And news."

"The coffee first, please." She led him across the bare floor to her tiny dining table.

"What happened to your rug?"

"I had a flood." She snapped the plastic lid off one of the containers. "It's funny, in a grisly sort of way. I was coming home late yesterday, wishing . . ." She stared into her coffee. "Wishing . . ."

"What is it?"

She blinked. "Nothing."

"So what were you wishing?"

"I forget." She waved at the air in front of her. "It wasn't important. Well, what's your news?"

Zack took a piece of paper out of his shirt pocket. "Aubrey sent me a telegram."

She felt her bowels constrict. "Listen, Zack, I don't think you should see him any more. I know I've said that before, but now—"

"Relax. He's moved to Morocco."

"What?"

I wish he'd just go away.

"He left this morning. That's what the telegram says." He began to unfold it, but Kate was choking on her coffee. He jumped up and smacked the middle of her back. "You all right?"

She held up a hand for him to stop. "He's gone? Just like that?"

"Yeah. Just boogied on out without saying a word. Weird, isn't it?"

You don't know how weird, she thought. She looked up at him. "Zack," she said softly, "if you could have everything you wanted just by wishing for it, what would that be?"

"What?" He cocked his head.

"Just . . . tell me, all right?"

"Well . . ."

"Besides me."

He smiled. "Okay. Actually, it's something I just thought of last night. And the damndest thing—"

"What is it?" she demanded impatiently. "The wish."

Zack folded his hands primly in front of him. "I've been thinking that I'd like to open a place for people to live."

"An apartment building?" she asked, surprised. "You never seemed like the landlord type."

He laughed. "This would be a different kind of building. A place for people who work full time at helping others. There's a lady a few blocks from here who goes around to restaurants in midtown in her spare time collecting leftover food that she distributes to homeless shelters. And I know a couple that does errands for old people who can't get around very well. They only do it on weekends, though, because they have to work the rest of the week. I was thinking that if there were a place for people like that to live without paying rent or buying food, they could really do a lot of good."

"A rent-free apartment building," Kate mused skeptically.

"Not an apartment building. A center. A center for agents of God."

Tears came to Kate's eyes. Aubrey hadn't gotten to him, after all. And never would. "Oh, Zack, I hope . . . no, I *wish* you get a place like that." She closed her eyes and spoke deliberately: "I wish you could have a place to show people how to be agents of God." Then she opened her eyes and smiled at him. "It'll happen, Zack. You'll see."

"It already has." He spread the telegram out flat. "Aubrey's bought an apartment building in midtown, and he wants me to manage it. He says I can do anything I want with it, as long as I leave the basement for him. I guess he'll want to store stuff there. The place doesn't even have to make money—he'll pay me anyway." He could barely contain his excitement. "Isn't that great?"

Kate felt as if the wind had been knocked out of her. "Yeah," she said in a whisper. "Great."

CHAPTER TWENTY-FOUR

That had been more than three years ago.

Kate left her apartment unseen and headed across town. It was a warm night, and the neighborhood smelled of food from thousands of apartments with their windows left open after supper.

The cup was in her handbag. It thumped against her with every step. Even through the leather, she could feel its strange vibration, throbbing, throbbing like a distant heartbeat.

It's not the Grail, she told herself as she crossed Eighth Avenue.

It couldn't be, because Aubrey had made an exact duplicate of it, which she had placed in the old man's room when she took the original. If the Grail even existed, how would anyone—even Aubrey—know precisely what it looked like, down to the last dent and discoloration?

The thing was probably some valuable artifact Aubrey had seen in a museum somewhere, or in a book. Something that had been photographed from every angle. For all she knew, the old man had stolen it himself. Or maybe he didn't know how much it was worth, and simply liked how it looked.

God, she wished . . .

No. She didn't wish anymore.

She had at least learned that much.

With Aubrey's disappearance, the group which had met at his apartment disbanded, Zack took over the maintenance of the building on West 55th, and Kate moved in. For three years, life had almost returned to normal. Almost, because Kate had never again been entirely certain whether Aubrey had told her the truth about her soul or not.

She wished a pizza would appear one evening when she was too tired to go out, and one was mistakenly delivered to her apartment; but it was covered with anchovies and green peppers. On another occasion, she wished for an A on an exam for which she was woefully unprepared, and the professor's assistant, a geeky graduate student who was grading the papers, offered her one—on the condition that she permit him to "tutor" her in his apartment.

So it seemed to go. Each time something she wanted came to her, the gift was somehow twisted, tainted. She had longed for a pair of red boots in Macy's window and had paid two hundred dollars for them before discovering a flaw in their construction that cut her toe. She had helped a lost kitten find a home with a cat-loving friend, only to learn that the animal had feline leukemia and had given the disease to her friend's other pets. She had even wished for world peace, and was delighted when the evening news reported that, for the first time in more than twenty years, not a single shot had been fired in battle that day. Unfortunately, on the same day, a civilian in New Jersey had taken an automatic rifle into a crowded shopping mall and opened fire, killing seventeen innocent people.

And so she stopped wishing. At least she thought she had.

When she heard that her father had been shot in Tangier, Kate was tormented for days by thoughts that she might have inadvertently caused an assassination attempt on her father half a world away. Even after she learned that he was unhurt except for the residual aftereffects of a heart attack, she ceaselessly went over every moment of every day in recent memory to see if she had done something, said something . . . *wished* something . . .

"Kate, your wishes aren't coming true any more than anyone else's," Zack said gently on the drive home from her parents' house after she finally confessed to him the torment she'd been suffering. "Use your reason."

"Reason! You're the one who thinks the nut bowl Daddy saw was the Holy Grail!"

Zack laughed. "I told him the truth. There are stories about a cup that heals wounds, and miracles do happen. If your dad was shot and a cup healed him, I'm ready to believe that was a miracle. But not everything is. If you've got a cold and you recover, that's not a miracle. You know what I'm saying?"

"My red boots?" Kate asked sheepishly.

"Exactly. Lots of people buy shoes that hurt their feet. Not me, of course." He pointed to the ratty sneakers he'd been wearing for the past four years. Kate smiled. "And lots of stray cats are sick. And even I was bound to get a job sometime."

She leaned her head against his shoulder while he drove. "I always thought you were the crazy one," she said.

"At one time, you might have been right," Zack said. "Like those nights at Aubrey's. I really thought he was teaching us how to make our dreams come true by using magic."

"Wasn't he?"

"No! That's what I'm trying to tell you. He'd let everyone go on about all the stuff they wanted, and then he'd give us spells to make them happen, and we believed, we believed, we believed."

"Well? Did they ever come true?"

He shrugged. "Sometimes. Remember Geoffrey? The one who inherited a million dollars? He used the money to open a club. It's called Sparkles."

"I've heard of that."

"Who hasn't? It's the hottest place in New York. And Sean, the actor—"

"I just saw him on TV! He won a Tony award. I thought he looked familiar . . ." Her forehead creased. "So the spells must have worked."

Zack laughed. "Unless you consider the others. Have you ever heard of them again?"

"No, but . . . What are you getting at?"

"The fact that some of their wishes came true, and some didn't. Just like the rest of the population."

"Huh?"

"That's the way life works. Sometimes you get what you want, sometimes you don't. But what I'm saying is, it's the *belief* that keeps you going. I think that's what Aubrey was trying to show us. And we all probably would have come to that understanding, if he hadn't left so suddenly."

"But I wished for that, too. For him to leave."

"Yeah. You wished he'd leave. And I wished he'd stay. Either way, life went on. Here we are. Maybe that was part of the lesson."

"He told me he'd taken my soul."

Zack ruffled her hair. "Let me tell you a story," he said gently. "It's a zen koan about a student who walked miles through the forest to spend a day with his teacher. By the time the session was over, the sun had gone down, and the student was afraid he wouldn't be able to find his way home.

" 'Why do you hesitate to leave?' the teacher asked.

"The student answered, 'Because it's dark outside.'

"So the teacher gave him a candle. The student thanked him and began to leave. Then, when he reached the doorway, the teacher blew out the flame."

Zack sat back and drove in silence.

"Well?" Kate asked. "What happened then?"

"Nothing. The student understood, and bowed to his teacher for making him understand."

"Understand what? That he had to spend the night there?"

"No. The student went home."

"Did the teacher at least give the guy a match?"

Zack laughed. "No."

"That's the dumbest story I ever heard! What point is there in giving somebody a candle if you're going to blow it out before he can use it?"

"He didn't really need it, Kate. That's the point. The candle made the guy believe he could find his way home. So once he had that belief, he didn't need the candle anymore. It's like Dumbo and the magic feather. Don't you see? Aubrey was trying to teach you the same lesson he was trying to teach the group—that the magic we're looking for is inside us."

"He didn't take *your* souls," Kate argued.

"And he didn't take yours, either," Zack said, smiling. "He was just blowing out your candle."

She inhaled sharply. "So that I would . . ."

"So that you would believe in yourself," Zack finished for her. "Aubrey was telling you that you didn't need him anymore." He kissed the top of her head. "And then he left."

Kate thought about that for a long time. Finally she sighed. "You make everything seem okay."

"Everything *is* okay," he said.

"Even Aubrey Katsuleris."

Zack grinned. "An agent of God. Just like the rest of us."

"I wish I could believe that." Kate sat up with a start. "Oh, no, I mean—"

Zack laughed. "Try wishing for another pizza. I'm getting hungry."

Two weeks later, Aubrey came back into her life.

Zack brought him. "Look who just breezed into town," he said.

Kate could only stare.

"Aubrey wants to do some work in the basement," Zack said.

Neither of them said anything.

Zack turned to Aubrey. "You're so famous now, having your studio here will put our center on the map."

Again, there was no response. Kate and Aubrey were doing battle in each others' eyes.

Zack cleared his throat. "Well, I guess I'll leave you two alone. I've got some things to do." Quietly, he let himself out.

When the door closed, Aubrey spoke. "Did you miss me, Kate?" he asked softly.

"No."

"Good." He took her in his arms, and for Kate, it was as if no time at all had passed since the last time the evil bloom inside her had stirred. He pressed her downward to the floor, to the same place she had submitted to him the first time, and with a moan of shame, she opened her legs to him.

CHAPTER TWENTY-FIVE

"Kate," he whispered afterward, inhaling the fragrance of her hair. "Sweet, sweet Kate."

"Get out." She pulled herself up, straightening the rumpled folds of her skirt. He had not bothered to undress her.

"Don't you like my company?" he asked, smiling.

"Please leave," she whispered miserably.

"Zack tells me you're concerned about your soul." She turned away, but he grabbed her by her hair and forced her to face him. "It's a little late for that, Kate. That part of you belongs to me."

"Zack . . . says . . ." She squeezed her eyes shut, trying to remember. "He says that you were trying to teach me . . . to believe in myself. . . ." Tears coursed down her cheeks. "You blew out the candle . . . so that I could find my way in the dark." Still weeping, she began to laugh, high and hysterical. "He thinks you're an agent of God." She shrieked with wild laughter.

"An agent of God?" The idea amused him. "Well, perhaps I am, at that." They laughed together, two hyenas crouching on the floor.

Then Kate started to scream. She screamed without point or purpose, shrieking the sound of her unnameable fear and her knowledge that all along, Aubrey had been telling her the truth.

Her soul was gone.

Calmly Aubrey locked his hands around her neck until the scream quieted to a gurgle of panic. His nostrils flared. With his thumbs he stroked the tender indentation at the base of her throat. "Does death excite you?" he asked conversationally. "Of course it does. Death and sex—both are natural and fundamental to all living creatures. Yet for human beings, these two occurrences are at the vortex of our fears. They have become the origin and consequence of sin, inextricably entwined. They make up the forbidden zone of our psyches, that place of guilty delight where you've found such contentment, Kate."

Kate kicked her legs futilely. Her eyes rolled back in her head.

"If I were to crush the life out of you, I expect I would experience a magnificent orgasm."

With a smile of regret, he released her. The air rushed into her lungs with a honk. For several minutes she choked and coughed.

"Your nose is running," he said, dabbing at it with a linen handkerchief. "Now be a good girl and keep quiet for a bit. I have to talk to you, and you have to listen. Understood?"

Kate's chest heaved once, then she nodded.

"I suppose I should begin by telling you that I've been asked to kill your father. A political matter, you understand. Now, now—" He held up an index finger. "You're not going to speak, are you?"

Kate felt the muscles in her neck cording, but she forced herself to lean back against the wall.

"That's fine. You're doing perfectly," he said. "Needless to say, I haven't killed him yet. And I won't, so long as you cooperate with me in another matter." He raised his eyebrows. "Yes?"

"What . . . what is it?" she asked, her voice raspy and hoarse.

"A simple task. In three days' time a ship, the *Comanche*, will dock at the Port Authority in the early afternoon. There will be three stowaways on board that ship, an old man and two children, a boy and a girl, both young teenagers. The old man and the girl will be killed. You are to bring the boy back to the center."

A look of horror crossed Kate's face.

"The boy will have in his possession a cup. I want you to get it from him, preferably without his knowledge. You may replace it with this." He took a knobby, spherical metal object from his jacket pocket. "They're identical." He pressed it into her hands.

"The cup," she said, the words little more than puffs of air.

"Incidentally, if he doesn't have it, he'll want to go back to the bodies. . . ."

"Stop it!" She slapped her hands over her ears, letting the cup drop to the floor.

Aubrey yanked her hands away. ". . . He'll want to go back to the bodies to retrieve the cup," he said deliberately. "If that is the case, let him." Aubrey let go of her hands. "As soon as you're in possession of the cup, bring it to me immediately. I'm back in my old apartment. Now, repeat back to me what you're going to do."

For a moment, Kate said nothing. He slapped her.

"I'll tell you what I'm not going to do. I'm not going to watch you kill two—"

He slapped her again. "I can be at your parents' house in an hour," Aubrey said.

"So can the cops."

He laughed softly. "How sheltered you must have been during your White House years," he said.

Kate knew what he meant. She remembered her mother's constant worry whenever Marshall had to travel as President, worry so severe that on several occasions the First Lady was rendered too sick to leave her bed. She had begged her husband not to seek a second term, and though she pretended to be disappointed when he lost the election, it was obvious to everyone close to Mrs. Marshall that she was secretly ecstatic about the outcome.

Even after Marshall ostensibly retired from public life, his safety was never a thing taken for granted. Secret Service agents continued to tail the family for five years, until Marshall could no longer bear their presence in the small town where he had grown up. Kate's mother had wanted them back after the incident in Morocco, but Marshall had been adamant on that count.

"Four Secret Service men were with me in Marrakesh, and they didn't do a damn bit of good," he argued. "If someone really wants me dead, nothing we do is going to stop them."

He was right, Kate knew. She could alert the local police, the FBI, and the Secret Service that her father's life was in danger, and it wouldn't make any difference. If someone wanted William Marshall dead, it was just a matter of time.

And accusing Aubrey Katsuleris before the fact would elicit nothing but scorn from the authorities. Aubrey was a famous man. Kate was just another woman he'd slept with and then abandoned. Even Zack would tell them that.

"Did you shoot my father in Tangier?" she asked.

"Please don't bore me with tiresome questions, Kate."

She set the cup down. "How do I know you—or someone else—won't kill my dad after I bring you the cup?"

"Because it's no longer necessary that he die. The peace mission in Tangier was thwarted, and your father's reputation is in disgrace. My employers are content."

"And you?"

"I will be, too. After I get the cup." He touched her face. "And so will you."

Only if you die by tomorrow, she thought.

"Now, Kate, that isn't nice." He stood up. "But you'll change your mind, I promise you."

"How are you going to arrange that?" she asked drily.

Aubrey raised his eyebrows. "Have you made any wishes?" When she didn't answer, he smiled. "They didn't turn out the way you'd thought, did they," he said with mock pity. "That's because you haven't yet accepted the loss of your soul. But you will. After you get me the cup, it will be easier for you." He pulled her upright. "I'll help you to embrace the darkness, Kate," he said softly. "I'll take you fully into the forbidden zone."

He kissed her then, and her blood coursed wildly, her arms longed to encircle him, the place between her legs grew damp. She hated herself.

Woodenly, she opened the door.

"It will get easier," Aubrey said in parting.

That night Kate tried to pray. It was difficult. She hadn't prayed since her mother had stopped dragging her to church for appearances' sake, and even before that, she had never prayed with any conviction.

"Please help me," she began. "Let this all be some kind of nightmare. Let my family be safe. Let Aubrey leave me alone. . . ."

Mother bring us life from death

". . . alone . . ."

Mother bring us life from death

She shook her head, trying to rid herself of the strange words that rang in her mind. "Don't let anybody get killed. . . ."

Life from death
Life from death

She buried her face in her hands and wept.

Mother bring us life from death . . .

Aubrey shook with rage and contempt. The ancient gods were calling. After sixteen hundred years, the useless deities of the druids were crying for life. They screamed so loudly that even ordinary people like Kate could hear them.

The blood with which he had smeared his body—a vagrant's blood, spilled with a sharp knife in a remote area of Central Park—rose rank to his nostrils. Aubrey sat in a pool of darkness within the basement of the building where Zack and Kate lived.

The Center for Cosmic Consciousness—Aubrey had nearly laughed aloud when Zack proudly announced his plans for the place. If the fool had possessed any Cosmic Consciousness at all, he would have known what sort of spirits dwelled here.

In the earth beneath the building's foundation were scattered the ashes of a colony of druid priests and priestesses, killed by the first black magicians in Europe. These had learned their art from masters in Arabia, who had learned from the Egyptians, who had been practicing magic for three thousand years.

Beside him in the circle of darkness which Aubrey had created with his mind was an ancient femur, grown brown and brittle with age. It was the leg bone of one of the druids, a necessary relic to conduct the rites of his order. Saladin himself had brought it to New York from the forgotten island of Mona, where the massacre had taken place.

According to him, the initiator of the holocaust that wiped out the druids had himself been one of their number, raised among the holy ones since birth. His name, Saladin explained, had been Thanatos. Aubrey had been given his name at his own initiation into the coven in Tangier as a mark of honor.

To whom did that first Thanatos give his soul, Aubrey had often wondered, this druid who, in the midst of a community devoted to serving the ancient Celtic gods, had discovered the bright flower of evil within himself?

What did he get in exchange for his monumental betrayal?

Perhaps it was the sheer thrill of killing. Aubrey understood that. Murder brought with it a certain exultation. The moment of inflicting death was an evanescent treasure to be savored like fine wine, or the scent of sex.

But there must have been something more to make this born druid turn against his own, to destroy the seat of his religion.

Whatever it was, Aubrey's namesake had done well, this ancient ancestor. By killing the druids, he had destroyed their gods. Their power was gone, even in the hidden repositories their followers had set aside to keep their magic until they rose again.

Even in the sword of Excalibur, now reduced to a handful of metal fragments.

No, those gods, for all their noise, could do nothing to Aubrey. They were powerless, their droning song no more than ancient echoes of their death-cry.

Holding the druid's leg bone in both hands, Aubrey turned his mind into the darkness. He produced an image for himself of the old man. There was not much to begin with; Aubrey had only caught a glimpse of him before he disappeared into the hold of the ship with the two children. But he would try: First, the eyebrows. Yes, he had a good fix on the eyebrows, bushy, white, high-arched. And the eyes, blue, intelligent, now an aqualine nose, long and aristocratic, the nose of a nobleman. Bony fingers, long and graceful, yes, yes, it was coming . . . The fingers played an instrument, they plucked strings, and now Aubrey heard his voice. Ah, it was young; the old man was remembering his youth. Good, good. He was singing.

> *A maid from the north sighed from her sad heart*
> *And the wind grieved low to mourn*

Aubrey sighed in disappointment. The old sod must be feebleminded, or drunk.

"*Think*, fool. I want to know who you *are*."

He was no one of consequence, most likely. A kindhearted stranger whose help the American enlisted to keep the boy out of harm's way at the dock in Tangier. The old coot had probably been more surprised than the rest of them when the ship he'd been hiding in with the children pulled out of harbor.

Still, it was best to be sure. From Saladin's private writings, Aubrey knew who the boy was, and knew it was of utmost importance not to kill him yet. Aubrey would not repeat Saladin's mistake of taking the cup while Arthur Blessing still held the spirit of the Forever King.

He was quite sure of what to do with the boy.

The girl was another matter entirely. She had merely stumbled into Arthur—if the workings of fate could be couched in such terms—and had delivered the cup to him, however accidentally.

So the girl had fulfilled her function in the scheme of things. She was expendable.

And Hal Woczniak was probably dead, although Aubrey had heard no reports of a body being found in the waters around the docks in Tangier. The bullet-ridden corpse of an American ex-FBI agent would have attracted some attention, and Aubrey had eyes and ears within the Moroccan government as well as as the police department. Nevertheless, the current had been strong that day, and the boy may well have washed out to sea to become a meal for the fish.

In any case, the American was not in New York with the boy. The old man was.

Zack had told him the stranger's name was . . . Taliesin. Taliesin, yes, like the ancient bard.

Aubrey added this piece of information to the picture forming in his mind. Taliesin . . . and he was singing ancient songs. The tonality of the music was . . .

Suddenly the melody stopped. The old man was thinking of something else.

"Yes, yes," Aubrey purred. "Let me in, Taliesin. Bring me into that foggy old head of yours."

Suddenly there was an image, scattered as a dream, of twelve arrows streaking across the sky above a castle on whose grounds a lone figure walked.

He is your destiny, a voice speaks to Taliesin.

And he follows that image blindly, travelling all night on horseback, guided by the moon, until at last he reaches an island, a sacred island rising in the mist of dawn.

Mona . . .

"Mona!" Aubrey whispered, nearly dropping the relic in his hands. "Who are you, old man?"

Mother bring us life from death

Mother bring us life from death

The yellowed legbone seemed to vibrate in Aubrey's hands. "A druid?" he asked aloud. "But that cannot be. They've all been dead for more than a thousand years."

Can the gods die?

A beating of drums. The flesh of a woman. Ecstasy, and then release, his spirit spiraling upward, toward a crystal mountain where a king waited to be born. A king with a magnificent sword . . .

When they go, they will take their magic with them.

The bone fell from Aubrey's hands. He knew. Saladin's letter had mentioned a magician. A king's magician.

"The Merlin," he said softly.

It would take more than a bullet to end the old sorcerer's life, with the cup or without it. The Merlin had died before, "died" in the way that men perceived death. But this was not a man, but a creature born of magic. To destroy such a one, nothing less than magic as powerful as his own would do.

An hour later, Aubrey contacted a man he had met six years ago at a coven in Madrid. The Spaniard was a simple man; he had embraced the Dark Power to become wealthy. He had never been troubled with Aubrey's scruples about exchanging his soul for the life he wanted on earth. He was a good second man.

Once Aubrey had determined when the ship carrying Taliesin and the children would dock, he prevailed on the Spaniard to collect the same twelve magicians who had assembled to destroy the sword Excalibur. They were in place now, and would assist Aubrey when the time came.

It would cost him, he knew, probably many millions. Men who had forsaken eternity did not work cheaply. But with the cup, money would always come easily. Money and everything else, for all time.

"Call them together," he told the Spaniard. "Tomorrow we shall kill a wizard."

CHAPTER TWENTY-SIX

Kate took Zack to the Port Authority the following morning, ostensibly to help the homeless who sought shelter there.

"I told you there wouldn't be any homeless people here," Zack said after they had scoured the place for half an hour. "This is a container port, for cargo ships. We'd have better luck on the street."

"Maybe they're outside," Kate said, pulling his sleeve.

"Why do they have to come from the Port Authority, anyway? There's an OTB right around the corner from the center . . . Oh, my God, what's that guy doing?"

A moment later, a young blonde girl screamed as her assailant grabbed her by her hair and tried to drag her into a van parked across the street. A hundred feet or so away, a redheaded boy crouched beside the body of an old man.

Jesus, it's happening, Kate thought as she ran with all the speed she could muster toward the killer. *Just the way Aubrey said it would.*

At that moment nothing mattered to her—not her father's life nor her own, not the loss of her soul and her god—nothing mattered except stopping the killer from finishing his task. With a wild shriek she leapt on the man, beating him with her fists, her pocketbook, gouging at his eyes. The old man had been shot. At least Kate thought he had until he sat up, covered with blood but without a single wound, to hide a small metallic cup inside his clothing.

A cup she knew even then, despite her logic and her reason and all the lies she had told herself, was the single most sacred and powerful object on the face of the earth.

She'd stolen the Holy Grail.

Stolen it for a man who took her soul.

As she approached the entrance to Aubrey's apartment building, she clutched her pocketbook against her chest. She could feel the cup inside it, throbbing, singing to her.

Mother bring us life from death

If she didn't give it to him, her father would be killed.

Mother bring us

Would he? Or was that just an excuse to do something she really wanted to do anyway?

Aubrey appalled her; that was true enough. Yet there was a part of her that cried out for him with every breath she took, a part of her that longed to explore the darkness where he lived.

That part had thrilled when she had turned Zack's key in the lock of the old man's apartment. It had rejoiced when she found the bat-tered cup inside a flower pot on the window ledge and replaced it with Aubrey's imitation. With each forbidden act the evil, alien flower that Aubrey had planted in her bloomed, gorgeous in its monstrosity, and caressed her from the inside out.

A thousand images bloomed with it: Sitting quietly at recess while the other children played because she was afraid to get her clothes dirty. Pretending to romp unselfconsciously with her dog on the White House lawn while surrounded by news photographers. Giving away her birthday presents to charity because it was the "right" thing to do. And later: Stumping around for some good cause or other with the sons and daughters of senators, hating them for their cheerful public-spiritedness. Dating only boys of good stock, whose eyes assessed her potential as a political wife.

Katherine Marshall, the Good Girl. Good, dull, and false.

All her life she had longed to tear off the mask forged for the Pres-ident's daughter. She even thought she had, after she left her parents. Working with the Peace Corps in Zaire, she had thrown away her virginity to a boy from Holland, and had smoked pot for the first time. In college she argued with professors, joined militant women's groups, and explored Zack's New Age silliness. She kept her own apartment, paid her own bills out of earnings from summer jobs, volunteered at soup kitchens, occasionally took unsavory lovers. Most people she met nowadays didn't even know whose daughter she was.

And yet she still felt the marks of the mask on her face. Despite her efforts to become her own person, Kate had remained at heart the Good Girl, the princess who escapes the palace for a brief taste of ordinary life, knowing that she must eventually return to the charity balls and good works and marry an ambitious man of good stock.

Until Aubrey.

Aubrey had shown her that the palace door could be closed, that the mask could be torn off forever.

Was she only afraid, then, to take that first step into the darkness? Had she gone along with Aubrey because he had recognized that her own deep and secret wish had been to *lose her soul?*

"No!" she screamed. "I didn't want it! I didn't want it!"

Other people sharing the sidewalk turned to look at her while passing her by as quickly as possible. The doorman in front of Aubrey's building folded his arms across his chest, his face set with an expression of grim determination.

Mother bring us life from death
Mother bring us life from death

"There is no life from death, not for me," she whispered. "But I will not give this holy thing to the devil."

She turned back the way she had come and ran.

"Mr. Taliesin!" Kate's breath came in gasps. Her knees were cold and shaking as she pounded on the old man's door. "It's Kate. Please open up. It's important."

She heard the slow shuffle of feet approaching. "Hurry, please," she hissed desperately. "Someone may have seen me."

With infinitesimal slowness, the door opened.

"Mr. Taliesin, I've got—"

A hand reached out, grabbed her by the wrist, and yanked her inside.

"What—"

Someone slammed her against the door, jamming a cloth into her mouth, while another took her pocketbook.

Wildly she bucked against her attackers. There were five of them, all operating together as smoothly as a piece of machinery. As they dragged her through the hallway of the apartment, one of them, the tallest, spoke.

"I see you're still wearing the barrette," he said laconically.

Kate twisted around to look at him, and instantly recognized them all. Four of them had belonged to the group that had once gathered in Aubrey's apartment: Geoffrey, as arrogant and rarefied as ever. Sean, with a mouthful of capped teeth. Harold, the balding man who had dabbled in the stock market, was leaner than he had been, and deeply tanned. On his pinky finger he wore a thick gold ring with a diamond the size of a raisin. The man with the twitching fingers who had run down a man with a car while Kate watched was also present, but now he was sporting an Armani suit and a manicure. And the last, a new addition, was the thug who had tried to drag the English girl by her hair into a waiting blue van. He smiled at her.

Zack had been dead wrong when he said that some of their wishes had come true. Kate knew at a glance that they had *all* come true. These men were no longer the desperate losers who had gathered like disciples to learn magic spells at Aubrey's feet. They were rich, successful, confident. And something else, something Kate could read in the eyes of each of them:

They were soulless.

The men dragged her through the living room to the fireplace. The brick wall behind it appeared to have been blown inward, as if from an explosion.

Kate was shoved through the opening, her legs swinging in empty air as she clung to the broken brick. Screaming into the gag in her mouth, she finally found a foothold on what felt like a ladder. She tried to climb back up, but one of her assailants pressed his foot over her fingers. When he released her, she willingly scrambled down the ladder into the basement below.

Even though the place was ringed with candles, Kate's first impression was of darkness. *Darkness*, not as a function of light, but as an entity. It seemed to fill the very air she breathed. She felt a strong impulse to scream out of pure, unfocused terror, but that was only momentary. Her eyes had still not adjusted to the light. After the men who had greeted her at Taliesin's door had descended the ladder and prodded her forward, her fear became real.

In a large circle stood twelve men, hooded and dressed in long black robes, holding thick candles. They stood so still, so silently, that they might have passed for wax dummies. Occasionally Kate caught a flickering image of a face, staring out at nothing through dead-looking eyes.

What the hell is going on, she wondered. It looked like some sort of stage set, almost beautiful in a macabre sort of way. But there was something . . . an odor . . .

God, yes. Now that she thought about it, she nearly gagged. The place was infused with a cloying, sickly-sweet snell, strong and repulsive and . . .

Unwholesome, yes. Unwholesome, like rotted meat, like disease.

The men who had brought her here pushed Kate through the circle of monklike creatures, where she found Taliesin. The old man, garbed in a white robe, knelt in a pool of blood on the floor. His arms were bound to his sides by a length of rope. His head sagged on his chest, and he weaved uncertainly on his knees, as if he had been drugged. Surrounding him were the corpses of animals—cats, birds, a puppy, an exotic striped goat. They had all been disemboweled, and their entrails entwined around Taliesin's feet. In yet another circle, around the animals, were bones that were too large to be anything but human.

With a low cry, Kate turned away from the sight and tried to fight her way back to the ladder, but the men with her held her fast. One of them bound her hands, while another tied her legs together. In an instant the cloth stuffed in her mouth was replaced by a black silk band wound tightly over her jaw.

Then, before she could react, someone sliced up the length of her sleeve with a knife, laying her arm bare. As the blade was moving, another knife slid up her other arm, and two more up the length of her legs.

She looked at them through wild eyes, shrieking her muffled protests into the gag, but the men were like automatons. None of them was smiling now, and none spoke. They simply peeled the clothing from her body as if they were paring a large piece of fruit. And when they were finished, they carried her, nude, to the middle of the circle and deposited her there, then retreated to stand in silence against the wall.

She sat there for a while, hunched and shivering and acutely aware of her nakedness, until she realized that the odor in the room came not from the newly killed animals, but from the floor beneath her. She lowered her face to sniff, then immediately retched, struggling to keep from vomiting into the gag. It was as if the earth itself were dying here, poisoned and putrid.

Scrambling to her feet, she saw that the area in the center of the monks' circle was stained darker than the rest of the floor. Also, there were four crude iron stakes, like railroad spikes, protruding upward in a square.

Ritual sacrifice. The words popped into her mind with a sickening certainty. The stakes had been used to tie down the disemboweled beasts surrounding Taliesin.

While she was in West Africa, she had witnessed the sacrifice of a goat by a Bantu shaman with the objective of bringing rain to the village where Kate had been assigned. The stakes there had been made of wood, and the ceremony had been carried on outdoors, but the earth looked the same—discolored from years of spilled blood—and the odor, now that she had made the connection, was identical.

Kate closed her eyes, swaying, feeling lightheaded. *Oh, my God,* she thought. *My God, my God.*

Someone began to sing. It was faint at first, a low chant sung by a single bass voice in a language Kate had never heard. The music itself was chilling—disharmonious, as though each note were from a different melody and none belonged together.

The robed men in the circle around her still held their candles, though the wax from the thick pillars had dripped over their hands and onto hardened mounds on the floor. They took up the chant, and the eerie, tuneless music swelled with their voices.

Kate looked over at Taliesin. The old man was struggling to open his eyes. The clothing on his right side was stained with blood. He must have fallen over the animals and then righted himself.

I did this to him, she thought, her heart aching. *And to the children, too.*

What would happen to Arthur and Beatrice now? It was just a matter of time before they came back. To this.

Because I once made a wish, she thought bitterly. But it was more than that, she knew, more than a single errant wish. From the first, Aubrey had recognized her for one of his own, like these others, these false monks, these horrors. She had condemned an old man and two children to death for a few nights of pleasure with a madman so that she could think of herself as free. There was nothing separating her from Harold or Geoffrey or the others except for the price she had asked for her soul.

It had been, she realized, pitifully small.

Tears streamed down her face into the silk band around her mouth. The evil vision around her blurred until she could see only the flames from the candles, dots of wavering light. And then, abruptly, the music ceased.

Kate swallowed, suddenly electrified with fear. The very air seemed charged with some unnameable, unknowable terror. And then she saw: Descending the stairway was the thirteenth monk, a silver reversed pentacle suspended over his chest. His hair had been slicked down with oil, and his entire being seemed to be suffused with power. It was Aubrey Katsuleris, and in his eyes was the fire of ecstasy.

He pointed at her. The five men standing against the wall rushed into the circle to lift her up. They untied her hands and legs and removed the gag from her mouth. When they were done, they backed out of the circle in five different places, unobtrusively as spiders in the night.

She looked about her frantically. She was free now, she could move. The ladder was some distance away, but if she could only break through those men . . .

"Where is the cup?" Aubrey asked. His voice was soft, but it carried through the chamber like the howl of the wind.

A fleeting thought crossed her mind: Could it be they didn't know? But the attack . . . Had they . . .

Aubrey laughed, booming. "That's twice you betrayed me, Kate. Three times if you count the evening when you wished I would die."

And then she saw it, a lump at his feet, its metal glinting in the candlelight.

They stood facing one another for a long moment, Kate clenching her jaw. *You won't get into my mind, you jackal! I won't let you in. I won't . . .*

And then one word, unspoken, delivered from Aubrey's mind directly to her own with the force of a hammer:

Bitch!

Kate reeled backward with the sheer physical pain of it.

"I trusted you," Aubrey said aloud, though his voice was far softer than the weighty blow from his mind. "You were to bring the cup to me. Do you think any of these others would have turned his back on me if I'd offered him half of what I promised you?" He held his hands out in front of him in mock supplication. "Anything, Kate. You could have had anything you wanted—riches, fame, success, love—without limit, and with no effort beyond proving just once your loyalty to me."

She felt so cold. While Aubrey spoke, she rubbed her arms, trying to warm the gooseflesh on them while struggling to maintain her balance. Her head throbbed with pain.

Out of the corner of her eye, she saw Taliesin lift his head. The old man was obviously drugged, but looked as if he were coming out of his stupor. If he could get out of here, Kate thought, it didn't matter what happened to her. If only he could get to the children . . .

Quickly, before the idea had a chance to plant itself firmly in her mind, she ran up to Aubrey, snatched the cup, and hurled it into the far corner of the basement, where it disappeared into the darkness.

All twelve of the robed heads turned. The five men from the group ran after it. Aubrey himself momentarily forgot her and pushed his way through the monks.

Without wasting a second, Kate went to Taliesin and yanked the thin rope up over his shoulders so that he could move his arms.

"Get up," she whispered, pulling him to his feet. "You can get out of here. Just climb up the ladder. I'll fight them as long as I can—"

Then she screamed as she was pulled up bodily over the heads of the monks. The old man craned his neck slowly to look up at her, then sank to his knees again in a swoon.

Again the five men from the group were on her, this time tying her wrists and ankles with ropes to the four stakes in the floor.

Ritual sacrifice. Not a goat this time, but a human being. Herself.

"No!" Kate shrieked, the sound welling up out of the fear deep in her belly. She pulled at the ropes, her arms and legs struggling vainly to yank out the stakes, her muscles straining with the futile effort.

At last, exhausted and panting for breath, she lay still. Aubrey stood over her, holding the cup in one hand and a dagger with an elaborately wrought hilt of iron in the other.

"Do you know what happens to people who die by magic?" he asked softly.

Kate turned her head away. Her whole body was trembling violently.

"They become discarnates," he explained. "Spirits who never ascend beyond the physical plane. Poltergeists, boogeymen. The dark, formless creatures that haunt the dreams of frightened children. That is what you shall become, Kate. A fitting punishment for a traitor, don't you think?"

She turned back toward him, her eyes wide. "You said I had no soul," she rasped. "That this would be my last life, and there would be nothing afterward."

Aubrey shook his head. "Sadly, you never gave it willingly. I had hoped you would redeem yourself this time, but you failed me. And your father. And yourself. I no longer want your soul. It is worthless to me."

He raised the dagger and brought it down. With Kate's scream of agony, the monks took up their chant once more.

CHAPTER TWENTY-SEVEN

The old man shuddered. There had been enough of whatever drug was injected into his heart to kill another man, but it was clear that the magician knew who he was, and just how to dispose of him.

The drug was just a precaution. It would keep him quiet long enough to set up the real instrument of his death.

First came the animals and the cheap blood-spells which kept Taliesin from expelling the poison. These were accomplished magicians; they had performed the spells without a leader, and the spells had held his body in a numb stupor while they awaited their master.

But now the real magic had begun. Taliesin knew as soon as he saw the girl what was intended. He had seen it before.

Aubrey drew the blade from right to left across Kate's belly, deep enough to cut the muscle without killing her. The pain would be excruciating, but she would remain alive during the entire length of the spell.

Then he cut upward, and down again at an angle. Kate screamed as if possessed by a demon; then, on the next upward slash, when the pain became too terrible, she fell suddenly silent. Taliesin was relieved for her. Unconsciousness was the only mercy she could hope for.

There would be two more cuts, he knew. Six incisions, forming a reverse pentagram, the symbol of the magicians' perverted art.

The Innocent had explained the procedure to him once, long ago, during what Taliesin thought at the time was an idle conversation.

How blind he'd been not to know that the Innocent never said anything idly.

"It occurs in the Eastern lands," she told him. "At least it does now. One day the dark magic will be everywhere."

"How can we fight it?" he'd asked.

The Innocent had smiled sadly. "When that time comes, there will not be enough of us left to even try."

Taliesin felt a surge of relief. "It will be a long time in the future, then."

"Yes," the Innocent said reassuringly. "A long, long time."

They had been walking through a field of wildflowers, picking medicinal herbs. The Innocent had greatly expanded Taliesin's knowledge about healing, and he followed her eagerly whenever she invited him to accompany her.

He was constantly astounded by her ability to pick exactly what she was searching for, because not only did she not possess the faculty of sight, but she seemed to use no other senses to find what she was looking for, either.

"How do you know?" he asked.

She inclined her head toward him slightly, her eyes as blank as water and moonlight. "About the magicians?"

"About everything. About which herb to pick, without touching the leaves or smelling it. That asphodia was in the middle of a patch of thyme. How did you know it was there? How do you know that the sun shines through the two top lintels of the observatory precisely at dawn on the morning of the vernal equinox? How can you explain the black arts to me, when you—as you yourself have told me—have never set foot outside the island of Mona?"

She laughed softly. "Don't you believe me, little bard?"

"I do. That's why I ask the question."

The Innocent was silent for some time, moving like a tiny wraith in her white gown among the spring blooms.

"There are matters which may strain your belief," she said at last.

"In you? No, Master. I question nothing you tell me, even that it is possible to walk through rock."

"Ah. I see you are still trying to learn how to do that."

"I will never stop trying."

"Then, child, one day you shall walk through rock." She handed him a batch of foxglove. "But though you may become the greatest of the druid wizards, you will not share in all my knowledge during your lifetime. And for that you should be grateful, because you would not be able to bear the pain of it."

"Are you not mortal, then?" He realized that he sounded impertinent, perhaps even mocking, but he could think of no other way to ask the question he had been pondering for so long. "Not in any sense?"

"Oh, certainly, in a sense. I have a body, such as it is. One day it will fall away to dust. The span of my life, in fact, will be much shorter than yours."

Taliesin wondered at that, since he guessed that the Innocent must already have lived more than ninety years. "Then you are saying there is a part of you which is not mortal," he prodded.

"Come now, my logical one. Even you, who are guided always by your intellect, must know that we all have a soul. Even the rock you wish to walk through is, in the essence of its being, immortal."

Taliesin sighed, and the Innocent laughed at his frustration. "Ah, but you are thinking 'that is not what I mean.' " She sat down on the meadow grass. "But it is."

He sat down beside her, trying to fight off his irritation. For someone so wise, the Innocent always spoke in riddles. Perhaps it was because she was a woman, he thought. In his experience, women lacked the directness of speech necessary for clear communication.

Suddenly she laughed, as heartily as a peasant. "Oh, my, you are so impatient! I want to walk through the rock, now! Quickly, tell me all your secrets, that I may not wait a single moment longer!"

He felt immediately ashamed. "I am sorry," Taliesin said, hanging his head. "Forgive me, Master. If you do not wish for me to know—"

"But I do wish for you to know, little bard. I wish for you to know everything. But one cannot calculate the movements of the stars without first grasping the elements of mathematics."

He frowned, confused. "I don't understand. . . ."

"Tell me, Taliesin," she said, patting his hand. "Have you ever met one who has come back from the dead?"

"From the dead?" He tried to follow her train of thought. This seemed like an odd way to explain how she had identified a flower. Or perhaps she had simply changed the subject. "No," he answered dutifully. "Well, once a man told me that he had drowned and been revived. But he was not quite well in his mind. He had been a fisherman, and even his family said that he never recovered his senses after his accident—"

"In other words, you did not believe what he told you about his death."

"It was the dream of a simple man, Master. He claimed that he fell through a dark tunnel to a place where a spirit made of light greeted him and reviewed with him every moment of his life. Afterward, he was led to a great city made of glass. . . ." He shrugged. "For the poor, eternity is always grand and filled with riches. That is why they call it the Summer County, I suppose."

"And how do you picture it, little bard?"

Taliesin felt uncomfortable. He believed in the gods; he had seen their work in action. He even believed in a great universal order, in which every molecule of matter existed for a definite and specific reason. But he had never, despite his commitment to the holy life on Mona, quite been able to accept the notion of a life after death.

"I cannot picture it," he said miserably.

"Ah," the Innocent said. "Then you are not immortal? Any part of you?"

He blushed at the way she had twisted his words. "The components of my body, perhaps. When I die, my flesh will return to feed the earth. My breath will become free air. The water in my blood will return, eventually, to the sea. That much I can understand."

"And your soul?"

He lifted one hand, palm up, in a helpless gesture. "I do not know. I have felt the presence of my soul. I have perceived with my mind its connection to a greater whole. And yet I cannot be certain that the thing I call a 'soul' is not simply my mind itself." He looked earnestly into the old woman's blank eyes. "How can one think without a mind? And how can the mind live without a body? After death, how can we know anything?"

The Innocent smiled. "How can we be certain that we know anything before death?"

"Because we perceive!" he snapped, momentarily forgetting that she was his superior in all matters. "I know you're here because I *see* you. . . ." He blinked. "I see you . . ."

"But I do not see you," she finished.

"And you didn't see the asphodia. Nor did you hear it or touch it. . . ."

"Or smell it," she added.

"Then how? Do you possess senses which I do not?"

"Yes," the Innocent said gently. "And so did the fisherman who tried to tell you about his city of glass. It was not glass, and he did not see it with his eyes. He was trying to explain an experience which you had no capacity to share. It was as if you tried to explain the color red to a dog, which sees no color and speaks no language."

Taliesin tried to grasp the idea. "Do you perceive color?"

"There is a vast spectrum, above and below yours, with which I am familiar. But that familiarity is not a visual experience. It is a perception of the soul. A perception I could not grasp until this lifetime."

Taliesin found he could hardly breathe. "Are you saying that you have lived before?"

"Many times, little bard. But the cycle of birth, death, and rebirth has ended for me. I am part of a larger cycle now, which encompasses, in part, this time on earth."

"Then you are alive . . . voluntarily?"

She nodded. "I suppose you could say that. I have come for a purpose."

"To teach us," Taliesin said.

The corners of her mouth drooped. "No," she answered softly. "For the path we walk will soon be overgrown, and the druids will disappear from the face of the world. My teaching will be as nothing."

Taliesin felt a terrible sadness descend on him because he knew that, as little as he understood the Innocent, she always knew the truth. "Nothing," he repeated. "Then why . . ."

"This is the beginning of a new time." she said quietly. "A frightening time, to you, because during it the gods will die. I have come to help lead them to their death."

Taliesin nearly sputtered. "But . . . the gods cannot die."

The Innocent's face lightened. She laughed again, her voice as silvery as a girl's. "Of course they can! They can do whatever they choose." She extended her arms to him. "Now help me up. My bones are old."

"Master . . ."

"Shh. First learn to walk through the rock. Then you will be ready to think about the death of gods."

They did not discuss her tragic vision again until the day Taliesin left Mona.

"May I come back," he asked, "from time to time, to see you again?"

"You will indeed see me again," the Innocent answered softly. "But you will have to be very wise to recognize me."

He frowned. "I don't understand. I will not wait so long that—"

"No, no, little bard. You are thinking with your intellect again. That is not enough." She cocked her head at him. "Have you a moment to spare before beginning your adventure?"

"Yes, Master," he said gratefully. He had, in fact, been dreading the day of his departure. During his ecstatic vision during that first celebration of Beltane, his future had seemed so clear: He was to find the great sword in the wood and give it to the man to whom it rightfully belonged. He was to create a king who would change the world. He had known at once that he must leave the island of the druids, and the years he had spent in Mona since then had all been directed toward that end.

Yet now that the time had come, he was no longer at all certain that he was doing the right thing. The vision itself, in retrospect, seemed a little foolish. But he had already announced his intentions. He had bade farewell to the order, turned in his garment, and collected his worldly possessions into a bundle. There was nothing left to do but leave.

And so he welcomed the Innocent's invitation to spend a few more minutes in the world he had come to love, which had enclosed him like a mother's womb, a world to which he would never again be a part.

She led him to a small lake only half a mile or so from the shore. In the pre-dawn darkness, they waited in silence as the mist rose from the surface of the water toward the full moon above.

"The lake rises as vapor, falls as rain, rests as water, then rises again," the old woman said. "It is a cycle, like the phases of the moon, or the wheel of life. Do you understand?"

"There is no beginning and no end," he answered. "Only change."

"Yes, little bard." She seemed pleased. "My teaching was not wasted on you, after all."

He smiled slightly. "I wish I did not have to leave you."

"But you do," she whispered back, catching her hand in her knobby fingers. "You go now to begin a cycle, and I remain to close one, but in the end, they are the same."

He knew she was talking about her death. "Does it have to be that way?" he asked, already feeling the loss of her.

"Oh, yes. The gods have already fashioned the instrument of their destruction. One of our own shall kill them."

"One of our . . ." His voice trailed off in shock. "A druid? But why?"

She shrugged lightly. "Because it is their will. It is just a matter of time now, though I must admit the waiting is hard."

Taliesin fell to his knees before her. "Oh, Mother," he whispered.

She stroked his hair. "Do not mourn," she said, "for the gods we serve are old, as I am old. Let us rest for a while, like the water on the lake. In time, the wheel will turn again."

"And then? Tell me, Master, for I will surely not be alive to see that day."

"Ah, but you will," she said with a smile. "We shall all return then. You, me, the one who is your destiny, and whose destiny you will shape. All the ascended spirits, all the souls who fell on the darkened path to the source of All That Is. The seekers, the faithful, the blessed ones . . . We shall all be alive at the same time. We will have returned like the gods' lost children to celebrate a time of glory."

"The . . . the end of the world?"

Unexpectedly, the Innocent laughed. Her eyelids fluttered open. "No, no," she said gleefully. "There is no end, and no beginning. Only change, little bard. Only change."

His teacher had been called the Innocent because she had never known evil, Taliesin thought sadly as he was forced to witness the magician cutting the finished shape of the pentagram into Kate's flesh.

Taliesin, though, had known it too well. Even in ancient times, evil had risen all around him, like the stench in a slaughterhouse.

He had been at his brother Uther's castle in Tintagel, on the southeastern tip of Wales, when word arrived that the druids had been massacred on their own island. While the castle occupants debated whether Mona had been attacked by the Romans or the Christians, Taliesin raced for the stables without packing so much as a jug of water.

He galloped for three days and two nights, stopping only long enough to buy a horse when the one he was riding died from exhaustion beneath him. He reached the channel separating Mona from the mainland at sunset, and only by threatening a ferryman at the point of his dagger was he able to reach the island.

It was still smoking from the fires which had been set. No rain had fallen since the incident, and none among the herdsmen and fishermen from the mainland had dared to venture onto the place where so many powerful and angry spirits dwelled; and so it was that Taliesin was the first to see the carnage.

He noticed the trees first, from the boat. The massive oaks which had stood since before anyone's memory were charred sticks poking into the twilit sky.

"Come back for me tomorrow," he told the ferryman, who was looking around bug-eyed, as if expecting the ghosts of the dead to fly out at them. With a sigh, Taliesin took out a small leather pouch filled with silver and tossed it at the man's feet. "Tomorrow," he repeated.

The ferryman picked up the pouch and weighed it in his hand, considering if the silver were worth the risk.

"Daylight," he said. "Not night."

"Daylight," Taliesin agreed.

Finally the ferryman gave a curt nod and poled his craft back into the water.

And Taliesin was alone with his dead.

As he walked the familiar paths into the island's interior, the silence was so deep that it made his ears ring. There was no birdsong, no chattering of squirrels, no rustle of leaves. Every fragment of life here was gone. But as he walked deeper into the interior, the feeling that crept upon him was worse than the specter of death.

Something terrible had happened here. He could almost smell it.

The first sign was at the mounds where the holy ones had lived. On one of them, atop the scarred grass, lay a man's severed arm. Beside it was a large pentagram, its top pointing downward, drawn with blood.

"In this holy place," Taliesin whispered, numb with shock. Farther away, long gray objects swung from trees. They were the bodies of druids, still wearing what was left of their robes after the fire. There were dozens of them; most had fallen to the ground, the blackened ropes still around their necks, their faces distorted.

In what had been the sacred grove of oak trees—in the same sacred circle, in fact, where the rites of Beltane had been celebrated—five women lay naked, their throats cut.

"Who could have done this thing?" he rasped.

It is how the gods have chosen to die, came the answer. Taliesin did not know whether the voice had been the Innocent's or his own, but the thought of her sprang into his mind, and with it a pang of fear that felt as if his guts had been cleaved by an axe.

The cave where she lived was nearby. There was no sign on the outside that betrayed any violence, but he knew, he knew.

He walked slowly into the sacred dwelling, dreading what he would find. Breathing shallowly to keep from vomiting over the stench of corpses dead more than four days, he stepped over the bloated, maggot-riddled bodies in the entranceway. These were horrible enough, he thought, but at least they had been killed quickly, with knives or swords. A trail of blood led through the passage toward the high chamber where the Innocent had, not so very long ago, listened to the petitions of her charges.

"Don't be here," he whispered roughly, feeling sweat pour into his eyes. "Don't."

And then he saw her, and a moan like the wailing of the dead themselves rushed out of him to fill the profound void of silence there.

She lay on the flat slab of the altar stone. On her belly was the sign of the reversed pentacle, and from beneath it her entrails had been pulled to spill over the sides of the stone. Through her feet were the blades of black iron knives. Her eyes had been plucked out. In her cupped hands, placed over her chest, was her tongue.

Taliesin fell to his knees. "Why?" he shouted, his voice echoing through the empty cave. "You could have fled, become invisible, walked through the walls! You were magic, you could have done anything! Why did you remain here?"

This time her voice was unmistakable. *It was my time,* she said, somewhere between the echo of his words and the silence that followed them. *This is death in life, Taliesin, the black in the white. But the wheel will turn again. You will turn it. You and the one who lights your way. . . .*

"I cannot!" Taliesin screamed. "I do not possess enough magic to bring back the gods! There is not enough magic in the whole world for that, not in the whole . . . world. . . ."

She had never known evil, but he had.

And in the end, after all the Innocent had tried to teach him, Taliesin understood only one thing:

The gods were truly dead.

PART FOUR

THE
KINGDOM

CHAPTER TWENTY-EIGHT

"Lords and ladies, the tournament will begin in thirty minutes! Take your seats for the joust of the year—the year fourteen twenty, that is!"

"Fourteen twenty?" Kay chuckled. "The fool doesn't know what year it is."

"Time's passed since we last rode with Galahad," Curoi MacDaire said, snapping the map in his hands and squinting at it. "It's not four sixty-one anymore, Kay. Can't you see how things have changed? It's fourteen twenty now." Slowly he turned the map upside down. "It's damned hard to read by moonlight."

"Give me that!" Dry Lips snatched it away. "I told you Gawain should navigate. He's found our way through the whole of Britain, and now when we need him most—"

"Can't read," Gawain said, leaning against the side of the truck. "Map'd do me no good."

"Get away from the truck!" Hal shouted from beneath the hood. "Bedwyr's trying to change the tire."

Kay smothered a laugh. "That's one thing to be said for horses. You never have to change the legs on 'em."

Hal clenched his teeth. His life had become a nightmare since meeting these lunatics. On the plane they had behaved like wild men, guzzling every can of beer on board and then tossing the empties over their shoulders onto the heads of irate passengers. They spat peanuts at one another. Agravaine threatened a steward with his claw when he was told he couldn't have more pie. Lugh tied up one lavatory for several hours, flushing the toilet and running the water in the sink until the flight's supply was exhausted. Tristan, Fairhands, and Geraint Lightfoot serenaded a young woman at full throat, over the strong objections of a snarling executive trying to work at a laptop computer. When he broke the laptop over Fairhands' head, the resultant fracas almost caused the plane to go down.

They had been delayed at JFK for two hours while various complaints were lodged against the British Ski Team, and were able to leave only after Hal paid everyone, including the airline, for the damage they had incurred.

After finally renting a truck—a pickup with a removable top, which the knights removed instantly—Hal's charges demanded more food. He was heading for the nearest McDonald's Drive Thru when Dry Lips spotted a billboard for a restaurant in Jamaica, Queens, named The Round Table, advertising A FEAST FIT FOR A KING! and ALL THE ROAST BEEF YOU CAN EAT! When Hal refused to detour through Queens, the knights jumped out of the truck and began walking in different directions in search of the wondrous dining experience that awaited them at the Jamaican Round Table.

Five hundred and twenty dollars later (including damages), Hal was trying to find his way back to the expressway when MacDaire insisted on reading the map for him. Hal was inclined not to trust him at first, but the Irishman was so sure of the route—and Hal so exhausted—that he allowed MacDaire to guide him.

"To the right here, that's a good lad. You see, that'll be putting us on the way."

"The way to the city?"

"Aye, 'tis certain. Oh, and now here's a fine road to follow, right here you are, by Mithras!"

Half asleep, Hal followed the road until two things happened almost simultaneously: One was that he noticed that the urban landscape had changed not into Manhattan, but farmland. The other was that a tire had blown out with enough force to swerve the truck completely across the road into a field.

When he got out, the knights in the back of the truck were laughing heartily as Lugh swung his mace over the side. The right rear tire, directly beneath him, had a hole in it the size of a golf ball.

"What the hell are you doing?" Hal shouted.

Lugh looked crestfallen. The mace fell with a mighty thwack that punctured the truck's body in four places.

"Oh, shit," Hal said.

Lugh snickered.

"Crudely put, but a fine idea all the same," Tristan said, hitching up his ski pants as he stretched. "I won't be but a moment."

"Nor I." Geraint leaped out of the truck with the grace of an acrobat. Lugh lumbered after him, the mace swinging over his shoulder.

"Lugh! Leave that here!"

Lugh looked back, shrugged, and tossed over the weapon. It landed square on the middle of the hood, denting it with a deep crater. The radiator beneath it began to hiss.

"Great. This is just great," Hal said, throwing open the hood with a crash. Steam engulfed him. A stream of oil shot into his eye.

"The bloody thing's afire!" Kay shouted. "Hoses at the ready, eh?"

Following Kay's example, the remaining knights rallied around the engine, urinating copiously onto the radiator.

"Get away, you morons!" Hal yelled. He took a deep breath and backed away. "Just . . . give me some room, okay? I can fix this. Everything will be fine," he said in a voice that sounded far more calm than he felt. "Bedwyr, do you know where the jack is?"

"I do, Hal. And I can work it, too. I studied the pictures."

"Good. Go to it."

Proudly Bedwyr walked to the middle of the road, assembled the tool, and cranked it so that all his fellows might see. When the jack stood at its apex, he stepped back. "It is done, brother," he announced.

Hal peered out of the hood to see. "It's supposed to go under the truck, for chrissake," he snapped.

Correcting his error, Bedwyr had the fender raised and the exploded tire off by the time Geraint called to them. "It's a joust! A great joust, just over this meadow!"

Kay waved him away. "We've no time for it, boy," he said importantly, flicking his finger on the incomprehensible map. "The wagon may catch fire at any time, and we must be prepared to quench it." He leaned against the vehicle protectively. The jack fell over, and the truck came crashing down.

Bedwyr jumped up in a fury. "You near to killed me!" he raged, coming at Kay with arms outstretched.

"But the joust . . . There's more than twenty knights assembled on the field, all to fight at once." Geraint's announcement stopped even Bedwyr. "Twenty knights? Is it to be a battle, then?"

"No, a tourney! And they're clad in outlandish style, armored from head to foot."

"This I must see," Kay said, hulking toward Geraint, the rest following eagerly behind.

"Hey, come back!" Hal shouted. "We've got to get to Manhattan!"

MacDaire stopped long enough to retrieve Lugh's mace. "We'll be back by the time you get the wagon fixed." He took a few steps, then circled back to pat Hal on the shoulder. "Though to tell the truth, lad, I think we might have been better off with horses," he added with a wink.

Stretched across the entranceway between two large gray papier mache towers was a banner reading RENAISSANCE FAIR. Throughout the crowd of tourists milled ladies wearing conical hats and young men in doublets and hose. Occasionally a jester with bells on his hat jangled by, juggling and reciting silly poems. Stalls selling shepherd's pie and toad-in-the-hole reached to beyond where Hal could see, along with fortune tellers, quaint-looking games of chance, a puppet theater, jewelers, potters, glassblowers, leather workers, haystacks onto which children propelled themselves from swinging ropes, stacks of flower garlands, and a fire eater on a tiny metal stage.

Hal wandered through the huge crowd, straining for a glimpse of one of the Companions. He had given up on the truck after ten minutes, but the knights had already been well out of sight. By now they were thoroughly dispersed in what was possibly the only place in New York State where eleven men from the Middle Ages could wander at will without being noticed, at least until they killed someone.

His first clue was an overturned metal drum in front of an ale stall. "Thank God Lugh left his mace behind," he reassured himself as he headed toward it.

"Did you see a bunch of guys . . . uh, big, talk kind of funny—"

"Hey, you with them?" the stallkeeper demanded, tripping over the fallen barrel to get to him. Hal backed away. "Don't you go nowhere, Bud!"

Hal broke into a run. A thousand feet away and to the left he spotted a young man who looked like a jester, except that all the bells had been ripped off his hat and the knees of his hose were torn. He was sitting on a wooden bench talking and gesticulating with what might at one time have been a lute. The instrument's strings were severed and curling, and the neck swung at a broken angle from the wooden body. Several young women in costume stood around him, clucking sympathetically.

"Like I need this bullshit, you know?" he lamented to the women.

Hal almost hated to ask. "Bunch of big guys?" he ventured, unconsciously bowing out his arms. "Long hair . . ."

"No deodorant," the lutist finished. "They almost killed me."

"Consider yourself lucky," Hal said, but the lutist was preoccupied in recounting his tale. "Just because I didn't know a *song*. Jeez, I wasn't even asking for requests or anything. I was just walking along playing 'Greensleeves,' which is the only thing I know how to play on the lute, when this big dude with beer foam all over his face yells, 'You! Boy!' "

The lutist put his hand on his hip. "Now is that rude or *what*? He says, 'Play the Greasy Harlot's Jig.' I swear, that was the name. So I says, 'I don't know that,' like very polite and professional, you know, but then this guy starts to *sing* it, and I mean really loud, and the rest of them join in for like fifteen verses. I guess it's their club theme song or something. And then they start dancing."

"Which way did they go?" Hal asked.

"Oh, man, did they dance. It was like something out of a Fellini movie. And the whole time this lunkhead keeps smacking me and yelling, '*Play* it! *Play* it, damn you!' "

He wiped his forehead with his sleeve. "So finally I says, 'Sir,' like that, 'sir, I *said* I don't know it.' And he yells, 'Well, then you're a damn slow learner, you dickless bastard!' "

"Good old Kay," Hal said under his breath. "Which way—"

"Then he whips out this *sword*! Like this real *sword*, made of steel or whatever, and he says he'll skewer me like a chicken, and I'm trying to get the hell out of there because these other goons with him start whipping out their swords, too, except for one guy with a *spear*, for God's sake . . ."

One of the sympathetic ladies around him offered the unfortunate musician a bottle of water. He poured it over his head. "Hey, I can play piano at the Marriott in Long Island City anytime I want. I don't need a summer job with people threatening to kill me, you know?"

"Which way did they go?"

"Meanwhile, about a million people are gathering around, and they think it's all part of the schtick, they're clapping and singing the refrain about the greasy harlot while these guys are smashing my lute like it's a potato chip, and I'm sweating my ass off thinking these psychos are going to *murder* me and nobody's even going to know, everybody's going to think they're using retractable blades or something—"

"Which way did they go?" Hal shouted.

"Do you think I care?" the lutist shrilled. "I crawled between someone's legs and got up running."

"I think I saw them heading toward the joust," one of the costumed women answered. "That way, over to the left. It's like a stadium. You can't miss it."

Hal took off at a trot, trying not to imagine what the lutist's condition would have been if Lugh had been in possession of his mace.

From under the bleachers surrounding the tournament field, two men in fifteenth century armor rolled. As Hal ran toward the entrance, he saw them get up with some difficulty and then dash headlong into the crowd of tourists. Inside, more would-be knights lay dazed around the perimeter of the field. With a sinking feeling Hal spotted Kay and Gawain on horseback, knocking the armored men off their steeds with long, fancifully painted lances. Each time one of the hapless actors fell off, one of the Companions scrambled to take his place astride his horse. Bedwyr was climbing on a mount now, as the unseated "knight" clanked away, his metal-sheathed arms upraised in terror. Kay cantered his horse around the rim of the playing field, waving and bowing to the spectators.

Suddenly the crowd got to their feet, cheering wildly. Onto the field rode Lugh, grinning like an orangutan and swinging a prop mace over his head like a lariat.

"Oh, no," Hal groaned.

One of the actors threw his helmet and visor to the ground. He might have stomped off, except that the armor he wore was so heavy that the only part of him he managed to get to a standing position was one leg, from the knee down. He was working on the other when Lugh spotted him.

With a shriek, the actor toppled over sideways, his arms covering his head, while Lugh delicately jumped his stallion over him. The spectators roared. Hal looked for a place where he could throw up.

"A lavish tourney," someone said beside him. It was Launcelot, his sober demeanor for once lightened. He raised a fist in salute to Lugh for his feat of horsemanship. "These modern days are not so uneventful as I might have thought. It is a good time to be a man."

Dry Lips threw a spear over the heads of the audience. It landed with a thud on the roof of one of the food stalls, to the screams of those standing nearby.

"Galahad! Hal!" Launcelot ran to catch up with him. "Have we displeased you?"

Hal stared at him. He didn't know where to start. "Displeased?" he repeated. *"Displeased?"* He waved his arms. "Gee, you might say that, Lance. Now that you mention it, my life hasn't exactly been a barrel of laughs nursemaiding a bunch of medieval warriors whose idea of a good time is throwing spears into a crowd. I'm not really crazy about staying up all night wondering when you guys are going to kill someone just for the hell of it. You . . . Oh, never mind."

"Hal—" Launcelot put his hand on Hal's arm.

"Look, it was a dumb idea to bring you along, and I'm sorry to leave you to fend for yourselves over here, but I just can't wait any longer. There's a thirteen-year-old kid who needs me, and I've got to find him." With a final glance at Launcelot, he turned away. "Sorry."

He left the knights and walked through the meadow back to the road.

Arthur wolfed down his first hot fudge sundae within five minutes, and was working on his second one.

"Wuss," he mumbled between mouthfuls, kicking Beatrice playfully under the table.

She tried to smile as she stirred the liquid in her dish.

"What's the matter, Beatrice?" Zack asked.

"Nothing."

"Maybe it was the love bombs. They can take a lot out of you."

Beatrice's head snapped up. "I didn't make any love bombs," she insisted. "That was you."

He shook his head. "No, it wasn't. I wish it were, but I know better. You're an old soul, Beatrice."

"She is not!" Arthur said in the girl's defense.

"Wait a minute." Zack laughed softly. "I'm not insulting anyone here." He scraped the last of his ice cream from the bottom of his bowl. "Somewhere along the line, human beings got this idea that we all have to be just like everyone else, but the fact is, we're not. Some of us run fast, some of us play music . . . and once in a while there's someone like Bea."

"An old soul," Beatrice mused. "What exactly does that mean, Zack?"

"It means he spends too much time at the Center for Cosmic Consciousness," Arthur said between mouthfuls.

Zack was the first to laugh. "A lot of people feel that way about me," he admitted. "Anyway, an old soul is someone who's lived a lot of lives."

Arthur set down his spoon. Taliesin had explained the boy's own situation to him very carefully, and only after Arthur himself had experienced incontrovertible proof that he was, in fact, continuing a former life. But Taliesin was a very special being, whom Arthur had long suspected of being not exactly human. To hear a wizard's words parroted by someone as goofy as Zack vaguely offended him.

"Actually," Zack went on, "we've all been here before hundreds of times, sometimes thousands. We don't remember those lives because that would interfere too much with the lives we're living now. But once in a while there's a person who's learned so much in past incarnations that he—or she—just *knows* things this time around."

"Are you one of them?" Arthur asked sharply.

"An old soul? No, I don't think so. I make too many mistakes."

"Then how can you say that Bea's one?" He shoveled his ice cream. "I mean, how would you even recognize someone like that? And how would you know how many lives people lived, anyway?"

"Arthur, that's rude," Bea said quietly.

"No, it's important that we're honest with each other." Zack nodded to indicate he was listening to Arthur.

The boy rolled his eyes.

"Ah, to be young and eat anything you want," a fat man at the table beside them said as he lifted himself off one of the small wire-backed chairs. His table was strewn with papers and magazines, which he gathered together and stuck haphazardly under his arm. "Now I have a small dish of frozen yogurt, and feel guilty about that."

Zack smiled politely as the man waddled out the door, wheezing and sweating. Arthur continued eating, his face flushed with anger. "You could at least get mad," he mumbled.

"*You* get mad, Arthur," Zack said, smiling. "It'll do you good. You're too serious for a kid. . . . Oh, that guy dropped some of his stuff. Just a second." He picked up a magazine that was lying on the floor and trotted outside with it.

"He drives me crazy," Arthur said.

"But he means no harm." Beatrice wiped a chocolate spot off his nose. "Really, I think Zack has a good heart."

He came back in a moment later. "Took off in a cab," he said. "Hope he doesn't need this." He tossed the magazine onto the table. It was a month-old issue of *International Artist*.

Zack burst into laughter. "Hey, this is your landlord!" He read the caption beneath the picture of Aubrey Katsuleris. " 'The Warlock Women Love.' Too much. Wait till Kate—"

Beatrice dropped her spoon. "It's him," she said, looking at the magazine.

"Aubrey Katsuleris," Arthur read. He looked over at Zack.

"Yeah, he owns the building the Center is in," Zack said, grinning and shaking his head.

Arthur stood up and grabbed Beatrice's hand. "Let's get out of here," he said.

She began to rise, but her legs wobbled beneath her. "No, Arthur. We can't go back. Not yet."

"Why not?"

"I don't know. It's just a . . . a feeling. You mustn't go near that building, Arthur."

"But we've got to tell the old man."

"No. Stay with me. Please . . ." Then her eyes rolled back in her head and she slumped to the floor.

"Oh no, Bea, not now," Arthur moaned.

Zack leapt up from his chair and bent over the girl.

"Want me to call an ambulance?" the counterman asked.

Arthur shook his head. "She'll be okay in a minute."

"I think she just fainted," Zack said, listening to her chest. "She's breathing." He slapped her face gently. "Bea . . ."

"Get away from her!" Arthur shouted, pushing him aside.

For five minutes he knelt beside her. Finally Zack went over to the counterman. "Maybe you'd better call an ambulance, at that."

"I told you, she's all right," Arthur said.

"Better safe than sorry, son," one of the other patrons said. They had all gathered around Beatrice by now, as if they could make her come to by staring at her.

Arthur had no idea what to do. Taliesin was in the apartment alone, and he had the cup. On the other hand, Arthur had promised Beatrice that he wouldn't let anything happen to her.

"Come *on*, Bea." Arthur spoke into her ear with quiet intensity. "We've got to get back."

When the ambulance came, she was still unconscious.

Arthur stayed with her.

"Did this ever happen before?" the paramedic asked Zack on the way to the hospital.

"No," Arthur answered. "She's never passed out." He gave Zack a cold stare. The man had been permitted inside the ambulance despite Arthur's complaints that Zack was not a relative and not necessary. Adults, he decided, always sided with other adults.

"Her blood pressure's okay, but her heart's beating kind of slow," the paramedic said. "Is she on medication?"

Arthur shook his head.

"You kids been doing any drugs?"

"No."

"You sure?"

"He told you he wasn't," Zack said.

Arthur's expression softened for a moment. Zack put his arm around him. "She's going to be all right," he said.

Whom do you suppose he'll send next time? Taliesin had warned. *A room service waiter with a stiletto under his napkin?*

Or some guy who buys kids ice cream?

The boy shook him off with an almost violent gesture. He moved as far away from Zack as possible in the small space of the ambulance.

Beatrice was taken immediately for a CAT scan.

In the waiting room Arthur studied the floor map of the hospital. Somehow he would have to get Beatrice out of there. Since he couldn't very well drag her through the halls while she was unconscious, he would have to wait until she snapped out of whatever kind of trance she was in. But after that, they would need a route of escape.

The CAT scanner, he knew from the admitting nurse, was on the fourth floor, in the neurology wing. There were several elevators, as well as stairways on both the east and west walls. On the lobby floor there was a secondary exit off the Emergency Room, away from the waiting area. If Arthur could only manage to be alone with Beatrice for a minute . . .

"Relax," Zack said, startling him. "You're like a coiled spring. Maybe you need a hug, huh?"

"Get lost." Arthur backed away from him.

Zack held up his hands. " 'Scuse me, I forgot. Tough guys aren't into hugs. Hey, we have to call your grandfather and tell him we're here."

"Who?"

"Mr. Taliesin. Isn't he your grandfather?"

"No. And there's no phone in the apartment you gave us."

"I can reach him through Kate."

Yeah, right. I know who you're calling. The International Artist with the gun.

While Zack was on the phone, Arthur asked the nurse at the desk about Beatrice's CAT scan.

"They usually take about thirty minutes," she answered with a smile. "Your sister will be out in no time."

"She's not—" he began, then thought better of it. He might not be allowed on the neurology floor if they knew he wasn't related to Beatrice. "Thanks," he said.

A security cop strolled by, a genial looking man with white hair and a paunch, and tipped his hat to Arthur.

Big fat help you'd be if a killer got in here, Arthur thought. As for the city police, he knew there was no chance they would even believe him if he told them about Aubrey Katsuleris.

He turned back to the floor map until Zack returned.

"There was no answer at Kate's, so I called Mrs. Neumeyer in the room next door to find your . . . you said Mr. Taliesin's not your grandfather?"

"Where is he?" Arthur demanded.

"Don't know. He doesn't answer the door. Maybe he took a walk with Kate."

Arthur felt himself shaking. *And maybe Katsuleris killed him.*

"Hey, lighten up," Zack said. "I asked Mrs. Neumeyer to leave a note. Meanwhile, we can get a soda, if you want."

Arthur pushed him away, then ran straight into a balding man in a white lab coat. "Are you here with Beatrice Reed?" the man asked Zack.

"I am," Arthur said, swiping at his nose with his sleeve.

"I'm Dr. Coles," the man said, still addressing Zack. "Beatrice has been admitted."

"Is she conscious?" Zack asked.

"I'm afraid not. She appears to be in a coma, although her tests are very inconclusive on that score."

"How can you be inconclusive about whether someone's in a coma or not?" Arthur asked.

The doctor's eyelids fluttered irritably. "Beatrice is very fortunate in that one of the leading neurologists in the world, Dr. Shanipati, is in the hospital and is taking an interest in her case." He smiled proudly as he touched Zack's arm. "He's with her now, but you can wait in the visiting area of the neurology wing. I'll take you up."

"You can take me up," Arthur said. "I'm her brother."

"I'm afraid children aren't permitted—"

"I said I'm going up. Call an administrator if you want, but I'm all Bea has, and I'm going to be with her." Arthur pointed to Zack. "He stays here."

The doctor stood indecisively for a moment, his eyelids fluttering wildly. Arthur strode past him. "Never mind. I'll find my own way."

He walked into an open elevator, pushed the fourth floor button, crossed his arms over his chest, and stared defiantly at the two men as the doors closed.

Then he cried.

The priests of the Black Mass chanted.

Inside the circle of blood, the air grew thick, charged with the magic of the dark forces which had been appeased by the sacrifice of the animals and the suffering of the woman. Already the Merlin was weakening; Aubrey could feel the sorcerer's power draining out of the old man.

Yes, the dark ones would be pleased.

He thought of the Mass as an offering for the cup. Aubrey's gods were mercenary; they had demanded many souls as its price. But what the cup brought with it was worth everything Aubrey had paid.

And he had paid a great deal, even more than he had realized. The Merlin had shown him, for the first time, just how much he had sacrificed for the cup.

With the heightened perceptions brought on by the ritual, Aubrey had followed the old man's thoughts with absolute clarity. He had walked with him through the charred forest on the island of Mona, felt the scorched earth still warm beneath his feet. He had seen the bodies of the druids hanging like ornaments from the burned oaks, dangling by frayed ropes. He had seen the women in the grove, their white bellies exposed for the first time to light.

But it was not until he beheld the remains of the hag whom the druids called the Innocent that Aubrey realized that the memory he was experiencing was not only the Merlin's, but his own as well.

He had been Thanatos then, as he was now. With his hands he had cut the pentagram into the witch's body during that distant time, in precisely the same proportions that he had just used to mark the American girl. His arms had felt the Innocent's cloying blood as he sank them into her bowels to remove the viscera. His ears had heard her cryptic dying words, Mother, bring us life from death.

But there had been no life from death for her and her kind. Nothing remained of the old religion. Its servants, killed by magic, had forfeited their souls.

It had been Thanatos' mission to destroy the gods, and in this he had succeeded.

CHAPTER TWENTY-NINE

He did not at first know why he had been given the mission. He had been raised, in that other life, as one of the holy ones, familiar with the ways of the druids since birth.

His mother told him before her death that he had been born on the sacred island of Mona, and had been sent with her to the ancient grove in Gaul, which had been their home ever since.

This, she explained, was the practice for children conceived during the rites of Beltane, as he had been, because no one was permitted on Mona who had not made a conscious decision to serve the ancient gods. In the lesser groves, however, these special children were trained from birth to become druids, as they were the only ones who would be considered to replace the Innocent when that time came.

"It will be you," his mother said, straining to speak in her extremity. "I felt your destiny in your soul as it entered my body at the moment of your conception. The gods have great plans for you, my son."

And so they had.

At fifteen, he was expelled from the order for raping a girl several years his junior. He was led before dawn to the field outside the druids' forest and left there with only a short tunic and a pair of rope sandals, to make his way or be eaten by wolves.

He spent the day weeping and cursing those who had done this thing to him, but by nightfall he had formed a plan. He gathered a great bundle of sticks and twigs together, and two pieces of flint, and waited. Then, at the midnight hour, when the wind howled mournfully over the dry autumn grass, he stole back into the druids' deep wood to their sacred grove.

It was the time of the new moon, and the first spark of the flint lit the dark sky like a jewel. The twigs caught quickly, blossoming into flames that scurried among the ageless oaks like living beasts.

He stayed long enough to watch the oaks catch fire, imagining he could hear their screams. Then he heard the sound of running footsteps, and he left the way he had come, silent and triumphant.

From more than two miles distant he could see the bright blaze. By the time he reached the nearest village, he heard talk of nothing else.

"They must have angered the gods," an old man said in a tavern where he had gone to ask for work.

He had laughed aloud. *Yes, indeed,* he thought. *They have angered the only god I worship.*

He killed for the first time a year later, in the tavern where he worked. It was a worthless stewpot whose life he took, a smelly, feebleminded old pederast with no family to mourn him or seek out his murderer. The man had come into some money—he sold carvings of religious figures to the Christians—and was stupid enough to show it to him.

"Malva," the man whispered, for that was the boy's birth name, "take a look." The old man was grinning lewdly at him as he jingled a pouch heavy with coins.

Malva had been chopping wood behind the tavern, and was lathered in sweat. He knew his appeal. More than half of the married women in the village, and a fair number of unmarried ones who still called themselves maidens, had squealed in delight under his weight. So, although it was the first time a man had looked at him with that particular sort of longing, he was not surprised.

He smiled, being sure to display his even, white teeth, then sauntered over to the man, the ax still in his hand. The old man, having drunk enough to sway on his feet, did not even react when Malva picked up the ax near its blade and cut his throat with it.

Several days later the body was discovered behind the woodpile, after the tavern had become overrun by rats.

Meanwhile, the pouch of coins was hidden in a corner of the root cellar, where only Malva went. In time, it was joined by others—one quite large pouch, from a foreign sailor who had actually enjoyed Malva's body before dying, and several smaller ones—before the villagers began to look at him with something like distrust.

He left in the night, after relieving his employer of his savings, his horse, and his life.

Gaul was a large country. There were many places for an enterprising young man to establish himself. Malva worked at many trades and learned many skills, but his way of life remained unchanged in the essentials. He robbed men and then killed them, all the while leading an ordinary life in every other respect.

In time, he no longer even needed the money. His victims' prestige and wealth had grown along with his own, so that every death yielded considerably more than the first bag of coins he had taken from the village sot. On one occasion, he murdered the garrison commander of a Roman fort right under the noses of the man's personal guard, and walked away with a box of Arabian jewels.

By the time he was twenty, Malva had grown weary of only one aspect of his life—that of masquerading as an honest man. On the southern shore of Gaul, he bought passage on a ship headed for the east, where he no longer had to work, and killed purely for profit.

It was in Egypt that he first encountered the dark magicians, and in the Black Mass he experienced a state describable only as bliss. Murder, in its ritual form, was not a secret act, like the elimination of one's waste, but an art. One killed with delicacy and refinement, and in a state of ecstasy. In the Black Mass, he discovered for the first time in his life that there was a force greater than his own will, and he bound himself to that force with the devotion of a lover.

During his initiation, the dark ones spoke his true name. "Thanatos," they whispered to his inmost heart.

For that gift, he gave the dark ones his soul, and they smiled on him.

Thanatos was never certain of the precise moment when he knew he had to return to the place of his birth. The idea grew as he embraced the dark way more and more completely. There was the question of payment—he felt his demon gods demanded more from him than merely his devotion and the sacrifices he was able to bring them. They wanted supremacy, not only among the esoteric few like himself, who were drawn to them from birth, but in the hearts of all who walked the earth.

So, in time, he came to understand his life's true work: He would become a harvester of souls.

That would be easy enough in a place like Gaul, where the people had long accepted foreign occupation and the loss of their gods. The sacred grove of the druids, where Thanatos had been reared, was hardly known to exist by the general population. Since the triumph of the Romans, the Gauls had adopted the ways of their conquerors to the point where they looked down on the Britons, who had never willingly changed anything about themselves, as savage barbarians. For their cooperation, the Gauls enjoyed a booming commerce, a settled government, wide, paved roads, vermin-free homes, and luxuries such as the Britons could not even imagine.

Yes, the Gauls would be an easy harvest.

But the Britons . . . That was another matter. They were stubborn, rough people, accustomed to the rain and cold, stoic about the suffering of life, and indifferent to death. They laughed at the Roman deities, deriding their gorgeous flesh-painted statues as harlots. For the Britons, who still walked miles through snow-covered mountain passes to offer bread to the ancient gods while their own bellies growled with hunger, their souls were all they had.

And their souls were fed by Mona.

Mona. The last stronghold against the dark ones, led by an old wraith of a woman who, it was said, was more spirit than flesh . . . perhaps one of the ancient gods herself.

Yes, it would have to be Mona. Thanatos would appease his greedy demons by giving them the greatest gift possible—the souls of Mona's gods, bound by magic in the dark realms so that they would never rise to live again.

It took him nearly six years to establish his coven and formulate his plan. Then, on a night the omens had foretold would bring strength to the dark forces, thirteen magicians, led by Thanatos, sailed from southern Britain to reach the shores of Mona at the hour of midnight.

They killed in an orgy of passion, chanting the ritual of their mass as they struck down the druids one by one. Each death was an offering to the dark ones; over each body the rite of sacrifice was said so that their souls would be bound forever to the power of the demon gods.

Only in one instance did he fail. When they reached the Innocent, she was waiting for them, unafraid.

"So you have come for us at last," she said calmly, even as the corpses of her closest attendants lay still warm around her.

"You and your gods will die by my hand," Thanatos said.

"I know. I have lived long in order to fulfill their destiny."

"Crazy old harridan," he said. "You don't even know enough to be afraid."

"It is you who should be afraid," she answered. "Do you not know what awaits you in the dark realms?"

"Nothing awaits me. After my death, I will be free. My gods have promised it."

"Your gods lie, Thanatos," she said quietly.

"How do you know my name?"

"The gods have spoken it to me. Your gods, and mine, for they serve the same purpose."

"To see you dead?" he asked with a smile.

"Perhaps." She gave him a small bow. "You will know soon enough." Then she walked, lightly as a feather, to the great altar stone and lay down upon it, offering herself to her gods.

"Mother, bring us life from death," she murmured, and then her breath stilled.

Thanatos watched the life go out of her. For a moment, a white aura, like the thinnest smoke, surrounded her. Then it gathered itself up into a light so bright that Thanatos thought he would be blinded for life by it. He threw his fists over his face, but it was as if his hands were transparent and his eyelids did not exist. He cried out in pain.

Then, in the hundredth part of a moment, the light was gone. The Innocent lay lifeless on the altar, safe from his magic.

"Did you see it?" he demanded of his initiates.

The black-robed men only stared at him, their expressions bewildered.

Thanatos ran to the corpse, lifted an arm, and dropped it again with a shudder. "She's already cold!" he bellowed in a fury.

Two of the magicians looked at one another. "Cold?" one asked diffidently, but Thanatos never heard him. Shrieking with rage, he ripped the Innocent's thin garments off her until her body lay naked, her withered little dugs of breasts hanging above the loose flesh of her belly, her arms and legs like sticks, her white hair streaming around her face, wispy as mist.

"Witch!" he spat, drawing his dagger and thrusting it deep into her bowels for the first cut of the pentagram.

Hesitantly, unsure of what to do, the priests formed a circle around the altar and began the chant for the rite of sacrifice, which Thanatos performed with a vicious exactitude upon the body of the Innocent, who had deprived the demon gods of her soul.

On the way back, after they had set the fires, Thanatos did not speak, or even look up from the dark water of the sea.

Though Thanatos' ambitions never vaulted so high again, he lived for many more years. While forming new covens around Britain, he learned that the destruction of Mona had produced just the effect he had hoped for. Without the island at the heart of their religion and no member of the order qualified to succeed the Innocent, the druids slowly died as a spiritual force.

There were occasional wanderers wearing the long gray robe of the old religion, but they came to be regarded as little more than beggars. After all, the druids had not touched the common people in any real way for centuries. Their magic was complex, and required years of study. They talked about the movement of the stars, and other things which were of no interest or use. While it was true that they had once given their blessings to tribes going into battle, there were now many holy men who were willing to enlist the aid of any number of new gods, from the Roman pantheon of deities to the Christians' merciful Father.

In the decades following the massacre, there were other raids on the sacred groves throughout Britain and Gaul. It was all the same to Thanatos whether these places were burned by Christians or Romans or his own initiates or even rowdy youths with nothing else to occupy their time. What was interesting to him was that they were never rebuilt, and their inhabitants hardly mourned. Some ignorant mountain folk still set out offerings of food for the ancient ones, but for most of the people, the stories of the druids and their magic were little more than folk legends.

At the age of seventy-three, Thanatos died of gout in Egypt, in his mistress' bed. He was a wealthy man, and left no heirs.

The last sound he uttered was a scream.

Down he fell, through a tunnel so dark that it caused him pain. He had no body—he perceived himself as a dim shape throbbing with sound, but a sound unlike anything he had ever heard. He in fact did not hear it, any more than he saw the darkness, but rather felt these conditions with some sense that he had never before used.

Had his gods had lied to him, then, as the Innocent had warned? In exchange for his soul, they had promised him no retribution at the end of his mortal life. He had expected, when he closed his eyes for the last time, to enter the void outside the wheel of life, where he would rest without thought or pain or punishment. Instead, Thanatos found himself on a turbulent journey through what looked like what the Christians called Hell.

Here he encountered all manner of beings, many of whom looked quite human, although he passed through them as easily as if they were made of dust. And when he did, he understood everything about each of them during the instant that their spirits met. One was a suicide who had killed her child at birth and then taken her own life in remorse. Another was a drunkard who craved a tankard of mead above all other things, even though he no longer possessed a body to drink it. He met the first man he had murdered, the leering old pederast, and one of his own initiates, who had died young in a fire.

"What is this place?" he asked.

"Why, it's home," the pederast explained as he wandered out of the tunnel and back into the village in Gaul where Thanatos had cut his throat with the blade of an ax. The man tried to speak with people on the street, showing them some wood carvings he had made, but the people walked right through him, unaware of his existence. The woman who had killed herself sat by a river, rocking the body of her drowned infant. The drunkard stood inside a tavern, his throat parched with thirst, futilely attempting to grasp the cup set before him. The initiate ran repeatedly out of a burning barn, his hair afire.

But Thanatos continued through the tunnel. Floating shapes passed by, the spirits of the druids he had killed, bound by magic to this dark place, struggling to free themselves.

"Mother, bring us life from death," they chanted, and still he did not understand what the words meant.

Then he met the ancient gods themselves, vast pools of thought, deep as oceans, crackling with energy. A shriek rose from Thanatos' innermost core as he rushed through them, and he felt their mocking mirth.

"You cannot harm me," he said. "You are not my gods."

"All gods are the same," they answered in colors, shades of blue and green. "We are channels to the source of All That Is."

"Then why are you here, in this odious place?"

"We are our own place," they answered, "complete in ourselves. You experience us because we have created you. Come into us now, and stay until it is time for us to create you again."

Then he was swallowed, tumbled end over end into a void a thousand times darker than the blackness of the tunnel. In time he slowed, floating free, so much a part of the darkness that he could no longer discern where he ended and the void began.

So the demon gods had not lied. He had found the void. And it was more terrible than the worst punishment that the human mind could invent.

"Where are my gods?" he pleaded, his voice the merest vibration in the numbing space.

He waited. For a year, or ten. Or a hundred, or a thousand. At last he heard an answer.

"We are here," came a whisper from within him.

When was he set free?

No one had warned him that he would be leaving the void. Suddenly he was thrust upward—or downward, or sideways, he really had no idea—to slide through a warm, wet tube into a world he had nearly forgotten, and continued to forget. With the first inrush of air into his lungs, he lost all remembrance of Thanatos' life; by the time he was two weeks old, he had even forgotten the void.

Only one idea remained with him, and in thirty-two years of his new life as Aubrey Katsuleris, it had never approached consciousness. Once, in a state of hypnosis during his teens, he had spoken the idea in a trance, but the therapist had utterly misunderstood. And once he had awkened from a nightmare screaming it. But it was not until now, when he stood in the magic circle with the Grail in his hand and

Taliesin's memories in his mind, that he understood it completely, and was able to give voice to the prime directive of his life.

"I will never go back there," he said aloud.

Now it was within his power to fulfill that promise to himself. So long as he possessed the cup, he would never again have to languish in the nothingness of the void in which he had purchased a place at the cost of his soul.

The Grail was in his hands now, throbbing with its great power, conferring its immortality to him with every beat of his heart, which would beat forever.

Aubrey Katsuleris had, at last, beaten the demon gods themselves.

CHAPTER THIRTY

Taliesin felt himself weakening. After his final, strong remembrance of the last time he saw Mona, his thoughts had loosened like thread on a spool, winding out of control. Mingling with his last horrible image of the Innocent were other thoughts—the vision at Beltane, when he saw Arthur as a king; the memory of the boy Arthur, when he pulled the sword out of the stone, both in that other life and in this one; the thought of Beatrice, who harbored the Innocent's soul, yet had not awakened enough to realize its power.

Beatrice. At last Taliesin understood why the Innocent had come back. It was for Arthur, because the time of the millennium was draw-ing near.

We shall all be back, she had said, *the seekers, the ascended masters, the ones who have fallen on the path leading to the source. We will all be alive at the same time. . . .*

Of course. They were all here now, each soul poised to bring about a new era in the history of mankind, and they would be led by a great man, a king past and yet to be. Arthur, the man who was Taliesin's destiny, the fulcrum on which the lever of the gods would rise again.

Only Arthur would not live to accomplish the task set before him. He would die before his time, just as before.

In his lifetime, Arthur of Britain saw only one of his dreams, the unification of his country, realized. Granted, it was a big dream, and no one had ever accomplished so much before. Under Arthur, the tribal chiefs who had warred among themselves since men first walked upon the land drew together to live in peace and fight their enemies as a whole nation.

But this was only the beginning of Arthur's vision. What he had wanted, what the petty kings under him found so shocking and unacceptable that they eventually splintered apart and brought about Arthur's death, was to stop fighting their enemies as well.

The Saxons had been raiding Britain's coastline villages for decades. In the beginning of his reign Arthur, who was a brilliant military tactician, had led the petty kings and their soldiers in a series of counterstrikes that had effectively rid Britain of the foreign menace. The only Saxons who remained were those who had settled in the land they could not conquer, who had married British women and tried to set up small farms on raw land which had never been cleared.

These were butchered regularly. The petty kings, now that they were at peace with one another, found their only outlet for the arts of war in the raiding of these Saxon farms. It did not matter that the heads of these homesteads were more often than not men who had lost an arm or a leg, or were otherwise too infirm to continue as warriors, or that their farms barely eked out an existence for the man and his family. It did not matter that many of them paid taxes to the nearest tribal chief, whether or not he owned the land on which the Saxons lived.

The chieftains regarded these raids as sport, and objected strenuously when Arthur, as High King, asked in council that they stop.

"How would you expect me to treat these savages?" roared Lot, king of Rheged, in whose vast tracts of wild land many of the Saxons had settled. "They have raided our coastlines—"

"Not *your* coastlines," said King Cheneus of Dumnonia, whose lands occupied the southeastern shorelines of Britain. Rheged was to the far north and east, where the Saxon raiders even at the peak of their invasions, had rarely waged war. "It was not your people they murdered, nor your women they raped."

"They do worse! They not only rape the women of my land, but take them to wife! They spawn their barbarian whelps right under my nose!"

"Since we have banded together as one nation, the Saxons have not invaded us at all," Arthur explained patiently. "Those who remain in Britain have cleared wild land, and cultivated soil where once nothing except rocks existed."

"And how long will it take these savages to attack us, their masters, so that they might clear yet more land for their brothers who wait across the sea, measuring the High King's weakness?"

Arthur took a deep breath. "If you think it a weakness to ensure peace—"

"At the cost of our land, yes!" King Lot bellowed, and the others pounded the table with their fists in agreement.

"Look at Gaul!" one of the petty kings shouted. "Its kings have become nothing more than Roman whores! For four hundred years we fought the Romans, and we are a free people as a result. Would you have us give away that hard-fought freedom to a band of hulking savages?"

"These Saxon farmers do not wish to impose their will upon us, as did the Romans," Arthur said. "They want only to join us, to become a part of Britain."

"Bah!" Lot spat. "Let their foreign blood wet Britain's soil, for that is all it is good for."

The others cheered their assent.

Arthur waited, stone-faced, for the noise to die down before speaking. "Can you not see beyond the contents of your closed fist?" he asked tightly. "If we accept the Saxon farmers as countrymen, they will fight with us, when the time comes, to protect the land they have come to think of as their own. Instead of waiting each day, as we do, for the Saxons to rebuild their fleet and train new soldiers in preparation for a new wave of invasions, we can enlist our Saxon population to help us make treaties with them, establish trade—"

"What do barbarians have worth trading for?" someone shouted. There was a general grumbling in the assembly. Several men spat on the floor.

Arthur waved them down. "We know little about them," he said quietly. "But I have seen on the corpses of their slain leaders ornaments of silver fashioned with workmanship to rival the Celts'—"

"Ornaments!" Lot exclaimed, his voice dripping with disdain. "Are we jewelers, then?" The kings all found this terribly amusing, sloshing the mead in their tankards and wiping their beards with their sleeves. "Their silver is worth nought to me, save for its weight when melted down."

"Would you melt down their weapons, too?" Arthur argued. "For they are fine, as we have all seen. Perhaps they know more about metalworking than we do." The kings bristled at such a suggestion, but Arthur went on. "They may be knowledgeable in many areas where we are ignorant. They may produce wine, like the Romans—"

"We do not need foreign wine," Lot said.

"I would spit it from my mouth!" one of the kings vowed.

"If it be made by the Saxons, it will taste like horse piss," the king of Dumnonia said, and the council swilled down more mead, to show their appreciation of their national drink.

Arthur sat down, defeated. The kings were too drunk to continue the discussion.

"I wish I could force them," Arthur said later to Taliesin. "Instead of killing one another year after year, we might all learn and profit from peace. And yet they will not listen."

The Merlin put his hand on Arthur's shoulder. "War is the natural state of man," he said. "To ask your kings to do without war is to strip them of all they know."

"They should know other things," the king said sullenly. "For all their talk about barbarians and savages, they behave little better than such themselves."

"And so you see how miraculous it is that they will even consent to sit together at one table. The tribes these men represent have been fighting one another for more than a thousand years. Peace is a concept that takes time, Arthur. You cannot expect them to change so much overnight."

"If we do not change soon, we can expect to be invaded again and again until, like a stag pursued by dogs, we are worn down by lesser men. That is already happening in Rome and, despite what my kings may say in their arrogance, the Romans are far superior to us in their knowledge of warfare."

Taliesin poured them both a drink, trying to find a delicate way of framing what he had to say. "It is better, at times, for a leader to take his men along the long path to their destination, lest too many fall on the short one."

Arthur looked up, annoyed. "What are you trying to tell me, Merlin?"

"Only that it would be better to lose a few Saxon farmers than the throne of the High King."

Arthur seemed stunned. "Do you think they would turn against me over this?"

The old man shrugged. "You are not an absolute ruler. The petty kings must give their consent to any enterprise. If you insist in the face of their objections, it would not take much for these men to go back on their oaths of alliance and revert to a state of constant civil war—a state, I may add, in which they are quite comfortable."

The king shook his head. "That is why we have no roads, no currency, no trade with other nations. . . ."

"One thing at a time, Arthur."

"I do not wish to spend my life nursemaiding a pack of drunken louts!"

"And yet you must, for if any of those drunken louts takes your place, all of your work will be undone."

Taliesin had not known then how prophetic were his words.

That day marked the beginning of the end for Arthur's dream of peace.

The Saxon farmers and their families continued to be murdered in their fields for the amusement of their local lords until they abandoned their meager plots of land and took to living like fugitives in hidden colonies among the caves and forests, or adopted the life of highway brigands. And when the mainland Saxons once again attacked Britain, in larger and ever larger numbers, those who had attempted to carve out a new life for themselves on British soil felt not the slightest loyalty to the kings who had treated them worse than slaves. They gave their Saxon countrymen every assistance, from drawing detailed maps of Britain's interior to hiding whole battalions of soldiers along the inland routes. When the Saxon soldiers reached the great fortresses of the petty kings, they were joined by a waiting army of men whose greatest pleasure it was to join in the triumphant destruction of their former masters.

"They are winning," Arthur told Taliesin in despair. "We can fight them on the shores, we can take back the strongholds of our nobles after the Saxons have taken the booty from them, but in the end our land will be lost to us."

It was only then, when it was already too late, that Taliesin realized his folly in counselling peace with the petty kings rather than with the Saxons. For the kings, though they relished being able to make war with a foreign enemy again, had used the confusion created by the Saxon attacks to consolidate their own holdings as soon as the invaders left, raiding one another's lands as their ancestors had done. The greatest coup of this kind was accomplished by Lot of Rheged.

When the king of Dumnonia and all his sons were killed in one fierce skirmish, Lot—who had maintained his own holdings by hiring a thousand German merceneries—picked up the pieces of the fallen kingdom, marrying Dumnonia's queen so that he could lay legal claim to both the northern and southern extremes of Britain.

The other kings, fearing Lot's immense power, dared not oppose him. When Arthur questioned the king of Rheged's annexation of Dumnonia, Lot slyly drew attention away from himself by bringing up the matter of succession.

"In these troubled times, a man's life—even that of the High King—is a fragile thing, my lord," he said smoothly in front of the council. "For proof of that, look to the ashes of our colleague, Cheneus of Dumnonia, who left behind no heirs to protect his lands from the savage hordes."

Arthur knew where this was leading. In nearly twenty years of marriage, his wife Guenevere had produced no children. Clearly it was to Camelot and the throne of the High King himself that Lot now cast his greedy eye.

"Had I not arrived in time to save Dumnonia and her widowed queen, they would now both be in the hands of the Saxons."

"It would have been better had you come when first I summoned you," Arthur said dryly, "so that the king of Dumnonia and his sons, as well as the queen, might yet be alive."

Lot shrugged expressively. "An army the size of mine," he said, looking carefully at each member of the council, "cannot march down the length of Britain in one day."

His threat was not lost on the petty kings. They looked down at their hands, each unwilling to be the first to speak against Lot. They understood, without a word being spoken, that the combined forces of Rheged and Dumnonia could crush any one of them in peacetime, and all of them at once if he should choose to attack them during a Saxon invasion.

"If you cannot produce an heir," Lot continued, "you must name one of us as your successor."

There was a collective hush among the council of kings, for they all knew who among them would have to be chosen as successor if a full-scale civil war was to be avoided. Some of the members were already thinking of ways to ally themselves to Lot against the rest of the kings; others, who possessed the foresight to realize that Lot, as High King, would have them all executed as his first act of office, ventured at last to speak.

"There is still the possibility of an heir," King Owain of Deira said, studiously avoiding Lot's gaze. "If you were to put Queen Guenevere aside . . ."

The sigh of relief from the other kings was audible. "Yes," one of them answered quickly. "A new queen . . ."

"An heir . . ."

"My lord, if you would consider one of my daughters . . ."

Lot could only fume in silent rage. At last, when the decision to eliminate Arthur's queen had been made by all except Arthur himself, the king of Rheged rose to leave.

"Felicitations, Highness, on your forthcoming marriage," he said with a mock bow, "and on the hopeful birth of your son and heir. May he live long." He added, "And grow quickly."

"It was a threat!" Taliesin paced the floor of the solar at Camelot as the High King reviewed a pile of parchment scrolls piled on the table in front of him.

"I don't need a wizard to tell me that."

"Both to your own life and to that of your unborn heir."

"Unborn and unconceived," Arthur reminded him, signing his name to one of the scrolls.

"Who will you choose as queen? The alliance will be crucial." The Merlin's mind was whirring, ranging around to see all of the ramifications of a second royal marriage. "Not to mention the reaction of Guenevere's family. If they were to rebel—"

"They will not rebel," Arthur said, "because I will not put Guenevere aside."

Taliesin stopped in his tracks, blinking. "What did you say?"

"I said I will not forsake the queen." His voice was like steel, and his eyes even harder.

"But . . . but the tribal chiefs . . . Lot . . ."

Arthur set down the quill in his hand. "Guenevere is my wife," he said quietly.

Taliesin had to reach for the arms of a chair to steady him as he sat down. "Arthur, she is . . ." He dreaded the word, but it had to be said. "She is barren."

"Yes, she is barren!" the king shouted. "Yet she is my woman, and I will not cast her away like an object of scorn!"

Taliesin rose quietly. "Then take the cup," he pleaded in a whisper. "The cup of eternal life. I have offered it before—"

"And I have refused it," Arthur snapped.

"Arthur, you must listen to me. If you do not wish to live forever, then keep it only long enough to outlive Lot and his schemes. Keep it to bind the kingdoms of Britain together, to further your plans for trade with other nations. Keep it, for the sake of the gods, Arthur! Keep it." He could barely speak now, so great was his emotion, but still the king was not moved.

"It is for the sake of the gods that I cannot keep it," he said. He smiled at the Merlin's confounded expression. "Our lives are short, too short to see the end of the gods' plans. And yet we serve those plans according to their will, whether we wish it or not."

Taliesin could only stare. He had not thought the king capable of such abstract thought. For a moment, Arthur's words had seemed to echo those of the Innocent.

"If the gods have a use for me, they will put the yoke upon me in their own time. I would not cheat them of their sport."

They will put the yoke upon me. Taliesin thought of the old woman who had known everything, even the terrible nature of her own death.

"What if the gods are dead?" he asked in a whisper.

"Then others will replace them," Arthur answered. "Man is far too interesting to be left alone."

The next few years were a time of relative peace for most of Britain. The Saxons continued to raid, but their forays, though frequent, were small and usually restricted to the coastline of Dumnonia. This was probably only because Dumnonia's shores were more accessible than the rocky coastlines of other kingdoms, but the petty kings liked to think that Lot of Rheged had been personally singled out by the invaders for his ill treatment of the Saxons who had tried to live peacefully under his rule.

For a time, Lot struggled proudly to fight the invaders alone, using much of his treasury and all his storehouses of food to feed huge numbers of mercenary soldiers while his neighbors grew rich from their bountiful harvests, but finally he was forced to ask the High King for help.

Arthur had been waiting.

"The members of the council, including myself, will each provide you with three hundred armed men. You will have eighteen hundred trained fighters within a fortnight to secure your entire border," he said.

It was a most generous offer, and not one of the petty kings had even grumbled. In fact, the whole well-fed lot of them smiled serenely as the High King spoke.

Lot's eyes narrowed. "What is your price?" he demanded.

"Your colleagues wish only to help you in your time of strife, King Lot," Arthur answered. "That is the purpose of a federation such as ours. For this reason, we are concerned with more than the state of your warfare. We have noticed that while you and your knights have been valiantly fighting the invading hordes, your tenant farms have been failing. Between the Saxon raids and the needs of your army, the peasants who till the soil of Dumnonia are near starvation."

"While the rest of you have harvested bumper crops," Lot added bitterly. "If you are offering me grain, I will take a hundred wagonloads as my due for keeping the savage foreigners from your doors."

"We are not offering you grain," Arthur said coldly, "for we know how you treat your tenant farmers. Many of them have sought refuge in our lands, offering themselves as slaves in exchange for animal fodder, such was the state of their hunger. They claim you denied them even that."

"The livestock was necessary to feed my soldiers!" Lot seethed through clenched teeth.

"So they are worth more to you than the people who have given their lives to you in labor in exchange for your protection."

"That could not be helped. There are losses in war. If any of you had come forward sooner—"

"We are coming forward now," Arthur interrupted. "As High King, it is my judgment that one third of your lands in Dumnonia, excluding the coastline, be parceled out equally to each of the four other members of the council . . ."

"What!" Lot was nearly beside himself with rage. Flecks of froth appeared at the corners of his lips. His clenched fists shook at his sides.

The council members beamed.

". . . who will appoint overseers to manage the farms in their territories with fairness and humanity. Though I will not share in the division of this land, I retain the right to have these farms inspected at reasonable intervals. If the tenants have been treated poorly, those lands now given to the council members will revert to me."

Lot laughed wildly. "Why, you'll take it all, then!"

"I think not," one of the council members said.

"Aye, the High King's shown himself to be an honest man. I'll take my chances with him." As each man agreed to Arthur's terms, Lot was reduced to silence, standing in their midst like a supplicant who had been denied his petition.

"I'll expect my soldiers in a fortnight," he said before stomping out.

CHAPTER THIRTY-ONE

It was during this time of goodwill—among everyone except Lot—
that Arthur grew closest to his personal guard, the knights of the
Round Table.

There were twelve of them. Their names and faces had changed
often over the years—Arthur always insisted on fighting at the fore-
front of battle, and the elite dozen always suffered heavy losses—but
in their loyalty, honor, and ability as soldiers, they were an unchanging
unit.

During this time they were led by Launcelot who, like Arthur himself, had so distinguished himself both in battle and in peacetime that
his life had already become, by the age of forty, the stuff of myth. To
the common people he was half man and half angel, a being raised by
water fairies at the bottom of a magical lake. Here, according to legend,
Launcelot learned the art of swordsmanship—in which he had no
equal—and the discipline of piety, which found such favor with the
Christian god that he was able to bring people back from the dead.

Taliesin had grumbled resentfully when this last bit of fiction began
circulating. He could not deny that Launcelot wielded a sword like
none other; he would even admit that the man was that rarest of

individuals, a born soldier who was as comfortable in court circles as on the battlefield. What irked Taliesin was the peasants' claim that Launcelot was some sort of wizard, perhaps the Merlin's equal—or better, since the old man had never been able to bring anyone back from the dead.

Of course the Merlin had, in fact, done just that, and more than once. But he had used the cup, and so was obliged to keep its accomplishments secret. As for the altogether too-handsome knight and his supernatural powers, he could only scoff. The son of King Ban of Brittany, Launcelot had been reared not as a fairy, but as a royal prince. He had never learned magic, neither from the druids nor his Christian priests. He did not even consider himself a holy man, and was continually abasing himself on his knees before his peculiar god, weeping and begging forgiveness for such miniscule sins as thinking impure thoughts or absentmindedly honing his sword on the god's holy day.

Still, even the Merlin could not fully deny the miracle that had prompted these stories, since he had witnessed it with his own eyes.

During a tournament in the early part of Arthur's reign, Launcelot, who was still in his young twenties and not yet a member of the Round Table, was slated to joust with a knight named Naw of Catraeth, a man in his middle years with the experience of fifty battles behind him. Like many of his fellows, the old soldier regarded the pious "foreign" prince (Brittany, across the channel separating Britain from the mainland, was considered too far away to be really British) with a certain disdain for his fastidious habits. Launcelot's armor was always gleaming, polished until it appeared white in the sunlight. That in itself might not have been so offensive to the other knights, had he not kept his hands and fingernails in the same condition. He was always washing, it seemed. Perhaps his love of bathing sprang from his upbringing in the lake country, or from his strange religion, which demanded a good dousing as a sign of one's faith, but the battle-hardened soldiers found it inconceivable that a man of any merit would go about with hair as shining as a maiden's and a face so smooth-shaven that he might have passed for a eunuch.

The women loved him for it, of course, and many of the knights suffered battles with their wives more fierce than any they had fought in the king's name over the odor of their armpits.

Then, too, was the question of Launcelot's Christianity. Most soldiers were willing enough to pray to any god that seemed appropriate on the night before a battle, but for the most part they were practical men who were more concerned with keeping the lives they had than in speculating about what awaited them after death. Not so Launcelot. For him, every spare moment was spent either in prayer or doing all manner of good works, apparently to keep his soul in the same condition as his armor.

Camping out of doors, even on the coldest nights, he would offer his sleeping blanket to soldiers of lower rank than himself, or even to peasants, who fought with no more than a pitchfork. He could not see a woman without assisting her in some way, and spent an inordinate amount of time pandering to one court lady or another, even going so far as to challenge the husbands of these troublemaking females to combat over some bit of behavior that was, more often than not, none of Launcelot's business. On one occasion he even killed some provincial idiot simply for beating his wife, which had been the man's right.

This was the only time any scandal had been attached to Launcelot's name, not for killing the nobleman in the provinces—the king was quick enough to forgive that—but for allegedly bedding his widow.

This was no more than a rumor, since Launcelot's chastity was such that he would not even tumble with a tavern whore while on campaign, but that rumor was fueled by Launcelot's frequent and secret forays into the part of the kingdom where he had killed the hapless nobleman. He spoke to no one about his visits, but upon his return, he would always spend the remainder of the night on his knees in penitential prayer.

Had it not been for the praying, the other knights might have thought better of him for at least possessing the manhood to use his seed for something other than watering the fields; but they grew disgusted over his constant and obvious guilt over doing something that all of them considered perfectly normal.

And so when the time for the tournament came, Sir Naw of Catraeth expressly requested that young Launcelot be his opponent. He had chosen to joust because, even then, Launcelot's sword was nothing to trifle with. The joust, though it was taught to young boys, was one event in which an older man had a distinct advantage over a younger one. Agility counted for nothing; the event centered around a man's horsemanship and the strength of his arm, back, and shoulders. Once the lance was in place, all that mattered was keeping it—and oneself—aloft.

Too naive to realize he was about to be taught a lesson, Launcelot actually thanked the older knight for granting him the honor of jousting with him, while the other knights exchanged mirthful glances and tried to find anyone simpleminded enough to place a friendly wager on the young prince.

When the two men faced one another at the outset of the joust, the ladies in the stands chirped their dismay. Not only did Naw outweigh his slender opponent by thirty pounds, but the stallion he rode made Launcelot's spindly foreign steed look like a lap dog. But even then, the young knight was unable to envision the broken ribs he was about to sustain. He smiled to the crowd, his fluffy hair blowing indecently in the breeze, then bowed in reverence to his opponent before donning his blindingly polished helmet.

Then they charged. The older knight, gripping the lance tight against his side with a hand the size of a ham, kicked his great horse to a gallop. Launcelot, on the other hand, did nothing for several seconds. Whether this was out of courtesy to his opponent or sheer, bone-freezing terror, no one knew; but it was not until the onlookers started hooting and shrieking that he moved.

But what movement it was! With an earsplitting scream that would have done justice to the wild Scots, Launcelot and his mount seemed to fly into the air, so fast were the beast's legs. They met Sir Naw before he had even gone halfway down the field.

The suddenness of Launcelot's attack must have surprised his opponent, because at the first contact the older knight fell off his mount and lay sprawled in the mud. The other knights groaned with disappointment. A collective sigh rose from the ladies in the stands as they realized that, through a stroke of luck, Launcelot's comely features would not be marred.

The squire of the fallen knight ran over to accept his helmet, but Naw did not rise.

"Sire," the boy said softly, putting his hand on the big man's shoulder.

A crowd gathered. Finally Launcelot himself removed the man's headgear. Beneath it, Naw's normally red face was waxy white and his eyes glassy.

"He's dead," the boy said, aghast.

At that he was quickly pushed aside by the other knights, who removed Naw's armor with the swiftness of men who understood the urgency of battle wounds. On the fringes of the commotion, both still kneeling and facing one another, were Launcelot and his opponent's squire, who stared in what looked like utter terror at the man who had killed his knight with a single blow. The boy was doubtless too shocked to be thinking of anything, but Launcelot felt in that stare an accusation so painful it was as if the lance had pierced his own heart.

Finally, the king and queen and Taliesin, followed by some noblemen from the court and their wives, made their way from the stands onto the field. The knights moved aside so that the newcomers could view the old soldier, dressed now only in breeches and a sweatstained tunic, lying motionless on the ground.

Taliesin could see by the man's skin color that his heart had probably failed. He had the characteristics of the ailment: tall, of middle years, with a large body and a big gut. He placed two fingers on Naw's neck. There was no pulse.

"I'm afraid he's gone," the Merlin pronounced.

In silence the other knights stepped forward to gather their comrade up in their arms, but they were stopped by Launcelot's pleading cry.

"My Lord!" he shouted to the king, his voice choked with agony, "Allow me to pray for this man, whose innocent blood is on my hands!"

Taliesin was about to say that the young man's hands probably had very little to do with Sir Naw's death, but Launcelot looked to be in such extremity, still on his knees, his hands clasped before him like a beggar's, that the king's wizard remained silent.

"Here?" Arthur asked.

"Yes, Majesty. It must be now."

Arthur hesitated for a moment—the span of perhaps one breath, during which Taliesin knew he was considering the large crowd in the stands, and how they would begin to saunter into the castle and disrupt the food preparation in another moment unless the tournament continued—and then nodded resignedly. "Very well. We'll wait."

Launcelot moved to kneel over the fallen knight, his head bowed. "Dear Father in heaven," he began, "I know well that this good man who lies before me was struck down because of my own wickedness."

The other knights exchanged a weary look. Toward the back of the crowd, someone said, "What'd he do, fart in church?" and a ripple of suppressed laughter ran through the gathering, but Launcelot continued, undeterred.

"It was because of my sin of lust that you brought this tragedy upon me, for you know I would rather die myself a thousand times over than to kill a man unjustly."

This time it was the ladies whose eyes strayed toward one another. Launcelot's sin of lust? It was almost too delicious to believe. Several noblewomen of the court had, for one reason or another, offered their favors to the handsome knight, but he had refused them all. If it were not for the rumor about the passionate widow in the provinces, it would have been easy to believe that the man's appetites were, as was said of those who preferred the the charms of their own sex, contrary to nature. *Now we'll know,* each of the women seemed to say without a word being spoken.

"I beg you, Father, do not consign my soul to the burning fires of hell, but permit me to atone for this grievous offense. Let Sir Naw of Catraeth but live, and I will never again enjoy the touch of a woman. . . ."

One of the court ladies fainted at this moment, and the moan she emitted as she fell drowned out Launcelot's next few words.

". . . devotion only to You, to the king I serve, and to Queen Guenevere, who is the fairest of your creations. Let . . ."

The eyes of the court ladies narrowed into hard slits as they turned toward the queen, who blushed so deeply that even her chest reddened down to her bodice.

"I will forsake Elaine, never to allow my eyes to look upon her countenance. . . ."

"Elaine!" someone whispered.

"Elaine of Parsifal! I knew it!"

The name ran through the crowd with the speed of wildfire. So the woman who had managed to trap Launcelot between her legs did exist, even though her lover was now swearing before God that he was cutting her loose. Still, if one could do it, so could another. . . .

Again they looked at the queen. *Camelot might see an heir, after all,* they thought.

"Hear my entreaty, O Lord of Lords. Take all the days of my life to come as an offering of repentance, and allow this man to live."

Launcelot lifted his arms and his face skyward, and remained in that position so long he might have turned to stone.

Arthur glanced at the stands. After such a long gap in the entertainment, the guests were losing interest in the tournament. He saw the king of Cornwall striding out onto the field with a roasted turkey leg in one hand and a silver Saxon goblet which had stood on the mantel of Camelot's Great Hall in the other. He sighed.

In the group gathered around the body, some of the women began to whisper, then titter. The knights had all loosened their armor during the course of Launcelot's lengthy bargaining session with the Almighty, but their faces were still dripping with sweat in the heat of the sun. Sir Kay had already sent his squire for a bucket of mead, and was cursing under his breath as he scanned the horizon for sight of him.

And still Launcelot knelt.

Near the castle, someone had dragged the musicians onto the lawn, and their tinny music, along with the singing—some of it already rather drunken sounding—floated toward the field.

Taliesin caught the king's eye and gave a subtle signal that it was time to end the vigil for the dead. With an audible sigh of relief, Arthur complied. He stepped forward, his arms outstretched solemnly to lift Launcelot to his feet. The gesture had no effect, as Launcelot was gazing heavenward with such rapture that he would not have noticed if the earth beneath him had opened up to swallow him whole.

The king cleared his throat and waited, wondering how the Prince of Brittany managed to have any blood at all in his arms after so long. He turned to Taliesin, who rolled his eyes.

Finally the king spoke, using the booming voice he normally reserved for issuing orders to troops during battle. "Noble knight," he shouted, slowly and deliberately.

And then a woman screamed.

She screamed because the dead knight's eyes had popped open. As the king peered into them with amazement, Sir Naw coughed gruffly and sat up, his face once again assuming its beet-red color.

"Begging your pardon, Majesty," he said, feeling his ribs. "Must have got cracked on the head."

The crowd which, aside from the screaming woman, had stood in stuporous silence during his remarkable recovery, now cheered frantically. The knights slapped Launcelot on the back. His face, still radiant in its earnestness, streamed with tears. The formerly dead Naw of Catraeth was handed the bucket of mead which had finally arrived, and guzzled it with noisy relish.

Then the queen fell to her knees, and the crowd's resultant gasp could be heard all the way to the castle.

"I wish to become a Christian," she said.

In the ensuing silence, several of the women—the prettiest, Taliesin noticed—and even some men, particularly courtiers who sought the queen's favor, did likewise. But neither Launcelot nor Guenevere saw them, for the look that passed between the two of them was like a river of fire.

CHAPTER THIRTY-TWO

With Launcelot as her champion, the queen's popularity among her people grew tremendously. Her subjects everywhere followed her example in converting to Christianity, particularly since Guenevere did not immerse herself completely in its harsh strictures, as did Launcelot. On the Christian holiday of Easter, she enlisted the help of the farmers' wives to dye hundreds of eggs with the red blossoms of the gorse bush, just as the druids had since antiquity, to celebrate the vernal equinox.

Holding a basketful of them, Merlin remembered the eggs piled high in the sacred circle at Mona, glinting red as jewels in the dawn light.

"We shall set them out on the castle grounds for the peasant children to find," Guenevere said. "And afterwards, they can take them home for supper. It will not hurt the king to be held in esteem by his subjects."

"No, it will not hurt," Merlin said with a sad smile, knowing that the queen was trying to preserve some of the ways of the old religion for his sake, even though the druids were no longer even a thought in men's minds.

Likewise, at what had once been the festival of Lammas in autumn, Guenevere had dozens of human-size Corn Mothers made from the first cuttings of wheat, effigies of the earth goddess who had been foremost among the ancient gods. In the days of Taliesin's youth, a Corn Mother had stood in every grain field as an offering, so that the harvest would be bountiful.

"They will offend the Christian priests," Merlin warned.

"Nonsense," she answered blithely. "I have had them made to frighten away the crows." She regarded him slyly. "So that the harvest will be good."

She even kept a trace of Beltane, erecting a maypole hung with colored ribbons, for the village maidens to weave as they danced around it.

How the people had loved her, Taliesin thought later, after Arthur's dreams had been shattered beyond rebuilding. They had loved her, yet eventually they turned against her with the hatred of a mob.

But that was not to come for some time.

The two decades following Launcelot's miracle—though the Merlin never discovered whether the "dead" knight had ever really died at all, and cursed himself daily for pronouncing Naw of Catraeth deceased after doing no more than taking his pulse—marked the true flowering of the Round Table.

Much of it was due to Launcelot himself, who was named to serve with the king's personal guard shortly after the incident on the jousting field. Here, at last, he was accepted by the other knights, since Naw's son, known for his prodigious drinking ability as Dry Lips, was among them and had vowed to torture any man who dared speak against the one who had restored his father's life.

With this recommendation, the younger members began to emulate Launcelot immediately, shining their armor, performing good deeds for commoners and nobles alike, disdaining the pleasures of the flesh when they could, and purifying themselves in the icy waters of a lake when they could not.

The older knights, too, though they smiled at the zealous antics of their youthful brethren, began to moderate their rough ways. Kay, who had been a member of the Round Table from the time Arthur first conceived of it, made a valiant effort to control his usually colorful language while leading the new recruits who came to Camelot in a steady stream through their daily drill. Unfortunately, this restraint made him so ill-tempered that he instigated a brawl nearly every night in the Great Hall after dinner until the king ordered him to begin cursing again.

Gawain, the second-oldest of the group—and the most indispensable, since he knew every town, village, forest, and field in Britain—had few faults to correct. He spoke little, thought less, noticed everything, and forgot nothing. Yet even he began to wash his hair and beard with passable regularity, and even bought a wooden comb to use on special occasions.

But the real change Launcelot wrought was in the way the Round Table knights fought. The members of Arthur's personal guard had always been brave men, prepared to throw away their lives in an instant to protect their king, but their valor had been a series of individual acts.

It was the way the tribes of Britain had always fought, each man a self-contained army, charging the enemy as if he alone were fighting. It was also why the Britons lost almost every battle with the Romans during their four centuries of occupation. In the end, Caesar's legions had left the island they called Britain not because the native fighting force was so effective, but because the Britons were too stubborn to accept defeat, whatever their losses.

Launcelot saw at once that this was not the way for fighting men to gain their objective, when that objective was to keep one of their number alive. Nevertheless, he kept silent for several years, grieving each time the knights returned from battle carrying one of their own upon their shields, learning the faces and names of their replacements, knowing that those faces, too, would soon be gone.

He kept silent until Arthur himself was wounded after eight of the twelve men in the unit were killed in a single battle against the Saxons at Badon Hill. It had been a terrible fight, but the Britons had won despite the near loss of their king . . . or perhaps because of it. There would be peace for some time, Launcelot knew. Peace and, once again, an entirely new King's Guard.

It was then that he finally spoke.

Hesitantly at first, counting on Arthur's word that at the Round Table all, including the king himself, were equal, Launcelot suggested that they change their tactics. "We cannot continue to fight like wild men," he said. "We must organize ourselves into a more effective formation."

"Fight like the Romans?" Kay spat. "Bah! I'd sooner eat the offal out of a pig's arse."

"It would not be like the Romans," Launcelot argued. "They depend on vast numbers and perfect discipline. I'm talking about twelve men. Twelve men who think and act as one."

"How do you propose to learn that?" Arthur asked, amused.

"We must practice fighting one another. Constantly, so that we understand in our bones every strength and weakness, not only in ourselves, but in each of the others, whatever our weapons."

Gawain wiped his forehead, his eyes closed. His weapon of choice was the light spear, meant for throwing. He did not want to imagine what would happen if he killed Launcelot—or, God help him, the king—on the castle grounds.

"Practice fighting, eh?" Kay beamed at the idea.

Dry Lips thumped the table with his fist. "I like it. Though I pity the man to put his sword against mine." He cast a challenging stare at Launcelot.

"I, too, would pity him," Launcelot said genially. "For this reason the weapons should be made of wood, and the spears blunted with cloth as well."

"What?" Kay roared. "Are you suggesting that the knights of the Round Table play with wooden swords, like children? Have you no pride, man?"

"My pride is as nothing compared with the life of my king. Or my brothers at this table." Lancelot looked to each of them in turn. "Of the eleven knights who accepted me at this table when I first joined them, only three are left. The losses in this unit are terrible. And unnecessary. We are all willing to die when our time comes, but only a fool dies when he can live just as easily. The longer we keep ourselves alive and together, the better we will be. I promise you this."

"Hear, hear," Gawain said, noticeably relieved.

"I think it's a good idea," young Geraint Lightfoot ventured. "Fighting as one, we'd be better able to protect the king. And ourselves."

"I agree," Arthur added. "I'd like every one of you to stay with me until we're all old men, and our weapons hang rusting on our walls."

"But . . . but . . ." Kay's mouth opened and closed like a trout's. "By Mithras' balls, every butt-stuffing courtier in Camelot will see us!"

"Let them watch!" Dry Lips shouted, laughing. "And they shall see that the knights of the Round Table can fight better with wooden swords than the combined armies of a hundred kings!"

So it was that, while peace stretched through the long summer and the autumn harvest and into the following winter, the noblest of Arthur's knights spent day after wearying day thrashing one another with toy weapons.

Kay, who led the drills, came to understand the wisdom of Launcelot's precaution as soon as they started. At the end of a fortnight, each man was covered with splinters.

But at the end of three months, they had learned one another's moves so well that their strikes were no longer marked by wounds, but by kills. The cloth-blunted tips of the swords and spears were smeared with berry juice, so that each could see where another had struck a blow to him which would have been fatal had the weapons been real. Each knight was killed almost daily.

In six months' time, there were no injuries and no kills. Each knight knew himself and his fellows so well that they could neither harm one another nor be harmed.

"Still playing at being soldiers?" one of the knights from Arthur's regular army jeered when Kay walked in to dinner, red-nosed and shivering after another day of practice on the snow-covered practice field. "Or did you lose your stick?"

On the instant, twelve pairs of hands reached for the man and hurled him across the Great Hall.

They had become one mind as well as one body. When the Saxons invaded again, the Round Table had no losses through seven months of fighting.

Twelve years later, only three members of the king's personal guard had been carried back to Camelot on their shields. Once a commonplace occurrence, the funeral of a Round Table knight was now marked with great ceremony, as if a member of the royal family had died.

And for Arthur, the pain was just as great, since the knights had taken the place of the brothers and sons he had never had. When Bors, a brilliant soldier who had served as Launcelot's second-in-command, had fallen in the battle of Tribruit, both Arthur and Launcelot had been nearly inconsolable with grief.

Bors had been one of the new recruits to the King's Guard during the time of Launcelot's change in training tactics—a change which the commanders of the army's other divisions had adapted after his success. The only son of a wealthy noble, Bors had sold most of his vast estates upon the death of his father and come to Camelot to serve the king, in whose name he distributed bags of silver—enough to purchase life's necessities for a year or more—to destitute women wherever he found them. He marked no difference in age or social status among the beneficiaries of his largesse: Widows, scullery maids, even tavern harlots from one end of Britain to the other found their lives changed by the young knight who asked for nothing—not even thanks—in return, but reminded them only that their good fortune came from their king.

When the other knights explained to him that the women would most likely throw the silver away in drink or hand it over to some vermin-covered lout with a thick pole between his legs, Bors only shrugged and said, "What do I care what they do with it? At least it isn't burdening my back any longer."

He had lived only to serve as Arthur's sword, and when he died, it seemed no one would ever take his place at the Round Table.

"But we must find a replacement," Launcelot said, trying without much success to raise a heavy pewter goblet to his lips. The king had invited him to share a drink in Bors' honor on the evening before the funeral. For the occasion, a cask of old Roman wine had been opened, and the two men had reminisced about past battles until the first streaks of dawn illuminated the sky.

"Bors cannot be replaced," Arthur said with the deliberate slowness of a man who has passed through all previous phases of drunkenness. "His chair at the Round Table shall remain empty, for all time." His chalice hit the table with a thud. "Under pain of death! Thus decrees Arthur, High King of Britain."

Launcelot's eyes clouded with tears. *"La siège perileuse,"* he said in the florid accents of his native Brittany. "To be occupied by none . . ."

"Under pain of death, remember."

". . . under pain of death, except he whom the hand of God shall place there." He looked blearily at the king. "We have to leave some room for God."

"Oh, very well." Arthur waved the detail aside. "I'll make the pronouncement at the funeral."

* * *

"What do you mean, you're going to leave Bors' seat empty!" Merlin snapped as soon as the mourners had left the gravesite. "How much wine did you drink last night?"

"It will remain unoccupied, as a sign of respect," Arthur said with as much dignity as a man suffering from the effects of ale-head could muster.

"Respect!" the wizard shrieked. "We're not talking about a dinner party, Arthur. This is your personal guard, responsible for your life. You can't leave a spot empty because of some sentimental—"

"Enough." Arthur pressed his thumb and index finger against his eyes, hoping to stem the throbbing that threatened to pop them out of their sockets. "I've said that the seat will not be filled, and that is the last I'll speak of it."

With a sigh, Merlin followed him into the castle. There was no point in discussing Bors' seat—or, as the young knights were already calling it, the Siege Perilous—with the king until he was in a better temper. Merlin shooed away the servant who was waiting to remove Arthur's ceremonial robes.

"Bring a glass of wine," he instructed, unclasping the king's heavy fur-trimmed cloak himself.

"That's not for me, I hope," Arthur said.

"Indeed it is. If you were more of a drinking man, you'd know that it's the only thing that will allow you to survive the rest of the day." When the wine came, Merlin added to it some powdered burdock root from the medicine bag he always carried with him. "Here," he said, handing Arthur the drink. "Although I've half a mind to let you suffer."

"Hah! It's your constant prattle that makes me suffer, not the wine." He quaffed down the potion, then looked through the morning's documents. Merlin, meanwhile, found a bound copy of Plato's *Republic* and leafed through it absently while reclining on a settee. The two of them were so accustomed to the other's presence that each felt as comfortable as if he were alone.

"By God, I do feel better," Arthur said after a time.

"I said you would, didn't I?" Merlin's eyes never left the book. "Rome is dying," he said absently. "It's inconceivable—the glory of the world destroyed by shoeless barbarians." He turned another page.

Arthur's eyes narrowed. "That sounds like chat."

"It is chat."

"No, it isn't. You never chat. What point are you trying to make, Taliesin? Your subtlety infuriates me."

Merlin closed the book and sat up. "The point, Arthur, is that you must avoid civil war if you are to have any hope of containing the Saxons."

Arthur closed his eyes slowly and opened them again. "I've just buried a friend. Do I really have to talk about this now?"

"I am sorry about the loss of Sir Bors," Merlin said softly, "but you are the king, and the affairs of kings do not cease because of sadness. As for having to talk, you do not. But I would appreciate it if you would listen."

Arthur leaned back in his chair. "All right. Be brief."

"I have heard stories about Lot of Rheged. One of them is most disturbing—"

"Are you referring to the one about his using magic to kill me?" Arthur laughed.

Merlin's eyebrow arched. "It is not a matter for hilarity," he said. "Two of Lot's serving girls fled Dumnonia for their lives after seeing a room in his castle draped in black and filled with bones and all manner of relics. . . ."

"A likely story," the king said, unimpressed. "Who told you this?"

"A farmer who gave the girls shelter for the night. I spoke to him myself, while I was out gathering herbs."

"And the girls? Where are they?"

"Dead. The farmer found them drowned in the river the next day."

"Which, of course is proof that they were killed by sorcery."

"Well, hardly proof . . ."

"Thank you," Arthur said. "Taliesin, I hear a dozen of these stories every day. They mean nothing, except that we've been at peace so long that the people don't know what to do with their time."

"Arthur, there is such a thing as black magic—"

"Don't tell me you take this nonsense seriously! Besides, my wizard is better than any Lot can drum up." He grinned.

"King Lot does not have a wizard. He has a wife." Merlin added with a shudder, "A most dreadful creature."

"Queen Morgan? She's considered a great beauty. Lot got more than one prize when he seized Dumnonia from under the noses of the Saxons."

"He may have seized it from under the nose of its rightful ruler, as well," Merlin sniffed. "As you may recall, there were many reports that King Cheneus died with the black tongue of a poisoned man."

"Yes, but the six Saxon arrows in his belly were a more likely cause of death."

"He might have been poisoned before he ever left his castle to fight," Merlin persisted.

"Good God, you sound just like the petty kings! What possible reason would the queen of Dumnonia have to murder her husband while he was engaged in battle? Do you think she relished the prospect of being carried off across the sea as a Saxon slave?"

"Cheneus was an old man. Morgan may well have poisoned him to ensure that he would not return from the battle. Remember, she had four sons. I doubt if she'd anticipated that they would all be killed alongside their father."

Arthur shook his head. "Well, you may believe what you like, but it's all too far-fetched for me. At any rate, it was some time ago. Even the other kings are happy since they received a portion of Dumnonia."

"Four of the other kings," Merlin said. "Lot certainly was less than delighted."

"He got six hundred troops for his inconvenience."

"But Queen Morgan got nothing. And Dumnonia was originally her land."

Arthur picked up the empty wine goblet, then set it down again. "Just what are you getting at, Taliesin? You're giving me a headache."

"I am trying to remind you to be prepared. Lot and his queen are powerful enemies."

"They are not enemies, Taliesin. Lot is a member of the council of kings. If he were to strike out against me, the others are bound by oath to fight him."

"But would they? For a king with no heir?"

Merlin's words struck deep into the king's heart. Arthur's gift of Dumnonia's farmland to the petty kings had temporarily stilled their demands for him to take another wife, but those demands had not been forgotten. The kings knew that if Arthur died without an heir, Lot would eventually rule as High King. For them, it was a question of whether to ally themselves with Lot before the bloodshed of civil war began, or to risk losing their kingdoms after it was ended.

"I cannot put my wife aside," the king said softly. "It would shame me as a man. As a human being."

"Then take the cup. I still have it."

"The . . . Oh, not that again." Arthur turned away.

"It is the only way, Arthur," Merlin pleaded. "Until you have someone to rule in your place, you must live."

"By sorcery? I think not. My problems are a matter of statecraft, not witchcraft."

"It is not witchcraft!" Merlin hissed. "The cup is a gift from the gods. From *your* god, if you will. Take it."

"I will not take it!" the king shouted, his voice suddenly echoing through the chamber. "You accuse the queen of Dumnonia of using magic to achieve her ends. Do you think I would resort to such means in order to rule if I am not fit to do so by my own abilities? Then you do not know me, Taliesin. You do not know me at all!"

The Merlin was silent. He did know the king; and so he knew there was nothing more to say.

Arthur held his head in his hands for a moment while the echo died away. When he finally looked up, his face was worn with care. "Please excuse me, old friend," he said quietly. "There are matters I must attend to."

Merlin nodded.

As he left the castle, he remembered his first vision of Arthur, years before the man had even been born. The gods had set before a young bard named Taliesin the task of helping a great king to change the world.

In that moment, he knew that he had failed both his king and his gods.

CHAPTER THIRTY-THREE

Taliesin left Camelot shortly afterward. Disappointed in himself, dismayed that the magic he had struggled so hard to learn had counted for so little in the outcome of his life, he put the intrigues of the court behind him and moved to a cottage near a lake. There he found a young student to teach and to keep him company during the long winters while he drifted contentedly into old age.

Most of those at court thought the old wizard had died. He had never announced his departure; he had simply left one day and not returned. Out of deference to King Arthur, no one mentioned the Merlin around him.

But they talked among themselves.

In some circles, they talked of nothing else.

"The High King's sorcerer is dead," Lot whispered into his wife's ear.

For the past six months he had been in Rheged, to the far north, attending to the lands he had neglected since the onslaught of Saxon invasions along Dumnonia's coastline. It had been a long time since he took his pleasure on Morgan's hot flesh. Even though his bed had rarely been empty during his absence from Dumnonia, the first thing

Lot had done upon his return was to ravish his queen as if she were a peasant in the fields, and she had not disappointed him in her response. Now he lay back, satisfied and sleepy. "I heard the news on the journey home."

"Sorcerer, bah! You mean that old fool they call the Merlin?" Morgan drank some wine from a goblet beside her bed and passed it to Lot. "He was never anything more than a druid, lucky to have had a roof over his head. No doubt King Arthur finally had enough of his doddering ways and had his throat cut."

"Many in the High King's army attribute his strength in battle to the Merlin's spells," he said, sipping the wine thoughtfully.

The Queen turned her head toward him with interest. "Oh?"

"And Arthur still has not put aside his barren queen. The provincial kings on the council are worried. Two of them sent emissaries to Rheged to talk about an alliance."

"With you? Then they're frightened."

"Oh, yes." He gave the goblet back to her and gathered the bedcovers around him. "Our time is coming, Morgan. Soon." He clasped her hand in his. Within seconds, he was snoring soundly.

Queen Morgan gently extricated her hand from her sleeping husband's. Lot had always felt himself to be the prime mover in the plans that were finally coming to fruition, she thought with some amusement. Actually, he had only been a tool to achieve her ends. Morgan's real partner was a man Lot had never met, a former lover of hers. The best lover she had ever had, although she had only had him once. Yet she had never forgotten the man with eyes as deep as the sea and a dark passion as powerful as her own.

His name was Thanatos.

He had been magnificent, and Morgan's beauty had matched his own. Even after the birth of three sons, her breasts were still full, and her face smooth as a girl's. King Cheneus of Dumnonia had married her for her beauty alone, since her family could offer him nothing in return for the honor of making her his queen.

The daughter of an impoverished provincial knight, Morgan had grown up in a house heated by dung fires and carpeted with straw. She had welcomed the opportunity to leave the drudgery of mending and weaving and tramping grapes with the farmers who worked her father's meager estate for the luxury of a queen's life.

At first, it was of no consequence to her that Cheneus was a widower nearly thirty years her senior, or that he had a fully-grown son with a wife of his own. It was not until she produced her first child that she understood that none of her offspring would ever wear the crown of Dumnonia. Worse, Cheneus' plain-faced but pedigreed daughter-in-law made it clear that when the king died, Morgan would be given rooms in a remote section of the castle, while her undistinguished son would be taken into the priesthood of the Christians, where he would live out his life in poverty and obscurity.

The daughter-in-law was the first person Morgan poisoned.

It was a clumsy affair. She had used nightshade, and far too much of it, so that the woman's eye sockets were as swollen and black as if she had been pummeled to death by a mace. Still, no one had questioned her passing, since she had never been particularly hardy. With a few sincere-sounding words and a torrent of tears, Morgan managed to convince both Cheneus and his son that the wretched creature had been suffering from the wasting disease for months and had bravely kept her illness from the men out of love for them. Morgan even showed them a pot of powder that she claimed the deceased had used to cover the ravages of her illness which were visible only now, after her death.

Cheneus' son followed her to the grave within the year. Morgan knew that a second poisoning so close after the last would cause suspicion, so she looked to Cheneus' knights for assistance. With a few inquiries, she determined which among them were in need of money, and among those, she found one who was also heavily in debt for a number of gambling losses.

This was the first lover she took. After he had spent his seed in her, she offered him a bag of gold in exchange for assassinating the prince. He was aghast.

"This is worth a great deal more than your life, at the moment," she said, drawing curlicues on his chest.

"But . . . the *prince!*"

She laughed. "Are you going to stand on your honor? If so, perhaps you ought to put on your breeches first."

"You would not dare tell the king of this." He squared his shoulders in what he hoped was, despite his nakedness, a posture of arrogance. "You would be condemned along with me."

"Would I? For being raped by a man who stole into my rooms disguised as a common thief?" From a locked box she took a dirty tunic and a well-worn hat, along with a massive necklace of gold links which her husband had given her as a wedding gift. "These will be found in the saddlebags of your mount." She put the items away. "Or you can accept the bag of gold."

The man had wept.

During a boar hunt three days later, he went with the prince into a thicket and emerged alone. The prince's neck had been torn open. There had even been a boar's tooth in the wound.

A nice touch, Morgan thought during the funeral. She was almost sorry when the knight was killed—some said by his fellow soldiers—during a raid the following month.

As consolation for the loss of his heir, Morgan gave King Cheneus another son, and then another, and yet another. Three new sons, all of them intensely loyal to their mother.

When the eldest was twenty and the youngest sixteen, she sent for Thanatos. One of her ladies-in-waiting had whispered of a magician who claimed to have killed the ancient gods.

"If you can kill a god, you can kill a king," she challenged him.

"Which king do you wish to kill, my lady?" the magician asked with a lazy smile. "I doubt that you require my services for your husband."

She had stared at him in silence for a moment, then shrieked with laughter. "You *know*," she said in amazement.

Thanatos shrugged.

She moved toward him until she stood with her face only inches from his. "Very well, then." Her eyes were glinting. "The High King."

He held up a finger. "Be careful, my lady. Is it the death of Arthur of Britain you want, or Britain itself? Speak your true wish, and none other."

Her mind raced. "But none can take the throne while Arthur lives," she said. "It will be afterward . . . when civil war ensues . . ."

"That Cheneus will fight the other kings for the High King's place?" he teased.

"Cheneus!" she spat with disdain. "My sons will win the throne."

"Will they?"

Morgan stepped back from him, her eyes cold. "What are you saying?"

Thanatos regarded her levelly. "Only what I have said before. Speak your true wish. Who shall rule Britain? Your sons? Or you?"

Morgan's breath sipped inward. "You can give me Britain?"

"Oh, yes." He smiled, his eyes undressing her. "But that is quite different from a mere murder. To kill a man—any man, even the High King—all you need is an assassin who is willing to die. But to change the course of fate . . . that is another matter entirely."

"I see . . ." She could not take her eyes from his. He had been waiting for her, she knew, perhaps for as long as she had been waiting for him. "What will it cost?" she asked.

"My fee will be high. But that is not what you meant, is it?"

"No."

"Ah. We understand each other." He bowed to kiss her hand.

She pulled him toward her, raising her face to his until their lips met. She wanted him badly.

"Your gods . . . What will they take from me?"

"All that you possess," he breathed.

"My sons?"

"Yes."

"My soul?"

"For all eternity."

He caressed her breasts. Her sex pressed against him, wet with desire.

"Done," she whispered.

The compact was sealed on an altar draped in black, surrounded by a coven of hooded magicians. As they chanted, Morgan approached the altar, naked, and lay upon it. One by one the magicians placed items around her: the bones of animals, a bowl of blood, a nugget of silver, two black candlesticks, a human skull. Two of them held a goat above the table while a third eviscerated it over the queen's body.

While the goat's blood streamed hot over her breasts and between her thighs, one of the magicians painted a pentagram of blood on her forehead. "She is fouled," he said.

Another held the bowl of blood to her lips. She drank from it. "She is fouled."

The two candlesticks were placed in her hands and lit. Black wax melted and ran over her hands, coating her fingers.

"She is fouled," the magician intoned for the third time.

Then Thanatos appeared at her feet, naked and erect.

"What is your true wish?" he asked.

Morgan raised her head from the altar table. Her golden hair, spread like a fan around her face, was streaked with blood. In the light of the burning candles, her eyes shone with a feverish glow. She reeked of death.

"I wish to be Queen of Britain," she rasped. "All of it."

Then she opened her legs to him, and he mounted her. With a moan, she arched her back to take him into her body, moving her hips faster, faster, her sweat mingling with the spilled blood of the goat, rutting in a frenzy as the magicians chanted louder, swirling around them like beings possessed.

"Take her, demons! Grant her wish, for she is your creature, she is unclean, her body has become foul in your name!"

Screaming at the apex of her pleasure, she squeezed the seed out of Thanatos' loins as her prize.

Then she lay back. The candlesticks dropped from her hands onto the floor, where they guttered.

"Will I lose this child, too?" Morgan asked later, in her solar, when she gave Thanatos a portion of his payment in gold. She knew even then, with Thanatos' seed still wet on her thighs, that she was pregnant.

"In time," he said. "But not before he has served your purpose."

She turned away. She had washed off the blood in the river, and the room felt cold. "They say King Arthur cannot be killed by a mortal hand."

"It will not be a mortal hand that kills him," Thanatos said, stroking the white belly beneath her dressing gown. "It will be his."

And so, protected by her new gods, Morgan poisoned her husband King Cheneus by giving him a cup of drugged mead while he was readying himself for battle against the Saxons.

Then she sent a messenger on a swift horse to Rheged, offering herself to King Lot in exchange for his aid. She had thought, at the time, that she would move to the north if Lot accepted her offer, leaving the kingdom of Dumnonia for her sons to rule.

As it turned out, Lot had plans of his own, and so had the evil gods. Morgan's three grown sons were killed in that same battle, as the magician Thanatos had foretold.

But one was left.

She could still picture Lot's face when she showed him the child. "You thought you'd killed them all, didn't you," she said bitterly.

Lot feigned innocence. "My lady—"

"The Saxons could not distinguish my princes from the other soldiers. But you could. You and your spawn, who wished to succeed you without interference from my sons."

His eyes shifted. Morgan knew she had spoken the truth. She was about to marry the man who had killed her children.

"The vicissitudes of war are not a woman's concern," Lot said coldly. "This castle is mine. I have won it. And you as well, by your own agreement."

"That is true. I have agreed to an alliance by marriage. With Rheged and Dumnonia as one kingdom, you will be more powerful than all others in the council of kings." She smiled slowly. "But do not think to kill this child of mine as you have the others, and do not think that you will rule alone."

"Oh?" he asked amused. "And how do you plan to rule, my lady?"

"Through my son, who will be the next High King of Britain."

Lot looked at the boy, a sullen, awkward little creature. "Him? Why, he doesn't even resemble Cheneus. I doubt if the old man could have produced him, anyway. Whose bastard is he?"

He had expected her to rage at that. Instead, she smiled at him in radiant triumph. "King Arthur's," she said.

Lot was so stunned that he could not speak.

"His name is Mordred," she said. "He will be useful to you."

"Arthur's bastard . . ." Morgan could see his mind working. "Arthur himself is a bastard; his father, Uther Pendragon, had dozens all through Britain. Still, it may not be enough of a claim. . . ."

"It would if Mordred's mother were also Uther's bastard," she said calmly. "The boy would have royal blood on both sides."

"You?" He could hardly believe his good luck. "Is it true?"

She shrugged expressively. "Does it matter? My parents are dead. It would be a small matter to create a document, a letter, perhaps . . . and I can be very convincing."

Lot stared at her for a moment. Then he strode toward her and kissed her hard on her mouth. "Indeed, you shall make a fine wife for me, Morgan," he said.

Thus was Lot of Rheged able to lay the final paving stone in his path toward the High King's throne.

*   *   *

He made the announcement at a meeting of the council of kings two years after the jackals had taken his land in exchange for the troops he had desperately needed to fight the Saxons. At that last meeting Lot had come a beggar, humiliated and starved out by war; but this time was different. Morgan was with him, and so was the boy named Mordred. Although the child was only twelve years old, he had been well schooled by his mother, and stood with the bearing of a king. In fact—and no one was more surprised by this than Morgan—he rather strongly resembled King Arthur.

It will not be a mortal hand that kills him, Thanatos had said, and over the years the queen had come to believe his words had been more than mere talk. The boy had never behaved like her other sons. He had never acted like a child at all.

With all of her other sons dead, she had felt especially tender toward the last of her brood, this child born of unearthly passion. But Mordred had never welcomed his mother's caresses. As he grew, he learned his lessons perfectly, spoke with eloquence, and grasped the arts of war with a cold intelligence that even Lot found admirable. Indeed, the King of Rheged came to look upon his wife's bastard, who shared not a drop of his own blood, as the most promising of his sons, although he was careful never to address Mordred as such.

"I am his guardian," Lot told the council, "nothing more. His father is Arthur Pendragon, High King of Britain."

The gasps in the council chamber could be heard outside the castle walls. A bastard son of Arthur's! The two members who had approached Lot with offers of alliance sighed with relief. The others stiffened in fear. With a claimant to the throne in his pocket, nothing would stop Lot from declaring war on any kingdom he wanted.

Queen Morgan followed her husband by confessing—as only she could—her indiscretions with King Arthur during the last years of Cheneus' life.

"He said that Cheneus was too old to service any but the worms in the graveyard," she said, her lips quivering just enough to betray her emotion, but not her dignity, "and that, as a servant of the High King, I was bound to do his will."

Arthur laughed at her histrionics. "Lady, please do these nobles—whom you have seen fit to regale with tales of my lust upon you—the honor of describing the marks I have upon my body."

Morgan blushed and lowered her eyes.

"What? Are you silent, Queen Morgan? But I have fought in many battles, and carry the enemy's scars in places you would doubtless have noticed had I been your lover, as you insist I was." He drummed his fingers on the table.

"I can think of none, your Majesty," she said quietly.

The petty kings shifted in their seats.

"Except for the large sword wound on your left shoulder."

Every eye turned toward Arthur.

"And the half moon upon your right thigh. And the bright red mark near your armpit."

Lot tried to cover a smile.

"Over your ribs, on the left side, there is a long, flat scar, colored white. . . ."

Arthur realized he had walked into a trap. A hundred soldiers had seen him in various states of undress on campaign, and not one of them would have hesitated to answer questions about their king's scars, which they considered badges of honor.

"Upon your belly, my lord, is one which you told me was inflicted by a dagger. . . ."

"Enough. It is clear you have come well prepared to this meeting."

"I did not wish to come at all, Majesty," Morgan said in her clear, lovely voice. "It was my intention to raise my son as Cheneus' child, as there is no other to carry on his name. Also, I wished to spare this young boy the shame of learning about the circumstances of his conception. However, since the country is beseiged by rumors of civil war owing to the lack of a legitimate heir. . . ."

"How kind of you to show such concern," Arthur said through clenched teeth.

". . . and since you yourself have told me of Queen Guenevere's infidelity with her champion, Launcelot, in order to get you a son by any means . . ."

"What!" The King leaped to his feet, reaching for his sword. Had he not been restrained, Arthur might have run both Lot and his wife through. "You are a liar, madam! And you, Lot, have broken your oath to this council by allowing this filth to be spoken here! The sight of you both is an offense against every honest man here!"

"Then we shall respectfully withdraw," Lot said smoothly.

But the damage was already done. Although Arthur tried to bring the meeting back to some semblance of order, the council members made their excuses, one by one, to leave so that they could discuss the matter among themselves and their advisors.

"The boy looks like him," they said.

"Lot will rule, one way or the other."

"If the queen does bear a child, it will be Launcelot's."

By nightfall, the news had travelled to every village in the countryside. Within a week it had spread throughout Britain.

CHAPTER THIRTY-FOUR

Launcelot knelt before the king red-eyed and nearly numb from lack of sleep. He had heard the rumor about himself and Queen Guenevere on the day of the council meeting. Since then, he had spent every night in constant prayer, ceasing only at dawn to train and perform his other duties.

"My lord . . ."

"Don't," Arthur said quietly. "We won't dignify this outrage with denials."

The knight lowered his head to his knee and wept.

"Come on, Lance, get up. We'll have a glass of wine." He drained the goblet already in his hand, then refilled it unsteadily and poured another, offering it to Launcelot.

"No, my lord."

"You won't drink? Very well. It won't go to waste." He set the cup down, spilling its contents over some documents scattered on his work table. "Well, isn't that a pretty mess." He looked around the room. "This place needs a woman's touch. That's it, I shall have to find a woman." He laughed mirthlessly.

"I believe I should leave your service," Launcelot said. "That would be best, in view of . . . circumstances."

"There's no need, not any longer." He took a drink. "The queen has consented to enter a convent."

Launcelot was stricken. "But she has done nothing . . ."

"I know." He drank the rest of his wine in one draught. "I know." From the outer bailey came the clanging of the armorer's hammers. "There will be war. The council members are already choosing sides."

"Then—Sire—why give in to them by putting aside the queen?"

"To fend off the fighting for as long as I can!" Arthur said with more vehemence than he had intended.

He missed Merlin and the old man's calm judgment. Launcelot was intelligent and loyal, but he possessed a soldier's clear-cut sense of right and wrong. He would never understand the necessity of discarding an innocent woman in order to fend off an inevitable civil war for a year or two.

He wished he didn't understand it himself.

"It was the queen's suggestion." He picked up the second goblet. "I suppose you find this all very un-Christian."

"A man's vow to his wife is sacred," Launcelot said.

"And to his country?"

"You should not have to choose."

"But I do, don't I," Arthur said waspishly. "I do have to choose, and I choose to betray my woman so that a pack of treasonous old men won't go snatching one another's land. Isn't that what you're thinking?"

Launcelot was silent for a long moment. "Yes, that is what I think," he said finally.

Arthur drank his wine. "Your show of respect for the king is touching."

Launcelot closed his eyes and took a deep breath. "I would die for the king. It is the man I cannot respect."

"Then get out." Arthur threw the empty goblet at him. "Get out, I said. I suppose you'll go next to offer Guenevere your consolation. *Consolation*—is that the term for what you do with other men's wives, Launcelot?"

The knight's eyes widened. He felt himself trembling.

"I didn't mean that," Arthur said. "It was the drink. Or the events of the week." He slumped into a chair. "Or my disgust at my own stench." He lay his head into his hand. "Go, Launcelot. We'll talk another time."

The king was not in attendance at the Round Table, but the other knights were in a state of high agitation.

An invasion, Launcelot thought. *Please, merciful Father, let the Saxons have come.*

More than anything, he longed for the mindless ecstasy of battle. Even if he were killed, hacked to pieces by a Saxon ax, it would be better than the slow death he was suffering now, waiting for the queen to be locked away in a nunnery like an adultress.

He loved her. With every drop of blood in his body, he had loved her from the moment he first saw her.

It was Guenevere's face he had pictured every time he took the widow named Elaine in his arms; it was to Guenevere that he had written so diligently, though he had addressed the letters to another. When he travelled to the provinces for his trysts of passion, he had pretended that it was to Guenevere's secret house that he was journeying. Guenevere was the center of his life, and he thought of her constantly, with the devotion of a barbarian to a stone idol.

He became the queen's champion and protector. He dedicated all of his tournament wins to her. His courage in battle had been for her. His service to the king, even the duties of his religion, had been born of his love for Guenevere.

And so, when he forswore his passionate liaison with Elaine of Parsifal after the resurrection of Sir Naw, Launcelot had only sacrificed the physical satisfaction of his love. But he had still possessed Guenevere herself, if only the sight of her.

Because he could never give her up entirely. Not even for God.

And that, he knew, not his dalliance with Elaine, had been his true wickedness.

At court, the ladies spoke of him in sighs, praising his pure devotion to his queen. But had they guessed how many nights he awoke from dreams of her, shamed and tortured and nearly willing to sell his soul for an hour in her bed?

Probably, he thought. They were all talking now, accusing him of the things he'd wanted to do for a lifetime, the passion he had tried so hard to disguise.

But God knew. God had known all along that Launcelot's sacrifice had been less than perfect, and now He was exacting His due.

Launcelot would never see Guenevere again.

Yes, he would welcome the butchering Saxon hordes.

Curoi MacDaire spoke first. "Launcelot, we wish . . . that is, the time has come, we think . . ."

Lugh Loinnbeimionach grunted and smacked MacDaire's ribs. MacDaire sat down.

Bedwyr tried next. "What MacDaire was saying is that we've been thinking about . . . well, about Sir Bors."

"What about Sir Bors?" Launcelot asked flatly.

"First off, we all knew him. That is to say, some knew him better than others. Tristan and Fairhands, I guess they didn't know him as well as some, seeing as how they were so young . . ."

"Get to it, boy," Kay grumbled.

Bedwyr fidgeted uncomfortably. "Get to it, yes . . ."

Gawain rose suddenly. "We want to fill Bors' place at the Round Table," he blurted, then immediately sat down again.

Launcelot looked around the table and had to smile despite himself. Of the hundreds of people at Camelot, these men were probably the only ones who were not consumed with Launcelot's supposed love affair with the queen.

They were the old fighters, Kay and Gawain and Dry Lips; stocky Bedwyr, who understood cavalry better than most men twice his age; Geraint the swift runner; Tristan, with a face as beautiful as a girl's, and Lugh, ugly as a winter boar. Agravaine, who lost a hand last year and then fitted it with a dagger and practiced until it was as much a part of him as his own flesh. MacDaire, who could charm a man out of his last piece of bread, and young Fairhands, who gave the others their souls. These were his brothers. Nothing Launcelot could do would ever make them turn their backs on him.

"Really," he said. "You don't like the idea of a Siege Perilous?"

"No, we don't," Dry Lips said, with a thump on the table for emphasis. "We need a full component, and a chair with a fancy name isn't the same as a man with a sword."

"By the saints' blue peckers, he's right," Kay said. "Now, no one had more respect for Bors than me. No one." He shook his jowls. "He was a fine man and a fine soldier. But he's dead now for two long years, and we're not going to bring him back."

Launcelot leaned back in his chair. "I see. And who has spoken with the king about this?"

There was a silence.

"We were hoping you would," Fairhands said at last.

Launcelot sighed.

"We'd come with you," Tristan offered.

"Thanks," Launcelot said. "But to tell the truth, I don't think that will be too difficult. I doubt if the king has even thought about the empty chair for a while. Do you have a candidate to fill it?"

"We do," MacDaire said. "A fine lad, the best of the young knights."

"And we've seen 'em all," Dry Lips added wearily.

Fairhands nodded. "We wanted you to look them over with us, but you were . . . well, busy." He lowered his eyes. Kay sniffed and gave Launcelot a hearty slap on the back, a gesture that brought the great knight close to tears with its crude eloquence.

"Very well," he said hoarsely. "If you like him—"

"You have to like him, too, or we'll kick the blackguard out on his arse," Kay said. "He's waiting outside."

"Out—" Launcelot laughed. "You blighters! Suppose I'd refused to fill the chair? We all have a vote at this table, you know."

"Oh, we'd have talked you into it," MacDaire said with a wink.

"Well, bring him in, then. That is, if he's not afraid the Perilous Seat will swallow him up."

"We'll tell him God picked him," Dry Lips said. "That's part of the story, isn't it? If God picks you, you're all right."

"Fine. Which of you is going to say he's God?"

"Lugh," MacDaire answered casually on his way to the door. "The devil himself wouldn't argue with him." He showed the young man in. "Sir Launcelot, may I present Sir Galahad," he announced.

The knight bowed. Launcelot squinted at him. There was something familiar about the fellow . . . more than familiar . . .

Then he rose and their eyes met. "Merciful Lord," Launcelot whispered.

Galahad was the very image of Elaine, the woman he had loved with his body while his heart had longed for the Queen. The eyes were Elaine's, serene, almost saintly eyes that had wept with gratitude when Launcelot prevented her husband from beating her to death. Eyes that shone with love for him whenever he came to her, filled to bursting with guilty passion for another woman. Eyes that he often suspected had known the truth without being told.

She had never accused him, never shown him anything but courtesy and kindness. When he came to her house without warning, Elaine had always greeted him as if she had been expecting him all day. And when he left again, after using her for a hour, she would say good-bye with a smile, never asking when he would come again. Even when he forsook her forever without a word, she had offered no recriminations—no letters, no gossip designed to reach his ears.

He saw her once again, several years after the incident with Sir Naw. She was picking wildflowers in a field with a small boy by her side. Her hair was bound by a kerchief, and she wore a long white apron that billowed like a sail in the summer breeze. She had looked beautiful.

Launcelot had hoped to ride past without being recognized, but the boy shouted, "Look, a knight!" and began to run toward him. Feeling like a thief who'd been caught, Launcelot halted his horse and waited for the terrible moment when he would have to speak with her, but Elaine called the child back with a word. Then she smiled at the lover who had betrayed her with such callousness and waved to him in farewell.

That was the image he had kept of Elaine from that day: a woman surrounded by flowers, waving farewell.

Of course she had not told him about the boy—this boy, now grown into a man and standing before him in the armor of a knight. Launcelot had never given the child in the field a second thought, but he knew now. Galahad's face was Elaine's, but his coloring and height were Launcelot's own.

"What is your surname?" he asked thickly.

"Parsifal," the young man answered. "Though my father died before I knew him."

"And your mother?"

"She died, too, sire. Last year."

Launcelot lowered his head in shame and regret. "I am sorry to hear it. She was a fine lady whom I had the honor of knowing."

Galahad's eyes shone. "Yes, Sire. She told me that once you chanced upon our lands, and slew a wicked man who was about to kill us."

"A wicked man," he murmured. *But not so wicked as myself.*

"And once again we saw you, riding past a fallow field. I was not yet seven years old, and had never before seen a real knight. My mother told me that you were Launcelot of the Round Table, and beloved by God." He blushed crimson. "It has been my prayer ever since to serve the king by your side."

Launcelot tried to speak but could not. At last he cleared his throat and rose slowly to his feet. "And so you shall, young Galahad of Parsifal. Take the seat that none except he whom the hand of God shall place there may occupy."

The other knights got to their feet as well, drawing their swords from their scabbards.

"By the grace of God," Kay said, holding his sword over the table.

The others touched the tip of his weapon with their own. "By the grace of God."

At the precise moment when Galahad sat in the long-unoccupied chair, a ray of sunlight appeared through the narrow window and beamed directly onto the young man. In the glare of the sudden light, the dust motes in the room seemed to swirl around him like moondust. A horn sounded—a call to some courtiers' hunt, no doubt, but for Launcelot, filled with memories of lost chances and broken dreams, it was the trumpet call of heaven itself. It heralded a new hope—not for him, for his time was past, but for the world.

"Sir Galahad," he said.

"Sir Galahad!" the others shouted in approval.

Tears streamed down the young man's face. The mission of his life had begun, and though he did not yet know what that mission was, he would serve it to the end of his days.

I was once the queen's champion, but he will be the king's, Launcelot thought with pride. *God be with you, my son.*

The queen left the next day. It was done without ceremony: Guenevere came out of the castle dressed in a plain black gown, like a widow. A serving woman walked behind her carrying a satchel in which a few of the queen's personal things had been packed. The woman was weeping; after the satchel was given to the equerry, Guenevere kissed her upon both cheeks, then ordered her back inside.

Two members of the King's Guard served as her escort. Launcelot had chosen himself as one, and Galahad as the other. Neither spoke as the queen mounted her horse.

She looked around, allowing her eyes to explore Camelot for the last time. The window in the king's solar was empty.

Did he ever say good-bye to her? Launcelot wondered. Or had the king simply pretended, as he himself had pretended with Elaine, that the woman who loved him no longer existed?

Guenevere's face was drawn, her eyes huge beneath the feathery brows. Launcelot had not noticed until then how thin she had grown, how fragile her alabaster beauty.

"Well, then," she said with a smile, "I suppose we had better be going."

With a nod, Launcelot led them out of the courtyard at a walk. When Camelot was a mile behind them, spread out over the hills it occupied like some fairy kingdom, she looked back.

"It feels strange to leave one's home," she said. "I've only done it once before, and that was . . ." She looked down at her hands.

That was to marry Arthur Pendragon, Launcelot thought. Arthur, who had pulled the magical sword from the stone to bring peace to all the world.

Dreams died the hardest death of all.

"I imagine this will be rather like a grand adventure for me. A little frightening, but . . . interesting. . . ." Her voice faded away.

"Yes, my lady," Launcelot said.

As they approached the convent, Launcelot felt an overwhelming impulse to grab the reins of her horse and gallop with her back to Brittany. He still had lands there; he could see that she lived in comfort for the rest of her life. It would be a place of gaiety, with parties and music and beautiful gardens blooming under Brittany's warm sun. Yes, it was possible! They would . . .

He actually reached for the reins, heedless of what would inevitably happen—the King's Guard coming to claim her, the necessity to fight and perhaps kill his sworn brothers of the Round Table before his own certain death, and perhaps Guenevere's as well.

He reached for the reins, but the queen stopped him. She put her small hand over his while she looked into his eyes as if he had spoken his reckless plan aloud. They said nothing; they did not have to. All of their unwritten history was revealed in that silent moment between them.

She loved me, too. The revelation struck him like the blow from a mace. *All those years . . .*

Then she released his hand and rode on, ahead of her knights, through the wide abbey gate.

"I'm glad you introduced me to Christianity," Guenevere said lightly as he helped her to dismount. "Otherwise, I should be quite an oddity in this place."

Overcome by emotion, he went down on one knee before her. "My lady . . ." he rasped, but could say nothing more.

She stood perfectly still. When he looked up, he saw that her eyes had welled with tears.

"Good-bye, my champion," she whispered. Her voice quavered for the briefest moment before she brought it under control. "I shall miss you."

She was gone.

The abbess had come out to greet her, and a stableboy had taken her horse, and she had walked through a heavy oak door. And then the door had closed.

Launcelot sat mounted on his horse for a long time, watching the door close again and again in his mind. Galahad sat with him in silence, though the sky clouded over and a strong October wind had begun to blow piles of dry leaves against the convent's outer walls. By the time Launcelot finally wheeled his stallion around, the first fat drops of rain were falling.

"I think it's going to be a bad one," Galahad shouted.

Launcelot looked into the wind, toward the northern hills. Beyond those hills were the ruined cities of the Romans, squalid ratholes inhabited by bandits who waited by the tumbled remains of roads for travellers whose throats they would cut for a piece of stale bread and spoiled meat. Past them lay the wide plain of Salisbury, where the druids' monument, Stonehenge, still stood, and the ghosts of their dead gods wailed for revenge. Above that were the lands of Rheged. Lot's men would enjoy catching the likes of Launcelot du Lac, he'd wager. Still farther north lay Hadrian's Wall, erected in the distant past by the first of the Romans who thought to conquer Britain. Launcelot had never seen the wall, but in his mind it marked the boundary of a land that had grown too small for him.

And what lay beyond that? The rough mountains of the Picts, who still painted their faces blue and fought like demons from Hell? Or the loch country of the Scots, where monsters sang in the mist, and warriors danced to their unearthly music by the light of the moon?

"Launcelot," Galahad prodded. "Sir Launcelot, I beg your pardon, but the horses are frightened. I think—"

"Can you find your way back to Camelot?"

"Yes," the young knight said, puzzled. "Of course."

"Good." His stallion pranced with impatience. "Galahad!"

"Yes, Sire?"

"Look after the king."

He turned his steed toward the north. It was all good country up there for a man with the time to wander and nothing left to lose.

The animal reared up and whinnied. Then, under Launcelot's spurs, it raced headlong into the wind.

CHAPTER THIRTY-FIVE

Galahad did look after the king, to the last breath in his body.

Long after the cup of immortality was lost, unwanted by the king and discarded by Merlin as a burden he no longer wished to shoulder, Galahad watched over Arthur with the devotion of a dog for his master.

But Arthur had already been lost by then, to himself and to Britain.

The banishment of the queen had broken him. After putting her aside, he could never again stomach the petty kings and their advice. He did not take another wife, even though many were offered to him, bringing with them powerful alliances which might have averted the catastrophe that was to follow.

He also never sat at the Round Table again. Launcelot's departure wounded him, and the wound did not heal. During every waking moment, the knight's terrible words rang in his ears: *I would die for the king. It is the man I cannot respect.*

Arthur, too, could no longer respect the man he was. For all the trappings of his office, he felt he was not worthy to sit among men of valor and unwavering loyalty.

His reign began to crumble. The Saxons continued their desultory attacks, gradually making inroads into Britain's interior to band with their displaced countrymen who had once tried to make their homes there. Together they carved out territories which they defended against the king's troops as if they were legitimate kingdoms.

"This is the final irony," Arthur told Merlin at the old man's lake cottage. "While Lot amasses his army and Morgan waits for her son to grow old enough to lead that army against me, I am losing my soldiers in a war against the same Saxon homesteaders I wanted to welcome twenty years ago." He tried to smile. "It does no good to fight them. When the tide of battle begins to turn against them, they vanish into the woods. They might as well be spirits."

"Unfortunately," Merlin said, "they are not spirits. I have heard that Lot has been paying them, and handsomely, to set up their encampments on your land and not his."

Arthur sighed. "Well, it's a way to keep his army intact, I suppose. Although he'll have to deal with the Saxons eventually, after I'm gone."

It pained Merlin to hear the king speak of his death. "Lot may not succeed you."

"Oh, he will. For a while, at least." He stretched his arms over his head. "Damn it all, I'd give it all to him right now, if I weren't certain that he'll drive the country into ruin. As it is, I've sent word to the farmers to put by any extra grain and dried meat they can spare against the day when he finally makes his move." He shook his head. "He'll gouge the very livers from their bellies, the poor devils."

"What about a peaceful transfer of power? You could name a new High King, if you want to take yourself out of things."

"It wouldn't accomplish anything. Lot won't serve another High King; he doesn't even want to *be* High King. He wants to rule all of Britain absolutely. The others know that, too. Some of them are already handing over their troops to him, hoping he'll toss them a bone later. Imagine their surprise when the hangman's noose is put around their necks."

He drummed his fingers on the table. "I suppose you're going to bring up that blighted cup again."

"No," Merlin said quietly. "The cup is gone."

"Who took it?"

The old man remembered his last sight of the miraculous relic, clutched in the talons of a bird, disappearing into the sky. "The gods, I think."

Arthur took a deep breath. "It's just as well." He examined his fingers. "Young Galahad's seen it, you know."

"He has?" Merlin nearly fell out of his chair. "Where?"

"In a vision."

"Oh."

"He claims to have them. Strange, for a fighting man."

Merlin shrugged, uninterested.

"He's a Christian, like Launcelot. He thinks it's the cup of Christ. He calls it the Holy Grail."

"It may be. I don't know its origins," the old man said. "But how does he even know about it? I never showed it to anyone except you. Did you tell those soldiers—"

"Of course not. They'd have all thought I'd gone mad. Besides, Galahad's vision isn't anything like the real thing. He pictures some gorgeous silver chalice worth a king's ransom."

Merlin smiled. "From what I've heard of the Christ, I doubt that he'd have used such a thing."

"Still, the boy's right about what the cup does. He says it heals wounds and confers immortality on its owner."

Merlin frowned. "And he got all this from a vision?"

"That's what he says. He's quite fervent about it. Wants to go looking for it."

"I can imagine," Merlin said with a sniff.

Arthur laughed softly. "No, I really think he means to find it for me. He's still young enough to feel that way about things."

"Ah. And will you send him?"

"I might. The others, too."

The old man blinked. "Have you changed your mind, then? Now you want it? Now that it's lost?" He could hear his own voice rising.

"No, no, I don't want it any more than I ever did. It's just . . . well, it might be a good way to disband the Round Table."

"Disband the King's Guard? There's a clever idea. Why don't you just chop off your head and send it to King Lot on a pike?"

Arthur waved him down. "I'll have a guard. But I'm thinking of these particular men. Kay's past fifty, and Gawain's not much younger. After they've given me so much of their lives, I'd hate to see them . . ." He didn't have to finish the sentence.

"You expect to lose, don't you," Merlin said.

"There's a strong possibility." He stood up and went to the window. "If I die, Lot won't have much use for the knights of the Round Table. He would make an example of them."

Merlin knew the king was right. Deserters from Lot's army were flogged to death. He could imagine what tortures the King of Rheged and his wife would come up with for Arthur's lifelong bodyguards.

"So you'd send them away?"

"On a quest. It's the only way I could get them to leave. 'Quest,' " he said, smiling. "The Quest for the Holy Grail. I rather like the sound of that, don't you?"

The old man smiled back. "Yes, I do," he said. "And who knows— they might even find it."

Galahad did find the cup, but not for many years, long after most of the others had returned to Camelot empty-handed.

The Grail looked exactly as it had in Galahad's vision, silvered and gilded and carved with Christian images. The plain metal half-sphere had come into the possession of a monastery in Sassa, far into the eastern lands of Gaul. The abbot there, having experienced no more of the cup's power than its warm, throbbing heartbeat, had ordered its adornment.

The abbot was about to take it to Rome as a gift for the Pope when it was stolen. At the place where the magnificent chalice had stood lay the body of a knight dressed in British armor, his throat cut.

"He was still alive when I found him," the young monk who brought Galahad's body to Camelot explained. His last words were, 'For you, my king.' "

Arthur's jaw clenched. Galahad's body had been wrapped in thick bandages for the journey, but his armor lay beside it. Painted on his shield was the red and white insignia of the Pendragon dynasty.

"I was charged to bring him here because we know of only one king on this island, and that is Arthur of Britain."

Arthur could not speak.

"Thank you," Merlin said to the young cleric, leading him outside, where he had the cook bring bread and a bag filled with dried apples. "You have journeyed far to bring our friend back to his home. Will you return now to your own country?"

"No, Sire," the monk said, brightening. "I am being sent by the

Church to Ireland, to bring the word of our blessed Lord to the savage Celts, who still follow the evil ways of the druids."

"Ah," Merlin said. "Soon the new religion will be everywhere."

"I hope so, Sire. I myself am a convert. I was born a Roman, named Padraic. But my name in Christ is Patrick."

"Well, godspeed to you, Patrick," the old man said. "But it might do you well to know that the Irish are not savages. They were writing books and making music centuries before our own ancestors learned even to weave cloth." He swallowed. "And the druids were not evil."

"Oh, but they were." Patrick looked shocked. "Perhaps on this island you do not have the opportunity to read the works of the great Christian scholars. They are all in agreement on that point. The druids were the most wicked of sorcerers, and those who remain must be put to the sword in the name of all that is good and holy."

"Good and holy," Merlin repeated softly, feeling a shiver. "How long, I wonder, will men's swords be bloodied in the service of what is good and holy?"

The young man smiled. "Why, until the ghosts of the dead shall return on the day of Resurrection," he said, repeating his catechism. He slung the provisions over his back. "Although I don't imagine that will be for a long time."

He waved cheerfully and set off toward the Irish Sea, two hundred miles distant.

"No," Merlin said, tucking his cold hands into the sleeves of his robe. "Not for a long time."

Galahad was the first to die, and Arthur was the second.

The Battle of Camlan was the only battle Arthur ever lost. Perhaps he lost it because he fought against his own countrymen. Some believed it was simply where the king had chosen to end his life.

"Civil war," he said as the first streaks of dawn began to color the sky. "Even the words are unbearable to me."

Already Lot's troops, augmented by the soldiers of three other kings in the council, were massing on the ridge overlooking the Camlan River as the king's men took down their tents and donned their armor.

"When did the gods desert me?" he asked.

They died before you were ever born, Merlin thought, but he said instead, "They have not, my king. They will fight with you today."

"That is just what Lot and his creature are telling their men at this moment," Arthur said. "Every king believes the eternal powers to be on his shoulder, as if our small lives were of consequence to any but ourselves."

"Yours is, Arthur. Long before you became a king, your destiny was written in the stars. You were born to bring mankind into a new age, an age of glory—"

"Glory!" he spat. He spread his arms to encompass the battlefield. "This is all we know of glory. To kill our brothers and be killed by them, until the earth runs red with our mingled blood. . . ."

"My Lord!" It was Kay, panting and furious. Gawain was beside him. "A pair of snot-nosed young pups claim to have taken our places with your personal guard. I ask your permission to kill them before the battle, Sire."

"I say they're spies, come from the army of Rheged," Gawain added.

"They're not spies," Arthur said. "I gave the order to replace you."

"But . . . but . . ." Kay sputtered, outraged. "We've served with you for thirty years. . . ."

"And that is too long." Arthur forced his voice to harden. "I tried to dismiss you gently by sending you on the Quest, but you gave up before a single year had passed."

"We believed you needed us here, Lord. With war brewing—"

"Well, it's come, and I shall be Lot's only target during the fighting. Under the circumstances, I would prefer not to be surrounded by incompetent old men."

"Incom . . ." Kay's head looked as if it were about to burst. "As children, we lived as brothers together! I was the first you asked to sit at the Round Table with you! Now this, this . . ."

Gawain went down on one knee before the king. Kay stared at him in astonishment for a moment; then his face blanked with understanding. "You are doing this to save our lives," he whispered, as if in accusation. "And I won't have it, damn your bones!" His words rose to a shout. Several infantrymen rushed to Arthur's side at the disturbance. "I'll not die in my bed like a woman, do you hear me? I am a sworn Companion of the Round Table of King Arthur, and my place is with you if you lead me to the gates of Hell itself!"

"Take him to the second ranks," the King commanded one of his officers.

It took four of them to drag Kay away. "Get your hands off me, you dung-eating ball-less swine! I vow I'll tear your worthless sausage out of its casing! Son of a whore . . ."

Arthur helped Gawain to his feet. "You were ever valiant, knight, and true," he said quietly. "When this is over, tell Sir Kay I said the same of him."

Gawain stood before his king with lowered head. Then he nodded curtly before loping away toward his horse.

The King watched him go. "I tried to surrender, you know. I offered my life to Lot in exchange for keeping the boundaries of the kingdoms as they are. He refused." Arthur looked up at the sky. "It's almost time," he said. "Will you watch the battle?"

"I will," Merlin said.

"Don't judge me too harshly, old friend."

"I cannot judge you at all, because your story has not yet ended."

Their eyes met. "Good-bye, old friend," Arthur said, embracing the old man.

Merlin carried the warmth of that last touch with him up to the crest of the high hill, where he stood to watch the man who had been his destiny live out his final moments.

Mordred, now a man of twenty-four, led the charge from the river, while Lot remained behind in safety.

From the beginning it was clear that the battle was to pivot upon single combat between Mordred and Arthur. The remainder of their armies fanned out into formation, preparing for the outcome of that first telling strike.

Surrounding the king, his personal guard screamed its war cry. The cavalry on either side of them charged.

Arthur was the first to use horses in battle, Merlin thought as the two armies flung themselves toward one another. From his vantage point, it all looked very tidy and planned, as if the components of war were wooden toys that moved by themselves for his amusement.

Yes, the horses. With his mounted knights, Arthur had brought every warring chiefdom in Britain together under one banner within ten years. And not a single tribe had been made to suffer the humiliation that usually follows conquest: After their defeat, Arthur had welcomed each chief into his federation as his personal equal. The country's division into six minor kingdoms had been to grant each portion of Britain its own rule, with the High King above them only to maintain peace.

Peace, he thought, was a fragile thing, perhaps too fragile to be entrusted to men.

The chieftains whose honor and lands Arthur had preserved had forgotten his gift to them. Kings have short memories. But the common people would remember. After war engulfed the land, when the farmers were reduced to eating their dairy cows and the women of the nobility forced to sell their jewels for bread, they would remember Arthur of Britain, the warrior who had been, above all, a man of peace.

Arthur was killed shortly after the battle joined. A sword seemed to snake through the King's Guard to reach its mark between the slats of armor shielding Arthur's heart. It was Mordred's sword, forged years before in magic to perform its single and unique task.

Mordred dealt the blow with cold resignation. *To kill a man—any man, even the High King—all you need is an assassin who is willing to die,* Thanatos once told Morgan, and her son had known this from his earliest years. The throne of the High King was never meant for him. Nor was it meant for Lot, though the king of Rheged was too arrogant ever to have seen the truth. Even Morgan, with all her knowledge of the dark forces, had never guessed in what manner her true wish would be granted.

But Mordred knew. He was the child of the demon gods, and he knew that he was their tool and nothing more. After he struck he waited, because his job, like his sword's, was done. He waited for the void which was his home to claim him.

Lugh Loinnbeimionach, whom not even the king's soldiers could dissuade from fighting in Arthur's personal guard, was beside the king when he fell. With a sound like the roar of a wild beast, Lugh leapt off his horse and onto Mordred.

With his huge hands wrapped tightly around Mordred's neck, Lugh tumbled to the ground. His thumbs pierced through the very flesh of his king's murderer, so that Mordred's blood spurted into his face with every beat of his heart, strongly at first, then feebly as his life ebbed away.

Lot's soldiers slashed at Lugh with their broadswords; still, he would not release his quarry, though Mordred was already dead. By the time Lugh finally gave up his spirit, his body had been butchered beyond recognition.

Nearby lay the sword Excalibur, the gods' sword which Arthur had pulled from a block of stone thirty-eight years before. It had not a drop of blood upon it.

"The king has fallen!" someone shouted.

For a moment, an eerie silence fell over both armies. The horses whinnied and stamped; the very air seemed suddenly to still with the weight of that news.

Then, from the second rank of Arthur's men, two aging knights, their gray hair shining like silver in the sunlight, galloped forward screaming their ancient war cry, and the rest of the king's army followed them into the bloodiest battle ever held on Britain's soil.

Kay and Gawain killed more than fifty of Lot's soldiers before they were cut down. The rest of the king's troops fought almost until the last man, even after the armies of Arthur's allies defected to fight with Lot against them.

When it was done, when the field ran red with blood and Lot's men cheered in victory as they put the wounded remnants of Camelot's army in chains, Merlin remembered Arthur's words.

This is all we know of glory.

He made his way down the far side of the hill, toward the place where he would wait for the judgment of whatever gods were left.

"Glory," he whispered.

CHAPTER THIRTY-SIX

Taliesin performed two final tasks before disappearing into the mists of time. The first he accomplished straightaway: He buried Arthur.

Lot had not shown the High King even the respect of burial, but had left him on the battlefield with the other corpses as food for the crows. Knowing this, the Merlin sent a student of his, a young woman named Nimue, with the first wave of women come to search among the dead for their husbands and fathers.

Nimue was clever and quick, and not at all squeamish about picking her way through a bloody field strewn with fly-covered corpses. To avoid any notice, she removed the thin circlet of gold which Arthur wore over his brow and tossed it into a coarse bag, then threw a ragged tunic over him to cover his clothing. Through sheer luck she also found his sword, which had been trampled into the mud during the heat of battle.

While Taliesin prepared the king's body for burial, Nimue polished Excalibur until it shone. "There," she said. "Now it shall be buried with Great Arthur."

"No, no, that won't do," Taliesin said wearily. "I plan to take every precaution to see that Arthur's grave is not disturbed, but if that should happen . . . Well, it won't happen."

After nightfall, just as they were about to leave the cottage disguised as a farmer and his granddaughter going to market with a cartload of vegetables, the old man brought the sword outside.

Is that going with us?" Nimue asked, tossing some pumpkins into the wagon.

Gently he stroked the burnished steel. "No," he said. "I'm going to take it to the middle of the lake and drop it there."

"The king's sword?" She put her hands on her hips, leaving black fingermarks on her apron. "I don't think he'd have liked that, wizard. It'll get all rusty." She shook her head in censure. "No, not the lake."

Taliesin sighed. The girl could be quite exasperating at times. "Well, what do you propose I do with it, then?"

"You must put it back where it belongs. In the stone."

"The stone? Are you mad? Lot owns Camelot now. We can't very well have Excalibur's hilt poking out of a rock right in front of his nose. He would burn it, or break it, or—"

"Then cover it over so he can't see it." Nimue bit her grimy fingernails, thinking. "But then, would King Arthur find it when he comes back?"

Taliesin stared at her, uncomprehending. "Arthur's dead, child," he said quietly. "He's not coming back."

"Why not? You've told me yourself that the life we know is rarely our last."

"Confound it, Nimue!" His eyebrows bushed out in irritation. "Haven't you learned anything? One doesn't return to live the same life over again. We grow through different existences. We . . . Oh, bother." He slapped the sword against his thigh, then stomped off toward the lake.

"How do you know?" she called out rudely to his retreating back. "You've never been dead. Why, I don't think you have any more idea about this sort of thing than I do."

His shoulders hunched near his ears. The girl was a horror, simply a horror.

"Isn't everything possible?" she asked.

Taliesin stopped in his tracks. He turned around to face her.

"Well, isn't it?"

The wizard held the sword up to the moonlight. *This is Excalibur,* he thought, *forged by the ancient gods for the use of one man alone.* It would take more than death to separate them.

"Good heavens, she's right," he whispered.

Nimue cupped her hands behind her ears. "What did you say?"

"I said you should get a bucket and clean yourself up," he snapped. "We're not trying to pass ourselves off as pig farmers!"

Then he ran down the rutted dirt road toward Camelot, the great sword gleaming in his hands.

The sun had just set two days later, when they reached the western shore of Wales. "What is that?" Nimue pointed to an island barely visible in the evening mist.

"Mona," Taliesin said. He listened to the silence, remembering the music from the isle of the gods. "The druids once lived there."

"Druids? You mean they were real? I thought they were imaginary creatures, like fairies and goblins."

He turned away. Nimue was very young; she had no idea how much her innocent words had hurt him.

"They were real," he said.

The ferrymen recognized him. After that first terrible night when he found the island a burned and desecrated ruin, Merlin had returned many times over the years to wipe away the traces of Mona's destruction. He had buried the dead, felled the charred trees, and cleaned the marks of evil from the rocks with sand and ash. Now, more than thirty years after the massacre, the island looked as if no human foot had ever trod upon its shores.

None of the mainlanders had, surely. They had feared Mona even while the druids had made it their home; after the slaughter, no one except Merlin—whom the ferrymen knew to be the king's wizard, and therefore impervious to the powers of spirits—had ever ventured there.

"Will you wait till morning, my lord?" the boatman whom Taliesin had selected for the journey to Mona asked.

"No. We must leave now."

The ferryman blew air between his teeth. "All right. Seeing it's you."

If he thought anything of the long wooden box which Nimue and Taliesin struggled to carry between them to the ferry, he did not mention it. Nor would he tell any brigands looking to rob a king's tomb about it. The ferrymen and their families were a close-mouthed lot, aloof and suspicious of strangers. They would guard the Merlin's secret well.

Taliesin dressed in his best robes for the short journey to Mona, as did Nimue, who wore a gown of shimmering silk. To accommodate the casket, they stood on the prow, still as statues, as the boat floated on the moonlit water toward the island shrouded in mist.

"Mama, look at Father's boat," a small girl whispered, pointing through a window at the vessel and its strange passengers.

"Shh." Her mother's arms encircled her protectively. "That is the wizard Merlin and the queen of the fairies, bearing the body of our king to the enchanted isle."

The little girl blinked. "Did he die, then, good King Arthur?"

"Aye. But don't you worry, he'll live again. The Merlin will see to that."

Taliesin and Nimue buried the king beside the Innocent, inside the sacred circle of the druids, and covered the grave with seedlings. By summer, the place would be grown over. Within ten years, it would be filled with trees. Oaks, infused with the magic of the ancient gods.

"Mother, bring us life from death," Taliesin sang, his voice hoarse with grief.

Uncomprehending, Nimue repeated the refrain.

They sang the long-forgotten words of the druids through the night, a thousand times and more until, at daybreak, the very woods rang with their music.

Merlin himself did not decide to die for several more years, during which he witnessed the destruction of everything Arthur had worked so hard to build.

The six kingdoms disintegrated almost at once. Lot ordered the executions of all his allied kings, and declared their lands forfeit to him. The ones who managed to escape before their arrest made open war on Lot in retribution for his betrayal. The families of the petty kings who were killed rallied what forces they could from among their troops. With the annexation of so much new land, Lot's original two kingdoms became unmanageable as well. Many of the old chiefdoms, melded together temporarily to form the kingdoms of Rheged and Dumnonia, now splintered off to become autonomous, as they had been in the years before Arthur the High King came to power.

Lot himself lived less than a year after his victory over Arthur. He died in his bed, poisoned, his black tongue lolling between his lips.

Queen Morgan—for she was, after Lot's death, ruler of Britain—waged a campaign to force the chiefdoms into submission, but they would not give in to a woman, even if it meant the death of every last member of the clans. A number of Rheged's soldiers found their allegiance torn between the queen and the tribal chiefdom to which their families belonged. Usually the chiefdoms won, especially when Morgan ordered her troops to destroy the seats of their own ancient clans. Desertion became commonplace, and what remained of the queen's army turned into an undisciplined mob that fed itself by raiding the farms of its own people, and sometimes of its queen.

And then the Saxons came.

They arrived in droves, their incursions into Britain now unchecked. They fought the chiefdoms, the petty kings, and Queen Morgan's army without discrimination. In the eastern part of the country they settled in homesteads and built rough villages which the warring Britons seldom bothered. To supply themselves with tools and food, the Saxons looted whatever they needed from their hosts, riding off with the horses and women which were now theirs for the taking.

Fires raged in the villages after each Saxon raid. The fields, once ripe with grain, now grew nothing but weeds. Medicine of any kind ceased to exist. Cloth for bandages was no longer woven.

Soon it became impossible even to bury the dead. Corpses lined the roads. Whole families lay butchered in their homes, left for predators to eat. The rivers clogged with rotting human bodies; the wells became poisoned with the putrefaction of the dead.

Then, on the heels of the civil war and the Saxons, came the plague.

It was called the Yellow Plague because of the color of its victims after death. Thousands dropped from the disease, their skin bubbling with yellow lesions, their bodies wasted; but by then, no one was counting the dead any longer.

Queen Morgan became infected. When her once-beautiful face grew hideous and misshapen and her luxuriant hair fell out by handfuls, one of her physicians suggested a treatment of warm salt water to heal her pustule-covered skin. For this she traveled to the ruined Roman city of Aquae Sulis with a contingent of royal guards, whom she ordered to repair one of the old public baths for her use. Here she spent her days trying to soak away the vile odor of her sores while she exhorted the demon gods to restore her beauty.

Some people who lived in the debris of the city's fallen stone buildings came out of curiosity to see the woman who called herself a queen. Most of them had the plague themselves. After a brief scuffle with the soldiers who had been ordered to guard her, they poured inside the ruined building to squat along the sides of the large tiled pool.

"Guard!" she shouted. "Where is my guard?"

The onlookers pointed at her, cackling. A woman found her cloak, made of velvet, and rubbed it over her face until someone cut her with a knife for the garment.

"Don't touch my things, do you hear me, you filthy offal!" Morgan tried to pull herself out of the bath, but the crowd pushed her back in. Someone threw a rat at her. It clawed her chest, drawing blood and pus down her body before it fell in the water and drowned.

"I am the Queen of Britain!" Morgan screamed. "Don't you understand, I am your queen!"

Another rat swam toward her. The crowd was amused. Several children scurried outside to find more.

It didn't take long; rats were the only things in Aquae Sulis which were not in short supply.

"Guard! I command you to attend me! Guard!"

"They're dead, poppet," a woman said, shaking her head sweetly.

"Those what didn't ride off," another added.

The children returned shrieking with glee, holding fat, squirming rats which they flung into the water. Morgan was the only other object in the pool, and the vermin all rushed toward her.

Screaming, she slapped them away with her hands. The people surrounding the pool laughed at the naked woman bobbing up and down in the water trying to force the creatures away. They splashed to propel the rats back toward her, cheering them on.

"Go get her, Whip! Attaboy!"

"Mine's named Lightning. See how fast he's going?"

"Well, let's give old Lightning a hand, eh? There you go, the wave'll push him."

"Hey! You're drowning Whip! Quit it!" Soon everyone was soaked, the water churning white under their busy hands, the domed building echoing with coarse laughter.

Morgan looked at their faces in despair. These people were the dregs of the world. She did not want to die here, among such creatures.

Yet these, these ugly, mindless animals, this wreckage of humanity, were what now populated the land that she ruled. There was no more civilization. There was no law. There were no boundaries, no ethics, no order, no aspirations for a better world. There were only these grinning, lice-covered ghouls.

These were her people.

"I am your queen," she whispered.

When she finally understood the truth of her words, she sank beneath the surface of the water and breathed it in. She convulsed once, twice. Her eyes bulged out. She swallowed her tongue.

I wish to rule Britain, she had told Thanatos. *All of it.*

Her last thought was that her wish had come true.

"Looks like Whip's dead," someone said.

"Where's the lady?"

Some time after they had all left, Morgan's body floated to the surface. It spun idly around the pool for a while, then came to rest in a corner, with the bloated carcasses of the rats.

CHAPTER THIRTY-SEVEN

The dark gods had won.

When Taliesin had seen enough of what they had done to his country, to the people whose wild purity had once repelled the mighty Roman legions, he bade farewell to Nimue and traveled on foot to the hill country of Wales where he had spent his boyhood, there to perform his final task as the Merlin.

It was Nimue who had given him the idea for it. *Isn't everything possible?* she had asked in her patience-stretching way while the two of them were taking Arthur's body to Wales.

She had been right, of course; everything *was* possible, if one knew how to accomplish what needed to be done.

In this case, what was required was the Merlin's very life, and even that might not be enough.

But he would try.

For you, my king. Those had been Galahad's last words. *Let them be mine, too,* Merlin thought. *I shall make this magic for you, and for the forgotten gods who made you.*

* * *

Taliesin did not wish to die on Mona. It would have been unfitting to lay his lowly bones beside those of the Innocent and the king. He chose instead a cave on the Welsh mainland, near a stream just above the shrine of the ancient god Mithras. He had been there before, on the night he had first heard the music of the druids wafting on the wind from Mona.

There would be no more music, he knew, and no old gods to bring him the visions he had seen in his youth. But there was still magic here—enough, at least, to ready him for the long journey into eternity.

He began by picking the mushrooms which had been sacred to the druids. No one ate them now, and they grew in profusion all over the countryside. He painted his body with woad and anointed his eyelids with fragrant oil, just as he had for the ritual of Beltane so many years ago.

Then he fasted. From one full moon to the next, he took nothing into his body except water from a nearby stream. He sat naked outside the cave for every moment of that time while the rain purified him and the wind scrubbed clean his soul. Like a toad, he luxuriated in the warm sun when it came. The cold he welcomed as well, shivering with life like a new blade of grass. He watched the moon wane and wax while the stars beyond it travelled in their endless voyage, their light burning hotter than fire through the void of space.

Among those who chanced to see him—a few superstitious old people still brought offerings to Mithras at his derelict shrine—some thought Taliesin to be the god himself, with his blue-stained body and his windblown white hair. Others recognized him as the king's great sorcerer, who had spirited away Arthur's body to an enchanted island where a fairy queen would watch over it until the High King's spirit returned to call him back to the world.

"The Merlin has gone mad," they whispered, staring at the grizzled old hermit who sat, naked and unblinking, before them.

Perhaps they were right. He knew he was changing, although he was uncertain as to what he was in the process of becoming.

He had been transformed once before, during his early years on Mona, from an ordinary man into an initiate into the mysteries. He had never thought about what state of being lay beyond that, but whatever it was, he was experiencing it. *Light* might best describe how he felt. Light—weightless, insubstantial, luminescent, fragmentary. He felt as if he were made of moonbeams; his emotions were in a constant state of detached, unwarranted joy. He danced in the high grass, his spindly limbs strutting gaily. He sang loud and clearly the bawdy ballads he had learned in his youth. He spent hour after hour looking at stars through the spaces between his splayed fingers.

When the moon sat full again in the sky, he bathed by its glow in the cold water of the stream. "Gods of my spirit," he called out at the top of his voice. "Gods of the earth and the universe, thank you!" He ducked his head beneath the bracing, fast-flowing stream and came up sputtering and laughing. "Thank you for giving me so much pain and so much ecstasy. This life has been a glorious gift. Thank you!"

Then he went into the cave and walled the entrance closed with rock. He lit a single candle and ate the mushrooms, one by one, until the bowl was empty.

In the candle's flame he saw Arthur die again, but this time his heart did not break with the sight, for it was beyond breaking. With the eyes of the ancient ones he watched Lugh fall, and Kay and Gawain. He saw the other knights of the Round Table as they met their fates, going each to the Summer Country of the dead.

Agravaine and Geraint Lightfoot, returning from their failed Quest, were captured by Lot's men and tortured, the skin flayed from their bodies as a mob cheered. Dry Lips was also captured. He was taken to Rheged and imprisoned there, but cheated Lot out of a third execution by selling a gold ring to a guard in exchange for a dagger, which he plunged into his own heart.

Bedwyr, the young Master of Horse, went back to his family's estates, only to find they had been confiscated during the civil war which raged for decades after Arthur's death. Bedwyr died defending the turnip field of one of his former tenant farmers during a raid by some of Lot's soldiers looking for sport.

After hearing of the outcome at the Battle of Camlan, Curoi MacDaire headed back toward Ireland, but was waylaid by thieves. He bled to death by the side of a road.

Tristan, the beautiful one, found his way home to his family's lands in the northeast where, through careful politics and heavy bribes, his father had managed to keep an uneasy peace with the new king. Seeking to keep his son out of Lot's reach, he sent Tristan to Ireland by sea as the escort of a young noblewoman named Iseult, who was betrothed to one of the Irish kings. Tristan accomplished his mission, but drowned on the voyage home.

Gareth Beaumains, called Fairhands, entered a monastery. He succumbed three years later to the plague.

Launcelot died a madman in the land of the Picts, unable to serve the king to whom he had sworn his lifelong allegiance, yet unable to forgive himself for deserting that king. After years of living like a beast in the forest, he ran to the top of a high cliff one morning in summer and hurled himself onto the boulders below.

And Galahad. Galahad had been the first of them. And the best.

Gone, all gone.

"For now, perhaps," Merlin said softly. He held out his arms to gather in the forces of energy inside the cave. Then, clearing his mind of thought, he shot that energy out again.

The crystals within the limestone walls glowed faintly. Their color dimmed as the wizard drew their power from them once again, and brightened as he released it. Each time he sent the cave's energy back the power grew stronger, augmented by Merlin's own life force. And each time it returned to him, the cave's living spirit brought with it more of the power of All That Is.

The power came from the rock of the cave and from the trees beyond it, from the green grass and the soil and the air; from the sun and moon and streaking comets and galaxies too far distant to see. From the black void of space it came, crackling through his bony fingers. From beyond the void, from places too dense and secret to belong even to the universe, and to other places yet deeper, reaching, reaching past the gods, past time, past being, reaching to the source itself, energy without matter, infinity, nothingness, All.

Reaching to the Mother.

"Mother, bring us life from death," the Merlin prayed.

The cave glowed with white light. It burned him blind; it turned his body to ash. His soul was all that was left, glowing with the light and dispersed into it.

Pure spirit now, Merlin traveled to the realm of the dead, to the Summer Country where long ago a fisherman had told him he had seen a city made of glass. Merlin had not believed him then, but he saw it now, a city not of glass but of dreams made real. And before his eyes which were not his eyes but something else, as the Innocent had tried to explain, a perception of the soul, the city became a field of flowers, a shining lake, a planet of exotic beauty, a grandmother's lap, an angel's enfolding wings. There was music here, and silence, and joy in the sky like a rainbow.

The fisherman's soul passed through him with perfect understanding. So did the spirit of his father, Ambrosius, and his brother Uther. He experienced the essence of his mother and his old nurse and the druid priestess on whom he had fathered a child after the rite of Beltane. The child was lost, doomed to the dark regions, but Thanatos would cheat his gods and live once more, and Merlin would know him.

He ranged through the realm of the dead searching for the Innocent before he realized that this place, wonderful as it was, served merely as an entranceway to somewhere else, to dimensions where his primitive soul could not venture. The Innocent was an ascended master, and between the lives of her choosing, she rested with her own kind.

Merlin possessed no magic strong enough to find her, but she had taught him enough to complete his task alone. Reaching out with tentacles of thought, he plucked the spirits of eleven men who had served King Arthur—Launcelot and Kay, Gawain and Bedwyr and Dry Lips, Tristan, Agravaine, Geraint, MacDaire, Lugh, Fairhands—and placed them into a vision of Camelot which he constructed on the infinite plains of the Summer Country. When they were in place, he found Galahad, whose shining soul had led him to the Holy Grail in the service of his king.

"You, faithful one, shall protect him in time to come," Merlin said, the words pouring in a silver thread from his spirit.

He was filled with warmth. A thousand jumbled memories buzzed through him—a boy in the forest, the sword in the stone, the building of Camelot, the marriage to Guenevere . . . It was Arthur's soul, entering his own. Arthur, who had waited so long to be born, and who would have to wait again.

"Your time will come once more," he said, catching the silver threads as he spoke. "Perhaps then, your light will not shine alone in the darkness."

He bound them together with the thread so that they would never be parted, not in the life to come, nor the ones after that. "It may take awhile. You both have lessons to learn. But Arthur the King will live again, and Galahad shall ride by his side."

"And you?" Arthur asked. "What of you, old friend?"

Merlin felt himself disintegrating. The magic was leaving him. "I cannot chart my own fate, my king. That is for a power greater than mine. But the love I bear you has no end. No end . . ."

"No end," he spoke into the flickering candle's light.

It was burned nearly to the end. He was back in the cave, his body wrinkled and white with age, but alive.

The task he had set for himself was done. The last task, the Merlin's final service to the king. Now he could die in peace.

The candle guttered and went out. In the darkness, the old man lay down upon his back and closed his eyes.

Then the crystals in the wall began to glow. Through the wall of rock came the form of an animal. It was a she-wolf, its blind eyes filled with light.

"Master," he said, feeling his heart leap. "Have you come to lead me to the Summer Country?"

But you only came back a moment ago. Do you not remember the way?

"You saw me?"

Certainly. I was beside you most of the time.

"I looked for you there."

Yes, but you do not yet know how to see the ethereal things.

"With the perception of the soul."

Indeed. It must be developed. But you've made a good start.

The wolf lay down beside him. Its fur felt warm against his bare skin. "Was I right to do what I did?" he asked, stroking the thick pelt. "To put the knights away on their own plane, to tell Arthur . . . ?"

It was the will of the gods that you help them.

"I thought the gods were dead."

Am I dead?

"Well, yes and no . . . I don't know how to answer that."

Ah, she said.

"Are you a god?"

You can see for yourself that I am a wolf.

"Then how . . ." Taliesin sighed. "I never could get you to answer me directly," he grumbled.

The Innocent laughed, her voice as lilting and gay as he remembered. *Sleep,* she said. *I will awaken you when it is time.*

"Am I not to die, then?"

Death, life, waking and dreaming, the black in the white . . . Have you not yet learned that it is all the same?

"Oh, bother with you."

The wolf licked his face. *You have done well, little bard.*

He harrumphed and turned on his side. His eyes brimmed with tears of joy.

He had done well.

Filled with hope, with a heart as light as a child's, he slept.

PART FIVE

THE
LEGACY

CHAPTER THIRTY-EIGHT

"Thanatos!" the dark magicians chanted. The ritual was almost complete.

"Help me," Kate moaned, coming to in agony. She raised her arms. They dripped with blood from the wound in her belly. "Oh, God, help me."

The cuts Aubrey had made were deep; the segments of the pentagram his knife had drawn were already shrinking, pulling away from one another.

"Thanatos!"

He held the knife high over her.

"Please kill me," she whispered.

"Yes," he answered, his eyes gleaming. "Yes, my darling. I will." He bent low to kiss her lips. Then with one massive swoop, he thrust the blade into the center of the pentagram and up, deep into her heart.

Kate shuddered once, then was gone.

Taliesin closed his eyes in pity. His tears fell onto the dirt floor, and he had not the strength to wipe them away.

"Thanatos!" the priests boomed. "The power is yours!"

Using the ceremonial knife, Aubrey opened Kate's mouth wide. From it issued a vapor dark as woodsmoke. "Take the spirit of the sacrificed one, O demon gods," he intoned. "Use it to destroy the last of your enemies."

Slowly the magician withdrew the blade and pointed it toward Taliesin. The foul vapor trailed after the knife, then snaked of its own will in a circle around the old man.

Taliesin felt himself choking, strangling on the thickening vine of Kate's tainted spirit. Images of the druid priestesses hanging from Mona's charred oaks spun dizzily in his mind. Kate was one of them now, one of the dead whose souls had been taken by magic, twisted into evil by the magician named Thanatos and his dark gods.

Those gods had won once before, and now, Taliesin knew, they would win again. Arthur would not have a third chance to live out his desiny. Even the Merlin did not have enough magic for that.

But there is Galahad, bound to the king by a silver thread.

The old man looked up, his breath catching.

Galahad.

Hal might still find the boy. Even with Taliesin dead, Hal might yet be able to keep Arthur out of the magician's snare.

"Hal . . ." he said weakly. He could not focus. The spell Thanatos had produced was growing stronger, the vapor now spinning, sucking the old man's life force into it like a vortex.

"Hal!" he called out with all his strength, but his voice could not be heard above the whirling wind that surrounded him. He tried to clasp his hands to work what energy remained in his body into them, but they would not move.

"I cannot," he whispered in despair. "I cannot do this alone."

You are not alone.

The voice that spoke was clear and loud. Its very sound, if it had even been a sound at all, pushed the whirlwind's core away from Taliesin, leaving him in an eye of calm space.

We are never alone.

In the old man's mind appeared a gossamer thread of silver, shining, stretching like a river from the sprawling city to the rolling hills beyond.

"Come, Hal," he commanded softly. "Come in service to your king."

*   *   *

The truck was a lost cause. With a final kick at the tire, Hal walked into the gathering twilight.

Ten minutes later he heard the sound of marching behind him. It was the knights. Kay, the Master of Drill, counted out time.

"No," Hal said, sweeping the air with his hands. "Absolutely not, guys. From here on in, I'm on my own."

"We serve the king," Launcelot said, running ahead of the others. "All of us, together."

Hal shook his head. "I can't look for Arthur and keep you out of jail at the same time."

Launcelot moved up next to him. "Their behavior was my fault," he said, his eyes haunted. "I was their leader once, but I left them. If you must punish someone, let it be me. Cast me out, and complete the Round Table with another. But do not forsake the others, for they have already given their lives once for their king, and would give them again without hesitation."

"No," Hal said adamantly. "They don't know how to act like civilized people."

"They can learn," Launcelot persisted. "For their sovereign, they would consent even to be slaves." He looked back at the approaching knights. "Take them back, Galahad. They have waited an eternity for you to lead them to Arthur."

"Arthur." Hal exhaled. "Yeah."

"Together you can find him, mayhap more easily than you alone. We have already come so far, nearly to the New York—"

"There are ten million people in New York," Hal said. "How are we going to find him there? Hell, I don't even know if we can *get* there. The truck's dead, our money's almost gone, we're lost . . ." He jumped. "What the hell's this?"

From the center of his chest sprouted a thin silver thread that stretched for miles down the road. Hal tried to touch it, but his hand went right through it, as if it were made of light. "Can you see this thing?" he asked.

"Aye. 'Tis a wonder." The thread flickered and dimmed, like a faulty string of Christmas bulbs. "Methinks it is a sign for you to follow. From the Merlin."

Hal nodded slowly. He tried to gauge the distance to the farthest point where he could see its light. "Wherever it's going, it's damn far for twelve guys on foot."

"Twelve?" Launcelot asked. "Then you will have me stay?"

Hal laughed. "It'd take a better man than me to kick Sir Launcelot out of the Round Table."

The knights strolled up to them. "Ho, Galahad!" MacDaire called. "This marching is getting to be thirsty work. I say we set about finding a pub for a taste of grog, to keep off the chill of evening."

Hal gave Launcelot a black look. "If I'm stuck with them, then you are, too." Launcelot smiled as a motorcyclist on a fat Harley zoomed past.

"Did you see that?" Bedwyr asked in astonishment.

"I'll eat my balls, it's a headless horse," Kay said.

The motorcyclist made a right turn just beyond them. His rear lights flashed, then went out. In the silence, Hal could hear party sounds.

He jogged ahead. In a copse just off the road were parked a dozen motorcycles. *Thank you, God,* he thought, although he realized that getting these people to part with their hogs would not be easy.

The cyclist who had just pulled in was popping open a can of beer. He wore a sleeveless denim vest with a patch on the back reading NO FEAR in lightning bolt lettering. On his head was a World War I German officer's parade helmet with a pointed spike on top. Nearby, fiddling with a boombox that poured out heavy metal music, was a woman with chalk-white hair arranged into eighteen-inch projectiles around her head. She wore a pair of skin-tight jeans and a bikini top. Above her ample breasts was tattooed the legend HOT MAMA.

The others in the group were equally unorthodox in appearance. One man sported a bushy, grizzled beard that reached to the middle of his chest and ended in two points over his nipples. Another had a bright red tattoo of a tongue running the entire length of his back.

A woman with pendulous armpit hair and a ring through her nose pointed at Hal with a cigarette. "Whatcha looking at, Slick?"

Hal moved forward uncertainly. "Well, I know this is going to sound like an odd request, but . . ."

"In the name of the king, we are requisitioning your headless horses!" Launcelot boomed.

The woman made a face. "Come again?"

"What about the king?" a red-eyed man in chaps asked. "Somebody seen Elvis?"

The other knights walked quietly into the copse behind Launcelot, gazing with awe at the colorful assemblage. "What do they want?" the man in the pointy helmet growled.

"Something about the headless horseman. Hey!" She waved a green fingernail at Bedwyr, who was looking over the dials on one of the motorcycles. "Spike don't like anybody screwing with his Harley."

"Somebody messing with my machine?" Spike roused himself enough to turn his head toward the newcomers. He threw an empty beer can at Bedwyr. "Yo, numbnuts."

Kay strode up to him. "And who be ye calling my young brother numbnuts, thou peckerless fiend?"

Spike winced. Then slowly, deliberately, he stood up to face Kay. The two men were built exactly alike.

"Wait a minute," Hal said. "We don't want any trouble, okay?"

"Then maybe you shouldn't have crashed our party," Spike said, twisting a steel chain around his knuckles.

"Yeah," chirped the platinum blonde. "What do youse want, anyway?"

"Well, actually, we came to see if we could, um . . . borrow your motorcycles."

The man in chaps laughed so hard he sprayed beer all over himself. The blonde popped her gum, smiling.

"Why, sure," Spike said. "We're neighborly folks." With that, he smashed his chain-covered fist into Kay's face.

Kay went down momentarily, then got up grinning through the blood that flowed from his nose. "Ah, I thought you had not the look of a truthteller about you," he said before smashing his knee into Spike's groin.

"Here we go," Hal said flatly.

The man with a tongue tattooed on his back came at him with a tire iron.

"Launcelot spoke with us," Agravaine said somberly into Hal's ear. "Would it be considered ill-disciplined if we fought with you, Galahad?"

"By all means, be my guest," Hal said, ducking out of the way of the tire iron. He chopped his assailant at the knees while Agravaine knocked out one of the man's teeth with his hook.

"Well, what are the rest of you waiting for?" Hal shouted, shaking the pain out of his knuckles.

With a ululating battle cry, the knights threw themselves on the charging motorcyclists. For a full ten minutes the forest copse rang with curses, groans, and the thud of flesh pounding flesh. A tree was felled by the weight of Dry Lips' flying body crashing into it, and Gawaine lost a fistful of hair to a dagger; but otherwise, the Companions took the day. While the cyclists lay sprawled on the grass, Hal gave a crash course on motocycle riding.

"This is the key," he said. "Make sure it's on. Then you squeeze the clutch with your left hand while you shift gears with your left foot." He demonstrated. The Harley purred. "To go faster, turn the throttle—right hand." The motor revved. The knights listened appreciatively. "The right foot's for the brake. The brake makes you stop, got it? That's very important."

"Right foot, brake," Bedwyr said. "Makes you stop." The knights nodded.

Hal looked nervously over at the heap of unconscious men. No one had been seriously wounded, so it would just be a matter of time before they came around. With their vehicles stolen, they weren't going to be happy when they did.

"Okay, Bedwyr, give this one a try."

"Left hand, clutch," Bedwyr said intently. "Left foot, gear. Right hand, throttle." He wobbled off slowly down the lane.

"Shift up to second gear!" Hal shouted. Bedwyr's motorcycle responded with a satisfying roar.

"Ah, that one's the master of horse, and no mistake," Fairhands said.

"The rest of you are going to have to learn this, too . . . Where's Lugh?"

An obscene laugh came from the direction of the campsite. Lugh was stepping over the bodies toward them. Over his shoulder was slung the woman with the octopus-shaped hair. Spike's pointy helmet was perched on his head.

"Put her down," Hal said irritably.

"But she's the spoils of war," MacDaire objected. Leaning closer in, he added, "The other one's too much of a dog, even for Lugh."

"This isn't a war, and we're not taking prisoners." Hal pulled the woman down. She popped her gum in his face. "When your friends come to, tell them we're going to bring the bikes back."

"Sure," she said. She winked at Lugh.

"Okay, guys, mount. Just remember that—" He was interrupted by a scream as Bedwyr flew over the front handlebars of the Harley. "—the brake makes you stop."

He stuck a helmet on his head and mounted another bike. "I'll meet you at the end of the road," he said, and peeled away.

While he waited for the others to accustom themselves to their new steeds, he tried to follow the silver thread which mapped out his route like a string in a maze. In the darkness of the moonless night, the thread was at times very pronounced, and sometimes barely visible.

A sign from the Merlin. "Hold tight, old man," he whispered as the knights came rumbling up behind him. "We're coming."

At a signal from Hal, all twelve of them laid rubber onto the two-lane highway.

CHAPTER THIRTY-NINE

"Amazing."

Dr. Rasheesh Shanipati took notes as he studied Beatrice Reed's electroencephalogram on the monitor above her bed.

"It's looked like that for the past forty minutes," Dr. Coles said. "I didn't want to disturb you during dinner. I know you prefer to be left alone before—"

Shanipati made a small gesture meant to set his colleague's mind at rest. "I'm glad you called me in on this. It is most interesting." He turned to a nurse. "Could you please arrange to have a glass of milk brought up for me? I would like to remain here for a time."

"Certainly, Doctor."

Arguably the foremost neurosurgeon in the world, Shanipati had flown into New York that evening to deliver a talk to the AMA on the brain waves of individuals in states other than consciousness. His research on the effect of prayer on brain activity had been the focus of hundreds of magazine articles and television programs.

He had just sat down to a solitary room-service meal with his papers spread around him to review the talk he would give the following morning, when the hospital called.

"The entire configuration is baffling," Coles said, picking up a printout from an electrocardiogram, one of several machines to which Beatrice was attached by wires. "Her heart appears to be beating only once per minute."

"The resting rate of a marmot during hibernation," Shanipati mused.

"Er . . . yes. And the alpha waves!" He looked back up at the screen "I've never seen anything like this. Have you?"

"Theta," Shanipati corrected. "Between four and eight Hertz cycles, the reading is for theta waves. And yes, I have seen it before. Once."

Years ago, in his native New Delhi, he had recorded the vital functions of a ninety-year-old yogi. The yogi, who had lived in solitude in the mountains for more than two decades, had agreed to participate in the tests in order to prove that his followers' claims that he could control even his autonomic responses with his mind were correct.

Shanipati himself had tested the equipment and affixed the wires to the yogi, so he knew that the results had been accurate, even though they were later refuted on the grounds that what they reported to be occurring within the yogi's body and mind were incompatible with life for a ninety-year-old man, and therefore must have been erroneous.

The yogi, he remembered, had gone into a trance state fairly quickly, in which his pupils dilated and his reflexes no longer responded to external stimuli. His heart rate slowed dramatically, almost to the rate Beatrice's monitor was showing, while his EEG slowly went berserk.

First it slowed from the beta, or waking, range into the alpha, where the brain waves of individuals in a state of meditation occur. From there it slowed further, into the mysterious realm of dream activity, sudden insight, psychic receptiveness, memory recognition—the theta.

"For most people, the theta range is a kind of no-man's-land to be passed through uneventfully on the way to deep sleep," Shanipati explained to the resident. "It is the place where dreams occur, where the dreamer can run or fly or leap from buildings while his body remains locked in rigid safety on his bed. But for others, the theta is the very seat of the mind itself."

The yogi's brain waves did not slow further into the delta, or deep sleep state. Instead, some fifty minutes into the test, they began to take on an entirely different character. They no longer resembled waves at all, but a dense band of solid color from one extreme of the theta range to the other.

This was the condition currently reflected on Beatrice Reed's EEG.

"Is she *dreaming?*" Coles asked.

"No, the theta in this structure is not indicative of dreams. Not exactly." He struggled to find words the American neurologist would understand. "It is more like a perception . . . a perception of the soul," he said.

"A . . . I see." Coles cleared his throat.

He didn't see, of course. What made neurology so difficult to grasp at Shanipati's level was that everything known about the human mind was communicated by doctors, who understood its science but refused absolutely to recognize its divinity.

After his study on the yogi was deemed unacceptable, as Shanipati had suspected it would be, he had not further blackened his name in the medical community by disclosing that twenty-six letters had come to his office after news of the experiment appeared in the newspapers. From all over India, people had written him about having seen a very old man, naked except for a loincloth, who had performed some sort of miracle before their eyes.

Many of the letters reported healings: A twelve-year-old boy who had collided with a truck while riding his bicycle and suffered a concussion had sat up, smiling and hungry, after the yogi's visitation. A woman, suffering from bone cancer, told her family that the old man had taken away the horrific pain with which she had been living for years. The headman of a remote village in Uttar Pradesh wrote to tell Shanipati of an ancient stranger who had stood ringing a bell in the marketplace, warning the villagers of an avalanche. Despite the fact that the area was not mountainous and a heavy rain had begun to fall, the villagers heeded the stranger's warning and fled upcountry in time to see most of their homes destroyed by a massive mud slide.

In all cases, the mysterious old man's arrival had coincided with the period of the yogi's trance state during the experiment; and in all cases the stranger disappeared after performing his miraculous acts.

Twenty-six letters, Shanipati remembered. How many other occurrences involving the yogi had not been witnessed, how many letters not written?

A perception of the soul, he thought, drinking the milk which had been brought for him. He sat down, a notebook on his lap, to watch

the theta waves of the comatose girl in front of him, and wondered to
what distant realms she was travelling.

A river of silver.

Taliesin saw it stretching over miles of highway to the place where
Hal rode with the knights of the Round Table in search of their king.
Light! he commanded, and the band which he had forged in the Sum-
mer Country glowed bright as his strengthening soul.

He trembled with the power that surged through him, filling him,
dispelling the drug in his body and the magicians' dark spells. The
whirling vortex which had threatened to strangle him dissipated to a
mere breeze. Beyond it, unaware, Thanatos began the complex and
subtle ritual designed to kill a being such as himself, a human versed
in magic. It was the ritual that had been performed on the body of the
Innocent, though she had willed herself to death before the sorcerers
could take her soul.

Nor will they take mine, Taliesin thought. He raised his hand,
knowing that with one thought he could shatter these magicians' puny
spells. With one . . .

Yes, Merlin.

He pulled back. The magic that grew inside him could not be coming from the room around him. This place was dead, contaminated by
evil. Nothing but the filthy spells of the demon gods could thrive here.
Yet something was moving, swelling, shooting directly into his mind
from some other source. Someone was sending it to him, someone of
great power.

Innocent?

Use my power, Merlin. You have need of it.

He remembered the magic he had made in the cave. To achieve it,
he had destroyed himself. After it was done, he had slept for sixteen
hundred years.

I cannot do this thing to you, Master—

Do it!

But Beatrice . . . She will die. She is no more than a child. . . . Taliesin pictured the young English girl whose life he had saved in Tangier. For what had he saved it? To take it away for his own uses, like
one of the black magicians' sacrifices?

He had never taken a wife. He had never had a family, or enjoyed
the simple, profound pleasures of an ordinary man's life. He had given

up these things without a thought, because what he possessed in their place had always been of greater importance.

He had the magic.

You became the Merlin, Beatrice had told him. Beatrice, who did not even know whose magnificent soul she carried within her. Yet she had asked the great question: *Was it enough?*

That question had been a test, he knew now, as the Innocent had always known.

Was the magic enough to give up the life of another for it, the physical life of one whom he had loved for sixteen centuries? The Innocent had been his master, his friend, his mother. It was she who had taught him the mysteries of the druids, and the magic of the immortals. She had given him everything, made him everything he was. She had come back from death itself, from far beyond the Summer Country, to be with him.

And now she was asking him to send her into death again, for the sake of the magic.

Was it enough? Was it?

No, he thought. It would never, ever, be enough for that.

Then you betray the gods who entrusted you with their existence, for it was through you that they died, and only you can bring them back.

Through me? How could they have died through me?

Their assassin was your son, conceived during the rite of Beltane. He has come back here, to this very place, to complete the circle, as you must . . . if you are strong enough.

My son . . . Through eyes glazed with shock and horror, Taliesin watched the dark magician perform the first incantations upon him. *This evil beast . . .*

Thanatos. His name is Thanatos, god of death.

My son . . .

Use my power to close the circle.

Please! Do not—

I have come into this life only for this moment. I have come to offer you my gift, and you must take it, Merlin, for Merlin you truly are.

Oh, Innocent, what you ask of me!

A force like a thunderbolt entered through the top of his head and surged through his body.

Take my fire, take it, and with it light the world.

Her voice fell silent.

The old man knew what he had to do.

With tears streaming down his face, Taliesin raised himself up off the floor to his full height until he stood rigid, filled to bursting with the Innocent's profound energy. The cords binding his arms and chest fell away like ash. "I will do as you bid me, Master," he whispered.

The power exploded within him. He felt it burning from the inside out, a force like the fire of a thousand suns, searing away his thoughts, his emotions, his soul itself. Taliesin stepped out of the vortex of the dark spell and quelled it with a gesture. Then, fixing his gaze on Thanatos and his sorcerers, he made a sound like the roar of the sea.

Aubrey looked up from his work, startled. The magicians with him cowered, shielding their faces. The curved dagger flew out of Aubrey's hand to shatter against the wall. The bowls of blood and other accoutrements of ritual smashed to fragments. The carcasses of the dead animals that had encircled the old man scattered to the corners of the room as if a great wind had swept them away. The blood on the floor was blasted clean. The candles blew out, leaving the room in darkness except for an eerie, otherworldly glow that surrounded Taliesin like a halo. The magic burst like starlight from him.

He was the Merlin.

"The cup," he commanded.

Inside Aubrey's sleeve, the metal sphere glowed red, burning through the fabric of his robe until he cried out in pain, his garment ablaze. As he struggled to put out the flames, the cup floated over Kate's body, then came to rest upon the great wound that had stilled her heart.

Immediately her flesh knitted, the skin growing smooth over the place where the deep marks of the pentagram had been. She opened her eyes. Her cracked lips moved.

"Mother, bring us life from death," she whispered, holding the cup in her hands like precious water. She sat up, transfixed. "Mother bring us . . ."

". . . life from death," the Merlin finished, understanding the prayer at last. This was why the Innocent had given him her power. For this single moment, when the destiny of mankind would change forever, healed by a cup which had been forged in the depths of the universe by the ancient gods.

It was their time to live again.

"Mother, bring us life from death," he breathed.

Kate repeated the words. "Mother, bring us life from death."

Aubrey lunged at them. A wall of fire rose to stop him. Gasping, the black magicians recoiled into the shadows, fleeing from the flames that licked at them.

"Mother, bring us life from death."

Kate stared, slack-jawed, at the inferno rising up around her. "M—mother, bring us life from death."

The magicians scrambled for the ladder leading out of the building, tearing at one another like wounded vultures, but the fire was always a step ahead, extending, traveling where the Merlin bade it, encircling them finally in a ring of fear.

"Mother, bring us life from death."

"Mother . . ." Kate staggered backward. Along the far wall, a long human bone was slowly ascending toward the ceiling.

Mother bring us life from death

The earthen floor beneath them shook.

Mother bring us life from death

Merlin closed his eyes. The prayer came no longer from him, but from the earth itself. The souls of the dead gods had stirred at last.

Mother bring us life from death

Mother bring us life from death

It grew louder, reverberating through the chamber, thundering. The black magicians quaked behind their wall of fire as Merlin called out the names of the vanished gods:

"Mithras! Cerridwen! Arianrhod!" he shouted. "Hearken to me, for I am the Merlin come to resurrect you with the souls of the long faithful! Rise, Scathach, Mannannan, Dagda, Bran! Rise, LlewLlaw Gyffs, Eostre, and the Cailliach! Selene, Gwion, Elphin, Forgall, rise, for the wheel has turned and your time has come at last!"

With a keening wail, the walls began to craze and crumble. Huge cracks appeared in the old stone masonry, and from them poured forms like zephyrs, the ghosts of the desecrated dead. They had been druids, each of them, killed as the old gods themselves had been killed, by the followers of the darkness. Their bodies had been defiled, their bones brought from their sacred island across the ocean to this sub-terranean place; but their souls were free now. Sighing, they rose, reaching up with skeletal fingers, flying upward, filling the room, twist-ing like smoke among the screaming black magicians.

Kate had fallen to her knees, shaking with fear, her hands clutching the cup which had brought her life back to her. Taliesin lifted her gently. His touch was cold as ice.

"Take everyone out of the building," he said.

She offered him the cup. "The Grail," she said. "This belongs to you." With a final look at the old man and the terrifying magic he had conjured, she ran toward the ladder and climbed up.

Around him swirled the chaos he had wrought. By sacrificing the Innocent, he had brought about the rebirth of the gods. It was the greatest magic he had ever known. He regarded the cup in his hand. The Holy Grail, vessel of eternal life, a suitable possession for the Merlin.

He tossed it on the floor. There was nothing more of life he wanted.

Yes, he thought, this was a fitting way to die.

Facing the magicians who had brought him here, he spoke in a voice like the wind: "Now we shall go into the void together, we killers of the holy ones."

The walls bellied in. First a trickle of earth, dry as sand, seeped from behind the foundations of the building. Then it poured into the room, throwing up billows of dust, the deep cracks splitting open with a sound like thunder.

The magicians shrieked. The fire that had surrounded them spread to the ceiling, evading the inrushing earth. They scrambled for the ladder, but it was too late. The timbers supporting the structure cracked with a boom and caved in.

Through the rising dust and flames, Merlin saw Aubrey Katsuleris crawling toward him.

"My son," the old man rasped, choking in the unbreathable air. "Come die beside me, Thanatos, so that we may be judged together." He sank to the floor, gasping. "Our crime was the same, you know. We both killed her, you in your time, and I in mine." He laughed bitterly. "What a fine joke the gods have played on us both."

Then the last of the beams gave way and the building folded in on itself, filling the room with brick and rubble.

CHAPTER FORTY

Dr. Shanipati was still in attendance when Beatrice called Arthur's name.

"That's her brother, I think," the nurse said. "He's outside."

"Bring him, bring him in quickly," Shanipati ordered, scribbling in his notebook. He had never seen such a thing, even with the yogi. The girl had spoken, *spoken*—positively a beta wave function—while the EEG still registered in the theta range. "Are you certain this is working correctly?" he asked when the nurse returned. He tapped the monitor hesitantly with his index finger.

"I wouldn't know. Would you like me to call a technician to check it?"

"Yes, please. Do that." He looked at the young boy in the doorway. "You are named Arthur?" he asked.

The boy nodded.

"Please." The doctor gestured for him to come by the bed. "I think she is asking for you. Of this I cannot be certain, however, because . . ." He looked up at the monitor, still reading intense theta activity, then at the boy, and decided it would be too difficult to explain. He moved to the chair at the foot of the bed. "Go ahead. I will not disturb you."

Arthur bit his lip. "I think the old man's in trouble," he said softly. "I have to help him, but I can't leave you here because . . ." He stole a glance at the doctor. "Well, you just have to take my word for it, you've got to wake up. We can't do anything until you wake up." He shook her. "Oh, please come back, Bea. He needs us bad."

Shanipati grabbed hold of his wrists. "You must not touch her!" he cried out. "She is in a very delicate state. If you disturb—"

"Leave him alone." Beatrice opened her eyes. They were milk-white.

Babbling in a torrent of Hindi, Dr. Shanipati leaned over her with an opthalmascope. This was impossible, he thought, quite certainly impossible! He had examined her eyes not a half hour earlier, and there had been no trace of blindness then. Yet these were the eyes of an individual who had been sightless from birth. A very old individual at that, judging from the retinal scarring. Very old . . .

"Do go away, Rasheesh. No one will believe this report of yours, anyway," she said with the voice of an old woman.

Shanipati fell back, scattering the notes he had left on his chair. "What did you say?" he asked in a whisper.

"You've been trying for centuries to convince people that there's more to them than flesh and bones, but they've never believed you." She waved her hand at him idly. "That's just as well. It is not important to prove the existence of the soul." She smiled. "All that matters is to perceive it."

"All that . . . One moment, please. I wish to write that down." He bent to pick up his papers.

"Come quickly, Arthur." Beatrice waggled her fingers. "Time is short, and I must be certain that you know what to do before I say good-bye."

"Good-bye?" the boy whispered. "But you can't—"

"Shh. I can do whatever I like. Everything is possible, child. Try to remember that." She clasped his hand. "Now listen to me. A great deal of trouble has been taken to bring you back into the world and keep you here, but now things are up to you. What you do, how you live from this moment on will be of immense consequence. Do you understand?"

He took a moment to find his voice. "Yes," he answered. "I know who I am."

"Good. Taliesin did a fine job." She smiled at him. "This is your time, Arthur. The wheel of destiny has come full circle, and you are at its center." She closed her eyes, then opened them again slowly. "I'm afraid living is getting to be rather too much of an effort for me."

"Bea . . ." his voice broke. "Bea, don't die. Please don't die . . ."

"Remember how to be a king, and how to be a man. Be strong. Do good. Bring honor to your soul."

With a soft sigh, she lay back on the pillow. The EKG above her registered a flat line.

"Nurse!" Shanipati shouted, knocking Arthur out of the way to begin resuscitation procedures on his patient. "Call at once for defibrillators!" He glanced at the monitor. What he saw there nearly caused his hands to still. Within seconds, every life sign registered by the bank of machines had ceased, with the exception of one: Beatrice's theta wave was still coming through as a dense, fast-moving band.

The doctor continued to pump her chest while his eyes remained transfixed on the monitor, watching the evidence of a mind functioning without a body.

"Crash cart's coming," the nurse announced. "Son, you'll have to wait outside—"

"Be quiet!" Shanipati snapped. The nurse left the room.

Arthur moved silently to Beatrice's side while the neurologist struggled to revive her. Above them both, Beatrice's theta wave continued to expand until it filled the monitor. As they watched, a light appeared in the center of the black screen and then grew to fill it, a light so intense that they both had to shut their eyes and turn away to keep from being blinded.

Shanipati shouted something in Hindi. Arthur picked up Beatrice's hand and held it tight while the light burned through the room like lightning.

Then, in an instant, it was gone.

The monitor beeped. Eight functions appeared, all normal. There was no theta wave.

Beatrice sat up. "Oh, dear," she said. "We're not at Planet Ice Cream, are we?"

Equally stunned, Shanipati and Arthur looked at each another as the crash cart lumbered in, accompanied by the usual army of doctors, nurses, technicians, and students.

Dr. Coles was among them. Holding a pair of electric paddles, he approached Beatrice, frowning in bewilderment. "Are we in the right place?" he asked.

Shanipati flicked on his opthalmascope and peered into Beatrice's eyes. "She can see," he whispered. He turned toward Dr. Coles. "A most extraordinary recovery." He bounded toward the electroencephalogram. "I will show you on the printout. The patient, as you recall, was comatose. . . ." While he was speaking, Coles gestured for the resuscitation team to leave.

"That was a monster zone-out," Arthur said quietly into Beatrice's ear. "You sounded like an old lady—"

"I saw her, Arthur! She's the one I always dreamed about. Only this time she didn't tell me I was going to die. She said she doesn't need me anymore." Beatrice looked at their hands, still entwined.

Arthur blushed, disengaging himself. "Well, now that you're okay, we've got to get out of here, and I mean right now." He peered over her shoulder at the two doctors conversing with one another. "I'll explain everything to you on the way. You can walk, can't you?"

Beatrice nodded.

"Can you run?"

Shanipati was tossing the unscrolled printout over his head like a lunatic. "There! You see? Heart rate zero. But the theta! Look at the theta!"

While he spoke, Beatrice pulled off the contact points connecting her with the monitoring machinery. The printout halted abruptly.

"What are you doing?" the doctor squealed, whipping his head around toward them. "You must not disconnect yourself. It is very important—"

"Let's go," Arthur said, throwing off Beatrice's bedsheets.

The two of them ran past the doctors at breakneck speed, then wove through the route Arthur had designed to take them out of the hospital and into the city streets.

CHAPTER FORTY-ONE

"Arthur! Beatrice!"

The taxi stopped at the red light as the children dodged through the night traffic.

Zack would not have known they'd left the hospital at all if he hadn't gone up to the fourth floor in search of Arthur, where he was told by a harried-looking Indian doctor that the boy had run out a moment before with his patient. Alarmed, Zack had jumped in a cab and headed for the Center. He'd spotted them turning down 55th Street.

"Hey, guys, wait up!" he shouted as he paid the cabbie, but Arthur and Beatrice roundly ignored him. "Kids," he said.

Halfway up the block he heard a tremendous noise, like some slow, sustained explosion, and shifted into a sprint until he caught sight of the Center. Surrounded by a nimbus of dust, the building was crumbling into the ground like a sand castle.

"Kate!" he shouted, pushing past the people gathered in the street.

Dressed in a yellow bathrobe, she was kneeling on all fours on top of the wreckage. Beside her were Arthur and Beatrice. The three of them were digging through the debris with their hands, throwing aside bricks and pieces of broken timber.

"Oh, Jesus," Zack said, running toward them on the shifting, rubble-strewn earth.

"He was standing right here," Kate sobbed.

"Who?" Zack asked, his eyes tearing with the flying dust.

"Taliesin. He's buried under this." She wiped her nose with a grimy arm.

"What happened?"

"Just dig, okay?"

The debris settled, opening up a hole near Arthur. He and Beatrice jumped into it, scooping up armfuls of broken wood.

"It's not safe here," Zack said.

"Then leave!" Arthur shouted. "It was your friend who did this, and you were probably in on it!"

"My . . . who are you talking about?"

"Aubrey," Kate said. "You don't know what he was into, Zack. But no, he didn't do this. Taliesin did."

Arthur looked up momentarily. "The old man?"

Kate nodded, swallowing a sob. "He was no ordinary old man, Arthur."

The sound of motorcycles filled the street. "That must be the police," Beatrice said, picking a long shard of window glass from the ground. "I asked someone to—"

"Arthur!" one of the motorcyclists shouted as he dismounted.

The boy scrambled out of the hole where he had been digging. "Hal! It's Hal, Bea! He's come back!" He ran down the hill of rubble, waving frantically as Hal loped up to meet him, followed by eleven very unusual looking men. "Hal, you've got to help us, and we don't have any time to lose," the boy panted as they neared one another. "Taliesin was in the basement when the building came . . ." He glanced at the motorcyclists behind Hal. For some reason, they had all fallen to one knee and bowed their heads. ". . . down . . ."

"What?" Hal yelled. "He's under this?"

"We think he was over there, where Bea and those other two people are digging. Please, Hal, we've got to hurry." He ran back to join the others.

Hal swivelled toward the knights. "All right, men, follow me," he ordered. "Move it!"

Like an army, Hal and the knights swarmed over the wreckage, using boards and window casings as shovels.

"What be we searching for, treasure?" MacDaire grunted as he helped Lugh move a massive block of concrete.

"The Merlin," Hal said, unable to disguise his hopelessness.

Arthur looked up, wiping the sweat from his eyes. "Curoi Mac-Daire," he said softly. "And Lugh."

"We'll find your wizard for you, Majesty," MacDaire said reassuringly before he moved on.

A young blond man gave him a quick smile as he gathered up an armload of bricks. "Fairhands, the standard bearer." Arthur squinted. "Gawain's here, too. And there's Kay."

Hal stared at him. "You know their names?"

"I remember . . ." *Remember how to be a king,* the old woman who spoke to him through Beatrice had said. With those words, he knew, she had given him a gift, the final piece of the puzzle Beatrice had envisioned. "I remember everything," he said.

The other tenants and bystanders jumped in to help. While they worked, Kate went to the neighboring apartment buildings to collect any tools available. By the time the police arrived, they had dug nearly to the foundation.

"All right, everybody clear out!" an officer ordered, but no one paid him any attention. Finally the police, too, joined in the excavation.

"We've got one," a neighbor called. The diggers moved to the spot and worked until the first of the bodies was pulled out. It was a man, his charred face no longer identifiable as human. Everyone stepped back in silence as the police extricated a second body in the same condition.

"Must have been a fire," one of the officers said as a third body was found. This one had a face. Its expression was one of abject terror.

The grim excavation went on in silence as an ambulance and fire trucks pulled up, followed by a TV news van. Within minutes the site was ablaze with lights. A reporter, having hastily gathered her material from one of the neighbors while applying her lipstick, related the story of the building's mysterious collapse to the television camera.

A few feet away, Arthur and Beatrice spotted a hand beneath a pile of broken concrete. "Hal!" he called. The TV cameraman waved at him for silence as the reporter continued her narrative. "Over here! Help me, please! Hurry!"

Hal and the knights rushed to his side. The fingernails of the un-covered hand were blue. The rest of the body was buried too deeply to pull out.

"It's him," Arthur said.

Twelve pairs of hands thrust into the dirt. When they came out, they were holding Taliesin's lifeless body.

"He has not the look of a living man," Dry Lips said gently.

A paramedic squeezed between the knights to check Taliesin's eyes and pulse. "This one's gone, too," he said, signalling for a stretcher.

"No!" Arthur hugged the old man, lifting his shoulders off the ground like a rag doll. Taliesin's head lolled to the side. "He's not dead, he can't be! He had the cup!"

"Get a shot of the kid," the reporter hissed. Bright light flooded over Arthur.

"Get the hell out of here, you ghouls," Hal snapped.

"Keep rolling."

Two paramedics came by with a stretcher. "We'll take the body," one of them said.

"Don't touch him!" Arthur screamed. At his words, four of the knights stood to face the paramedics like a wall between them and the boy.

"Suit yourself," one of the men holding the stretcher said with a shrug. "We got too many for the wagon as it is."

As they walked away, Launcelot knelt on one knee before Arthur. "My lord," he said quietly, "I would pray, if I have your permission."

The boy looked at him through eyes weary with suffering. "Laun-celot," he said softly. "You've come back, too."

"Aye. And to stay, if you can find it in your heart to forgive me."

Arthur touched his shoulder. "I do, friend. Now, pray. Pray for the Merlin, who is beyond the help of even his own magic."

Hal closed his eyes. *He remembers,* he thought. *The knights have returned, and so has their king.*

As Launcelot bowed his head to pray to his god, the other knights knelt also, Kay and Gawain, Lugh with his spiked helmet, Dry Lips and MacDaire and the young men who had died before their faces had weathered. They all knelt to call upon what gods they knew to bring King Arthur's wizard back from the Summer County.

* * *

Fog, that was what it was, the kind of thick milky fog that used to enshroud Camelot after a heavy winter rain. Taliesin felt himself tumbling through it like a seed.

"Blast it all, I know I'm dead, and I know where I'm headed," he shouted. "This pointless charade is wasted on me, I tell you!"

But his journey continued uninterrupted, his body circling end over end. After a time he began to think that perhaps this was the void he had been expecting. If so, death apparently involved a great deal of movement. He tucked his hands inside his robe and waited.

"Ah, there you are," came a woman's voice.

"Indeed, and I've become damned dizzy getting here, wherever that is."

His endless spinning slowed, then stopped. The fog around him cleared.

"Is that better?"

Taliesin tried a few tentative steps. He felt rubber-legged, like a seafarer standing on solid ground for the first time in months, except that the ground under his feet was anything but solid. It was the same milk-white fog, surrounding him on all sides, leaving only a globe-shaped space around him.

He touched the fog experimentally. It sent out tendrils of vapor between his fingertips.

"Well?" he demanded. "Is this home?"

"No, Merlin." The ball Taliesin stood in glowed with golden light. When it subsided, the Innocent stood beside him.

He staggered backward. "I . . . I didn't recognize your voice."

"That's because it wasn't a voice at all. Nor is this your body." She poked him in the area of his navel. Her fingers went right through him. "I'm afraid you left that buried under a heap of soil and building materials."

"Yes, I had no . . ." He choked on his words as he felt his heart breaking all over again. "I had no wish to keep it any longer." He went down on his knees before her. "Innocent, if this is to be the state of my death, it is too good for me."

"This is not death," the Innocent said gently. She put her arms around him and cradled him like a baby. "This is love."

He felt her soul pass through his own, filling him with her forgiveness and joy. "You were so young," he whispered, weeping into her bosom. "I killed you . . ."

"I am old beyond counting, Merlin. And do not presume to know more than the gods you serve."

"The gods ask too much," he said bitterly.

"Ah, yes. They ask for all you are, and all you may be. And for your reward, all they give you is yourself."

With her hand she swept away a patch of fog. In the space, far below, he saw his body, held in loving arms just as he was being held now. But the arms around him were not the Innocent's, but Arthur's. And kneeling around them both were the knights of the Round Table.

"Why, they're back," he said. "There's Tristan and Bedwyr and that rascal MacDaire . . . They're all down there with the boy."

"The circle has closed, Merlin. You have closed it. The Age of Arthur has begun again."

"Good heavens, it's . . ." He looked over at her in astonishment. "It's Beatrice!" He leaned back over the hole in the fog. "But that's quite impossible—"

"Everything is possible," the Innocent said. "I should think you'd know that by now."

"But she was you! Your vessel. When you gave me your power, her body was supposed to expire. It *had* to!" He shook his fists in agitation. "Yours was the spirit inside her, and you're gone."

"Perhaps she has another spirit now."

"Whose?" he demanded belligerently.

She shrugged expressively. "It might be anyone's. Your student Nimue's, perhaps."

"Nimue? The one with all the questions?"

"A student is supposed to ask questions. You certainly did."

"But she never washed."

"Oh, come now. She was lovely when you brought her to Mona for Arthur's burial. The locals thought she was the Fairy Queen."

"Hah! Fairy Queen indeed. She used to eat frogs, heads and all."

"But she loved you, Merlin. I felt she was a good choice."

"Nimue." His face was a perfect blank.

They sat in silence for a moment. "Well?" his teacher asked finally. "Would you like to go back?"

"Under the circumstances, I'd have to think about that." He turned to her and grinned. "Is it too late?" he asked, squirming to his feet. "Have I decomposed?"

"I think not," she said, smiling.

"Then I must . . . I must . . ." He poised himself at the edge of the clearing, his eyes squeezed shut, his hands curled into fists, preparing for the jump but too frightened to take it.

"Is it enough?" she asked.

"Is it what? Is what enough? Confound it, you're talking in riddles again."

The Innocent laughed with a sound pure and tinkling as a bell. "Enjoy your life, little bard," she said, and pushed him through the opening.

He felt himself falling, floating languidly through space, drifting formless toward the place where Arthur held the body of a dead man, refusing to let it go. With a shudder the Merlin entered the body again, and was immediately assaulted by all manner of aches and infirmities— wheezing lungs and sprained ribs, a bruise the size of a man's hand on his thigh, a tooth knocked loose, a broken toe.

"By the gods, life is a trying condition," he grumbled.

"Taliesin!" Arthur's face, just coming into focus, was filled with happiness. To the other side was Launcelot, weeping into his chain mail.

"You again!" Taliesin muttered. "Still praying, I see."

"Welcome back, old man." It was Hal, of course. None of the others would have the effrontery to address the king's wizard as "old man."

"It certainly took you long enough to get here," Taliesin complained. He looked around at them all. Launcelot, Galahad, Arthur, all of them brought out of the mists of time to try the dream once more.

Perhaps this time they would succeed.

"Hello, Mr. Taliesin." Beatrice squeezed between two of the knights to stand shyly before him. She was wearing a hospital gown with a man's leather belt around it. She was covered with dirt from head to toe. Her hair was wild.

"Good evening, child," he said. "I'm pleased to see you again."

Is it enough? The Innocent's question rang through Taliesin's mind.

He felt laughter, like bubbles, pouring out of his chest. He hugged Arthur, then stretched his arms as far as he could all around to touch the others.

"Yes, it is enough," he said, fairly leaping to his feet. "Oh, my, yes."

CHAPTER FORTY-TWO

The television cameras caught it all. A bevy of reporters from news organizations all over the city had arrived on the scene in time to film what they called a "street-tough motorcycle gang" on their knees in prayer around a dying old man. And when Taliesin had come to and then leaped up to embrace them, every edition of the next morning's news had its lead story.

"People here are calling it a miracle," a woman shouted, thrusting a microphone in Taliesin's face. "What do you have to say about what happened to you?"

"Why is it so blasted bright here?" the old man groused, squinting into the camera lights. "Go away, all of you."

"Forget him," another reporter said. "Get the boy."

The lights shifted to Arthur. "What's your name, son?"

"Buzz off," Hal said. Lugh growled. For a moment, millions of television sets throughout the Tri-State area were filled with his snarling visage.

"I am Arthur," the boy said calmly, "and these are the knights of the Round Table."

"Cut!" one of the reporters yelled. "The kid's cracking jokes. It'll wreck the human interest angle."

The lights swivelled back to the excavation, where the police and emergency crews were pulling out still more bodies. Only one reporter, the woman who had arrived first, kept her cameraman trained on Arthur. He spoke to her.

"The time of horror is past," he said somberly. "This is a new era, and in it we will find peace and hope and true brotherhood."

The reporter exchanged glances with the cameraman. He shrugged, but kept the tape rolling while Arthur continued.

"This will not be easy for many of you to accept. You have lived in fear and pain for so long that distrust has become natural to you. Violence has become ordinary. Evil has become acceptable. But this will change. Slowly, and with effort, you will lose your fear, you will heal your wounds, and you will walk in the light of your own perfection. This is my promise to you."

He walked away toward the knights who were waiting by the motorcycles. The reporter's mouth hung open slackly.

Zack, who had been listening to the boy speak, ran up behind him. "Arthur, I heard you," he said earnestly. "I mean *really* heard you."

The boy kept walking.

"Look, I know you think I might have had something to do with this because I knew Aubrey, but I swear to you I didn't."

Arthur turned back toward him.

"Kate just told me what happened in there. . . ." The words dried up on his lips as the earth around the building shifted, whirling in a slow circle.

"The ground's giving!" the police captain shouted. "Get away!" Hundreds of people obediently scrambled onto the street.

On the site of the fallen building, tall mounds formed and erupted in the ground. Pieces of metal and wood and sparkling shards of broken glass churned as if they had been spat out of the mouth of some underground monster.

Then a hand shot out to the surface.

In it was a metallic sphere.

"The cup," Taliesin said, closing his eyes in despair. "He has the cup."

"Yes," Aubrey said, dragging himself out of the filth. "I have it still, despite your paltry gods." He shambled out of the pit, his bare feet treading on slivers of glass that left no wounds. His long black garment was burned to tatters in places, yet his face and body were unmarked. No one spoke as he staggered past the crowd to face the boy.

"So you're Arthur," he said.

"I am."

Aubrey laughed. "All this trouble, for a child whose neck I could have broken with one hand."

Hal and Launcelot stepped in front of the boy, but Arthur pushed them aside. "What do you want?"

"Oh, didn't your tame sorcerer tell you? He's seen to it that as long as the boy is alive, the cup will always come back to him." From the folds of his sleeve he took the curved dagger he had used in the ritual of sacrifice. "So, naturally, he can't remain alive."

Kate screamed. The knights got into formation around Arthur.

Twenty policemen drew their weapons. "Hold it or we'll shoot!" the captain warned.

"Fire away," Aubrey said, his eyes never leaving Arthur's.

The policeman fired. Aubrey winced as the bullet entered his body and left it, leaving two holes that healed almost immediately. The other officers emptied their cartridges into Aubrey's back. His garment flew apart to hang in ribbons at his waist, but he remained standing. When he turned to face them, the wounds closed before their eyes.

"Jesus Christ," the police captain muttered. Then, collecting himself, he called out, "Take him!"

When the officers rushed toward Aubrey, he raised one arm in their direction.

Tendrils of smoke poured from his fingertips. It flowed out of him in streams, puffing into billows. The policemen stopped in their tracks, gagging, as the foul cloud engulfed them.

Around the knights, the smoke thickened to form a solid wall encircling them, creating a barrier between them and the outside world. Inside that barrier there was no street, no city, no time. The air was still, and charged with magic.

"I thought we'd like some privacy," Aubrey said, smiling.

Preparing to charge, Lugh broke away from the others. "No, that's what he wants us to do," Hal said, wrestling him to a halt. "We can't leave Arthur open. Back up." He looked past Lugh to the others. "All of you."

The phalanx of knights, with the boy in the center of them, moved quietly toward the motorcycles, where Taliesin had stationed Beatrice. The two children would be safe there.

"Don't bother trying to hide him from me," Aubrey said casually, stroking the curved blade of the dagger. "This was forged from Mordred's sword. Do you remember him, Merlin?"

The old man's jaw clenched. In his mind's eye, he could still see that final, mortal blow that had set the world back by a thousand years. "Oh, gods of the sky," he whispered. "Gods of the sea and earth . . ."

"Go on, wizard, try your magic. Do you think that because you gave them what they wanted, they will rush to protect your boy-king who rules from behind the backs of his flunkies? Did they protect him at Camlan?" He chuckled. "No, Merlin, they did not, and they will not. This fight is Arthur's, not yours."

Taliesin's hands shook. The magician was right, he knew. Arthur had chosen to lose at Camlan, and the gods had been pitiless.

As your reward, you have only yourself, the Innocent had said.

The gods would give Merlin nothing for resurrecting them from death. After his great feat of magic, even the great wizard had been left with only himself.

Just as Arthur, in the end, would have only himself, now and always.

"Nothing could stop that sword from finding its way to you, little king," Aubrey taunted. "Do you remember its sting as it pierced your heart?"

Arthur's shoulders hunched, making him seem even smaller than he was.

"It will find you again," the magician whispered as he positioned the dagger.

"We'll see about that," Dry Lips said, squaring his shoulders.

Lugh lowered his eyes, and Taliesin knew what the soldier felt. Lugh had been beside the king on that last, terrible day. He had watched with horror as Mordred's sword flew past him with its own evil will. For all their courage, the knights would not be able to stop that blade.

"Yes," Aubrey agreed, "we'll see." With a quick, practiced motion, he let the dagger fly. "Get down!" Hal shouted. Arthur crouched. Following the trajectory of the dagger, every one of the knights expanded his chest, hoping to be the one the blade struck instead of the boy.

Zack was the only one who saw the sudden swoop of the weapon in the air, careening suddenly so low that it would pass between the knights' legs, directly to where Arthur was.

"Arthur!" he screamed, throwing himself to the street. As he hit the pavement at the knights' feet, the dagger struck him squarely in the chest.

His eyes opened wide in reflex, then slowly began to close. Kate rushed to his side, shrieking as she pulled the knife from his body. "Help! Someone help him!" She cradled his head in her lap, her tears falling on his face. "Oh, Zack, I love you, I love you so much. . . . Medic! Where's the ambulance?" she screamed into the wall of smoke Aubrey had created.

"Shh," Zack said, lightly resting his hand over hers. "It's all right."

Arthur crawled out from behind the knights' legs. "You saved my life," he said.

Zack smiled. "Then you believe me?" A trickle of blood seeped from the corner of his mouth.

"Yes, my friend," he whispered.

Hal grabbed the boy's collar. "Get back here," he said.

"No." Arthur wrenched away from him. Aubrey was walking toward them, his eyes blazing with anger and madness. The boy walked out into the street to meet him.

"Highness!" the knights rushed forward, but Arthur stopped them with a gesture.

"Enough of you have died for me," he said. "I'm done hiding."

Taliesin held his breath.

"Bravo!" Aubrey clapped his hands together as he sauntered forward. "How brave you are. We'll all tell our children about you." He splayed out his fingers. "Are you ready to fight me, Arthur?" he whispered, flicking his wrists.

The boy stopped. "I'm ready," he said.

Aubrey tapped his cheek with one of the long blades growing from his hands. "Dear, dear," he said with mock concern. "I can't help but think it's not quite fair this way. Perhaps you should have a weapon." He looked up suddenly. "Of course! Would you like your sword? I found it, you know."

"It wouldn't do you any good."

"Yes, that's true," he said with a sigh. "Perhaps it will serve you better." From around his waist he tugged at a small pouch suspended there by a black silk cord until it snapped, then threw the pouch at Arthur's feet. "Here it is," he said smoothly. "Or what's left of it. It didn't travel well."

The boy emptied the contents of the pouch into his hand and examined the dull bits of melted metal. "Excalibur," he whispered.

"Well, now I suppose we might as well begin," Aubrey said. He crouched down on all fours. From deep in his throat rose an inhuman growl. Before he leaped, Hal rushed forward, head down, arms extended.

A fireball shot out of Aubrey's mouth. It blazed through the air toward Hal, hitting him in the belly. With a scream Hal flew backward under its weight, landing on the pavement with a thud, his clothes scorched.

"By the gods, he's a demon!" Dry Lips rasped. Launcelot crossed himself.

"Anyone else want to try?" Aubrey asked, moving his head in spasms from side to side.

"Don't move, any of you!" Arthur snapped.

The magician beckoned to him, blinking his eyes lazily. "Come, boy. I'm hungry." He pointed to the dagger that lay on the street beside Zack, and it moved to his bidding. The blood-slick blade snaked along the pavement, then flew into his hand.

In answer, Arthur held up the pieces of the broken sword.

Aubrey laughed. "What are you going to fight me with? Marbles?"

The boy gazed steadily at him. "Faith," he said softly.

Moonlight struck the desecrated pieces of the ancient weapon. For a moment they sparkled like water. Then, while Aubrey rushed at him, the scraps of metal in the boy's hand danced upward into the shape of a shimmering cross of gold and steel, the living sword Excalibur, raised for battle.

"Go back where you belong!" Arthur commanded. "There is no longer a place for you among us. Go!"

In the sky, a bolt of lightning shot down to touch the great sword. It shimmered, incandescent and perfect, the glow of its magic surrounding Arthur like a nimbus. He was the heart of the fire, and Excalibur its soul.

The magician sprang, Mordred's dagger pulsing in his grip. Then, with a shriek, he was lifted up high off the street as if he were suspended on strings.

"I will not go back!" Aubrey screamed as he struggled in the air, his spindly legs jerking like an insect caught in a spider's web. A formless cloud, darker than the starless night, engulfed his flailing body. "Not there! Not again!" His voice sounded thin and flat. He grew smaller with each terrified breath. "I will not . . ."

Then he was gone.

The void that had swallowed him spun and collapsed in on itself, creating a wind tunnel on the street below. The wall of smoke Aubrey had created blew away in the sudden gust. With a sound like popcorn, the glass in the surrounding buildings cracked. Lights from the television crews smashed against the walls, and the vehicles parked on the street careened willy-nilly. Swept off their feet, the people at the scene rolled like dandelion puffs into the gutters and alleyways. The debris from the magicians' coven swirled overhead, planks and stone and crumbled mortar, leaving in its place only a flat expanse of earth blown clean by the wind.

In another moment, the cloud dissipated as unexpectedly as it had come. Through it all only Arthur had remained standing, the glow from Excalibur radiating into the night.

From the faraway dot where the void had taken Aubrey Katsuleris, an object bright as a comet tumbled through the blackness of the sky. Grasping the sword in one hand, Arthur held out the other, palm up, to receive this gift from the unknown places.

With infinite gentleness it gave itself into his possession: the cup of eternal life, the gift not even the vacuum of the dark gods could keep from its master.

Arthur knelt beside Zack. He was still alive. Kate had gone for the paramedics, who were running toward them down the street with her.

Zack's eyelids fluttered weakly as he tried to focus. "I saw what you did," he said in a harsh rasp. His tongue was covered with blood. "You . . . you were an agent of God."

"So were you," Arthur said, placing the cup in Zack's hands. He held his fingers over Zack's as its power coursed through them both.

"Oh," Zack whispered. Tears filled his eyes as the wound in his chest closed and healed without a mark. "The Grail. It's *real*. The magic was real."

Kate arrived with the paramedic, who could find not even a scratch on Zack's body. "You always believed," she said, sobbing into his arms.

"I thought you were a fool for believing, but you were the only one who saw the truth."

Zack stood up, the precious Grail cradled in his hands. He held it out to Arthur.

"I think you should keep it," the boy said.

Merlin's eyebrows rose in consternation. "Arthur—"

"This will be the beginning of my work," he said. He turned back to Zack. "You'll know what to do with it better than I would."

"But . . . but . . ." Zack looked at the object in his hands. "The Grail . . . "

Arthur closed Zack's hands around it. "Be strong," he said softly, repeating Beatrice's words to him. "Do good. Bring honor to your soul."

"Honor . . . yes. Yes, I'll try. I promise you, I'll try."

Hal came up behind the boy. "I think we'd better get out of here," he said. Down the street, the reporters were scrambling to their feet, racing to get their equipment. At his signal, the knights mounted their motorcycles.

"Wait!" Taliesin loped over. "Where in blazes are you going?"

"Somewhere in Long Island," Hal said. "We've got to take these bikes back. They were sort of . . . borrowed."

Arthur slipped his hand in Beatrice's. "And then we've got to get Bea home." He smiled shyly at her. "Unless you'd like to stay with us."

She pressed her lips together. "Arthur, you're the best friend I've ever had. My whole life has changed since I've known you, and I'd love to ride with you and your friends. . . ." She blinked away tears. "But I think Mr. Taliesin needs me," she whispered in his ear.

"The old man? He doesn't need anyone. He's a . . . well . . ."

"A wizard, yes. I know. He's probably the only one of his kind alive. Can you imagine how lonely he must be?"

Arthur stared at the ground. "I never thought about that. I suppose I could stay—"

"You know you can't," she said. "But I can." She kissed his cheek. He blushed furiously. "I'll miss you, Arthur."

"You'll see me again."

"Yes, I'm sure I will." She turned to Taliesin with a happy sigh. "It's settled, then. I'll stay with the old man."

"*Old man?*" Taliesin repeated, bristling. "Allow me to inform you, Beatrice—"

"I'm sorry. I meant elderly. That sounds more polite, don't you think? Oh, we'll have lots of adventures together!"

"We'll have nothing of the sort. Hal, tell this person—"

"I'll make cookies for you and see that you don't forget things, and you can teach me how to walk through fences, the way you did when we first came to New York. Do you suppose if I concentrated very hard, I could learn to walk through rock?"

"I'll take her back to England," Taliesin said, rolling his eyes heavenward. "Immediately."

Arthur smiled. "Would you do one more thing for me?"

"Of course, Majesty."

"Take the sword."

"The sword?" Taliesin asked incredulously. "But—"

"Please. I'm only thirteen years old. Which is why I'm asking you to take Excalibur back where it belongs." Arthur placed the sword flat across his forearm and offered it to Taliesin.

"I should have known it couldn't be destroyed," the old man said, accepting it.

Arthur climbed on the Harley behind Hal. "I think maybe you did," he said knowingly.

Half a block away, the news vans were rolling through the tangle of emergency vehicles. Alongside them ran a flock of reporters, their microphones already extended.

Beatrice wriggled with excitement. "I'll bet they want to interview us!" she exclaimed. "Goodness, where shall we begin? With Arthur, I suppose. Only how does one explain to Americans that they have a king? Particularly since he's still in the eighth grade . . . Oh, dear, are you feeling all right, old man?"

Taliesin sucked in his breath and covered the girl's mouth with both hands. Then, just as the reporters reached them, the two of them faded like an old photograph and then disappeared into thin air.

"Did you get that?" one of the journalists screamed. "Is the tape rolling?"

"I told you, damn it, nothing's working. That wind shorted out all the electronics."

"What about them? Talk to the guys on the motorcycles. They must have seen it."

"The kid's there, too. Hey, you!"

Hal jumped on the gas. With a roar, the twelve knights tore down the street, leaving the press and the police and the fire fighters to sort things out for themselves.

"Where'd Taliesin go?" Arthur shouted over the din of the engines when they stopped for a traffic light.

Hal gave him a telling look. "Wherever he wants."

The boy grinned. The old man would find them in his own time. Meanwhile, he and Hal would have their hands full looking after the knights.

They were such good men, Arthur thought. Kay, Gawain, Bedwyr sitting tall in the saddle of his mount, Lugh with his spiked helmet, Fairhands the standard bearer, who had tied a red-and-white neckerchief he'd found along the side of the road to the sissy pole behind his seat, Tristan, Agravaine, Dry Lips, crafty Curoi MacDaire . . . Good men, valiant and true, the Companions of the Round Table at last restored to their former glory.

But it was Launcelot he had missed the most. Launcelot, who had thrown away his life after leaving Camelot because he had not been able to bear the shame of having abandoned his king. Arthur had deserved to lose him, of course—even then, the king had understood that with perfect clarity—but Launcelot had never forgiven himself. He had waited through sixteen centuries to atone for what he perceived to have been a great sin.

Now, at last, he would have his chance. He would stay with Arthur to the end of his days, and they would both be better for it.

When the light changed, he nodded to Launcelot to take the lead. The knight obeyed, speeding past the others to turn right onto the big avenue leading north, out of the city. North, toward forests and vineyards and the wild sea, where a man could find all manner of marvels.

The motorcycles raced into the wind. It was all good country out there.

EPILOGUE

Merlin sat beside the stone in the thicket. He was worn out. It had taken some very tricky magic to get Excalibur into the boulder. People always assumed such things were easy for a wizard. . . .

He laughed out loud. *People assumed!* Why, it was just like the old days, when everyone he encountered feared that he would turn them into toads. Since the incident in New York, he had become quite famous. His picture—hideously unflattering, unfortunately, as it showed him lying unconscious on Arthur's lap, with the knights on their knees around them—had appeared in nearly every magazine and newspaper in print. Evidently it was the only photograph available, as most of the photographers' equipment had been destroyed during the windstorm.

Pundits on the subject of wizardry, and there were apparently a number of them, wrote all manner of opinions about his spectacular disappearance, ranging from outraged cries of fakery to treacly tracts of adoration.

But that was nothing compared with what they were saying about Arthur. None of them could forget the sight of the boy holding the glowing sword over his head as a madman vanished into a black hole.

A few had even guessed Excalibur's location. That was why it had taken Merlin so long to get around to bringing it back. For weeks after Arthur's dazzling introduction to the world through television, fanatics of all stripes had come snooping around Cadbury Tor—and every other place that claimed to be the site of Camelot, if what he read was true—looking for the sword in the stone. Merlin wondered what these silly people would do if they found it. Would they bring tanks and demolition balls to try to break it up again? Or did they believe that somehow one of them would actually manage to pull it out, to take Arthur's place?

Human beings, he decided, were quite ridiculous.

It took the fools a long time to go back to their own business. One particularly persistent woman came every day for several months, much of the time encumbered by plaster casts on her limbs. Merlin was beginning to think she would pitch a tent on the Tor and take up permanent residence with an intravenous drip to sustain her, but at last even she decided to look elsewhere for her heart's desire.

Finally, after nearly a year, the wizard was able to bury Excalibur firmly and seamlessly inside a solid granite boulder that was taller and wider than most men. Then he placed some other good-sized rocks around it and covered the whole business with an acre of brush and thorn.

Soon the curious would forget entirely about the great sword, and perhaps about the boy-king who had wielded it, as well. Sensational though the events of that midsummer night in New York City had been, they paled beside the lurid artifice that made up the daily fare of modern man. These were not the Middle Ages. People nowadays were accustomed to the bizarre. Every supermarket carried a variety of chronicles detailing encounters with alien beings and sightings of popular musicians ostensibly risen from the dead.

Arthur's work would not be easy.

But it had begun. Zack married Kate, and together—along with the inestimable help of Kate's father, former President William Marshall, they raised fifty million dollars for a new Center. The facility, located on ninety acres of rambling grassland in upstate New York, had already become a mecca of healing and spiritual renewal for people of all religions from all over the world.

When he last spoke with Zack, more than five thousand people were coming each day to drink the curative water from a deep pool inside the Center's main building. Wisely, Zack had encased the cup in concrete and then submerged it at the bottom of the pool so that no one—not even himself—would be tempted to use it for his own purposes. The water was available to all without charge. For this alone Zack, as the Center's director, was currently regarded as even more of a rarity than either Merlin or Arthur.

"They'll learn," Zack had said. "It'll just take people awhile to accept the idea that not everyone wants to cheat them or hurt them."

"There are still some nasty sorts around," Merlin had suggested.

"Oh, I know that," Zack said, laughing. "But I'll take my chances."

Yes, he would. Arthur had chosen wisely.

In keeping with the all-encompassing nature of his enterprise, Zack had not insisted on calling his new creation the Center for Cosmic Consciousness. Instead, it was named the Rasheesh Shanipati Center, for the brilliant physician whose groundbreaking work on the continued existence of the soul after death was changing mankind's entire concept of existence.

Beatrice Reed, the patient whose brain waves served as the springboard for Shanipati's studies, was not found after her flight from the hospital. Indeed, after six months of diligent effort, the Reed family solicitors were obliged to step down their search for the missing heiress and begin the years-long wait before Beatrice could be declared legally dead and her considerable property turned over to the British government.

"There!" Beatrice announced, emerging from the boulder that encased Excalibur. "The sword looks lovely."

Merlin gasped. "How many times do I have to tell you not to do that?" he shouted. "One day you're going to give me a heart attack!"

"I'm terribly sorry," she said, genuinely penitent, as she always was. "I just enjoy it so . . . Would you like some fudge?" She reached into the pocket of her jeans and pulled out a flattened chocolate smear covered with grass and dirt, encased by a leaf.

He stared at it, appalled. "I think not," he said.

The girl was quite impossible. He should have taken her straight home, as he'd intended from the beginning. She was very well off, and would have been sent to a reputable boarding school while her solicitors managed her fortune. True, with no family, she would have had no visitors and nowhere to go on holidays, and, after what she'd been through, no one to confide in . . . rather like himself . . .

He groaned as she helped him to his feet. "I suppose I ought to be used to it by now," he groused. "After all, it's been bothering me since before the turn of the sixth century."

Ah, well, he thought, that's what comes of being reborn when one is already nearly eighty years old. With the girl gently guiding him, Merlin limped out of the thicket, bending and stretching his knee to get the kinks out.

The Innocent had done that, brought him into that long sleep when he had been prepared to die. She had done it twice, in fact. He doubted that his last encounter with her in the fog had been by accident.

He had not seen her since. Perhaps he would never see her again, not until he was finally permitted to enter the Summer Country.

If he could even find her then.

With a sigh, he led the way across the grassy, rock-strewn plain where Camelot had once stood. Camelot, the place where Arthur's dream was born, where knights jousted and ladies danced and everything was possible.

"He will build the dream again," Merlin said aloud.

Yes, little bard. You shall build it together. All of you.

He scanned the horizon, his heart thumping like a boy's. "Look!" Beatrice called, pointing toward the ragged tip of Cadbury Tor. "A wolf!" She clasped her hands together. "A wolf with eyes like moonlight."

Merlin's breath caught. "Wait for me," he told Beatrice, loping off toward the bluff, his arms waving wildly over his head. "Innocent! I'm here!"

Of course you are, dear. That's why I've come.

"Is it Arthur? Is he—"

He's fine. He'll be a splendid young man the next time you see him.

"That long?" He jogged to a stop. "Why? Is there something you'd like me to do?"

There may be. High on the tor, the wolf cocked its head. *We have company.* Beatrice ran up to him, red-cheeked and out of breath. "It talks," she panted, her eyes sparking with wonder. "The wolf can talk."

"What are you doing here? I told you to . . ." His eyebrows shot up. "You heard her?"

An apt pupil, the Innocent said.

"Hardly." The old man's gaze slid toward Beatrice. "She carries sweets in her pocket."

And she can walk through rock.

"Well, yes. She learned that rather quickly."

More quickly than you, I'd say.

The eyebrows formed a hard wedge.

Now, now. I'm only saying it took you a long time to learn that first lesson.

"First? That was only the *first* of my lessons?" he sputtered. "But I'm a wizard! The . . . the Merlin . . ."

And so you thought you knew all the magic you'd ever need? The tinkling voice laughed gaily.

"But I'm nearly eighty years old." He glanced at Beatrice. "She's twelve."

"Almost thirteen," the girl said, popping the fudge into her mouth.

"Oh, go away." He sank down onto the grass. Beatrice sat beside him and leaned her head on his shoulder. He moved away. "First lesson indeed. Bah."

The wolf sauntered down the hill toward them. *Well?*

"Well what?"

Would you like to learn the second lesson?

Both their heads snapped up. "Oh, yes!" They said together, scrambling to their feet.

Then follow me, children.

With a swish of its tail, the wolf bounded into a field of flowers. Behind her ran the old man and the golden-haired girl, hand in hand, their laughter bright as sunlight.